# The Woman from Kerry

## ANNE DOUGHTY

Allison & Busby Limited
12 Fitzroy Mews
London W1T 6DW
*www.allisonandbusby.com*

First published in 2003.
This paperback edition published by Allison & Busby in 2015.

A CIP catalogue record for this book is available from
the British Library.

10 9 8 7 6 5 4 3 2 1

ISBN 978-0-7490-1735-4

Typeset in 10/14.45 pt Sabon by
Allison & Busby Ltd.

The paper used for this Allison & Busby publication
has been produced from trees that have been legally sourced
from well-managed and credibly certified forests.

Printed and bound by
CPI Group (UK) Ltd, Croydon, CR0 4YY

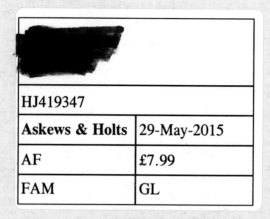

*For Don,*
*my red-headed cousin in Canada,*
*who also struggles with words*

# AUTHOR'S NOTE

In 1861, when our story begins, Ireland was ruled by Queen Victoria. Irish Members of Parliament went to London and represented all thirty-two counties. The internal divisions of Ireland were simply the ancient provinces, Ulster, Leinster, Munster and Connaught which every schoolchild knew. The northern province of Ulster was made up of nine counties, Armagh, Down, Antrim, Londonderry, Tyrone, Fermanagh, Donegal, Cavan and Monaghan.

Throughout the period of our story most people in all four provinces spoke Irish, unless they had come from Scotland or England in the first place. Many Irish speakers from Donegal went to Scotland each year to help with the harvest. There they learnt a second language which they called Scotch, but we would call English.

# CHAPTER ONE

Donegal
April 1861

The lough lay gleaming in the sunlight, its surface mirror calm. Not a breath of wind disturbed the stillness of the afternoon. No cart creaked on the stony track above the shore, no raven called from the mountainside. Close to the water's edge, a swan swayed on its eggs and stood up. As it stretched it's wings, minute ripples vibrated outwards from the tangled willow roots below the nest, running in ever-widening circles until they slapped noiselessly against a curving line of boulders.

For long minutes, stillness and silence reigned, as unusual in the length of this well-settled valley as the warm sunshine on such an early April day. Light glanced off new foliage, a column of midges rose and fell in the shadows beneath a gnarled hawthorn. Then came a sound to break the silence. A soothing, rhythmic sound, like the hum of bees around a hive. Flowing down the steep slope on the western side of the lake, the chant of children's voices moved out over the water.

'Ulster, Munster, Leinster, Connaught. Ulster, Munster, Leinster Connaught.'

On a low ridge between the rough track that ran along the lower slopes of the mountain and the boggy margins of Lough Gartan, a school house had recently been completed. It was so new, the grey-green mosses that mantled the encircling trees had yet to find a foothold on its dressed stone walls or slated roof. For yards around, the bare feet of children had tramped the ground so hard and so smooth that no growing thing could find a purchase on the dark, packed earth.

'Antrim, Armagh, Cavan . . . Derry, Donegal, Down . . . Fermanagh, Monaghan and Tyrone.'

The new refrain had more urgency, then stopped abruptly. A single peremptory voice rang out.

'You boy, Lawn. Stand up, turn your back on the board. Now tell me the counties of Ulster.'

'Donegal . . .'

'Yes . . .'

As the pause lengthened the class shifted uneasily in their seats. A big, burly lad, a good hand with a spade or a slane, Danny Lawn was no scholar. He could barely write his name and he had no memory at all for names and places.

'Yes, indeed, Lawn. It is quite fitting you should put our native county at the top of your list,' he said sarcastically. 'Now we should like the other eight counties in any order you care to choose.'

With his back turned away from the blackboard where the counties were inscribed in the Master's copperplate, only three of Danny's classmates remained visible. With the simple logic of smallest at the front, largest at the back, the Master's seating arrangements left him looking directly at two boys, his own older brother, Larry with his desk mate, Kevin Friel and one girl, Mary, the older of the McGinley girls from Ardtur, who sat by herself across the narrow corridor separating the boys from the girls.

Danny looked desperately from Kevin to Mary, knowing full well his brother would never lift a finger to help him. Larry might be the eldest in the family, but Danny was his mother's favourite. Larry could never forgive him for that.

Mary's eyes were fixed on the Master's face. She didn't dare move her lips in case he'd catch her. When the Master narrowed his eyes and fixed them firmly on Danny's hunched shoulders, she glanced across at Kevin, hoping he'd help Danny out.

'Aaa,' began Danny slowly, as he tried to read Kevin's lips. But Kevin's lips stopped moving the moment the Master stepped from behind his desk and strode down the narrow aisle.

As soon as the Master left his desk a small child in the front row moved cautiously in her seat and followed his retreating figure with dark, troubled eyes. Rose McGinley knew the Master disliked

11

Danny. It was not the first time he'd found an opportunity to disgrace him in front of the class.

Rose shivered. From where she sat she could see only the backs of Danny and the Master, but she could see her sister Mary, her face flat and expressionless, her eyes wide. She was frightened, she could see that quite clearly, though she'd never yet admitted it to her. She went on watching cautiously, perfectly aware that turning round could bring the Master's wrath upon her if he was to glance behind him and catch her. None of the other children with whom she sat had dared take their eyes away from the blackboard.

'Ah what, Lawn?'

'I can't mind, sur.'

'Well, we'll have to see if we can improve your memory, Lawn, won't we? Sit down and stay sitting down,' he barked, as he looked up at the clock. It was half past three exactly.

Seconds before he turned on his heel and strode back to his desk, she had swivelled round again and was sitting perfectly still, her hands folded, her eyes firmly fixed on the counties of Ulster as if they had never strayed for one moment.

'On your feet, up.'

In a single practised motion the class rose, repeated a lengthy Irish prayer, said 'Good afternoon, sir,' collected their few possessions and filed out without a word, the back rows leading the way. Not a soul spoke even as they turned away towards their homes. They knew better. The Master's ear was sharp. As they moved towards the scattered clusters of cottages that lay between the track and the mountainside, the swish of the cane and Danny's muffled grunts were the only sounds to be heard.

By the time Rose emerged into the sunlight her sister was well ahead of her, walking quickly along the track, her head down, her practised eye picking out the worn boulders and humps of grass kinder to bare feet than the rock the winter frosts had splintered. She dawdled, looking around her and kept an eye on Mary's purposeful stride.

Before and after school each day, Mary visited her father's aunt, an old woman, strong in spirit, but unable to walk more than a few steps. Without her help there'd be no water from the well, no turf for the fire and no potatoes for the evening meal.

Moving slowly along the track behind her, Rose was surprised she hadn't looked back. Usually she stopped as soon she was out of range of the Master and waited for Rose to catch up with her. Today she hadn't paused. Rose glanced at her brothers as they ran past, walked a little more quickly as if she were following Mary, then slowed down again as soon as they were gone, her eyes darting from side to side of the rough track. Away ahead of her now, Mary strode on, wrapped in her own thoughts.

13

As she watched her sister's retreating figure, her long-lashed dark eyes grew bright with excitement. As the last of her school fellows dispersed and Mary moved out of sight, she stopped dawdling, shot across the empty track, climbed nimbly over the ditch and crept along it till she reached the thread of path that ran between the grain and potato patches surrounding the small cluster of houses known as Ardtur.

Not yet eight years old, Rose was a fragile-looking child with pale skin and a mass of black, wavy hair. She carried no satchel, for only the oldest scholars were trusted with the National School's battered reading books. Dressed in a worn shift, she moved with quick, light steps, her excitement growing as she made her way through rough, marshy ground and headed for the piles of boulders that marked the foot of the steeper slopes ahead.

They were much further off than she imagined, but she hurried on, thrilled by her good fortune and determined to get out of sight before anyone could call her back. Minutes later, she scrambled triumphantly through the tumbled remains of an old wall built from the stones dug out of the tiny fields that now lay behind her. She glanced behind her and hugged herself in glee. There was no sign of Mary or of anyone else.

She had never been so far from home by herself. Sometimes her mother took her for walks down by the lough or up the hillside beyond Aunt Mary's small, dilapidated cabin, but she'd never been on the mountain before. Though she'd looked up at it every day for as long as she could remember, this was the first time she'd set foot on its worn and craggy slopes.

The bare patches of rock were easy on the feet, but the wiry stumps of burnt heather were best avoided. Here and there, tangles of briar had dropped dry, thorny twigs among the fresh shoots of bracken. She tramped on one, twisted her face in pain and stopped to pull out the thorns. After that, she moved more cautiously, her eyes no longer fixed upon the crest of the mountain's long shoulder, until now the boundary of her world.

Despite the tiny breeze she met as she climbed higher, she was soon damp with perspiration, her face prickled with heat. She paused for a moment, wiped her forehead with one slender arm and stood listening. If there'd been rain at all in the last few days, the narrow gullies seaming the mountainside would be tumbling with water. She could make a cup with her hands and have a drink and splash water on her face to cool it.

The thought of it filled her with longing. She could almost feel the water sliding down her parched throat and the coolness on her hot cheeks, but there'd been no rain for over a week. Her only hope was a spring. She looked around her, but saw no sign of one. All those she knew came out low down, at the bottom of a hill or under a hedge bank.

She kept going, the cool breeze encouraging her as she climbed. Then she heard a call. It must be a bird, she thought. But when it came again, it sounded too like her own name to be a bird. She stopped and looked behind her. She was amazed at how far she'd come, the whole valley now spread before her. There was no one in sight on the slopes below or in the fields beyond.

She picked out the roof of her own house. Standing a little higher than those of their neighbours, it had pale gold streaks in the weathered thatch where her father mended it last autumn, then the roof of the school glinting in the sunlight. A little way from the gable end, a sapling with fat, grey-white buds raised its thin branches to the sky.

The day the school was opened, a man in a uniform had planted it. He was a nice man with a wife in a long dress and a big hat. He'd smiled at them and made a speech most of the scholars couldn't understand, because they only had Irish. But she did because her mother had the Scotch. He'd said he was sorry it would be a bit too soon for them to benefit themselves, but he hoped his tree would give apples to their children and their children's children.

The call came again. Startled this time, she turned abruptly from the green and sunlit prospect below to the bare rocky slopes of the mountainside. She shivered. The voice was above and ahead of her. Uneasy now, she searched for signs of movement, but nothing stirred in the stillness, neither bird nor animal.

Could it be a banshee? she asked herself. She wasn't entirely sure what a banshee was, but she knew it was a bad omen if you saw or heard it. Most people said it's cry was a sure sign of a coming death. Others said the banshee itself was death to travellers, it's human voice leading them to their doom in bog or quicksand, over cliffs or precipices.

She paused, uncertain what to do. Aunt Mary said you couldn't be too careful when you were dealing with the Other World, but you must always try not to give offence. She would do as Aunt Mary did. She crossed herself quickly, said a prayer to the Blessed Virgin, and continued her climb.

'Where in the name of goodness are ye goin' Rose. Are ye lost?'

She leapt backwards and nearly fell over.

'No, I am *not*,' she replied crossly, as she gathered herself up.

Owen Friel was leaning back in the shade of an overhanging rock, his worn, peat-stained shirt and trousers as dark as the rock itself.

'An' what are ye doin' here yerself?' she came back at him. 'Ye weren't at school. They'll come after ye.'

'Na.'

He shook his head dismissively and went on looking out over the valley below. 'I'm near the age to go. Da says they'll not trouble to come away up from Letterkenny. He's workin' on the new drains above Warrenstown. I brought him up a can o' tea a while back.'

Owen lived further up the valley in the same cluster of cabins as Aunt Mary. She'd seldom seen him at school, but when he did appear he sat silent, looking out the window whenever the Master took his eyes off him. He moved to one side and made room for her to sit beside him on a slab of smooth rock. Her legs already aching, she dropped down gratefully.

'Does yer ma know yer out?' he asked without taking his eyes away from the prospect below.

'No. She had to go over to Termon to get paid.'

He stared at her, puzzled.

'What put the mountain in yer head, Rose? It's no place for a wee girl. Ye might have hurt yerself,' he said, kindly enough.

She was about to protest that she wasn't 'a wee girl', but then she saw he wasn't teasing her. And she was wee, it was true. In the row under the Master's desk, she sat with the five and six year olds and she was nearly eight.

'I wanted to see the other side of the mountain.'

'What for?'

He sat quite still, a look of amazement on his face.

'To see where the landlord's goin' to build his castle.'

'Landlord', he repeated carefully. 'What's that?'

She frowned and shook her head. She'd done it again. She kept forgetting that if she used her mother's words no one would understand except her brothers and sisters and the tinkers who came to sharpen tools and mend pots.

'Tiarna,' she said quickly, 'the man Adair they talk about every night when the neighbours come in.'

'Has your father the Scotch then?'

'He has, but not much. Only what harvesters have. But my mother has it. She always says she has very little Irish.'

'Is she from Tullaghobegley then?'

'Where's that?'

'Over beyond,' he said vaguely, waving his arm towards the north. 'My father once got work with a man there. He says there's a whole lot o' them speaks the Scotch all the time. He tried to pick it up, but he wasn't there long enough.'

'My mother's from Scotland itself,' she said proudly. 'Her father had a farm and a house with six rooms and a byre and a stable. My Da went to harvest two years in a row and the third year she came back with him. She's told me all about

Scotland. She lived in a place called Galloway.'

Owen looked thoughtful as he took in this information. He had never heard of Galloway, nor had he ever known anyone who lived in a house with six rooms. Of course, she might be making it up. Children were always making up stories. But it wasn't very likely she could make up words he couldn't understand. And her such a wee scrap of a thing.

'Will ye come with me?' she asked, fixing him with her gaze.

He saw her dark eyes bright with excitement and smiled in spite of himself.

'It's a fair bit yet. Are ye sure ye can do it?'

She nodded vigorously. He got up, put out his hand, helped her to her feet and they set off.

'You've a big sister, haven't you?' he asked, as they stopped for breath.

'Yes, and two brothers. And a baby. It's got red hair and it's not walking yet.'

'Five of you. There's seven of us, or there was till Mike and Pat went to Amerikay.'

'I had another brother and sister too, older than Mary, but they got the fever in the bad time. My Ma is always talking about them. She's calling the baby for the boy, Samuel. The girl was Rose. I'm called for her. Ma says I'm like her when she was small, but then she grew tall . . .'

'Save yer breath, Rose,' he said, looking down at

her as she began to gasp. 'D'ye want to sit down?'

'No. Not till we get to the top.'

They climbed on in silence, their eyes fixed to the ground. There were no briars now, nor tufts of heather, nor plant of any kind on this windswept ridge. Fragments of frost-shattered rock littered the ground slowing their progress.

'There ye are,' said Owen, at last.

A few feet behind him, she looked up, stumbled and winced as her foot caught the sharp edge of a stone. She steadied herself, wiped the sweat from her forehead and stood staring down at the great ice-gouged valley that lay below.

'There's not many trees,' she said crossly.

The hillsides dropped more steeply and were even more bare and rugged than the slopes they had just climbed. A broad lough stretched from end to end of the deep trench between them. It gleamed in the westering sun like their own Lough Gartan, but no clumps of sally, or birch, or oak grew by the shore.

'An' there's no people,' she went on, looking up at Owen, who stood scanning the valley from end to end, his eyes narrowed in the bright light.

'Where's the people gone?' she demanded. 'An' where's the castle?'

'Sure he hasn't built it yet,' he said absently.

'I wanted to see the castle,' she said irritably.

He glanced at her upturned face, saw the bright

eyes fill with tears and turned away quickly. She was tired out. He should have had the wit to take her home when he found her.

'Look down there, Rose, down near the water,' he began trying to distract her. 'Do you see a bit that's paler than the rest?'

'Aye, on the ground that sticks out into the water.'

'That's right,' he said, relieved at her change of tone. 'And this side of it, can ye see the big stacks like haystacks, only dark?'

'Aye, a whole pile of them.'

'That's the whin and heather cleared off the bare bit. That'll be where he'll put the castle.'

'An' what'll he do down there all on his lone?'

Owen laughed wryly.

'He'll do what all the big folk do. Eat and drink and ride round in his carriage and invite folk from away. He'll not be lonely the same man,' he added reassuringly, for the dark eyes that challenged him had filled up again. Tears were dripping unheeded down her flushed face.

'We'll come back in a week or two and see how it's doin',' she said, sitting down abruptly. She rubbed her foot where it was bleeding.

'It'll take longer than that to get a castle going,' he said, half to himself as she pinched her foot. 'They have to dig deeper for a castle than for a house. An' he'll have to get a road made for the carts to bring in the stone.'

'But there's plenty of stone down there,' she protested, wiping her eyes with the back of her hand.

'Ach yes, but sure landlords don't use mountain stone, they send for quarry stone. It's a different colour and comes in blocks.'

'What colour will it be?'

'Sure how would I know, Rose, what's in the mind of Adair, except the rumours that go round.'

'Will he put us out?'

'Who told you that?'

'No one. I just heard it.'

He put his hands on her shoulders and turned her away from the prospect below. He knew now why he'd felt so restless and oppressed all day. He'd heard the same rumours and pushed them out of mind but they wouldn't let him be.

'Well, pay no attention at all,' he said hurriedly. 'It's just some story. Is yer foot all right?'

'Aye, it's stopped bleedin' now.'

He leant over and lifted her to her feet. She was so light the wind could blow her away. Her face was pale now she'd got her breath back and she was shivering in the breeze. If he was beat, he might be able to carry her. But not all of the way.

'Come on now,' he said, trying to encourage her. 'Yer Ma will be lookin' for ye. Ye don't want her to think you've gone and got lost, do ye?'

# CHAPTER TWO

Rose heard her mother call to Mary and felt the planks creak as the older girl got out of the box bed by the hearth, where once their father's mother had watched the comings and goings of the house by day and listened to the talk of neighbours in the evenings. She rolled over sleepily into the warm hollow Mary had left in the straw mattress and dragged the thin coverlet round her more closely. But it was no good. Without her sister's warmth, she soon began to shiver. She got up quickly and pulled on her shift and the wool smock her mother had made for her because she so often felt the cold.

There was no sign of her mother or father. All was quiet and dim. Newly-lit, the fire smoked on the hearth. Gusts of wind blew down the chimney every few minutes. They swirled the cold ash from yesterday's fire across the well-swept floor and sent billows of thick smoke from today's into every corner of the room. It was cold even with her clothes on. She wished she were back in bed with Mary.

She coughed, rubbed the smoke out of her eyes and peered through the open door. There'd been frost in the night and the ground was hard, the hen's water frozen solid in the old tin bucket. Ice had formed on the shallow puddles that spread out between the houses whenever it rained. She saw her parents standing outside Andy Laverty's house. Mary was with them and they were listening to the old man. She could see the baby wrapped in her mother's shawl, but there was no sign of her brothers.

'Ma,' she called several times.

She didn't hear, but her father did and waved her back indoors.

She moved out of the doorway, but went on watching, for she knew something was amiss. Andy was red in the face and waving his arms around in great agitation. Her father had an anxious frown on his face. He seemed to be asking questions because each time Andy spoke in reply he shook his head and stared down the track to the roadway. Andy was still talking when she saw her brothers, Patrick and Michael hurrying up the track. Danny Lawn was with them, striding out so fast they had to run to keep up with him.

'What's the news, Danny?' her father asked abruptly.

'They're on the road the far side of Warrenstown,' he blurted out. 'Da said to tell you there's no talkin'

25

to them. There's Adair's land agent and a whole lot of polis, and a gang of men with the ram and axes and the like forby. And they're all from away. All strangers, though they're talkin' Irish the same as us. They just say they have their orders, there's nothin' they can do t' help us.'

Suddenly, the baby started to bawl, so Rose only heard fragments of what her father said.

'. . . she'll have to go indoors if they'll give her a place.'

As her father went on talking Mary put her hands over her face.

'Danny, away back, good man ye are. Send me word if . . .'

The baby had only paused. Now he'd started again, as Danny set off at a run, struggling in her mother's arms, his small fists beating the air, his red hair catching the first pale gleams of light from the rising sun.

Rose slipped quietly across the room and sat on her stool by the fire.

'Good girl, you're up and dressed,' her mother began, her voice soft but firm. 'Now you take Samuel while Mary and I make breakfast.'

Her mother lowered the child into her arms, his face red with the fury of his crying, tears still wet on his cheeks. She cradled him to her, delighted by his warmth. Babies were always warm. She shushed him and rocked him and sang to him, the way her mother and Mary did. To her surprise, he went to sleep immediately. Through the open door, she caught sight of her father going into the byre with Patrick and Michael, the ice cracking beneath their feet.

'Is he puttin' us out?' she whispered to Mary, as the older girl leant past her and hung the pot to boil over the fire.

But Mary said nothing, her lips pressed tightly together, her face closed. She just glanced sideways at their mother, measuring oats from the sack in the corner of the room.

'We'll meet that if we come to it, Rose,' she said evenly. 'The day's not over yet,' she added.

From her stool by the hearth, the baby asleep in her arms, she waited, alert for any unfamiliar noise from outside.

As soon as they'd eaten their porridge, her mother despatched Michael and Patrick to take the donkey to graze by the wayside. She handed Mary a can of milk for her aunt in Warrenstown.

'See she drinks it all, but don't linger. Come straight back,' she warned. 'Don't pay any attention to the strangers. There's nothing you can do.'

She scraped the last of the porridge into a bowl and handed it to her husband. 'Take that over to Andy, like a good man. He's no fire lit yet to cook a bite.'

Rose watched her mother clear away the dishes from their meal. There was an air of busyness about her, but she did none of the jobs she usually did, like go to the spring for water, or bake bread for the evening. Even the floor was left unswept.

She stood still and silent in the doorway for a while, then turned back into the room and moved around, touching familiar things, picking them up, patting them and holding them.

A woman just turned forty, Hannah McGinley was still handsome. Taller than her husband Patrick and once as fair as he was dark, she moved with a kind of gracefulness that seemed out of place in such a humble home. Even when she bent to sweep the hearth with a goose's wing or add turf to the fire, she had none of the awkwardness of women worn by childbearing and the burden of hard work.

Her hands were still soft, the nails clean and trimmed though deep seamed with fine lines. Once, when Rose had asked her why her hands weren't like other women's hands, she said it was because of the embroidery. If you did white work you had to keep your hands soft by rubbing them with meal or buttermilk.

'Strange you should ask, Rose dear,' she began, a wistful smile on her face. 'An old woman who read fortunes once told me no matter how hard I worked, I'd always have the hands of a lady.'

Rose was just thinking about the hands of a lady when the baby woke up and cried again and this time there was no stopping him.

'Good girl,' Hannah said, taking him from her. 'Bring me the shawl. Do you want to go and do a pee-pee?'

When Rose came back from behind the byre, her mother was feeding him, the shawl draped over her shoulder, covering both child and bare breast. She was singing, a song about a lad that was born to be King going over the sea to Skye.

They started with the house nearest the roadway. Old Mary McBride had barred the door. She sat stubbornly by her fireside when the urgent knocking came. It took a man with a hatchet only a minute or two to smash the door into kindling. They gave her five minutes to collect her possessions and get outside while they lined up the ram on the lintel above the door. When it gave way, the central part of the roof fell in, dust from the collapse pouring out from the empty doorway like smoke from a fire.

She stood there, stunned, shaking from cold and shock as ropes were secured to the gable ends. Men hauled on the ropes till they gave way and crashed down outside the cottage walls. The last support of the sagging roof removed, the remainder of the thatch pitched inwards to extinguish the fire on the hearth and obliterate all trace of a life that had survived even the Great Famine itself. Having ensured the cottage could no longer provide shelter, the men moved on. A tall, gaunt figure in dark clothes stepped forward and approached the shivering woman.

He bent down towards her and spoke slowly and carefully.

'As you now have no home or any visible means of support I am to tell you that you are entitled to relief in Letterkenny Workhouse. A cart has been provided for transport. It is waiting over beyond.'

Only when old Mary McBride's cabin was a heap of rubble did Patrick McGinley finally accept he was helpless.

'Hannah, there's nothing for it. What'll we do?'

Rose thought there were tears in her father's eyes, but she couldn't be sure. When the smoke was as bad as it was today, they all had red eyes and now there was dust drifting through the open door from Mary McBride's. She could almost taste it on the back of her throat, a stinging dryness.

'Get me the box, Patrick, my love, while there's time,' she said softly, putting a hand to his cheek. 'We're not the only folk to suffer like this. It's not new. Adair is only another Sutherland. He'll only defeat us if we give in. We'll not let him do that.'

Her father turned away without speaking, took a pronged fork from the tools by the open door and went into the tiny bedroom where he and Hannah slept. He returned moments later with a battered old metal box, its surface still dirty with tramped earth from the floor.

She opened it quickly and sorted through the contents. The largest item was a big fat book with a black cover. There was a packet of papers, a china tea cup and saucer decorated with flowers, a brooch and two little pouches with drawstrings.

Rose watched in fascination. She had never seen the box before.

'Ma, what's that?' she gasped.

'It's your great-grandfather's watch. You can hold it for a moment.'

But no sooner had Rose clutched the cold silver case of the fob watch that her eye caught the glint of coins.

'Not a word,' said her mother sharply, as she counted them and put them back in their pouch. 'None of you will say a word about the watch or the sovereigns.'

She turned to her husband and handed the pouch to him.

'When the Mackays were driven from Sutherland, they hadn't a ha'penny. Put it on a string round your waist and cover it well.'

The sounds of falling thatch were coming closer by the minute. Quickly, Hannah McGinley dispersed the precious objects amongst her children, showing them how to hide them in their scanty clothing. Young Patrick was entrusted with the silver fob watch, Mary with the cup and saucer wrapped in an unfinished piece of white embroidery. Michael put the papers under his shirt and Hannah pinned the brooch on Rose's shift below the woollen smock.

'Gather up the potatoes from the barn, boys, and bring them here.'

She turned to her husband. 'D'ye think they'll leave us the cart, or will they say it belongs to Adair? And what about the cow?'

Her husband shook his head.

'There was carts on the road earlier from Warrenstown going towards Glendowan. They must have let them go. But there isn't much room in it. Will I put straw in the bottom for Rose and the baby? What else can we take forby?'

'The sack of oats and the bit of flour left in the crock. A bit of turf and kindling for a fire.'

He turned to go and found the doorway blocked by a man about his own height.

'I must ask you to remove yourself from Mr Adair's property.'

For one moment, Patrick McGinley was overcome by blind fury. Sweat broke on his forehead and he felt every muscle in his body long to lash out at this man, this lackey, this miserable apology for an Irishman.

And then he heard his wife's voice, cool and polite.

'Patrick dear, ask the gentleman to step inside to deliver his message.'

He had never mastered the Scotch, but the way

she said 'Patrick dear,' he could understand in any language she would ever speak.

'No, *astore*, this man will never set foot over this threshold,' he said in his own speech. 'Come out with the children and we'll be gone.'

He pushed past the man, brought out the donkey and cart from the barn and lifted Rose up into it. The boys added the bundles of oats and potatoes and turf.

'Are you all right Rose?' her mother asked.

'Aye,' she said, bravely.

She was cold and the bag of turf was poking into her, so closely packed was the small cart.

'Can you hold the baby?'

The sun was setting and a thin rain was beginning to fall. The baby was warm in her arms as the cart moved out between the wrecked houses. The men had lit a fire and were feeding the flames with pieces of Andy Laverty's door. Andy was nowhere to be seen.

The flickering light reflected on sweaty faces and strong, dirty forearms, on the uniforms and helmets of the police who stood watching. All around, people were coming and going, some trying to get back into the wreckage of their houses, some sitting crying on the doorsteps.

'Don't look back, Patrick,' said Hannah, touching her husband's arm as he pulled on the donkey's bridle. 'Nor any of you,' she added, looking round at Mary and her brothers, who were following behind with the cow.

They made their way slowly down to the roadway in the fading light.

'Which way?'

In the twenty years since Patrick McGinley had brought his Hannah back to the mountain, he had come to understand that when times were really bad and all he could do was despair, it was Hannah who could see a way. While he had her, he knew he'd never give in.

'To the right. We'll find shelter tonight in Casheltown.'

The rain slackened momentarily, then turned to sleet. The sudden squall blew in their faces, bouncing icy fragments on their clothes, drifting on the rough surface of the road. Rose closed her eyes as the hail stung her face. She drew her mother's shawl closer over herself and the sleeping baby.

Above the creaking of the cart and the rush of wind, they heard behind them a shuddering crash. Though they all knew what it was not one of them looked back.

# CHAPTER THREE

The journey from Ardtur to Casheltown was no great distance, but the heavily laden cart and the reluctant movement of the cow made progress slow. Bent forward against the scudding hail, they said not a word to each other but tramped along the rough, potholed track, eyes downcast, knowing that when they turned towards the next random gathering of cabins there would be some relief from the particles of ice that stung the face, caught in the hair and clung to their worn and shabby clothes.

As suddenly as it had come upon them, the squall passed. Through a gap in the cloud, the sun poured golden rays around them and they were dazzled by bright beams reflecting back from the skim of hailstones that lay as thick as a light fall of snow.

'Thanks be to God,' said Hannah, lifting her head and straightening her hunched shoulders. She wiped the moisture from her face and smiled as the bitter chill passed away, the golden light streaming down from a widening patch of blue sky adding a touch of warmth to the evening air. She turned to the younger of the two boys.

'Michael dear, run away on up to Daniel McGee and tell him we're coming. If the door is maybe shut and barred, knock very softly and call his name.'

She tapped her long fingers on the wooden frame of the cart. Rose wondered if she was tapping out the beginning of a song.

Michael looked up at her, his face still damp from the melted sleet and solemnly repeated the rhythm on the rim of the cart. Rose knew he'd got it right, even before her mother smiled.

'Good boy, yourself,' Hannah said, as Michael took to his heels, pleased to be given a task after all the long hours of waiting.

Daniel McGee's door was open by the time they arrived. Born in the 1780s and blind from birth, he stood waiting for them, greeted each of them by name, though only Hannah stepped forward to press his hand, for he was uneasy when people came too close to him. He always said he could 'see' people better if they were further away.

'You've none of you taken harm?' he said abruptly, when he had studied each one of them. 'Are we to have one more night?' he went on, addressing Patrick McGinley, who stood by the donkey's head wondering what to do next.

'Aye Daniel, we are. Sure haven't Adair's fine,

strong men worked hard and long the day. Won't the factor want to see they've good food and rest against the work of the morrow?'

He spoke bitterly as he took the sleeping baby from the cart and put him in Hannah's arms. Then he picked up Rose, swung her into the air, twirled her round his head till she laughed with glee and set her gently down again on her own two feet.

A look of desolation passed over the old man's face at the sound. Wherever he ended his days, and those days might be few enough, Hannah thought, he'd never again hear the laughter of children in the valley where he'd been a child himself.

'Come in, Hannah, be ye welcome as ye always are. I've little to offer, but what I have is yours.'

Daniel McGee's house was about the same size as theirs had been, but there was no division to make a bedroom, so the single room seemed much larger than their own, its roof much higher, for it was raised in better times. Rose stared at the smoke-blackened sods that lay under the thatch. On the pale, silver-grey wood of the lowest laths St Bridget's crosses had been nailed up each year on her special day. Some were woven from rushes. Some carved from the whitened tree stumps dug up with turf from the bog. A few were just pieces of sharpened stick bound together with a piece of rag. She began to count them softly to herself as her brothers brought the bundles from the cart.

'Can I hold the child, Hannah?'

Rose was amazed when her mother lowered Samuel into his arms without a moment's hesitation. He sat rocking him gently and crooning to him while Hannah and Mary made up the tiny fire with turf from the cart and put water to boil for the potatoes they'd brought with them. Samuel opened his eyes, sneezed and then lay still, his arms waving gently, his large dark eyes attempting to focus on the face of the unshaven figure who looked down at him focused but unseeing.

By the time they'd eaten, the sun had dropped far behind the ridge of the mountain. Inside the big room it was shadowy, the only light the pale oblong where the door still stood open. Every so often, even that source of light was dimmed as another man or woman slipped through to join the growing company.

'Come away in and let ye be easy. There's no one but old friends among us tonight,' Daniel called out firmly. He greeted each of his visitors by name before they'd even spoken.

He'd insisted Hannah sit in the wooden armchair that faced his own across the flags of the hearth. Beside it, he'd placed a low stool for Rose. Here she sat, her back resting against her mother's legs, watching the silent figures settle themselves around the room.

Behind Hannah, Mary shared a bench with her father and brothers, but many of the people who arrived had no place to sit. They dropped down on the floor or stood leaning their backs against the walls. For what seemed a long time to Rose, no one spoke in the crowded room and no one came. Then two men carrying a wooden bench slipped into the back of the room and seated themselves. As if that were the signal he'd been waiting for, Daniel cleared his throat and began to tell a story.

It was a familiar tale of heroes she'd heard many a night, listening behind the bed curtains when she was supposed to be asleep. What was new to her was Daniel's way of telling it. There were long and elaborate descriptions of places and people, clothes and weapons, castles and great houses, she'd never heard before. Sometimes the hero would pause and break into verse, praising his friends and drinking companions, cursing his enemies, celebrating the beauty of a woman or the paces of a fine horse.

Often Daniel would pause and ask a question, as if to be sure he had their full attention. At critical points in his tale, he would ask his listeners to express their feelings. 'Ah bad luck to him,' they would chorus, if Daniel had spoken of treachery. 'God give you joy,' they'd cry, as ill-used lovers ran off together to the shelter of the mountainside.

Daniel spoke in Irish, for he'd never left the valley and had no Scotch at all, but there were many words and phrases Rose had never heard before. At first she didn't understand them, but as they were repeated, over and over again, slowly the meaning came to her. She wondered what her mother was making of them. For over half her lifetime, Hannah had spoken everyday Irish to her husband and her neighbours, her own Scots-English to her children. If asked, though, she was sure to insist she had little Irish.

Rose noticed she'd not joined in the responses and cries of encouragement. She wanted to look up at her and see if she could work out why she was so silent, but she knew she must move only very slowly and gradually, for there was no greater discourtesy to the teller of a tale than a fidget. Even if you got a cramp in your leg or wanted to scratch your back, you must put up with it till there was a break in the story.

When finally, during a burst of applause, she was able to turn towards her mother, Rose was quite taken aback, frightened even by what she saw, for suddenly she looked so old, her face pale and drawn, the wisps of grey hair usually drawn back into the still-fair tresses of her thick hair, straggling down on each side of her immobile face. Her eyes seemed quite dead and lifeless, though they glittered with moisture, her fingers locked tightly on her lap the knuckles poking out, white and angular, from the hands Rose so often admired for their softness.

A little later, the story ended. Cheers and handclaps greeted the triumph of the hero. There were cries of 'Good man, yerself. Well told, God bless you,' directed towards Daniel. Rose looked up at her mother again, saw her unclasp her hands and applaud with the others. At the very same moment, two large tears dropped silently onto the dark fabric of her skirt.

Daniel drew breath, the spell of the story broken. The forgetfulness it brought ended with it. The dark figures moved uneasily and took up again the burden that had haunted them for weeks and the fears became a reality this very morning with the news of the first evictions.

To Rose's surprise, the voices fell quiet again and a sense of waiting returned. She wondered if Daniel would tell another story or whether he would call on someone to sing or play, though she'd seen no sign of anyone bringing an instrument.

'Dear friends,' Daniel began, stretching out his stiff and twisted hands as if to embrace them all. 'I know what's in yer hearts and minds. I feel it all around me. And yet in the midst of this great anxiety and fear, I feel something stir, a whisper on the air, as light as the perfume of the hawthorn in May and yet as wholesome as bread baking on a griddle.'

He paused and looked from face to face, though

the soft glow from the orange embers would have been little enough for a sighted man to see by.

'There is something in this room that would sustain ye on a hard road better perhaps than a full stomach. I feel it near me, though I cannot put words on it.'

He paused and then threw out his arm slowly, his fingers still incurved towards his own body as he leant across the hearth.

'Hannah, good neighbour, is there something that speaks in your heart?'

For a long moment Rose thought her mother wasn't going to say anything. Then, at last, she spoke.

'Daniel, old friend, I have no skill at all in your art of storytelling and I have little Irish. Or so I thought, till I heard you speak tonight. You have brought memory to life for me and, though my mind is troubled as we all are, I will tell you what I have remembered.'

Rose had never noticed before how soft her voice was when she spoke Irish, but of course, she'd only heard her say everyday things to her father and neighbours. Perfectly at ease in herself now, she smiled and went on.

'I make but one condition,' she said, looking round the company, 'That you judge me lightly on matters of date for which I have no head and on words I may not have, though this little one here may well supply me,' she added, dropping a hand lightly on Rose's shoulder.

There were murmurs of assent and words of encouragement from every part of the room. Daniel himself nodded vigorously. 'Good woman, good woman yourself. We'll not fault you for what is no fault at all.'

Hannah drew breath and began, her tone light, her soft voice floating effortlessly over the silent company.

'My great-grandfather was John Mackay of Scourie in Strathnaver and his wife Hannah, whose name I bear, was of the same proud clan, but she was from Tongue on the north coast, a wild and beautiful place I've heard tell, for I was born in the south, in Galloway.'

Rose was entranced. When her mother spoke of her great-grandfather, her voice was full of a quality she'd never heard before. 'John Mackay of Scourie', she'd said. But it sounded more like 'Victoria, Queen of England.'

'My grandfather would be as old as Daniel, had he lived,' she went on. ' A strong-built man, but not tall. He had red hair and was a doughty fighter. He followed his lord into many a battle in a war that lasted for seven long years. He fought in Germany and in Denmark and many places whose names I never knew. But although the life of the camp was meat and drink to him, he always came home joyfully to his glen and to his wife and sons. He was wounded many times, but his lord gave him both money and land for his faithful service and he was content. His family flourished. They had plenty to eat and could always pay their rent.'

The silence had deepened. Hannah's tone was as light and as steady as ever, but something in the way she held herself upright in her chair seemed to warn her listeners that this pleasing picture could not last.

'I know little of the doings of great folk, those who live in castles and raise armies and fight wars against other countries. What I do know is that what little we hear of such people, their lives and loves, their friendships and enmities, are often more story than truth. Rumours flourish round a castle gate even more than at our own lane-ends. But what seems to have happened is that the great Chief of the Mackay made bad decisions or was cheated, so that he lost much of his land. The man that benefitted from his loss was from England, but he employed a Scotsman called Patrick Sellar to do his work for him, and an evil work it was for the land of Sutherland and, most of all, for the Mackays of Strathnaver.'

She paused, as if the mention of Patrick Sellar had been hard for her. Then she smiled.

'When I was a child I would have been punished for speaking that name,' she explained easily. 'But time moves on. He has been judged by God long since. He was a man, like Adair, that had no time for the little people. Perhaps he was cruel, as some said he was. Perhaps he didn't know the hurt and harm his action would cause. But whatever the truth of it, his agents sent thousands of people from the lands of Strathnaver to dwell on the rocky shores of the north. Men and women were driven from their homes, settled far away with no land to grow their food and no knowledge of the sea to provide what sustenance there might be. Many died trying to fish in the wild, northern waters. For the old and the weak, the children and the sick there was no future. They died, just as many of our friends and our family died in the bad time.'

Rose thought of her sister, who would be older than Mary had she lived, and her big brother Sam, who had red hair like the baby. Were they all going to die too, now that Adair had put them out?'

She looked up at her mother and saw that she was looking round the room, her dark eyes meeting those of everyone there.

'Yes, many died. That is the heartbreak that the great ones inflict upon such as ourselves. And it may come to that for some of us,' she said sadly. 'But not for all.'

She took a deep breath.

'My father and his brother walked the length of Scotland on burn water and berries from the hedgerows and the scraps of bread kindness brought them. My father found work in Dumfries and then bought land. He worked hard. He had fifty acres before he sold his farm, for he had no son. My uncle earned his fare to Nova Scotia and settled among the Rosses from Skye. He traded with them and became rich. They're both dead now, but while they lived they never forgot their family. It was not the hunger that took our Rose and Samuel from us,' she added softly.

There was a pause and Rose remembered the day she'd asked why her brother and sister had died.

'There was a fever that came when people got very hungry,' her mother had said. ' Even those who still had enough to eat could catch the fever. Many children caught it. Mary and Michael had it too, but they recovered. Rose and Samuel died in the same week.'

'And did I catch it too?'

'No, my love, you didn't. You were not born till the worst was well over and I fed you myself for a long time. Your father was poorly for a while, but he threw it off. He has always been strong.'

'And you Ma. What about you?'

'Me? I prayed I'd be spared to care for the rest of you. And I was.'

The room was silent and growing cold as the last embers of the turf fire shivered and fell to ash. Daniel was looking at her mother now, his face pale below the dark stubble of his unshaved face.

'And what words did your father and his brother leave with you Hannah, when they spoke of their ordeal?'

'They said they had found strength when they least expected it, they had found comfort in the most desolate of places and they had found the richest of hospitality in the poorest of places.'

'Did they now?'

Daniel repeated Hannah's words softly to the silent room.

'And did either of them give you any advice when you gave up your comfortable home to marry your chosen man and come to this hard place?'

'Yes. My father spoke to me before Patrick and I were married. He knew he would most likely not see me again. He was heart sorry that I was marrying across water and to a man of a different religion to his own, but he respected Patrick and knew he was a good man. What he said to me was this:

"Hannah, you have joy now in this marriage of yours. Long may it last. But none of us passes through life without hardship and great sorrow. Shed tears for your grief, but do not hold bitterness against any person or any situation. Bitterness stuns the spirit and weakens the heart. Accept what you cannot change and ask God and your fellow men for comfort. In that way you will live well however short your span. Give in to the bitterness and you will never fully live though you go beyond three score years and ten".'

The last orange sparks on the hearth glowed and faded as the wind blew down the chimney. The single candle that someone had lit and placed on the dresser flickered and steadied.

'There, friends and neighbours. There are words to put in your hearts when the men come tomorrow. Remember what Hannah has shared with us, both the ordeal of her father and uncle and the experience they gained from it. May God in his mercy watch over us.'

# CHAPTER FOUR

### May 1875

As soon as she'd climbed well above the coach road, Rose paused between the low, wind-bent fuchsia bushes and undid the top buttons of her blouse. The fine cambric, stitched into narrow pleats over her breasts and gathered with ribbon at the neck, dropped back and exposed her pale skin flushed with heat and gleaming with perspiration from the effort of the familiar, short, steep climb.

She turned and gazed back down the rocky hillside now patched with rich summer grass and dotted with early flowers. With a few deft movements she pulled out the long hairpins from the neat coil at the back of her head.

She felt the light touch of the sea breeze as it flowed in over the broad lake below. 'Oh, that's better, a hundred times better,' she said aloud.

She shook back her dark mass of hair and tucked away the few tendrils that were blowing across her eyes. All around her, the red tassels on the fuchsia bushes moved gently to and fro, tall stems of mayflower swayed easily above the smaller, brighter plants growing in their shadow. The breeze was a delight, cool, but with no edge of chill. She stood drawing in a deep breath of the clean, salt air like someone drinking spring water after a long, dusty journey.

After a few minutes, she began to struggle with the tiny seed pearls at her wrists. However much she loved the pretty buttons, they always made her cross when she was hot, or tired, or just wanted to pull off her clothes and fall into bed. She laughed at herself as she pressed patiently with damp fingers till they slid through the close-fitting buttonholes her mother had stitched with such patience.

None of the other servants at Currane Lodge wore such an elegant blouse. Even were they so fortunate as to possess one, they would most certainly not have been allowed to wear it. But then, none of them was lady's maid to the eldest daughter of the house. Given Lady Anne Molyneux's temperament, none of the other house servants envied her the privileges that came her way. She rolled up her sleeves and felt the soothing touch of the cool air on her warm body, threw back her head and stretched out her arms above her head as if to embrace the whole sunlit hillside and the blue dome of the sky above.

Suddenly, the air around her was filled with sound. Surprised and delighted by the shower of notes pouring down upon her she scanned the sky above. Dazzled by the light, all she could make out were two minute brown specks that shimmered and dissolved and then reappeared yet further away. She shaded her eyes. Immediately, the two specks became one as the lark rose higher in the clear air, its song bathing the quiet hillside where the only other sound was the murmuring of insects drunk with the first honey of the season.

She glanced around her, picked out a ridge of rock protruding from the midst of a flower strewn meadow and sat down, her long, dark skirt flapping slightly in the breeze, her well-polished boots placed firmly on the smooth turf, close-nibbled by the sheep that had moved on, up to higher pastures on the mountain slopes behind.

She sighed with contentment as she listened to the lark's song. She'd so very nearly had to stay behind with Lady Anne. Immediately, she put the thought out of mind. She was here now. That was all that mattered.

There'd been a few fine days recently and she'd already heard the lark, but today was the loveliest day so far this year. There was something about its perfection that made her want to drink it all in, every precious fragment. She needed the light and warmth to put against the damp and dark of winter, the breadth of the mountain and the sky against the confinement of the servants' hall and the rooms overlooking the stable yard where she lived with her mother and younger brother.

The road below clung to the edges of the lake where Thomas, the coachman, took young Sam fishing. Beyond the low wall bordering the coach road, its waters lapped gently on the stony shore. Her eye followed the line of the road westwards till it met the coast and the greater expanse of bay that merged with the Atlantic itself, a blue shimmering mass stretching to the far horizon.

'Nothing out there till ye reach Amerikay,' old Thomas always said, when they reached Ballybrack and he turned inland along the much narrower road that lay directly below her.

Time and time again, whether on a short outing for Lady Caroline, or on one of the many longer tours for the frequent visitors at Currane Lodge, she'd heard Thomas make the same remark. Something in his tone told her the simple words meant far more than they appeared to do. Certainly, never once did he fail to look out towards the far horizon as they came down from the pass and the whole of Ballinskelligs Bay lay before them.

Whenever he'd been away in Dublin with the family, she felt he was always relieved to be back. He never seemed easy far from the sea. She wondered if he needed the sea to be there, like herself, an infinite space in which there was no master or mistress, no call for the coach to go here or there. No relatives or friends of the family from Dublin, or Sligo, or the north, to be driven around the sights. No cousins from

England to be returned to Dublin or Rosslare for the boat. No gentlemen admirers from nearby estates to be conveyed on picnics with the young ladies.

Thomas never complained. In fact, Thomas said often enough that the Molyneux's treated their people far better than many he'd heard of who were richer and more important. They'd a lot to be thankful for besides a roof over their heads and decent food. He never tired of pointing to the plight of poor farmers, trying to feed a family on a few acres of land with the rent to pay even when the harvest failed.

Rose sighed. It might be true. Yes, of course, it *was* true. The master and mistress were kind people and not hard to please, but that didn't mean you didn't get tired of endless fetching and carrying, listening with one ear for the bell when you were trying to get a dress smoothed or shoes cleaned. You never knew when your work would be finished and you'd have a few hours to yourself. As for her own special problem, Lady Anne's changes of mood, that was an added burden. You never knew how or when she'd disrupt the ordinary business of the day.

Tears, tantrums or stubborn silences were regular occurrences, almost always unpredictable and feared by family and servants alike. Any small thing, something her four younger sisters would scarcely notice, could cause a total collapse. A speck of dirt on a muslin gown, a decision about what to wear, whether or not to have her hair up or down. But Rose had never feared her outbursts. From the very first day her mother brought her to the servant's hall, to begin her training as a housemaid, she'd sized up each member of the family and she'd grasped immediately that Lady Anne, a mere three years younger than herself, was a very strange girl indeed.

Short and squarish like her father, Sir Capel, when all her sisters were slim, fragile, and likely to be as beautiful as their mother had once been, she had fared well enough in childhood. Indulged as a lively and venturesome child, she'd would lead her sisters and cousins on wild expeditions round the estate and into the surrounding countryside, always emerging triumphant, despite the hazards that brought tears and torn clothes to her companions.

Childhood ended abruptly a few months before Lady Anne's eleventh birthday, when a new governess arrived. Miss Pringle felt it her duty to prepare Lady Anne for the sitting room and the ballroom. She set about it with vigour and unfailing determination. Before many months had passed, Lady Caroline was in despair of her eldest daughter. The once amusing and lively Lady Anne screamed and threw things, tore off her clothes and tramped on them, insulted the household staff, pulled her sister's hair and ran weeping from the schoolroom.

A gentle woman, whose health had been undermined by continuous unsuccessful attempts to produce a son who would survive for more than a few months, the mistress of Currane Lodge had neither the imagination, nor the energy, to make sense of the dramatic change. But Lady Caroline was quick enough to observe what was clear to all her servants. Only Rose, a very junior housemaid, could do anything with her.

'I nearly missed you today,' said Rose, lying back on the grass, focusing on the ever-diminishing lark, as it ascended higher and higher into the cloudless sky.

'Rose, where have you been? I've been ringing for an age. Didn't you hear? What am I to do? What am I to do? Today of all days. I'm not due for another week.'

Lady Anne was crouched on the stool in front of her dressing-table wearing only her shift. A pair of stained knickers lay at her feet.

'Have you a headache, then?' she asked quietly as she lowered an armful of freshly starched petticoats onto the bed.

'No.'

'Does your back ache?'

'No.'

'Then what's to stop you riding if you feel well?' she asked easily.

'Don't you know?' Lady Anne demanded crossly, her face red and blotchy from crying. 'Of course, you wouldn't know. Servants don't know anything about horses,' she said unpleasantly. 'A stallion can always tell when it's that time of the month. Conor'll play me up, I just know he will, and I'll look such a fool in front of him. Everyone says he's such a good horseman. All the O'Sheas are.'

'Then why don't you ride one of the mares?'

'I never thought of that,' she said abruptly. 'No, I can't,' she burst out, her voice rising ominously. 'It's impossible. Out of the question. He'll think I can only handle a lady's horse. It has to be Conor.'

'But what does it matter what Captain O'Shea thinks? Do you really like him?'

'No, I don't, but that's not the point.'

Rose saw a twist to the mouth, a droop of the shoulders, that always meant trouble. Say the wrong thing now and she'd start screaming and throwing things, or retreat into a tearful silence that could go on all afternoon.

'Well I think he's got bandy legs,' said Rose firmly. 'He can't possibly ride as well as you with legs like those.' She paused deliberately. 'Never mind anything else a man might want to do.'

Lady Anne put her hands over her mouth and giggled.

'Oh Rose, you do say the most outrageous things. Whatever would mother think if she heard you?'

Rose opened her eyes wide and looked at her with an air of innocence.

'I think Her Ladyship is in the walled garden at the moment.'

Lady Anne laughed aloud, stood up and kicked the knickers into the air, catching them deftly as they descended.

'Men are stupid. I don't care if I never marry. Let Lily and Mary go off and have crowds of babies. You and I can have fun without them. Can't we, Rose?'

'Of course we can,' said Rose reassuringly. 'If I were you, I'd ride whoever you fancy and forget about Captain Bandy Legs.'

'I'll ride Conor,' she replied, grinning broadly as she held up her arms to be undressed. 'I can wash by myself, Rose. You go down and find Tom, or your brother. Tell them to bring Conor round for me as soon as he's saddled up. Hurry on now. I want to be at the front steps before the men arrive. I'll show them how to ride.'

Rose stretched out more comfortably and propped herself up on one elbow, so she could look down the hillside.

'Poor old Conor,' she said aloud. 'She probably made him walk up and down the steps while she was waiting, just to show him who's boss.'

She sighed. The problem was you never knew what was going to happen. One day you'd spend a couple of hours persuading her to get into a dress for a ball she didn't want to attend, the next you'd have to do her hair, brush her riding jacket, lace her boots and tie her scarf in no time at all, while she twisted and twitched with impatience all the while.

Well, she'd managed it today. She was out. Away. Free for a few hours. Somewhere further up the valley, the party from Currane Lodge would be following a track across the estate which led up into the adjoining hills. Lily and Mary would be there, sitting neatly on their mares, their admirers in attendance. Sam would be following behind with Old Thomas's son Tom, the tea baskets, the rugs and the young ladies sketching materials.

She smiled to herself. Dear Sam was in love. Just turned sixteen, a handsome red-head, intelligent above his station, he'd discovered there was more to life than work in the stable or studying so that Sir Capel could send him to Dublin to train as his estate manager. She knew he'd be watching Lily's every move, thinking longingly of a warm glance from her lovely brown eyes, but Lily had never yet noticed Sam's existence, not even as a well-liked servant. With Captain Pakenham and his friend Captain O'Shea in attendance, as well as the eldest son of the Blennerhassetts, and the handsome young Lord Harrington it was hardly surprising she'd have other thoughts in her mind today.

An ideal day for a picnic, indeed, but she was glad it was her afternoon off and Sam, rather than herself, had been chosen for the job. Not that there was any problem with Lady Anne when she'd a horse for company. Once on Conor's back, she became a different person. Easy, relaxed and confident, she would be agreeable, even highly amusing, so much so visitors who stayed but a short time at Currane Lodge thought the rumours they'd heard about her were flights of fancy, stories that had gained in the telling as they passed from the drawing rooms of one county to those of another.

Once Lady Anne left the schoolroom, Rose had begun to see these drawing rooms for herself. If Lady Anne called for a scarf or a cloak, to go walking in the gardens, she'd slip into the large, ornate rooms and see little groups of elegantly dressed women settled by the huge fireplace, or standing in the deep embayments of the tall windows. Their heads would be inclined towards each other, their voices subdued, as they shared the latest gossip. It wasn't hard to imagine how rapidly and freely rumours would spread when women had little to do except entertain each other, drink tea, and dress for dinner.

The Currane Lodge drawing room was small compared with what she'd seen when the Molyneux ladies went visiting and only a fraction of the size of Martham Park in Cheshire, where she'd had her first experience of an English country house.

'Sure they're only middling rich,' Old Thomas declared when the magnificence of other castles, parks and lodges, were discussed in the servant's hall, together with the idiosyncrasies of their owners, the sources of their wealth and the suitability of their sons for one of the young ladies.

'But sometimes being rich is not the biggest thing. The Molyneux's are exceedin' well connected,' he continued, always pleased to have an attentive audience.

Thomas was an expert on the aristocracy. Having spent his life driving Sir Capel round London and the Home Counties in his younger days, he had then spent the next twenty years driving him from one Irish estate to another. Thomas never read books, but he read newspapers avidly and he observed. With time on his hands while he was waiting outside the places the family frequented, his eyes were never still. No detail of dress, deportment or behaviour escaped him.

Once started, he could weave the family connections up and down the generations and add a synopsis of the many families with whom connections had been made by marriage. Although it had taken Rose some time to tease out the main threads, especially when the same Christian names appeared time and time again, it was always perfectly clear to her that Thomas was quite right. The Molyneux might not themselves be related to everyone of importance, but they would almost certainly have a relative who was.

Sir Capel's sisters had all married well. Lady Violet, the eldest, was well-known in Dublin circles where she encouraged and supported young poets and playwrights, while her English husband conducted his affairs at Dublin Castle. Lady Jane, the youngest, had married a wealthy entrepreneur who was now a Cabinet Minister. Their London house in Lord North Street was a popular meeting place for Irish M. Ps. Lady Jane herself was frequently received at Court.

Lady Caroline's brothers, Harold and Rainham, had abandoned the small family estates in Cheshire and quietly made fortunes in the Manchester cotton industry. Harold had built Martham Park, in the countryside south of the city. On her only visit to England its scale and splendour had quite overawed Rose, but she'd been assured by Old Thomas that it was nothing compared to Rainham's mansion in Derbyshire.

One day, Lady Anne promised, they would go to London together, see the sights, visit the Queen and then go on to the Continent. She never spoke of France, or Italy, or any of the watering places frequented by the rich, but always of the Continent. But then, Lady Anne's knowledge of geography was distinctly limited, for she seldom opened her atlas or bothered to look at the books of engravings Miss Pringle brought down from Sir Capel's library.

Rose had first-hand knowledge of Lady Anne's weaknesses as a scholar, for it had been her task to sit with the sisters in the schoolroom, trying to help her with her work. But it had been a thankless and wearisome task. Unless she was in a good mood she would sit silent, waiting only for the moment when she was free to go down to the stables. Nothing held her interest unless it could be related to horses. A landscape with physical features to be jumped, forded or climbed, a historical personage mounted, a battle scene with charging cavalry. In the end, Miss Pringle too, gave up, turned her attention to the four younger girls and left Lady Anne to her silence.

Rose sighed. She'd ended up learning a great deal more than Lady Anne ever had, but what she'd learnt wasn't much use to her. No one in the servant's hall spoke French, nor could they recite the counties of Ireland, the main towns and their occupations, the rivers, mountains and lakes to be found in each of the four provinces. She could sketch rather well, do embroidery and drawn thread work, and read poetry and plays, but there was never time to practice what she'd learnt. The last sketch she'd done was a couple of years ago, a pencil portrait of Sam for her mother to send to her eldest sister, Mary, now married and settled in Donegal.

It was all very well, having nice clothes, and a comfortable place, the prospect of travelling to England and the Continent, but what was given with one hand was taken away with the other. What was the use of having all these things if you found you never had time to enjoy them?

The lark stopped singing. She gazed up again into the vast, empty vault of the sky. The tiny brown dot was dropping towards her. She followed it's descent intently, made out at last the narrow, brown wings as they unfurled. It came closer and closer, swooping down, silent now, quite indifferent to her presence and dropped suddenly into a clump of rich grass threaded with the bleached remains of last year's growth.

She listened. Barely audible above the gentle murmur of the breeze, she could just make out the tentative vocalising of tiny fledglings. The lark reappeared, this time only flying a short distance. Darting back and forth, it pursued the insects that swarmed in the heavy air and made journey after journey to feed the waiting youngsters.

So fascinated was Rose with the lark's domestic duties, it was some time before she noticed the sun glinting on the polished bodywork of a small coach that had stopped on the road immediately below her. Despite it's modest proportions, it was drawn by four well-matched greys, a sign it had come some distance, probably from Dublin itself.

Well, that was quite likely. Only that morning as they shared their early breakfast, her mother had spoken of the visitors who were expected in the course of the next few days.

'How many, Ma, did you say were coming?'

'Oh, a houseful and a half,' Hannah replied, wryly. 'The young ones will have to sleep in the schoolroom to leave the nursery for the ladies maids, Sam and Tom move into the loft to leave their room for the grooms and coachmen. Every bedroom's in use except the one where the damp got in with the storm. If I hadn't brought down sheets that have been turned or mended, I wouldn't have had enough for the girls to make up all the beds,' she said, shaking her head as she cut even slices of bread from a new white loaf.

'No wonder Annie's going round in a state,' said Rose, laughing, as she took the teapot from the hob and filled her mother's teacup and then her own. 'It must be like feeding an army.'

'Aye indeed,' said Hannah absently, a distant look in her eye. 'I'd hate to be a cook, making food for all those grand people. I sometimes think of our neighbours away up in Ardtur. They could have lived for a month on the scraps that go out of here to the dogs and chickens. Even the Rosses in Ramelton – you remember the people who were so good to us in '61 – wouldn't have had a Sunday meal the like of what these visitors get three times a day.'

'Do you ever wish you were back there, Ma?' Rose asked as she buttered her bread and spread it with damson jam.

To her surprise, her mother laughed.

'Sure there's never any back to go to, Rose dear,' she said quickly. 'Oh, yes, I'd love to have my time again with your father and your brothers and sister and Sam and Rose that we lost, but you can't have bits of your life over again. That's why you have to take the good of everything you have when you have it. That way you have fewer regrets when things change.'

'But are you not angry, Ma? You were so happy in those days. I know we hadn't much, but I remember you and Da were always laughing and talking away to each other and it was one man that put an end to it.'

'Aye, he did that, and put an end to a few lives forby,' said Hannah, her grey eyes suddenly dull. 'Your Aunt Mary for one,' she went on, 'and our neighbour Andy Laverty and dear old Daniel McGee at Casheltown. He was only in the workhouse a week, poor man,' she said sadly, putting down her bread and jam untasted.

She stared at the pretty china plate from the tea service Lady Caroline had recently retired from its life in the drawing room.

'What did happen Aunt Mary, Ma? I remember our Mary crying and crying for days that summer, but she wouldn't speak to me. And then the news came from Scotland about Da. To tell the truth, I forgot about her.'

Hannah smiled grimly.

'Mary had a bit of spirit about her. She wouldn't go in the cart to the workhouse. She went up the mountain. How she ever did it with her bad legs is a mystery, but your father and Patrick found her about a week after, crouched down behind a heap of stones with her rosary in her hand. It was so cold that first night she'd never have seen the morning.'

Rose crossed herself unthinkingly, then smiled suddenly as she realised what she'd done.

'I have to remember not to cross myself when we go to church with the family. It was Aunt Mary taught me, you know. She always used to say "When in doubt, cross yourself." She said it was a way of asking for help from above.'

'Good advice, Rose. There's times in everybody's life when they don't know how they'll manage to keep going. It doesn't matter what church you go to, or how it tells you to believe, it's all one when you're in need of help. Mary was wise enough. She trusted in her God and she was able to do what was right for her. I had to do the same when your father died, though my way was different.'

Rose saw a moistness in her mother's eyes and was sorry she'd mentioned Aunt Mary. Her mother seldom spoke about the past, unless you asked her a direct question, but then she would often say quite a lot, as if grateful to have the chance to share the thoughts she'd normally keep to herself, so Rose waited to see if she would go on.

Hannah cut her piece of bread in two, but made no move to pick up either of the halves. She sipped her tea.

'I think of your father every morning when I get

out of bed,' she said slowly. 'Every time I put food on the table. Every time I see you, or Sam, walk across the yard. I think how glad he would be that we're safe and well. And that comforts me. He was always so anxious we'd have enough. He worked so hard and he loved us so much. Nothing can take that away, Rose. If you've been truly loved, it stays with you forever.'

She'd looked at the clock then and reminded Rose it was almost seven, time to finish breakfast and leave all tidy before they went across to the servant's hall to start the day's work.

Rose looked more closely at the carriage on the road below. It still sat where she'd first seen it. She watched as the coachman and the groom climbed down from the box and came round to the front horses, stroking them and looking at their legs. One of them must have cast a shoe.

The groom was a tall fellow in a green livery that looked far too tight on his shoulders. She could almost see the fabric straining as he bent down to examine the leading grey's hooves. When he straightened up, she noticed he'd undone the glinting metal buttons and his neck scarf was busily unwinding itself.

He spoke to the coachman, looked around him, caught sight of her, and to her great surprise, looked up at her and waved. Without thinking, she waved back.

'Well, the cheek of him,' she said aloud, when

she saw he was now beckoning her to come down. She stood her ground and went back to watching her lark, still hard at work feeding it's family.

Out of the corner of her eye, she saw him conferring again with the coachman. A few moments later, he was striding up the hillside towards her. In no time at all, he stood before her, looking down at her out of candid blue eyes.

'Would you not come down an' give us a hand?' he said, agreeably. 'Sure what way's this to treat poor travellers?'

'You don't look too poor to me,' she retorted sharply. 'Were you wanting me to shoe your horse for you?'

'Well now that would be a great help, but you might get your nice hands dirty. I'd settle for a bit of information and a word or two to her Ladyship. I reckon she'll melt soon in thon wee box.'

Rose laughed. She couldn't help it. Whether it was the unperturbable smile, the northern accent, or the thought of his mistress melting away, she couldn't be cross with him.

'It's my afternoon off,' she said feebly.

'Aren't you the lucky one? I've never met one of those,' he said, laughing. 'C'mon wi' me,' he said, bending down and lifting her to her feet as easily as if she were a child. 'Do up your buttons like a good girl or m'lady might wonder where I found you.'

# CHAPTER FIVE

'Good day t'ye miss,' said the coachman, a tall, angular figure, dressed as if it were still the middle of winter. 'Can ye tell us how far we're off Currane Lodge?' he asked, as John swung her over the low wall that bounded the road and set her back on her feet. 'We can't be far, but I've niver been here afore.'

On the road itself it was hot and still and very dusty. Not a trace of a breeze. Pestered by the flies attracted to their sweating bodies, the four greys were swishing their tails and tossing their heads uneasily.

'You're not far indeed,' said Rose agreeably. 'About a mile perhaps to the main entrance, but the farm entrance is nearer. It's just a cart track but its bone dry at the moment and the trees make it shady.'

'An English mile or an Irish mile?' asked the coachman doubtfully.

'Is there any difference?'

'Ach aye,' said John promptly, nodding his head towards the coach. He dropped his voice to a whisper. 'Any sort of a mile would be too far for m' lady. She's not one for walkin'.'

From the coach itself came a loud banging. The small, shiny box vibrated on its springs, making the greys fidget even more. The door flew open, but no one emerged.

'John, John, where are you?' called a peremptory voice. 'What *is* going on? Come here this minute and tell me what's the matter.'

John looked from the coachman to Rose and back again, as if he hoped between them they'd solve his problem, but the coachman just smiled wryly and shrugged his shoulders. When she saw the look on John's face, Rose had to smile too. He couldn't have been doing the job for long if he'd let that tone of voice bother him.

'Pegasus has thrown a shoe, m' lady, an' hurt the frog of his foot forby,' he explained, standing by the open door and leaning into the gloomy interior.

'And what do you propose to do about me?' she asked crossly. 'Leave me to perish by the wayside while you commiserate with Pegasus? I'm sure I heard a woman's voice a few minutes ago. Who was it?'

'Yes, m' lady. I went to ask a young lady how far it was to the Lodge.'

'And how far is it?'

'About a mile.'

'Well then, one of you go and ask Sir Capel to send his coach for me. He can't be using it when we're expected. Where's this "young lady" of yours, John? Let her come up to me while I wait.'

Rose glared at John as he turned away from the open door and stepped over to where she and the coachman were standing, near enough to have heard every word.

'Lady Ishbel would like you to go up to sit with her while one of us walks to Currane Lodge for the coach,' he said, looking at her doubtfully.

Rose sighed. There was nothing for it. If Lady Ishbel was a guest at the house, the discourtesy of not doing as she asked would certainly be reported to Lady Caroline. She wiped her damp forehead and took a deep breath. When she climbed up the hillside, she thought she'd escaped duties for the whole afternoon. It never occurred to her she might be brought down again to spend the rest of it in a hot little box of a coach entertaining a cross old woman.

She waited by the open door of the coach for John to lower the step, but either he'd forgotten where it was, or he was in such a hurry to get away he made no move to release it. He simply came up behind her, put his hands round her waist and swung her up so that she landed neatly in the seat facing Lady Ishbel.

'Well, then,' said Lady Ishbel promptly, 'you're an elegant young lady for these parts. Who are you and where do you come from?'

Rose collected her wits. She was not used to being picked up and put down again twice in fifteen minutes, she was furious at the loss of her precious afternoon, and she couldn't imagine now why she'd ever agreed to come down to the road in the first place.

'My name is Rose McGinley and I come from Currane Lodge,' she said quickly.

*When giving your name to any guest, or member of the family always curtsy*. It was the very first thing she'd learnt when she'd started work in the servant's hall. You could hardly curtsy if you were already seated, so she folded her hands in her lap and looked attentive. At least it showed she knew how to behave, not like that idiot of a groom. How long he'd last in the job was a nice question.

'Yes, of course,' said Lady Ishbel, nodding vigorously, so that the dark feathers in her hat bobbed up and down. 'Your mother is the housekeeper who came from Donegal and you used to help the governess with the girls. Particularly Lady Anne, I gather. I hear you've been most useful to Lady Caroline,' she said approvingly.

'Lady Caroline is most kind,' Rose replied, as the coach suddenly jolted backwards, throwing Lady Ishbel forward in her seat.

'Whoa, whoa, steady there boys. Steady there. Easy does it.'

'Oh, what now? demanded Lady Ishbel irritably, as the coach continued to rock and vibrate and the voices of the coachman and his groom echoed around them.

'See what's happening, Rose.'

Rose stepped across to the heavily curtained windows on the sunny side of the coach, pulled one back and peered out. She found herself almost level with a pair of handsome black horses and a coach twice the size of the one in which they sat.

'Another coach, my lady. It can't pass at this point and the greys are giving trouble.'

'Oh well, that solves *our* problem,' said Lady Ishbel briskly. 'They *must* be fellow guests. Go and present my compliments to whoever it is. Ask them to drop one of their servants and give me their seat,' she added, as she picked up her gloves and began to draw them carefully over her bent fingers.

Rose caught up her skirt, jumped cautiously down from the rocking coach and made her way behind it to where the newly arrived coach had drawn up, its coachman and groom still on the box, the horses tossing their heads in frustration, having come to such an unexpected standstill. From the amount of dust on their gleaming flanks they'd been travelling rapidly for some time.

Rose nodded to the coachman who touched his

hat respectfully. The groom, however, gave her a dazzling smile, jumped down from the box, bowed to her, accompanied her to the door of the coach and opened it for her.

'Lady Ishbel presents her compliments and asks if you could give her a seat to Currane Lodge.'

'Why, of course, we can, can't we Katherine?'

'Yes indeed. If Jane comes and squeezes in beside Carrie and me, Lady Ishbel can sit with you, Aunty Ben. Do you know her?'

'Yes, I most certainly do,' laughed Aunty Ben. 'But it is so long ago since we danced the night away we may not recognise one another,' she said cheerfully, as she turned back to Rose. 'My compliments to Lady Ishbel. Tell her an old friend and her favourite niece will be pleased to see her.'

The two coachmen were now conferring. There was no possibility of passing at this point on the road. John was nowhere to be seen and the other groom was watching her every move as she delivered her message.

Lady Ishbel seemed spry enough once she was on her feet. She lost no time at all in moving from one coach to another and settling herself in the seat by the window which Aunty Ben had vacated for her.

Rose turned away as she heard the two older women greet each other.

'Oh my goodness, Ben, it's you! How extraordinary. And this is Katherine. My dear, I knew your father when I lived in Dublin, but you weren't even born then. Such a beautiful preaching voice. I can still remember it. But such an age ago. And your husband, Captain O'Shea, I hope he is well?'

'Oh yes, Lady Ishbel, he *is* well, but he hates coaches. He and his friend Lord Harrington are great supporters of the railway. They even persuade their unfortunate mounts to travel with them. I expect he'll have arrived at least a day before us.'

Rose stood in the small patch of shade cast by the empty coach and wondered if she could slip away unnoticed. Now that Lady Ishbel was safely settled, it was up to the coachmen to get them back to the house. There was no question of her being offered a seat for Lady Ishbel and Aunty Ben were generously proportioned. Only Jane and Carrie's slim figures saved one of them from having to walk.

She had just made up her mind to slip over the wall and go back up the hillside when a breathless figure appeared at her side.

'Rose, would you give us a hand and hold Pegasus for us? He's in a bad way.'

'Would you like me to uncouple the others and reverse the coach as well?' she asked sarcastically.

'Now, Rose, don't be unkind,' he said quietly. 'Wouldn't I help you if it were the other way round?'

Yes, he probably would, she thought to herself.

There was no doubt he was good-natured enough, but just at this moment she was not at all inclined to admit any of his good qualities.

'How do you know my name?' she asked shortly.

'Sure, I listened when ye went up inta the coach. I knew her ladyship woud ask ye.'

Rose laughed and shook her head. The man was as innocent as a child. That would do him no good in his present occupation.

'Come on then. Take me to Pegasus. Who in heaven's name called him that?'

'Oh, that's Sir Capel. He's a great one for books. Books and birds. Doesn't much like people. Hates visitin'. Always sends the wife first to make sure the beds is aired afore he comes. But he's a right sort. Never do anyone down, not even the boot boy.'

He paused, ran his hand down Pegasus's long, grey nose.

'Ach sure we'll soon have you right as rain,' he said to him reassuringly, as he began to undo the traces, more skilfully than Rose had anticipated.

'You're not afeard o' horses, are ye?' he asked suddenly, looking round at her, his blue eyes full of concern.

'I wouldn't need to be. I spend half my life talking up at Lady Anne on a stallion bigger than Pegasus.'

He looked relieved as he led the limping horse slowly forward to a patch of rough grass broader

76

than the one beside the coach. He handed her the reins and stood watching for a moment as she stroked his head.

'There ye are now, Pegasus. Aren't you the lucky one? Wasn't it worth a bad foot for all the attention yer getting'? Maybe if I had a bad foot, she'd come an' stroke my head, instead of bitin' it off.'

Rose opened her mouth to retort, but he'd already gone to help the coachman release the other lead horse.

It was not long before Lady Ishbel's coach had been drawn into the field entrance which John had located some small distance away, thus allowing the larger coach with its full compliment of ladies and servants to proceed. When it had passed, Lady Ishbel's coachman, O'Donnell, checked the re-harnessed greys, shook the reins and followed, leaving John and Rose with Pegasus and his companion.

'Are ye tired?' he said suddenly, looking down at her as she stood leaning against Pegasus, a quiet animal who now stood easily, his hurt foot slightly raised from the rough ground.

'Why do you ask?' she replied curiously.

'Sure I could put you up on Icarus and lead the both of them. No trouble at all.'

She laughed at the thought of a horse called Icarus and shook her head helplessly at the idea of riding him.

'And a nice pair we'd make coming into the stable yard with me on one of your Sir Capel's horses,' she said, shaking her head vigorously. 'You'd never hear the end of it in the servant's hall or the stables.'

'Ach sure I wouden care about that if ye were tired. It's powerful hot the day. Is it always like this in this part of the world?' he asked, as they led the two horses carefully back onto the carriage road.

'No, we get our share of rain and cold, but its probably warmer here than Armagh. It's certainly a lot warmer than Donegal.'

'How did ye know I wus from Armagh?'

'Your Sir Capel is my Sir Capel's cousin. When you meet Old Thomas, the coachman, you'll hear who everybody is and where they come from. And maybe you'll get as mixed up as I used to with them all having the same names.'

'We could call them Sir Capel North and Sir Capel South?' he offered.

'Or Sir Capel Armagh, and Sir Capel Kerry,' she added, smiling.

They paused to let Pegasus rest and she watched while he pulled off the scarf that had worked itself loose in the course of the afternoon and was now in danger of falling to the ground. He stuffed it in the pocket of his livery jacket, then took off the jacket itself. As he wiped the sweat from his brow, Rose asked the question that had been in her mind since she'd first laid eyes on him.

'How long have you been a groom?'

'A groom?' he repeated, an unexpected note of outrage in his normal easy speech. 'I'm no groom,' he said sharply. 'I'm a time-served blacksmith. As good a one as you'll find.'

'I do apologise, your honour,' she said, curtseying to him. 'You must forgive me if I was taken in by your disguise.'

He threw back his head and laughed.

'Sure, maybe I could have taken ye in if the coat had fitted, but that coat's been the plague o' my life. Even the buttons get hot. An' sure I niver was one for wearin' a coat anyway. Not wi' my work. Ye've no call for one in a forge, even in the wintertime.'

'So what are you doing here?'

'Ach, just helpin' out. The groom's old mother was took bad a few days before they were due to set out an' he asked Sir Capel for leave not to go. Sir Capel came to the forge an' put it to me that I was no stranger to Paddy O'Donnell or the horses, so it'd be a bit of an outing for me. Ah wasn't all that keen, I admit. But then I thought to m'eself "John take every opportunity ye get t'see yer own country."' He paused deliberately. 'If I'd knowed I'd meet you, wild horses wouldn't have stopped me, as the saying is,' he continued, with a broad smile, his livery coat thrown casually over one shoulder, his blue eyes fixed firmly on hers.

To Rose's amazement, she found herself blushing. She looked away and tried to think up a suitable retort, but before she'd managed it, John had asked his next question.

'Ye mentioned Donegal. I've heard tell it's powerful wild in winter up on the coast. D'ye know the place?'

'I do. I was brought up there, though not on the coast. We lived inland in the valley of Lough Gartan, a townland called Ardtur. Until we were evicted, that is. In '61.'

She paused and glanced up at him. He was watching her, his mouth open in amazement.

'There were good people in Ramelton cleared out their barn for us and fed us till we made plans what we'd do. We were better off than most. Some people had nowhere to go. Some build huts of sods for shelter.'

He nodded, encouraging her to go on with her story. She hadn't thought about it for so long, she wondered what best to say. Then the great plan they'd had came back to her, the one they'd talked about all through that summer.

'My parents thought of taking us all to Australia and making a new life there. There was a scheme got up in Sydney to help people get away in a ship called the *Abysinnia,* but then my father died and that changed everything.'

'Ach dear a dear. Sure what happened him? He couldn't ha' been very old.'

'No, not that old,' she agreed, she shook her head sadly. 'He took my two brothers with him to the haymaking in Scotland that same summer to help raise the passage money. He was throwing up sheaves of hay to my brother on top of a stack when he just fell to the ground. They got a doctor to him, but he said it was his heart. That he couldn't have done anything for him.'

'An' what about yer mother an' yourself?'

'And my sister Mary and wee Sam, the baby,' she added, not wanting them left out of the story.

'Och, Rose dear, how could anyone put out a whole family of you like that?' he asked, his voice catching with emotion.

'Easy, John, easy,' she said lightly, waving her free hand gently, careful not to startle Pegasus. 'No trouble at all. There was over two hundred people on that ship who'd been evicted from our valley alone. Do you not have evictions in Armagh?'

'Well, if we have, I've niver come across them. But then, we only know what we've met up with. Sure what would the well-off people know about the poverty of the poor souls that pays them rent? And how would those same poor people know there's many a rich person isn't as happy as they are?'

He fell silent as they turned into the cart track leading to the farm and its outbuildings. The trees provided welcome shade and Pegasus moved more easily on the bare earth track with grass growing up the middle.

'So why didn't ye go?'

'My mother's not a Catholic and the money for the passages had come from Catholics in Sydney. They'd got up a subscription when they heard what was happening. Ma thought it wasn't fair to take help that might not be meant for her. But she also said she could face anything with my father beside her. Without him, she hadn't the courage for going so far away.'

'Thank goodness for that,' he said warmly.

'What?' she demanded, startled.

'Thank goodness ye didn't go. Sure we'd never be walking here, now, in a lane in Kerry.'

Ahead of them the trackway opened out into a broad cobbled yard surrounded with whitewashed buildings. The two coaches had been towed away and grooms were already rubbing down the black horses. The two greys had their heads bent deep into a horse trough.

'When will you be finished your work?' he asked, looking her full in the face.

'When the cows come home,' she said, laughing.

'We could walk back up to your hillside and listen to the nightingale.'

'How do you know there'll be a nightingale?'

'Well, if there isn't, sure we can imagine one.'

She shook her head.

'I never know when I'm going to be let go. Especially when there's visitors. If Lady Anne doesn't need me, Lady Caroline may want me to see to some of the guests. You might wait a long time.'

'I'll wait all night if I hafta,' he said in a whisper, as a young lad with red hair came towards them.

The lad held out his hand and grinned at him.

'You're John Hamilton from Armagh,' he said firmly. 'I'm to show you and Paddy O'Donnell your quarters. The meal is at six in the servants' hall. Don't be late or they'll give you half rations.'

'I'll leave you now,' said Rose smiling. 'You're in good hands. This is my brother Sam,' she said proudly.

She turned her back on them and made her way towards the stone steps that led up to the rooms she shared with her mother. Just as she reached them, the clock on the stable block struck the half hour and the yard filled with noise as the afternoon's picnic party returned.

She slipped into the empty sitting room, grateful to have a quiet half hour before going down to the servants' hall. She moved the small table where her mother kept her lists of guests and rooms and went right up to the window, gazing down at the movements of riders, grooms and horses.

Directly below her, she saw Lady Anne smiling triumphantly as Conor walked delicately across the cobbles. Sam was staring up at Lily as he held her reins for her to dismount. She ran her eyes over the crowded yard and for a moment couldn't see the tall figure of John Hamilton.

Then, Captain O'Shea and his companion moved their horses to the water trough and she spotted him. He was standing exactly where they'd parted, looking up towards her window. He saw her and beamed, raised a finger in salute and turned away to join Paddy O'Donnell at the horse trough.

# CHAPTER SIX

John Hamilton was as good as his word. When Rose finally slipped down the back stairs and made her way across the stable yard in the gathering dusk, she saw him excuse himself from the circle of grooms and coachmen sitting outside the stables, listening to Old Tom and enjoying the pleasant warmth of a fine May evening. He strode across the yard and was at her side before she'd even set foot on the steps that led up to her room.

'Ye haven't done so bad,' he said cheerfully, beaming down at her, as he moved between her and the rising steps. 'It's only half nine. I thought it mighta been midnight if ye'd had wait up for her and unpin her hair and suchlike. Some women can take half the night to get to their bed. So I've heard, anyway. Will we go for a bit of a walk?'

Rose was tired. The hours since she'd last set foot on these same steps had not been easy. At six o'clock the servants' hall had been noisy and crowded. Cook was in a bad temper and the butler, Mr Smithers was standing on his dignity, afraid the presence of servants not under his direct control might undermine his rigid rules and regulations.

As always on such occasions, he'd insisted that Hannah should have her meal in his room as a member of the Senior Staff. Normally, he was quite willing to let her to eat in the servants' hall to be with Rose and Sam. And this evening, Sam too was missing from his usual place.

One of the young ladies had left her paint box at their picnic place and he'd been despatched to find it.

Rose ate her supper silently, avoiding the cautious glances of John Hamilton and the more engaging smiles of the groom from the O'Shea coach. Quite suddenly, the place, the known figures, the coming evening task, had all become part of a wearying round which no longer offered the comfort and support of routine and familiarity, but only the weariness of an endlessly repeating pattern.

As soon as supper was over she made her way to Lady Anne's bedroom. This was often the worst point of the whole day. She hadn't rung, for she could not expect Rose to do without her evening meal, but Rose knew she would be waiting impatiently. Although there was more than an hour to get her ready for dinner at eight o'clock, she would fuss and fret as if there were no more than a mere fifteen minutes before the gong sounded.

'What shall I wear, Rose?' she asked, the moment she entered the room.

The breathlessness of her voice was a warning that she was excited or overwrought. She'd thrown her hat and riding jacket so carelessly on the bed, they'd slipped on the silk coverlet and lay in a tumbled heap on the floor. Beyond that, she'd not bothered to undress further, even though her dressing gown was laid out waiting for her.

Rose put aside her own thoughts and prepared herself for whatever difficulties might lie ahead.

'What about the green velvet?' she suggested lightly.

'You say that every time I ask, Rose,' she began irritably. 'Why do you always say the same thing? Don't you like any of my other dresses, or is it just the green velvet is easier to clean?'

'No, it's harder to clean,' said Rose patiently, 'velvets always are. Specially if it's water or wine you've spilt.'

Lady Anne had a habit of being unpleasant, even insulting, that Rose had long ago learnt to ignore, but to her surprise, this evening, she threw her a contrite glance and said, 'You wouldn't ever leave me, would you, Rose?'

'What *do* you mean?' Rose asked, so completely taken aback by the question that she spoke with a quite inappropriate sharpness.

'Oh, go and work for someone else,' she began hastily. 'Go and join your brother in Nova Scotia, or the one in Scotland. Get married.' She paused. 'Leave me to manage by myself.'

With her shoulders drooping and her face crumpled almost to tears, she looked such a picture of misery it was all Rose could do not to smile.

'But you wouldn't be by yourself,' she protested. 'Your mother would find someone else to help you.'

She dropped onto the couch at the foot of the large, draped four poster. Mr Smithers would be apoplectic if he knew she'd sat down uninvited, but if Lady Anne was going to talk rather than get undressed there was no use waiting. You could stand all evening and she'd never notice, unless you stopped paying attention to her.

'But that's not what I mean,' she said, shaking her head violently. 'Any decent servant can do my hair and help me into my clothes. But . . .'

She paused awkwardly, looked around the room as if she had lost something.

'Sometimes *you* can tell me what I ought to do,' she burst out. 'Like ignore that silly Captain O'Shea. Did you know he was married, Rose?' she asked crossly.

'No, I didn't, not until I met his wife this afternoon.'

'He's horrible. Really horrible. He never even bothered to go and see her when he knew her coach had arrived. And he's so rude to Lord Harrington. I couldn't bear to be married to a man like that,' she ended, her voice rising ominously.

'But why should you marry someone you didn't like?'

'I might not know until it was too late and then there'd be all the babies and I might die.'

'You might die anyway,' said Rose crisply.

Lady Anne sat speechless, staring at her as if she couldn't believe what she'd heard.

Rose knew she probably shouldn't have said that, but now it *was* said it couldn't be unsaid. This was not an occasion to humour her or to scold her. She wasn't quite sure what sort of an occasion it was, but the signs were bad. The chances of getting her dressed and ready to go down by eight o'clock began to look very doubtful indeed.

'You can't do much about dying, no one can, so there's no use thinking about it. But you *can* choose the man you want to marry. Your father wouldn't dream of forcing you to marry someone he thought suitable if you didn't like him. So it's up to you.'

'But how would I know?'

It was not the first time Lady Anne had asked a question that amazed her. For all her education, her visits to England and other parts of Ireland, her questions could suddenly reveal how little idea of judging other people she had yet acquired.

'Simple. You'd go riding with him,' Rose began

quietly. 'You'd watch how he behaves. That's what you did with Captain O'Shea this afternoon, wasn't it? That's how you know you wouldn't want to marry a man like him.'

Lady Anne shook her head vigorously.

'That's all very well, Rose, but what if he didn't ride?'

Rose laughed and was grateful when the younger woman's face softened slightly.

'I don't think he'd stand a great chance with you if he didn't ride,' she said easily, 'but you could still test him out. Take him to the stables and introduce him to Conor. Get Conor to do his party pieces, like walking up the steps. See whether he's interested or not. If he's the right man for you, he'll pay attention *for your sake*, even if he knows nothing about horses himself.'

'Rose, how do you know all these things? You're only three years older than I am and you're a servant.'

Lady Anne's whole appearance had changed. She looked puzzled and she was smiling, sure signs the danger point was passed.

'I'm not sure how I know, but I *am* sure you'll be late for dinner if we don't get started,' Rose replied crisply, as she stood up and waited for her to do likewise. But Lady Anne made no move.

'Promise me you'll never leave me,' she said softly.

'I can't promise you that,' Rose replied, just as softly.

For one long, exhausting moment, Rose watched her face, saw the conflicting emotions chase across her features, observed the twist of her mouth, the anxious flick of her eyes. She had almost prepared herself for the scream, the brush thrown violently against the wall, when she saw her drop her eyes. She heard the deep intake of breath.

'I'm sorry, Rose. I shouldn't have asked that.'

Rose smiled, relief and amazement flowing over her. It was the first time in her life she'd heard Lady Anne apologise to anyone.

'Why do you always choose the green velvet?' Lady Anne continued, smiling, as if the words had never been spoken.

'Because it suits you. When you wear pink, or white, or blue, you try to look like your sisters. And you aren't like them at all.'

'Who *am* I like then?'

'You're not like anybody else, you're like yourself. But too often you try to be like other people. That's what makes you so unhappy.'

Startled by what she'd just said, Rose bent down quickly and picked up the jacket and riding hat. She'd no idea she'd been thinking about what made Lady Anne so unhappy until the words popped out, ready and waiting to be spoken.

'I'll wear the green. What about my hair?'

'Up.'

'Why?'

'Because you have good skin and fine eyes. When you smile they light up.'

'So *you* think I'm pretty, Rose?' said Lady Anne, turning from the dressing table to face her.

'No, I don't. I think your sisters are pretty. But you have much stronger features. *You* could be handsome.'

'How?'

'Just by being yourself and deciding what's right for you.'

Lady Anne stood up, pulled off her shirt and scarf, dropped them on the floor and held up her arms.

Rose lowered her petticoats over her head, one by one, slid the green velvet down to her waist and let the soft fabric fall into place over the petticoats. She did up the fastenings in half the usual time, Lady Anne stood quite still, staring into the large triple mirror of her dressing table. She fetched the matching satin shoes from the cupboard, as Lady Anne pulled out the long hairpins from the tight coil that fitted neatly below her riding hat. She handed Rose the hairbrush, sat down and regarded her closely in the mirror.

'You're much prettier than I am, Rose, and much wiser. If I promise to be good, will you help me stop being so horrible?'

\* \* \*

'You're lookin' tired,' said John Hamilton, bringing her back to herself with a jerk, 'but a wee breathe of fresh air would do you no harm. It's awful stuffy in that house.'

She looked up at the strong face regarding her so steadily. He was hardly what you would call handsome, but his features were pleasing, the skin tanned by sun and wind, the eyes bright and shining. She leant against the stable wall and laughed.

'Mind now, you've no Icarus to bring me back. You'll have to carry me if I fall with tiredness.'

'Sure that'd be no bother,' he said, lifting her up easily and setting her down again by his side.

'Will we give it a try?' he said encouragingly.

'We will,' she said promptly, suddenly aware that the whole collection of coachmen and grooms were watching them. She turning on her heel to lead the way down the stable yard. Despite the quickness of her movement John didn't so much as miss his step. To the experienced eyes of their fellow servants, they looked as if they'd been walking out for months.

'There's a wee bit of life left in ye yet,' said John as they came under the shadow of the trees and followed the cart track and towards the road.

'Don't depend on it,' she laughed. 'But I'm glad to be out.'

'Was her Ladyship in one of her moods tonight?'

'Who told you about that?' she asked sharply.

'A young gentleman with red hair and a quick wit,' he said, smiling at her. 'Goes by the name of Sam.'

Her look softened immediately.

'Did he find the paint box?'

'Aye, indeed. Just where she'd left it. Do they not teach these young ladies to gather up after themselves?'

Rose laughed heartily.

'Are you joking? Where would servants be if there was no gentry to drop their belongings all over the place for them to pick up?'

He smiled and looked at her thoughtfully.

'D'you like the job, Rose, pickin' up and fetchin' and carryin?'

'It could be worse,' she said honestly. 'There's plenty on the Kerry estates hard pressed to find a bite after a bad harvest. No one goes hungry at Currane Lodge.'

'Did you go hungry in Donegal?'

She caught the edge of anxiety in his voice. It was there too in his eyes. She had not known many men as friends and only once had she walked out. But never had anyone asked her about her life as if it were of such consequence to them.

'No, we came near, but father was always a hard worker and Ma was very careful to keep something for the bad times. Her uncle in Nova Scotia used to send her money and it was always put away.'

She paused and looked at him sharply.

'Do you not have poor people in Armagh?'

'To tell you the truth, I'm ashamed I don't know more about m'own country,' he said shaking his head sadly. 'I was listenin' to Old Thomas there after we'd finished our work and I thought to myself, "John aren't you the lucky one has never wanted?"'

He paused, looked down at her and went on.

'Ye see m' father and grandfather and indeed his father too, were all blacksmiths,' he said, throwing up one hand and bringing it down in a series of steps. 'An' sure there's always work for a blacksmith wherever there's horses, working horses or carriage horses, or where there's militia. What I like best though is working with machines, looms and engines an' suchlike, but I can earn a livin' wherever I go. An' that's more than your poor farmer can.'

They came out onto the carriage road and stood by a gap in the low wall that bounded the lake. Across the perfectly calm water two swans were sailing slowly by, a cluster of grubby-looking cygnets following behind, the ripples of their passage spreading out like a long train behind them.

The light was fading faster now, the sky a pale gold. Where the rays of the setting sun still caught the high, wispy evening cloud, the flimsy scraps where touched with orange and red.

'I think we'll get another good day, the morra,' he said gazing out over the lake. 'This is a lovely place. Everywhere ye look is water or sky. I'm not used to that at all. C'oud we rest here a wee while?'

They sat down side by side on the tumbled stones and watched the swans dip their long necks deep into the water. From the bushes nearby came the scuffle of small birds settling to roost. A deep silence settled around them.

'Whereabouts in Armagh do you live? Near the city itself?' she asked.

'About two or three miles outside, a wee townland called Annacramp.'

'Don't worry, it doesn't notice,' she said, grinning.

'What d'ye mean?' he asked, a look of complete bafflement on his face.

'You must know what Annacramp means,' she said, suddenly aware the more he said the more he seemed to live in a different world.

'Means? It's just a name, isn't it?' he added doubtfully.

'In Irish, it means *the place of the wild garlic*.'

'Oh.'

John dropped his head and looked at the grass growing up through the fragments of stone at his feet. He seemed dismayed and Rose wondered how such a light remark could have so dampened his good spirits.

'An' what does Salter's Grange mean?'

'That one's not Irish. Grange is French. It means barn. It must have belonged to a man called Salter,' she replied, still puzzled by the look on his face.

'Ye mean ye can understan' Irish and French, forby English?'

She nodded and watched the look of loss and sadness deepen.

'Sure ye cou'd pass for a lady yerself,' he said dejectedly.

'Thank you very much for the compliment,' said Rose laughing heartily.

'Ach no, I didn't mean it like that,' he said flustered. 'Ye are a lady. I meant, you could marry gentry if you'd a mind to.'

'An' then I'd have servants to run after me and dress me for dinner and drive me round in my coach to see the sights,' she said cheerfully. 'You could come and be in charge of all my coaches and horses. I'd pay you very well.'

'No. There'd be no payin' me. Not all the gold in Ireland would do.' He paused deliberately. 'I'd want ye for meself.'

Rose looked away. In all her thoughts of men and marriage, it had never occurred to her it might be like this. A man she'd only met hours before. A man from a different world. A man who was so direct that there'd be no way of dealing with him other than honestly.

'I'm not entirely sure it would suit me,' she said lightly. 'And I still haven't found a young Sir or Lord that I like. I'll maybe wait a bit longer.'

He smiled slowly, the sadness fading from his face as he drew her to her feet and put his arms round her.

'How long d'ye think this visit might be, Rose? Would it be long enough for ye to make up yer mind? For my mind's made up.'

# CHAPTER SEVEN

Rose was silent at breakfast next morning, her mind full of thoughts and images from the day just past. She could hardly believe it was only yesterday she'd slipped away to enjoy her free afternoon and made her way up the rocky slopes of her favourite hillside. It felt now as if the lark sang his song weeks ago and she'd known John Hamilton for most of her life.

Hannah too was silent, weary from the continuous demands of the previous day. Only when the last guest was settled for the night, all the requests for extra pillows, early morning tea, or breakfast in their rooms, duly answered, had she been able to lock up her housekeeper's room and the adjacent store rooms and slip away through the empty corridors and staircases of the darkened house to the privacy of her own small lodging place.

The first days of entertaining were always the worst. The guests themselves were still unsettled and their servants disrupted the regular routine of the house. Those guests who'd not brought their own servants had to be provided for. The senior house servants had to organise more carefully, maids and kitchen staff barely got time to eat their meals. It only wanted one member to fall ill, even of the junior staff and the boots and shoes would not be cleaned by eight o'clock, the downstairs rooms would not dusted before the ladies gathered after breakfast to write letters or diaries, the silver would have to be used unpolished and the meals would be delayed. After nearly fourteen years of summer visitors, seven of them as housekeeper, Hannah still breathed a sigh of relief when the last of the carriages departed at the beginning of August and Lady Caroline and Nanny took the younger children to the seaside.

'Ma, how long are the people from the north staying?' said Rose, her thoughts straying once more to John Hamilton.

'Lady Ishbel and Sir Capel?'

Rose nodded, her mouth full of bread and jam.

'Well *he* hasn't appeared yet. He usually gives his wife a week's start to make sure things are the way he likes them. It'll probably be a fortnight or three weeks from when he actually arrives,' said Hannah wryly. 'Not that their going helps very much. As soon as they leave, Lady Violet is coming with the three eldest girls and their governess, a coachman and *two* grooms. Poor old Sam and Tom won't get their quarters back till the end of August.'

Rose looked at her, grateful she hadn't asked why she'd been so late last night. Of course she would tell her she'd gone walking with John Hamilton, but she couldn't quite bring herself to mention his name just yet. For some strange reason, she could hardly say it over even in her own mind without blushing.

'Time we were moving, more's the pity,' said Hannah standing up and carrying their plates to the small sink in the corner of the room.

Rose drank up the rest of her tea quickly, her eyes never leaving her.

'Ma, you're limping. Is your back bad?'

'It's weary,' she admitted, turning back to face her. 'It was one thing after another, all day yesterday,' she went on, the tiredness plain in her voice. 'Never worry, you know as well as I do, the first day's always the worst,' she said, with a smile. 'How's Lady Anne taking it?'

'Better than I'd expected, so far. But it may not last . . .'

They tidied up the room with practised skill. Hannah donned a fresh white apron over her plain black dress and settled her cap on her head. As she tidied a few straggling hairs back from her face, Rose realised her mother was now not only grey but almost white. Only at the very back of her head was there any trace of her once strong fair hair.

'I'll maybe see you this evening, dear. She kept you very late last night. The poor girl's in such a bad way she can't really think of anyone but herself,' she said sadly.

They hurried across to the house, parting outside the servants' hall as the stable yard clock struck seven. Hannah went up to her room on the next floor to get cleaning materials ready for the housemaids when they came for their instructions. Rose turned into the short corridor leading to the boot-room. By collecting Lady Anne's riding boots herself, she could be sure she would find no fault with them.

As she made her way along the corridor, she heard a bell ring in the almost empty servant's hall behind her.

'Someone's up early this morning,' she said to the unshaven boot man. 'We don't usually hear much before nine, do we?'

A glance at the boots was enough. You could almost see yourself in the shiny toecaps.

'Thanks, Charlie. Hope the gentlemen are generous,' she said lightly, as she surveyed the other gleaming riding boots lined up on his bench.

'Rose, a word, if you please.'

The voice was intense, anxious and peremptory. It's owner equally intense and anxious.

'Mr Smithers,' she said surprised.

It was quite unheard off for Mr Smithers to leave the comfort of his room this early in the morning, unless something was seriously amiss.

'The bell, Rose. It's Lady Anne.'

'Good gracious,' Rose replied, too surprised to bother with the note of censure in his voice. 'She must be ill.'

'Ring immediately if you need assistance,' he said pompously, as he disappeared back into his room.

Rose hurried upstairs, gave a perfunctory knock at the door and was half way across the room before she discovered Lady Anne standing by the window in her dressing gown looking the picture of health.

'Oh Rose, I'm sorry to ring so early, but I'm going out riding at eight o'clock. Do you think I should have some breakfast before I go?'

'Yes, indeed I do,' Rose said, as she sized up the situation.

She'd never known Lady Anne breakfast in her room. By the time she went down, she was usually so late she would have to eat by herself, a copy of *Country Life* or *Hare and Hounds* propped against the teapot.

'What would you like? Your usual, or something cooked?'

'Oh, just my usual, Rose, but don't you go,' she said urgently, as she pulled vigorously on the bell rope. 'Let someone else bring it up. I want to talk to you. Come and sit by the window with me, there's a lovely view over the park and it's *such* a beautiful morning.'

Before Rose had quite recovered herself, there was a sharp knock at the door.

'Come in,' sang out Lady Anne cheerfully.

Smithers himself walked into the room. He looked around him coldly with the merest inclination of his head towards Lady Anne.

'Oh good, you have been quick, Smithers, I'd like my usual breakfast as soon as possible. I'm going riding shortly and I can't spare Rose to go and fetch it.'

'He did look cross, didn't he, Rose,' she added, with a giggle, as soon as the door had shut behind him.

Rose laughed. Cross was the mildest word for it.

'I think it's rather below his dignity to serve breakfast to anyone except your father and mother,' she said, as she sat down on the window seat.

'Never mind silly old Smithers, I have something to ask you.'

Rose had never seen her so animated. As she watched her trip lightly over to the window and lean back comfortably against the frame, she was sure she was even moving differently. There was a grace about her which suggested she'd just dropped off a heavy burden and was feeling enormous relief at being free of it.

'How can you tell, Rose, if a man likes you?' she began quickly. 'I mean apart from what you said last night about being interested in what you're interested in.'

Rose ran through a mental list of all the male guests at dinner the previous evening. It didn't help her to answer the question. The man who immediately came to mind was John Hamilton and you only had to look at him to know what he felt about you. But the men who had dined the previous evening at Currane Lodge were a different kettle of fish.

'Well, partly it depends on the man,' she began slowly. 'Different ones have different ways of expressing themselves. Some would be very complimentary. Some might be very attentive and fuss over you. I think I might need to know more about the man in question, if there is one.'

'Lord Harrington,' she burst out. 'He took me in to dinner last night and we talked and talked. I think horrible, old Captain O'Shea got quite cross. After dinner, when we were standing looking out the window together, he came up and clapped him on the shoulder so hard he spilt his wine on my dress. Lord Harrington was *so* upset, but Captain O'Shea didn't even apologise. I told Lord Harrington not to worry a tiny bit. I had a marvellous maid who could fix anything.' She paused. 'It *is* a bit of a mess,' she added, apologetically.

There was a tap at the door and breakfast arrived, the tray carried gingerly by the newest housemaid. Lady Anne gave her a smile, thanked her nicely, and asked Rose if she'd like some toast.

'No, thank you, I've had breakfast,' Rose replied, wondering if this miraculous transformation could possibly continue.

'Goodness, what time do you get up at? I've never been up this early before, but Lord Harrington says that early morning rides have a special quality that he particularly enjoys. He's training a new horse and he asked my advice about it. He's very shy.'

'The horse?'

'No. Lord Harrington.'

Rose restrained a smile and tried to focus on the problem in hand.

'Well, if he's a shy man and he's managed to ask your advice and persuade you to go riding this early, he must like you. Is Captain O'Shea or any of the other young men going too?'

'Oh no. Just us. He says Captain O'Shea plays billiards half the night and never gets up before mid-morning. I can't think why Lord Harrington bothers with him. I wouldn't. Would you, Rose?'

'Perhaps it's Captain O'Shea who bothers with Lord Harrington,' Rose suggested quietly.

'But why would he do that?'

'I don't know,' said Rose honestly, 'but friendships between men are often about advantage. Captain

O'Shea may want something from Lord Harrington. Perhaps he wants him to use his influence in some way, or help him to enlarge his estate. Something like that.'

Lady Anne's eyes opened wide.

'I do believe you're right, Rose,' she said excitedly. 'When the port came and we all went to the sitting room, Mrs O'Shea was talking to mother and Lady Ben about parliament. She said Captain O'Shea was looking for a seat and she mentioned Lord Harrington, but I wasn't really paying attention. Politics are *so* boring.'

Rose nodded thoughtfully. Old Thomas would know what Captain O'Shea's ambitions might be. By now, he'd most certainly have drawn out all there was to be got from the O'Shea coachman and matched it up with what he read in his newspaper. It would be easy for Sam to ask Old Thomas what he thought of his prospects.

'But Rose, how can you know so much about people you haven't even seen?

'I'm not sure *how* I know. I hadn't thought about it before,' Rose began. 'I think it's because my mother taught me to look at people and try to understand them. Even when I was little she used to say that was the best education I could have, even if I never opened a book. She's always helped me with whatever I couldn't understand.'

'You *are* lucky, Rose,' said the younger girl,

wistfully. 'But you promised last night *you* would help me, didn't you? You haven't forgotten, have you?'

'No, of course not. I said I'd answer all your questions if I could, even if you didn't like the answers.'

'And I promised I'd stop being horrible to everyone, because I was so stupid and ugly that no one would ever want to marry me,' she said firmly. 'Now, please, what do I do?'

'Finish your breakfast and get dressed. If you like Lord Harrington, then one way of showing it is not to be late.'

Rose didn't look at the velvet dress till after Lady Anne had gone and she'd done the rest of her morning's work. It was a disaster. One glance at it told her that no amount of careful cleaning would move the huge stain. The only hope of saving the dress was to insert a whole new panel in the flared skirt. Whether that could be done depended on what fabric might have been left over when the dress was made. If there was any, it would be listed in the inventory her mother kept in the room the dressmaker used when she came twice a year to make dresses for the girls.

It was early afternoon before she found her mother in her room, sorting clean table linen.

'How about this?' she said, holding up the soft green skirt.

'Oh dear. What a pity,' said Hannah sadly. 'We'll never get that out. Fetch me the dressmaker's book will you, Rose, and I'll see where my spectacles are.'

Hannah sat down wearily, sighed, and then laughed as Rose handed her the well-worn book neatly labelled in her own flowing copperplate.

'I think we might just manage a cup of tea, Rose, if we're lucky. It's gone very quiet since they all went off to Castlecove for their boat trip. If you make it for us, I'll see if I can read my own writing.'

Rose poked up the small fire, put the kettle down and took the biscuit tin from the cupboard. When she'd made the tea, she tidied up her mother's lists and notes, on the table by the window that looked out over the gardens. As John had predicted, it was another lovely day. She looked up at the perfect summer sky and wondered what he would think of the wide bay and the broad sandy beaches she so loved herself.

'We're in luck,' said Hannah, coming back into the room, a carefully wrapped packet in her hand. 'I'm surprised we didn't use this piece for a wee dress for one of the children. There's more than enough to replace the panel. Do you want me to do it?'

'No, I do not,' said Rose firmly. 'You've far too much to do as it is. She'll have to make do with my needlework,' she added, as she poured tea for both of them. 'Have you seen Lady Anne today?' she went on, as they settled themselves.

'I caught a glimpse of her this morning. She was having breakfast with Lord Harrington in the morning room. They must have been out riding, for the dining room was already laid for lunch. Why d'you ask?'

'I think something's happened. She's behaving quite differently. She's hardly the same person.'

'Lord Harrington?' said Hannah quietly, as she stirred her tea.

'Well, it might be. She's certainly talking about him. But she asked me last night if I'd help her to stop being so horrible to everyone.'

'Did she now? Well that *is* good news. The poor girl. She's been a sore trial to you, Rose, but maybe in the end you've helped her through her troubles. It's a hard thing when both mother and father want you to be something different from what you are, and can't value anything about you. Sir Capel never got over her not being a boy and Lady Caroline just let Miss Pringle do what she thought fit. That woman had neither heart nor imagination,' she said harshly.

'Do you think Lord Harrington might be interested?' she asked, after a moment. 'He's a lot older than she is, but that's no great matter.'

'Yes, I think he is. They seemed to have talked all last evening. That's usually a good sign.'

To Rose's surprise, Hannah smiled slyly at her.

'Would you say it was now, Rose?'

Rose hung her head and then laughed aloud.

'Oh Ma, I was going to tell you tonight. I only went for a bit of a walk. His name's John Hamilton.'

'Oh, I know all about the blacksmith from Armagh. When Sam brought in the vegetables for Cook, he came up to me. He's very impressed. He's calling him *Rose's man* already,' she said smiling.

To Rose's great surprise, she blushed.

'Sure he'll be away back to the north in a couple of weeks,' she said, flustered.

'And maybe you with him.'

'Ma!'

'Sometimes we think the big things in life take a long time to happen, like building a house, brick by brick, but sometimes your life changes in the shake of a lamb's tail,' she said, offering Rose another cup of tea. 'Oh, yes, both ways, good and bad, happy and sad,' she went on. 'When I met your father I knew the first time I talked to him that I loved him, though I was only seventeen. I couldn't face my father then. I had to wait till the third summer he came and then I could wait no longer. I was afraid my father would never forgive me.'

'And did he?'

'Not entirely. He was a very hard, rigid man. He loved me all right, but he couldn't stomach your father being Catholic and Irish, him being so proud of his Covenanter stock. He liked your father and your father liked him. But there was this bitterness they could never get over. Next to losing your father, and your brother and sister, it was the greatest sadness in my life,' she said simply.

'But, Ma, I couldn't leave you and go north, not with Sam off to Dublin in September. How could I, with no one of your own?' Rose burst out, her thoughts leaping forward, already accepting that what had been true for her mother might turn out to be true for her.

'Of course you could. Haven't I been to see Mary twice in Donegal? A woman has to make her own life, Rose. If she lets mother or father stop her, she'll always regret it. I've seen women do that, both gentry and ordinary folk, and it's a sad thing. They end up hating the parents they've stuck to and hating themselves as well.'

Hannah waited to see if Rose would reply, but Rose was so taken aback by what her mother had said and what it implied that she'd nothing to say at all.

'He's a good man, this John Hamilton. I watched him this morning with that horse that hurt itself. He's a man with no malice in him. He's innocent, but no fool. If you were to take him, you'd have to guide him on his way, for he's not sure of himself, but you'd always be well loved and cared for. Don't let anything but the man himself help you make up your mind.'

Hannah stood up and unwrapped the carefully folded swathe of green velvet.

'I'll hardly see you tonight,' she said smiling, as she handed it to her. 'I'll be in bed long before you, but I'll see you at breakfast time. If you've any trouble with the lie of the velvet, leave it and I'll give you a hand, but you're as good as I am with a needle these days, if not better,' she said easily. 'I think you'll get a fine evening for your walk.'

# CHAPTER EIGHT

Whether it was simply settling in, or the pleasures of a long spell of fine, sunny weather, life at Currane Lodge seemed happier for everyone as May turned to June and the freshness of springtime modulated into the luxurious growth and prolific flowering of early summer.

Almost every day the coaches lined up in front of the house. There were drives through sunlit countryside to places of interest, small villages, beaches and viewpoints. There was croquet on the lawn. Some guests walked or rode in the park, others sat in the shady arbours of the rose garden, a few, both male and female, pursued more private conversations on the less frequented paths through the woodland.

In the servants' hall, work settled into a more relaxed rhythm as maids and valets made friends with house staff and offered help with the routine work. Having upset everyone initially by scolding the newest housemaid for speaking Irish to her friend while they were dusting the drawing room even Mr Smithers felt able to retire to his quarters and stop supervising work going on perfectly well without him. The relief was palpable.

Hannah felt the easement as much as anyone, able to sit by her window and do the most difficult of the mending tasks without having to interrupt her work to comfort a tearful girl or reason with a young man, so angry he was threatening to give notice. After the first fraught week, even Cook began to smile again, responding to the light-hearted attentions of the young grooms and stable boys who had been drafted in to help her when they were not needed outside.

For Rose and John, it was the happiest of times. Lady Anne frequently insisted Rose accompany her on her outings, so they would find themselves together. Whatever the task to hand there'd always be moments when they were free to stand side by side, the sunlight warm around them, the brilliant greens of new foliage set against vistas of lake, or sea, watching the house party split up into twos and threes and disappear, leaving them to sit under a tree, or in the shadow of a coach.

John was impressed by Kerry.

'Sure it's just beautiful. There's no other word for it. I've niver seen the like of it,' he said, shaking his head.

Rose was puzzled by the hint of sadness in his

voice every time he commented on a new prospect. Not for several weeks did she discover what lay behind it, however.

'Rose, Rose, oh come in quickly. I've something wonderful to tell you.'

Whatever it was the effect on Lady Anne's appearance was quite marvellous. Her eyes bright, a winning smile on her face, she had an excited glow about her as if she were going to a ball. Her step was so light, so gay, as she ran across the room to meet her, Rose wondered how anyone, could ever have thought she was rather plain, if not actually ugly.

'My goodness, what's happened,' Rose gasped, as she clutched her hand and hurried her over to the window seat.

'We went up to see the cliffs at Hog's Head this afternoon. You know the place, Rose, where we leave the coaches,' she began hurriedly. 'Well, everyone got out and started to walk up,' she went on, so quickly she almost tripped over her words. 'Captain and Mrs O'Shea and Lady Ben were walking with us and I was so disappointed. I was sure they'd come all the way to spoil it. Lord Harrington always goes so quiet when Captain O'Shea tries to be amusing, but suddenly Lady Ben got tired and Katherine said they'd sit down and rest, they'd come far enough. So we went on, right to the very top and perched on a big piece of rock and looked out at all the islands,' she gasped, spreading her arms wide to embrace the whole extent of the bay. 'It's amazing, Lord Harrington knows all their names and he's only been here three weeks.'

She paused and drew breath while Rose waited, wondering if she'd guessed at what was coming next.

'Then he went very quiet,' she went on, dropping her voice to a whisper. 'He often does Rose, and I know now not to be upset. I used to chatter away when he went quiet, but then I realised it didn't matter, so I just sat there and looked around. I discovered there were little mauve flowers everywhere, growing in sweet little clumps in the cracks in the rock, and here and there in the grass there were little yellow ones I'd never noticed before. So I showed them to him. I was sure he'd know what they were.'

She paused, put her hand to her mouth.

'Oh Rose,' she said, taking a huge, gasping breath. 'He said I was the only flower he ever wanted. And then . . . and then, he asked me to marry him.'

'And what did you say?' Rose asked, anxiously, for her own future was as much involved as Lady Anne's.

'Well, I said yes, I'd love to. And he kissed me. I never thought he'd manage that. But he did and I didn't care one bit if wretched Captain O'Shea came up and saw us. He's going to speak to my father before dinner. And if he says "Yes", and I'm sure he will, we'll be married in August, so we can be back from our honeymoon tour before the hunting starts.'

Rose breathed a sigh of relief and offered her the warmest of good wishes. She was not totally surprised when Lady Anne immediately threw her arms round her and insisted she could never have managed without her.

'You know Rose,' she went on, releasing her from her energetic embrace, 'when he talked about our honeymoon tour, I'd have been absolutely lost if you hadn't made me look at the atlas and see where all the countries of Europe were. And then I asked where we would live and he talked about Easky Lough and the Ox Mountains,' she went on, laughing. 'Wasn't it a mercy you made me walk all round Sligo on the map. I used to think Sligo was in the middle of Ireland, but of course it's not. He says he has a house on Ballysadare Bay and a lot of his land overlooks Sligo Bay but it's not like Kerry at all. He's so kind, he asked if I thought I'd miss Kerry, even though we can come and visit every summer if I want to. And I said . . . Goodness, Rose, is that the time?'

Rose got up immediately, shocked that she could have been so absorbed she hadn't even glanced at the pretty porcelain clock on Lady Anne's dressing table.

'You can't be late tonight of all nights,' she said quickly, as she helped her off with her dress. 'What do you want to wear?'

'Oh Rose, the green, of course. He particularly likes it. He says he fell in love with me when he spilt his wine all over me and I wasn't cross with him.'

Rose smiled as Lady Anne sat down and pulled out her hairpins. She took up the brush and began to work and recalled what her mother had said the day after she'd first walked out with John Hamilton. *'Sometimes your life can change in two shakes of a lamb's tail.'* Well, Lady Anne's certainly had. By tomorrow there would most likely be an engagement, perhaps even a wedding date. There was no need for any delay other than the time needed to make the necessary preparations and provide a trousseau.

'Thank you, Rose. Do I look all right?'

'I've never seen you look so well,' said Rose honestly. 'I hope you have a lovely evening.'

'You too, Rose. Don't spend an age tidying up, will you? It can wait till tomorrow. Your John will be waiting for you and you only have the evenings,' she said warmly, as she paused, a hand on the bedroom door.

Rose picked up the discarded dress and inspected it methodically. It was still perfectly clean but the soft material had creased. She put it to one side to take down to the ironing room, then went through her evening routine, her mind completely engaged with all Lady Anne had told her and the implications it had for her own future.

John was waiting in his usual place, sitting

talking with the grooms and coachman, his eyes never straying far from the outside stairs leading up to the living quarters over the old stable block.

'There ye are, John. Time to go,' said Old Thomas cheerfully, as he caught sight of Rose coming into the yard.

There were teasing comments from many of the young men gathered round, for John had become popular among the outdoor staff, not so much for his skill with horses and metal, as his willingness to help anyone in difficulties, whatever the task might be. Even the young O'Shea groom now treated him in a friendly manner. Having seen Rose and John walk out on a second evening, he'd transferred his affections to Lady Ben's maid and thereby discovered John more agreeable than he had imagined.

'See ye in the mornin',' said John, raising his hand in salute to his companions as he stood up and strode across the yard.

They greeted each other, then walked in silence. The moment they were out of sight of all the following eyes, John took her in his arms and kissed her, holding her as if he could never bear to let her go.

'I've missed ye today,' he said softly, his voice full of a longing that touched her. 'When they all went off to look at the cliffs, I had only Icarus and Pegasus for company,' he said wryly. 'Paddy has taken to goin' to sleep in the coach as soon as they're gone.'

'I'm not surprised,' she said laughing. 'From what I hear, it looks as if all the wrongs of Ireland are put right outside the stables. Sam says it's after midnight many a night when they go up to the loft. And them has to be up at six.'

'Sure they're young. It'll not harm them a bit,' he said smiling. 'An' indeed, I've learnt a powerful lot since I come here. I was niver one for books, but I can remember things fine when I hear them. My, there's some great talkers here, men like yon Old Thomas that know their history an' can go back generations. Sure I diden know the half of it.'

He fell silent as they walked down to the lough shore and made their way over the stones to one of their favourite sitting places.

'I've somethin' to tell ye, Rose,' he said quietly, as they settled themselves.

She felt a sudden, unexpected pang of anxiety. She'd been about to tell him Lady Anne's good news, but the tone of his voice was alarming and the droop of his broad shoulders did nothing to reassure her.

'My Sir Capel's had letters from Dublin today. Business he has to see to. We're for the road at seven in the mornin'. He says he'll send Paddy an' me back in a couple o' weeks to collect Lady Ishbel.'

Rose's heart sank. It was so sudden. There'd been no talk of the Molyneux's returning to the north and it never occurred to her to think of Dublin.

'I'll miss you then, John,' she said, trying to sound calm.

He sat looking out over the lake, so still the tall grasses and rushes at the water's edge made a perfect mirror image.

'How coud I ask you t'leave a place like this?' he said, sadly. 'That first night we walked down here, I told you my mind was made up, an' indeed it was, but I didn't know then what yer life was like. I didn't know how well thought of ye were and the way ye were treated. Sure Lady Anne thinks the world of you,' he said, looking at her for the first time. 'All yer nice clothes and the outings to the coast and yer own wee place with yer mother, an' her such a nice lady. How coud I ask ye to give up all that?'

'Well, you could try,' she said briskly.

He stared at her in disbelief.

'D'ye mean t'say you'd give up yer life here to marry a blacksmith from the other end of Ireland?'

'I might if he asked me.'

'I'm askin' Rose,' he said, still sounding amazed. He paused and gathered himself. 'Will ye marry me?' he said, looking her full in the face.

'Yes, John, I will,' she replied smiling.


Three weeks later they were married in the small parish church a previous generation of Molyneux's had provided for those of their tenants who were not Catholic. The church was packed. Servants and guests alike had wished to be present and Sir Capel of Currane Lodge had declared their wedding day a holiday and a celebration. He provided transport for the bride and groom and for all his household staff. Furthermore, he gave orders for a buffet meal to be set out in the garden after the service and a dance in the servants' hall in the evening. So splendid an affair was this wedding of the lady's maid and the blacksmith, there were those among both guests and staff who wondered if Smithers would ever recover from the effort it demanded of him.

Lady Anne's excitement knew no bounds. Only with difficulty did Rose restrain her from ordering a wedding dress for her from a catalogue provided by one of the new department stores in Dublin. For the first time in her life, Lady Anne was preoccupied by fashion, wanting her to have the best. If she had to part with her, she insisted, it was the least Rose could do to make her happy by accepting all her gifts.

'You are so good to me,' said Rose, returning her embrace, 'but you see I must think about the life I'll have when I marry John. We'll not be as poor as if he were a groom, but I shall have very little money for clothes. If I had a lovely wedding dress, I could never wear it again.'

'But you could keep it for your daughter, like my mother's done,' Lady Anne protested. 'Not that I like it, and it doesn't fit very well, but she's been so kind since I got engaged, I think I ought to wear it.'

Rose laughed and shook her head.

'There's your answer, my dear. *If* I have a daughter, and *if* she marries, and *if* fashion hasn't changed, she might not like it anyway.'

'Oh Rose, you are so sensible. What will I do without you?'

Rose still found it hard to see the anxious look that came with the question, even if it was a pale shadow of its former self.

'Harrington says I can have anything I want,' Lady Anne said confidingly. 'When I told him I'd so love to have you come with me to Sligo, he said right away he'd find a good job for John, either in his own trade or supervising his improvement works. You know, drains and so on. You'd have a lovely little cottage on the edge of the park and you could help me make sure our children were brought up properly, not scolded by some horrible person who didn't really care about them.'

Rose shook her head sadly.

'I shall miss you so. But it wouldn't be right for you, or me, if John and I went to Sligo. You'll have to learn to be mistress of your own house and you must let Lord Harrington help you. I'll have things to learn too, with a new place and a new life. I'll write to you, if you like.'

'Oh Rose, yes. Yes, please. I've always hated having to write, but it would be different writing to you. I could still ask your advice then. You won't be a servant any more, so you can say what you like and not have to pretend you don't see things you've always seen. Think, only a few more days and you'll be Mrs John Hamilton.'

'And only two more months and you'll be Lady Harrington of Tobercurry.'

'I sometimes can't believe it.' She suddenly looked grave. 'Will I always be this happy, Rose?'

'I'm sure there will be many happy times,' she replied, carefully, unwilling to spoil the moment with too cold a touch of reality. 'What my mother says is that you must always gather up all your happiness in your hand and look at it and cherish it, because whoever you are and whatever your station in life, there will always be sad times.'

'Then I shall gather up all these days we've had since Harrington came and you promised to help me. I've never been so happy in all my life. I'll never forget them, Rose and you mustn't either, whatever happens. Promise.'

'Yes, I promise.'

'And you must also promise you'll wear the little veil I've found with the pearls round the edge to match the ones on your new silk blouse.'

'Yes, I will,' she said steadily, suddenly aware the days were passing so swiftly. In such a little while she would be gone into an unknown world to live amongst people she didn't know with customs she hadn't met, to live a future she couldn't possibly imagine at this moment.

She knew she would still have said yes to John, but it was only now, sitting in the window seat with Lady Anne, the picture of a wedding veil spread out between them, did she understand fully what had made him hesitate to ask her. Yes, she would miss so many things, the people she knew so well, the countryside she loved, the gardens and the sunlit rooms, the comfort of her own tiny bedroom, the small fireplace where she and her mother drank a cup of tea last thing at night. She knew that would be the hardest of all, saying goodbye to her mother after all these years, bound so close by ties forged in adversity.

'Well then, has the bridegroom arrived?' Hannah asked, as Rose came up the stairs and pushed open the door, her arms full of clothes from the ironing room and small packages from the fellow servants who'd just wished her joy.

'Yes, he has. And you'll be glad to hear he's bought a coat that fits him. He sends you his regards and says he hopes he'll not disgrace you tomorrow.'

'Ah, he'll not do that, good man that he is. But it's a big expense.'

'It was indeed, but he says it will do him many a long day if he only wears it for christenings, weddings and funerals.'

'Are you not going for a walk this evening, Rose?'

'No, Ma. Not this evening. I think perhaps Sam and his friends have plans to entertain John, but I said I would see him in church.'

They settled by the small fire that always burnt in the fireplace, even in summer, and waited for the kettle to boil. Usually she made their tea in the evening, but tonight Hannah told her to stay where she was and rest herself before she did her packing and washed her hair.

She did as she was told, leant back and let the weariness of a long day flow over her. Her last day in service. The last day on which someone might ring, someone might call her, someone might come to her and demand that she do what they wanted. From this moment on, she was free to make up her own mind. Free to say 'no,' even to those she loved. She could not imagine refusing John anything, any more than she could refuse her mother or Sam, and yet this new sense of freedom and power excited her.

'It's a long journey you have ahead of you,' said Hannah, as she handed her a cup of tea.

She nodded, thinking of the coach journey to Dublin with Lady Ishbel and John and Paddy.

'They came down in three days, but we don't start till four tomorrow, so it may take more.'

Hannah smiled and Rose realised she wasn't thinking about the journey back to the north. At the same moment, she noticed that the cup she was drinking from was just as familiar as the breakfast china, but smaller and prettier, and it was one they never used. It was the cup and saucer she'd seen for the first time the day the men came to put them out of their home in Ardtur. She looked up at her mother, surprised.

'I want you to take it with you. And maybe, sometimes, if things go a bit hard with you, you'll sit down by yourself and drink from the cup, even if it were only spring water you had,' she said quietly. 'My mother gave it to me the night before my wedding and I did as she asked, many a time, when I was anxious or perplexed,' she said, looking deep into the orange embers glowing in the grate.

'I planned to give it to your sister, Rose. But that wasn't to be. And then I thought to give it to Mary, but she married far away in Donegal. And maybe that's the right way of it after all. Maybe it was meant for you.'

Rose sat silent, tears welling in her eyes, but her mother leant across and took the empty cup from her hands and set it down on the nearby table.

'Sure we'd better start packing or we'll be up half the night. I can't have my lovely Rose wilting when she goes to marry the love of her life,' she said, dropping a kiss on her cheek and drawing her to her feet.

# CHAPTER NINE

The Molyneux coach with its well-matched greys, its experienced coachman, its newly-married groom and its two passengers, Lady Ishbel Molyneux and Mrs Rose Hamilton, made good time on the journey to Dublin, but once there, the uncertainty as to what was to happen next grew wearisome. The departure for the north depended upon Sir Capel's business in the capital and Lady Ishbel's decision whether to stay in Dublin, or return home ahead of him.

Rose longed to complete this longest of journeys. Until she reached her new home, her life was suspended. Though no longer a servant, she was still entirely dependent on the decisions of others and although Lady Ishbel treated her very courteously, it was her nature to be very demanding. Throughout each day of the journey from Currane Lodge to Dublin she'd talked continuously. Sometimes interestingly, at other times her monologues filled up with minute details of people and places quite unknown to Rose.

She'd responded as best she could, but the effort wearied her. It was particularly hard to bear when all she wanted to do was sit quietly and absorb the passing countryside, storing it up, delighting in its newness, its variety, its difference from all she had yet experienced.

There was a more personal reason too. The short nights spent in different hostelries on the long road brought pleasure and joy. John was as tender and passionate a lover as she imagined he would be. Sometimes when Lady Ishbel was in full flight and only required an attentive appearance, the occasional nod, she smiled to think she was separated from her lover only by the thin walls of a coach and the interminable chatter of an old woman who found travel tedious and boring.

After a week of delays in Merrion Square, only partly offset by visiting the sights of the city, Lady Ishbel made the decision to remain in Dublin. Anxious for John to return to his own work on the estate, Sir Capel decided to send them north by train, an unexpected gift which delighted them both.

'So where are we now, John?' Rose asked, as they stopped at a small station, somewhere beyond Portadown. There they'd left the great gleaming express gathering steam for the last stretch of its run into Belfast, while they made their way in the opposite direction on a small local train bound for Armagh, Monaghan and Cavan.

'Sure we're nearly home, Rose,' he said softly. 'This is Richhill.'

Rose glanced at the small station and gazed up the lane she could see running between the end of the platform and a nearby goods shed. A girl with ginger hair was leading a horse on a rope away from them, up the rising slope of the lane between high hedges. A dozen yards away, a handful of cows crossed the lane itself, moving slowly towards a long, low building, whitewashed, its thatched roof recently patched with new straw that caught the long fingers of evening sun filtering through the nearby trees.

'It's not a very big village, is it?' she said cautiously, as she watched John smile contentedly as he ran his eye over the familiar place.

The cows were followed by a man with a stick. As the whistle blew and the train creaked, vibrated and began to move, he spotted John, raised his stick and waved it in a vigorous salute. John lowered the window and leant out.

'Good evenin', Tom. Are ye well?'

'Aye, the best at all. An' yerself, an' the wife?' he asked, a broad beam on his face.

'Grand. Grand. We're on our way home,' he shouted, as the whistle blew again, the train now gathering speed, a cloud of smoke and steam enveloping their carriage.

By the time John had pulled up the window, the

grey-white cloud had dissolved and they were once again moving between green fields and orchards, the railway banks bright with ox-eye daisies, long-stemmed buttercups and the rusty spikes of sorrel and dockon.

'That was Tom Loney,' John explained. 'His brother James works for Sir Capel. He's a forester.'

'And that was Richhill?' Rose prompted him.

'Ach no, that's only Richhill Station. Richhill is a mile or more away.'

'That's not much good if you live in Richhill,' said Rose, laughing.

'It'd be worse if it weren't here at all,' he replied promptly. 'Sure when the line was built, talk was there was to be no station at all between Portadown and Armagh, but some of the big business people had their say. There's fruit growing all round this area,' he explained. 'A lot of farmers send boxes of apples and soft fruits up to Belfast in the season forby the milk and eggs that goes every day. There's a tannery too and furniture workshops at Stonebridge. Sure it's goods the railways makes their money on, not the likes of you an' me travelling around the place,' he said, shaking his head.

'I'll be quite glad to stop travelling around the place, John. It seems such a long time since we walked down our path to the lake and had a place to call our own.' She poked him gently in the ribs and said, accusingly, 'And we never did hear that nightingale of yours.'

'Aye, but we heard your lark sing the few afternoons we had,' he reminded her gently.

She fell silent, her eyes closing, weary from the brightness of the light. All day she'd peered through soot-stained windows to see as much of the passing country as she could, for there was little likelihood of her ever seeing any of it again.

'Look, John, look,' she'd whispered, when the carriage was still full of people as they made their way towards Drogheda. 'Wouldn't that just be Lady Anne?'

They looked down on a wide, empty beach, the blue water creating a leisurely fringe of white wavelets. A girl on horseback raced along it, clods of damp sand thrown back from the hooves of her mount. Following her, a black dog, tried to keep pace with her, its pink tongue just visible.

'Them's the wee hills I told you about,' he whispered, a little later, nodding towards the window on the other side of the train.

Rose studied the smooth, rounded hill that occupied the foreground, its summit outlined by a planting of young trees. A pleasing shape indeed, as if a giant hand had taken its time to mould the countryside, finding curving hillsides more appealing than low lying fields, however rich or productive.

The low hills came and went again. They

rattled over a railway bridge and realised they had crossed the Boyne, a harmless stream far below them, emptying itself into an estuary lined with tall, stone warehouses and smaller rows of houses. Soon afterward, the carriage now empty of fellow passengers, they'd picked out the Mournes, their south-facing slopes pale in bright sunlight as they swept down to the shores of Carlingford Lough.

As they drew nearer to the mountains, the train slackened speed and they found themselves travelling more slowly through country rougher and wilder than any they'd yet encountered. Here the fields were no longer green and pleasant, but rough and filled with rushes, invaded by bracken and bramble. The farms looked poor and mean and even on such a lovely summer day there was a bleak, windswept look about the place. This much closer now, the Mournes turned their northern faces towards them, sombre, pitted with deep gullies, full of dark blue shadows.

'Well, yer in Ulster now, Rose. Old Tom says it's always been different t' the rest of Ireland, but I can't see it myself. Sure it's the same wee hills, the same folk out workin' on their land. Can ye see a difference?'

'Ask me again when I've got my feet on the ground,' she began.

'It's different from Kerry all right. But looks aren't everything. It's the people that make a place different.'

'Sure you'll find nothing but welcome where we're goin'. My mother's that excited she'd have had the whole house decorated for ye comin' if I hadn't written an' told her to hold her horses till she'd ask ye what ye'd like. She's been lonely since the father died. An' forby, she always wanted a girl, an' didn't she have all boys, poor woman.'

'Well, if they were all like you, she maybe didn't do so bad. Were they like you?'

'Ye may ask her that yerself for I was young enough when they upped sticks for Canada,' he began. 'I always remember George, the eldest, said he'd never work in a forge. He was kinda particular. He said it was too dirty for him. When he left school he went and served his time in Elliott's of Thomas Street. They were grocers and thought themselves very superior. Nothing but the best. They brought in their own cigars and had a special whiskey. But he said he was fed up with the airs and graces of the customers. James always wanted to do what George did, but he couldn't get a place in a grocer's, though there's plenty of them in Armagh, so he ended up in Gillis Mill watchin' the looms, but sure he couldn't stan' the noise.'

The evening light was beginning to fade a little and the shadows were lengthening. In the orchards, every tree cast its outline on the long grass, the pale unripe fruit catching the light against dark foliage. The train slowed once again and came to a halt at an even smaller station. Here there was no building of any kind, just a platform and a sign. It said: The Retreat.

John helped her down, handed her the small bags and parcels they'd brought with them, the items Rose would need to keep her going till the coach came up from Dublin with the rest of her possessions and the wedding gifts they'd had from the staff and guests at Currane Lodge.

'Are yez right?' called the guard.

'Grand, thank ye,' replied John.

She stood looking round her as he banged the carriage door shut and waved to the guard who was watching to see them safely landed. Somewhere a blackbird was singing his heart out. He sounded just like the one who perched on the point of the eaves above the stable yard clock opposite the rooms she'd shared with her mother for so long. For a moment she felt so utterly desolate, a small figure in a completely unknown world. Then John put an arm round her and moved her away from the train as it began to make steam. They stood together on the rough stones by the track and watched it move slowly away from them, disappearing into a cutting where the line curved southwards before its next stop in Armagh.

'There now, love, it's not far now. There's a bit of a shortcut across the field here and then its about half a mile on the road.'

With one arm firmly round her, the other carrying their bags, a couple of parcels wedged under his arm, he set out across the field, humming quietly to himself.

They walked in silence for a little, grateful to be moving on their own feet, their limbs full of the weariness of the day, the crowded carriages of the Dublin train, the hard wooden seats in the Portadown waiting room, the creak and rattle of the elderly carriages on the local train.

Rose drew a deep breath of the fresh evening air, caught the aroma of turf smoke and found herself suddenly back in her childhood, sitting by the fire with her brothers and sister, her mother cooking bread on a griddle hung on a chain over the glowing embers.

How remote it all seemed, those far-off days. How much her world had changed. How widely they were scattered. She had come to Armagh while Mary stayed in Donegal. Michael was in Scotland and Patrick had settled in Nova Scotia. Her mother and Sam were back in Kerry, separated not so much by the distance between them, but by the expense of getting there.

They'd all survived, but not her sister Rose whose name she carried on, nor her eldest brother Sam, buried side by side in the sloping churchyard that looked out over Lough Gartan, close by the remains of Columbkille's small stone church. They lay among friends and neighbours whose names she could still bring to mind. Not so her father, lying in a churchyard in Galloway, surrounded by good Presbyterians, every one a stranger.

She felt tears well up in her eyes and blinked them away so that John would not see. How could anyone ever have imagined what would become of the little family gathered by that glowing fire? And now, she was setting out, just as her mother had done, travelling to an unknown place, a good and loving man by her side. For a moment, she was aware just how enormous a step she'd taken, but before fear or anxiety could touch her, she heard the sound of John's voice and her sense of loneliness and isolation dissolved. As her mother had said, she'd chosen a good man. That was all that mattered. What would come, would come. Together they would face it.

'There now,' he said, drawing her through a field gate and releasing her for a moment to shut it behind them. 'Yer so close now ye might even smell it,' he said, beaming down at her.

'No, not a sign of garlic,' she said, laughing up at him. 'All I can smell is turf smoke and mown hay . . . and flowers, but I'm not sure what flowers.'

'Ah, ye'll smell flowers all right when I get you home, sure it's only a wee bit now. Are your eyes all right?' he asked, looking at her closely.

'Its just the smoke and the brightness,' she said,

lightly, not wanting to dampen his good spirits. 'I could do with washing my face,' she said, laughing.

The road was narrow but well-used, the cart ruts mended with loose stones. On one side, tall trees shaded the worn surface from the setting sun, on the other, beyond low hedges and tumbled stone walls, fields and water meadows were still bathed in golden light.

Rose noticed John was walking faster, but she said nothing and saved her breath for keeping up with his lengthening strides.

'There ye are,' he said, nodding, his arms fully occupied.

Ahead of them they saw the gable end of a sturdy, two-storey house partly sheltered by trees. As they drew closer, the light glinted from small paned windows and glanced off the fresh whitewash. A trim little house, well-thatched and solid. Very much as he had described it to her sitting by Currane lake.

As they stepped off the road, through a small gate onto a cobbled path leading to the front door, she gasped in delight.

'John, you never told me about the garden.'

'Ach, I had to keep a wee surprise. My mother has great hands for plants. She can grown anything.'

Rose walked slowly up the path, the perfume of roses and the heavy scent of lilies lying on the cooling air, the blending colours of delphiniums and foxgloves, rich blues, mauves and pinks, a joy to the eye. Tired as she was, she could have stood and looked at the two broad herbaceous borders for long enough had the front door not been thrown opened, and a small, stooped woman with a stick moved awkwardly towards them.

'Ach Rose dear, I'm so glad to see you,' she said, throwing out her arms and embracing her. 'Sure you've had a long, long journey and you'll be thinkin' strange. Come away in an' have a bite to eat an' rest yourself.'

'Hullo, Ma,' said John quizzically, as he watched the two women embrace.

'Hullo, yourself,' Sarah Hamilton said, laughing up at him, as he bent down to kiss her. 'Aren't you the lucky one. Didn't I always say you were the one that would land on yer feet whether you were rich or poor?'

It took Rose only a few minutes to grasp that her new mother-in-law was simply an older, female version of her son. She had the same openness of manner, the same humour, and the same unwillingness to be bound by solemnity. Despite her obvious physical difficulties, she swept them into the house, despatched them with their bags to the largest bedroom and had a pot of tea waiting for them when they came down.

'Goodness knows when you last got a bite,' she said, waving them to their seats at a laden table.

On an embroidered linen cloth she'd laid out

plates of fresh baked bread, soda and wheaten, tiny scones, and slices of fruit cake. She put the heavy teapot beside John and bade him keep the teacups filled while she plied them both with questions about their wedding and their journey north.

'Sure it'll take me days to hear all I want to hear and the both of you tired out. I just wish I could've seen the pair of you in all your glory. I knew you must be the right woman, Rose, when he went out and bought a coat. I've been tryin' for years to get him to buy somethin' decent for a Sunday but I might as well have talked to the wall,' she ended cheerfully.

'Well, you *will* see us. But it'll be a wee while,' said Rose warmly. 'One of the guests, Mr Blennerhassett, had a photographic camera. He'd been practising on the family and he insisted on taking pictures outside the church. He promised us that our pictures would be his wedding present to us when he'd developed them.'

'Isn't that great. I was nearly goin' to ask you to go to Loudan's in Armagh and get them to do a picture for me, but isn't this far better? An' I'll see your mother and brother as well, will I?'

'Oh yes, he did us, then us with my family, us with Sir Capel and Lady Caroline, us and Lady Anne and Lord Harrington. In fact, I think he managed to get the whole staff in one picture. I don't know what he'll send, of course, but he's a very nice man and he said it was the first time he'd ever experimented with a wedding, so we may get more than just the one of us.'

'Oh, I hope so,' said Sarah, clapping her hands together in delight. 'Wouldn't I just love to see all the people John wrote to me about! You know, Rose, they did teach him to write at Grange School, but you'd never have guessed it,' she declared. 'I've never known him lay pen to paper till he met you. Even the postman came in to ask me was everything all right with my son when the letters started comin'. And now, of course, tell the postman and the whole world knows what a happy man he is,' she said, turning to Rose, and patting her hand.

Sarah, Rose and John sat over their meal and talked till it was so dark they could hardly see each other's faces. When John lit the lamp they sat on by the fire until finally Sarah stood up and said she'd talked far too long, and wasn't there all of tomorrow to talk, a long day and it not even started yet.

'I'll show you the parlour in the mornin', Rose dear. It's a nice enough wee room, but sure we never used it, so I've had my bed moved down. That'll give ye more room upstairs. Now away till yer beds children dear. Aren't ye worn out wi' all my talk.'

There was no need for the candle they'd lit to take them to bed for the room was full of bright moonlight. It cast the shadow of the window frame on the pale quilt. Even by its light, Rose could see that it had been made by hand, the fine white material sprayed with flowers and then quilted onto some firmer backing.

'Look John, look,' she cried softly, pointing to the centre of the spread, as she moved across to her side of the bed.

'Ach indeed,' he said quietly. 'She must have been at that from when I first told her.'

In the midst of a heart-shaped garland of tiny roses, the two initials J and R were lovingly entwined.

# CHAPTER TEN

On Rose's first morning in the little house at Annacramp, with John already gone to work, the breakfast dishes cleared away and the floor swept, Sarah made good on her promise of the previous evening. She led Rose out of the big kitchen across the narrow entrance hall and into the parlour. A room with some fine furniture, now cramped and crowded by the addition of Sarah's bed, it was immaculately tidy. From a great china jug full of roses and smaller vases filled to overflowing with sweet peas, verbena and mimulus came a heady mix of perfume that almost overlaid the musty smell of old floorboards and elderly rugs.

While Rose sat on the bed, Sarah moved awkwardly among the familiar well-polished pieces, picking up strangely assorted objects from the sideboard and mantelpiece. A picture of Niagara in a heart-shaped frame decorated with minute sea shells, a white mug in fine china sprigged with bunches of shamrock, a pink glass cake-basket, its handle made of clear twisted glass, a sea-green jug in the shape of a fish, a string of coloured beads, a crinoline lady embroidered in cross stitch, a crooked iron candlestick. Each object had its history and she learnt where it had come from, or who had given it to her.

Sitting watching this bright-eyed woman, so full of a vitality not completely taken away as yet by her difficulty in moving, Rose suddenly remembered a morning long ago, the last morning of her first life, when her father had brought out the tin box from under the earth floor of the bedroom and revealed the families few treasures.

*'That's your grandfather's silver watch, you can hold it for a moment.'*

She could hear her mother's voice, cool and calm, against a background of noise and shouting, the crash of gable walls, the crying of women, the rush of dust from each collapsing home. She shivered as she recalled how cold she'd been until her mother had given her Sam to hold. Warmed by the pressure of his small body, she'd watched, fascinated, as her mother had taken each object from its resting place and hidden them in their clothing. For her, there was a brooch pinned under her shift. The cup and saucer once wrapped in a piece of unfinished white work was now wrapped in her own clothes. It would come back to her with rest of her possessions when Sir Capel returned from Dublin.

She collected her thoughts and took the picture of Niagara, studying the faded colours of the tinted engraving. Sarah's sister had emigrated when she was only sixteen, married at twenty, raised six children on a farm in Indiana. She thought Niagara the most wonderful thing she had ever seen.

'And this was my grandmother's,' Sarah went on, putting the fish shaped jug in her hand. 'When you fill it with water and pour it out, it gurgles,' she explained, a broad smile on her face. 'We used to love it as children. Indeed, I've never met a child that didn't laugh at the funny noise it makes.'

She placed the jug carefully back on the sideboard and picked up the bent candlestick.

'Can you guess who made me this?'

From the soft tone in her voice, Rose was sure it must be her husband or John. It was indeed her husband, Tom. As a young apprentice in his very first weeks in the forge, he'd asked if he could make a present for his sweetheart. The smith said he could, on condition he made it entirely by himself. But poor old Tom couldn't get it straight. He tried and tried, but the smith just laughed and said a good smith spent his life straightening things out, so it was no harm at all to make a crooked piece when he'd have to earn his living putting straight what other people bent.

By the time Sarah had placed all the objects in Rose's hand and told their stories, she was quite sure she and Sarah would be friends. In everything she said Rose found both humour and compassion. She was so open about what gave her joy, what had brought her sorrow. Sarah had the gift of painting a picture, the colours still bright even when the people were far away or long dead. Rose found herself thinking once more of her first home, but this time what she remembered was the evening at Daniel McGee's house. The material of their stories might be different, what was just the same was the vividness of the telling.

The morning hours passed, the sun now so high the south-facing room grew shadowy, but Sarah continued unhurriedly with her task. From the drawers in the sideboard, she brought out pieces of embroidery and lace, some of it made by her own mother. She unfolded lengths of fabric and a parcel of baby clothes wrapped in plain, white linen. She took the lid off the Singer sewing machine her mother had acquired in the 1850s when she worked as a seamstress for a clothing company. Proudly she demonstrated how perfectly it still worked.

The very last item to emerge from the lowest shelf of the tall cupboard in the alcove by the fireplace was a worn, brown leather handbag with no handle. It was full of papers which Sarah pulled out in a bundle and placed in a pile between them on the bed. One by one, she unfolded them and handed them to Rose to look over. There were copies of her three sons' birth entries from the register of Grange Church. A copy of her marriage entry and a death certificate for her husband. A battered rent book and the receipts for the rates. Finally, there was a small fold of large, papery banknotes and an impressive document with a red embossed seal from a Friendly Society. The only documents in the bag not yellowed with age were the letters John had written from Kerry.

'There we are, Rose dear,' she said, as she got to the bottom of the pile. 'That money has to do me my day,' she said cheerfully, as she refolded the banknotes. 'And that's the wherewithal to see me off when I go,' she added, placing the bank notes on the battered cover of the Friendly Society pass book. 'There's a double plot in Grange Churchyard and room for me beside my Tom. There's no paper for that and I'm sure there should be, but there's a headstone up and ye can see plain where I'm to go.'

She took a deep breath and looked pleased with herself as she fitted the papers back into the handbag and snapped the catch.

'It's all yours now, my dear,' she said, dropping the handbag gently into Rose's lap. 'You deal with that as you think fit. This is your place now. I'll not be much good to you on the fetching and carrying work, more's the pity, but I'll not be idle,' she promised. 'Thank God my hands are all right and I have my sight. I can do any job that's sittin' down.

Aye, an' I can even get down and plant wee cuttings in the garden just fine,' she went on, laughing wryly. 'It's only the gettin' back up again is the problem.'

She patted her hand. 'You just tell me what I can do to help you about the house, an' when ye get fed up with my chatter, just say: "Sarah, would ye think of dustin' the parlour",' she added with a laugh.

Before many days had passed, it was clear Rose would probably never need to use Sarah's device. While she might not be as wise, or as deeply thoughtful, as her own mother had always been, she had a knack of knowing just when to leave her by herself. When John came home from work, she was able to sense when he was very tired or just wanted he and Rose to be left alone together. She'd kiss them both and slip away without a trace of awkwardness. She would sit and read, or simply sit in the room where she had gathered together the things that meant most in her life.

On the last day of her first week, sitting over a cup of tea when they had just finished making some new curtains together, Rose asked her if she didn't feel lonely or bored when she went off to her room, sometimes as early as seven in the evening. Sarah smiled and shook her head.

'No, not a bit of it. The thing is, Rose dear, life goes by so quick. So many things happen, you haven't time rightly to take them all in. Whenever

I sit in the parlour I go over things in my mind, walkin' out with Tom when I was a girl, playin' with the boys and cleanin' them up when they got in a mess. Nursin' them when they were sick. I even think of makin' the garden from the bit of waste out at the front an' savin' a few pennies from the egg money each week to buy a plant from the nursery at the Dean's Bridge. Sure, its like havin' a dozen story books an' I can read whatever I fancy as the mood takes me, happy or sad. Aye,' she laughed, 'an' I don't even need a candle to see by.'

It was the next day that Rose made her first visit to Armagh. One of Sarah's neighbours had made sure they would have enough butter, tea and sugar to keep them going while she settled in. The bread cart called every two days. The herring man came each Friday, one of the children from the big farm up the road brought their milk before school and there were plenty of potatoes and vegetables in the garden for John to dig up each evening. But after a week, the tea-caddy was nearly empty.

Rose dressed herself with care, counted shillings and pennies into her purse, took up Sarah's large wicker basket and set off, her sense of excitement growing as she made her way to Scott's Corner, turned up the hill past Thomas Scott's forge and the Robinson's farm. From the moment she breasted the low rise just before the forge, she could see the city, its two cathedrals set so proudly facing each other on adjacent hills just as John had described them to her, one old and dark with a solid, square tower rising above the surrounding trees, the other so newly completed its twin spires appeared a dazzling white in the morning sun.

It was a distance of nearly three miles to the level crossing on the outskirts of Armagh. With the morning warm but fresh, a light breeze taking the edge of the heat, she enjoyed every moment of it. As the sun climbed higher over the green countryside, her eye traced out the lines of the little rounded hills John had pointed out to her from the train before they'd even arrived in Ulster. Everywhere she looked, the patches of woodland cast heavy shadows on the rich grass, the apple trees raised their laden branches to the almost cloudless sky. The air was full of the mixed perfumes of cut hay and wayside flowers, ox-eye daisies, blue scabious and tall branching buttercups. Cattle grazed leisurely in the low-lying meadows below the gorse-covered banks of the railway that ran near to the road for much of her journey.

*'My name is Rose Hamilton. I'm twenty two years old and my husband and I live at Annacramp with my mother-in-law, Sarah. My old home was in Kerry, but I like it here very much. Everyone has made me very welcome.'*

Over and over again, like a litany, she rehearsed the details of her new life, as if she must not forget a single detail.

She laughed at herself as she paused to look up at Drumcairn mill's long rows of windows. The racket of the spinning machines vibrated on the warm air. From a tall brick chimney, a thick plume of dark smoke rose into the deep blue of the sky, laying a shimmering brown haze over the mill itself and the two rows of tiny houses that faced each other in its shadow. She waved to the children playing in the dust but they did not wave back, staring after her unfamiliar figure till she passed out of sight.

Hardly had the noise of the spinning machines receded when the roar of the power looms at Gillis enveloped her. Two hundred and twenty of them, John said. Now she'd heard them, she could understand why his brother couldn't stand working there. Suddenly aware of the confinement of the factories and the tiny houses that went with them, she strode out more rapidly, grateful for the sun and wind and the freedom to move as she pleased.

'*When I have my children they will have a garden to play in and flowers to enjoy.*'

Ahead of her, the white gates of the level crossing swung out into the road and clacked shut. She stopped among the ponies and traps and carts heading for the marketplace and listened to the huffs of sound as the train began to pull out of the station. Up in the signal box, a figure pulled on great levers. A few moments later, she was enveloped in clouds of steam. The train whistled as it moved across the road in front of her, disappeared under a bridge and headed for Monaghan. The gates swung slowly back, clicked more gently into place. The crowd surged forward, carrying her with it.

Her excitement growing all the time, Rose walked past the pillars and great silvered gates of the station itself, along Railway Street and up into the busy streets of the city.

*'I have my purse in my pocket and I'm shopping for my family, my husband and Sarah.'*

It wasn't that she'd never shopped before. Often enough she'd been sent in the trap with Lady Anne to buy ribbon or embroidery silk for Lady Caroline. Sometimes, she'd shopped for Cook. And sometimes she and her mother shopped for their few personal needs. But never before had she been out to shop as a woman with a household of her own.

'Good mornin' ma'am, can I be of any assistance to you?'

She smiled at the young boy in the boot-makers. He wasn't as old as Sam. And certainly not as good-looking.

'No thank you,' she said warmly. 'I'm just looking at boots for my husband, but he'll have to come himself.'

*'Boots for my husband.'*

As she finished her inspection and turned to leave, the boot-maker himself came and opened the door for her. He nodded politely.

'We'll be pleased to see you again, ma'am.'

She smiled as she thanked him, hurrying on her way, a new excitement almost overwhelming her. She had never before been called 'ma'am'. But then, never before had she been a married woman with her purse in her pocket and her basket over her arm.

'Well, what did ye think of Armagh?' asked John, as they strolled out, late that evening, through Ballybrannan and up the lane towards Cannon Hill.

'I was amazed,' said Rose honestly. 'I knew it would be bigger than Waterville or Cahirciveen and you'd told me about the cathedrals, so I was prepared for that, but I just couldn't believe it when I saw the shops. I'd no idea there'd be so many grocers and drapers,' she said, shaking her head. 'If you had the money, you could buy all the things Sir Capel and Lady Caroline had to order from Dublin.'

John smiled and looked pleased.

'I wondered what ye'd think, you bein' used to nice things.'

'I saw gowns and millinery as good as anything in Dublin,' she said firmly. 'I didn't look at all the grocers, there were so many of them, but I saw one with an Italian Warehouse. That's coffee and cheese and Parma ham and handmade chocolates,' she added, when she saw him look puzzled. 'Another one imported their own cigars and cigarettes,' she went on quickly. 'Oh yes, and another had their own brand of whiskey. It was Magowan's in English Street. I remember the name now. Eighteen shillings for a gallon of their own and twenty shillings for John Jameson. That was what Sir Capel used to drink.'

'Did ye buy me a gallon then?' he said, looking at her sideways.

'I did surely,' she replied promptly. 'And a top hat and tails, just in case you want to go for a groom again.'

He tightened his grip round her waist and hugged her.

'I did look in Carson's for some new boots for you,' she said, still smiling, 'but then I found a whole crowd of boot makers in Thomas Street, so I haven't compared the prices yet. It was the groceries I needed today. Sarah says she can't advise me on the shops any more. She only hears bits and pieces from the neighbours so I'm not buying anything else we need till I've looked at them all.'

'An' tell me, where did ye learn to go roun' comparin' the prices, an' you had all found where ye worked?'

Rose looked at him in surprise.

'John dear, did you not know the grand folk are just as sharp about money as we have to be? You should have heard Cook talk about some of the places she worked,' she said, shaking her head. 'She'd be up in front of the Master in his study, if she paid a penny a pound more for beef, or a farthing more a yard on butter muslin, or cloth for putting over the steamed puddings, than she need.'

'An' you'd think they'd never notice it, bein' rich,' he said, a look of amazement on his face.

'But don't forget John, the quantity. A penny isn't much, it's what you multiply it by over weeks or months. It mounts up.'

He laughed and looked down at her.

'I had a copy book at school,' he said, nodding. 'It was all good advice now I think of it. But I was so busy tryin' to get the letters right I diden give much attention to what it said. Now ye mind me there was something about "Look after the pence and the pounds will look after themselves".'

He stopped abruptly.

'Are ye sure ye can manage on what Sir Capel gives me, Rose? I don't want ye to go short. An' I want ye to have nice things, like thon blouse with the wee pearl buttons, an' the dress yer mother made for ye.'

'We'll manage fine, John,' she said gently, seeing the anxiety in his face. 'Sure, if we're short I might go into business myself. In fact, I'm thinking of it anyway while I've time on my hands.'

'What sort o' business?' he asked, the anxiety returning to his face.

'Women's business, John. What women have always done when they can. Hens for egg-money

156

and needlework to buy the children's shoes and coats. The same as your mother did,' she went on reassuringly. 'Sprigging or embroidery, or drawn thread. Whatever's the fashion. There's nearly always someone wanting home workers. They don't pay well, but it's convenient.'

'An' you'd not mind doin' that?'

'No, why would I? Haven't I time and company and my own fireside?'

'An then you could buy your dresses at Leeman's?'

'Not if it's the shop I think it is,' she said, laughing. 'You'd need to be Lady Anne to be a regular customer there.'

'Expensive?'

'Very.'

They walked in silence for a few minutes, pausing to watch a flight of linnets as they moved from bush to bush.

'John, tell me, where does all the money come from? You can't have shops like those in Armagh unless you have plenty of customers to buy. There must be a lot of people with money to spend.'

'Aye, you're right there,' he said thoughtfully. 'As far as I can see, it has to be the linen. There's all these factories. Wherever you go, even places that were wee villages not so long ago like Milford, or Tassagh, or Darkley. You get a big mill and that's employment. Two or maybe three in a family earning every week. And then there's the bosses, of course. Sure some of them's so rich they can't count it all.'

'Wouldn't that be strange, John?'

'Wouldn't what be strange?'

'To be so rich you couldn't count it all.'

'Sure what would the good of that be?' he responded promptly. 'What's the use of money if you can't use it to some purpose. No good just hoarding it up.'

'But what about a rainy day, John?'

'Indeed, there was something about that in the copy book too, but I can't for the life of me remember what it was.'

'*Always put something by for a rainy day*. That's what mine said,' she replied thoughtfully.

'But doesn't everyone do that anyway?'

'No, love, they don't. There's plenty live from hand to mouth and then there's nothing for the day when there's no money for bread.'

'Well, we'll not be like that. Don't you worry your head. I'll see we never go short, however hard I hafta work.'

He turned her round in the fading light and they retraced their steps towards home falling silent now. It was a fine, warm evening, the land settling into the deep quiet that only comes with the approach of night. She matched her pace with John's longer strides and thought of his last words. At times, the things he said were so like what her father said to her mother.

'*He was so concerned about you all. He wanted to make sure you always had enough.*'

Hannah always spoke with such warmth of their father and the efforts he made to provide for them, but each time she had added a note of warning. '*No one could have worked harder than your father, but he couldn't foresee what came to him, either at the hands of others or of God himself.*'

Rose shivered in the warm evening air. Her mother's words had reminded her of her blessings. Since she'd met John, so many of her wishes and dreams had become reality. She was happier than she'd ever been in her whole life. Yet it was scarcely possible life should go on just the way she wanted it. Sooner or later she might find circumstances took away her joy and no amount of striving could bring it back. She pushed the thought out of mind. Well, if that were to happen, she'd meet it when it did.

# CHAPTER ELEVEN

Annacramp
1885

Rose looked out the window for the third time in ten minutes. The rain still poured steadily from a leaden, grey sky. The long, narrow puddles on both sides of the road had grown wider. In the deep herbaceous borders leading away from the front door, tall stems of delphinium, monk's hood, foxglove and lupin dipped over, heavy with moisture, showers of fallen florets strewn across the paving stones of John's newly-laid garden path.

She glanced at the clock. Nearly four and no sign of the children. She smiled suddenly. Of course, the new assistant would keep the children in the schoolroom till the rain was over. Master McQuillan would never think of the weather but May Todd was a local girl. She knew how many of her pupils had a mile or more to walk after school.

Rose pulled the kettle forward on the stove, sat down and picked up the child's dress she was making. She stroked it smooth and sighed. She felt again the strange sadness that had come upon her so often in the last weeks. 'Are you lonely?' she asked herself. No, she couldn't say she was lonely. She'd made friends easily enough. There were half a dozen houses where she was warmly greeted, brought in to drink tea by the stove and share her news. She enjoyed her visits to Armagh, was well-known in her chosen shops. She enjoyed studying the fashion in the more expensive shops, seeing what was currently in favour. It reminded her of the days when she went shopping with Lady Anne in Dublin.

Then there was the library on The Mall. She'd made friends there too. When she'd discovered a whole section of books on machinery she knew would delight John, she'd paid her five shillings' yearly subscription and brought them home for him along with her own. Often, they'd read together in the evenings. Sometimes John would move to the table and make sketches and plans. He was especially interested in the possibilities for self-moving vehicles and he'd explain to her the working of steam pistons or the use of heavy belts to transfer power.

She enjoyed listening to him, but, when he became absorbed in his study, her thoughts would often move back to Kerry, to her mother and Sam. Or she would think of Lady Anne's new life in Sligo as Lady Harrington. In this year past, she knew she'd missed them in a way she'd never done before.

She put her sewing down and listened to the silence. The house was so quiet. Too quiet. The change in her days was so obvious. Sarah was not well. The arthritis was not much worse, but she'd developed pains in her chest as well. When they came on, she found it hard to breathe, could barely walk at all.

The doctor had been sent for more than once. He said sadly the only advice he could give was that she should rest. The pain could be avoided, but not cured. So Sarah had done as she was bid and retreated to her own room. She said she didn't want to cause Rose any extra work, for she'd enough to do, cooking and cleaning, making clothes for four little ones, milking the cow, feeding the hens and getting the eggs ready for the weekly collection.

She spent more and more time lying down and her youngest grand-daughter, her namesake, Little Sarah, insisted on keeping her company, even to the point of falling asleep on the bed beside her. With her other three at school, it was no wonder Rose had more than enough time for her own thoughts.

Restlessly, she put the small garment down on her worktable and went back to the window. There was no sign of the rain easing off and no sign of the children. Yes, children were hard work, Sarah had been right, but she never counted the cost. They were far too precious, for they had not arrived without much heartache.

Her first pregnancy had miscarried at three months. Sarah comforted her and said it often happened with the first and Rose trusted her long experience. Then the second miscarried at six. Despite all Sarah's reassurances and explanations, John had been distraught and when she became pregnant for the third time he was beside himself with anxiety. But this time all went well and she carried James to nine months, a robust little baby with red hair and bright eyes when he arrived. He was followed by Hannah a year later, then Sam, who had just gone to school, and little Sarah, who had been born on her own birthday, June the twelfth, just two years earlier.

Rose moved around the room, put coal in the stove, folded up some towels drying on the rack above. She looked at the child's dress on her sewing table. It was so grey outside, it was almost too dim to see the fine work she was doing to complete the little garment. She went and looked up at the sky, a new anxiety stabbing at her.

This chill, grey rain reminded her of the summers of '79, '80 and '81, when day after day was wet, there was little warmth and very little sunshine. Sarah had watched her geraniums die of cold and damp, something she hadn't seen since the wet summers during The Famine. The farmers round about had had to keep the cattle indoors long beyond their usual time, buying fodder they could ill afford. The subsequent harvests were late and meagre. Hard enough years for many of their neighbours, but desperate for poor tenant farmers elsewhere. Either they could feed their families, or pay the rent, but not both.

They themselves had not suffered hardship, for John's wages were as steady as always. Her own small income from keeping hens was reduced when the price of eggs dropped, but from the time of her first pregnancy she'd made children's dresses and the demand for them was as steady as John's wages.

Her mind moved back to those hard years. She remembered how often she'd counted the shillings into her purse to go shopping and given thanks that their table was still well provided, the children properly clothed. As she set aside a little for unexpected bills each week, she thought of those left with nothing. Just like the 1840s, families faced eviction and the bitter choice between starvation and emigration. The newspapers were full of heartbreaking accounts of distress and the outrages desperation gave birth to. Rent collectors ambushed and beaten, big houses robbed or burnt, shops looted.

She'd her own sources of information too. Her mother wrote from Kerry and Lady Anne from Sligo, but it was her brother Sam, studying land management in Dublin under the sponsorship of Sir Capel, who had most to tell. He'd been drawn into the circle of the Land Leaguers and made friends with Michael Davitt. When the cold, wet weather and the downturn in prices began to take their toll in the late summer of 1879, his regular letters suddenly became more frequent and more urgent.

Week after week, he poured out his troubles to her, for he was torn apart trying to decide what to do. Sometimes within the same letter he would resolve on two different courses of action, arguing clearly and lucidly for one, quite unaware he'd argued as clearly and lucidly for the other.

As a wet and cold autumn followed on from the disastrous summer and the shadow of famine loomed ever larger, suddenly his mind was made up. '*I can't do it, Rose. I just can't be Sir Capel's land agent,*' he wrote, his usual neat hand jagged and difficult to read from the speed with which he was trying to write it all down for her.

*I don't remember, Rose, what it was like to be evicted, I was too young, but Michael remembers his home in Mayo and the day they were put out. His family went to Lancashire and got work in one of the mills. That's where he lost his arm. Rose, can you believe that when the British put him in jail for being a Fenian they harnessed him to a cart to pull stones because he had only one arm for breaking them?*

*I know he's right, that the land of Ireland must be owned and tilled by the Irish, not used to raise rents to keep the rich in comfort, not even the Molyneux who are kind people*

*and have been good to us. I am going back
to Kerry to see mother and to tell Sir Capel
himself that I cannot be his land agent. I
certainly owe him that. However good he
may be to his tenants, it is the principle that's
at issue. I shall be joining Michael and going
wherever the organisation sends me to help
the poor folk who are in such dire straits.*

Within weeks of writing to her, Sam was travelling
round Ireland, distributing money raised by the
Fenians in America. Wherever he and his colleagues
went, it was their job to encourage farmers to resist
eviction, to support families who'd been evicted, and
to show their hostile disapproval for anyone who
tried to benefit from the eviction of others.

Soon Sam was writing in glowing terms about
the success of Michael Davitt's achievement. There
was no repeat of the devastation of 'the bad years'
of the 1840s. Through his success in raising money
in America and distributing it where the need was
greatest, the potential famine had been averted. Rose
shared his delight in all that had been achieved, but
for her, a dark shadow of anxiety lay over his part
that Sam could not have appreciated.

Sam's vigorous activity meant his name would
now be linked inseparably with Davitt and therefore
with the Fenians, who had made Davitt's work in
Ireland possible. Both Rose and Hannah knew the

threat of imprisonment, or exile, now hung like a shadow over him, whether he'd actually sworn the Fenian oath or not, just as visibly as the shadow of famine had hung over the tenant farmers to whom he was committed.

When Sam first joined Davitt, Rose wrote to Hannah and Lady Anne and spoke of her anxiety for him, but what made it worse for her was John's reaction. He was quite distraught at the thought of Sam being jailed, or punished. When his letters came he'd read them over and over again, as if he were searching for some clue to relieve his distress.

'Ah know he's right,' he said, shaking his head and shuffling the close written pages between his large hands. 'An' sure didn't we talk about the whole land question in the stables with Old Thomas and the outside staff back in '75. We all agreed then it weren't right, but sure I niver thought young Sam would take it so much to heart. I'm afeerd Rose, he'll get himself into trouble. Can yer mother not persuade him away from it? There's some bitter men among the Fenians. They'll do things Sam would never think of, but sure he may get tarred with the same brush. Has he thought of that d'ye think?'

'I think he's thought long and hard,' she replied, shaking her head. 'And so has my mother for that matter. She says she'll not stand against him. She knows she couldn't anyway, now he's made up his mind. But she also thinks he's right,' she went on, calmly. 'She says in her letter she's told him that provided they use no violence, she'll stand by him whatever happens.'

'And so will I,' she added, more softly.

He smiled bleakly as he folded the sheets, fitted them back into the envelope and tucked it behind the clock.

'Maybe I'm a coward, Rose,' he said slowly. 'All I want is to live in peace. I want no argument with any man. Aye, or woman either. Sure what would ye do if I were out drilling with the militia or planning to murder some land agent or other an' I was caught an' put in prison? What would become of ye then?'

She'd no words to ease his distress, so she went across to his chair, leant over and put her arms round him. As she held him close, the child in her womb moved. He put his hand on her stomach and drew her head down and kissed her.

'I'd lay down my life for you and for them, Rose,' he said, his voice husky, 'but I couldn't go out to threaten any man. It just isn't in me.'

Rose wondered if this were the first time in his life when John had met a problem he couldn't solve by hard work or good spirits. She asked Sarah what she thought one morning after he'd gone off to work.

'Perhaps our John *has* had his life too easy, Rose,' she said thoughtfully. 'Sometimes you can protect children too much and they think everything will come their way. And often it does for a time,' she admitted. 'But sooner or later, they'll come up against something they can't mend. He's a lucky man has you, Rose, to keep him straight. You and your mother had your share of troubles.'

'We did, Sarah, we did. But compared to most folk, we had an easy life. The conditions weren't bad or harsh. We always had enough to eat and wages that kept us in decent clothes . . .'

She saw Sarah watching her and paused.

'But what you didn't have, Rose dear, was your freedom. You were like a bird in a cage, well-cared for, much appreciated, but not free to fly. For some, that's the most important thing there is.'

When she thought about Sarah's words and the look that went with them, suddenly she saw a link with John's distress and frustration over Sam's situation. Did he feel caged, lacking in freedom to act on his own part? Could it be his work on Sir Capel's estate was not all he'd hoped for? Was he was frustrated by the repetitiveness of the tasks when he had such an interest in doing new things?

She often asked him about what he'd been doing during the day, what jobs he was working on, the people who came to the workshop and forge, but he was reluctant to talk about his work. Only when there was some amusing story, or news from the big house, or from Dublin, or Kerry, did he talk at any length about the events of the day.

But then, one evening, there was a lightness in his step on the path and his eyes were shining as he walked into the house.

'Rose, d'ye mind we met Thomas Scott last week when we went for that walk up by the church and round home by Riley's Rocks?'

'I do indeed. What about it?'

'Ah, I've a story to tell you, but we'd best wait till we've the we'ans settled.'

She remembered the lovely summer evening only too well. The air warm and still, like some of those evenings they'd walked by the lake down in Kerry. They'd met Thomas coming up the hill as they shut the gate of the churchyard where they'd laid a posy for Sarah on Tom's grave.

'Ah, a great evenin',' Thomas agreed, when they stopped to talk. 'But sad enough for some,' he went on. 'Did ye's know our friend Alex is havin' to give up the manufactory. 'Tis a hard thing an' him wrought there all his life an' his father before him.'

'Ach dear,' said John, 'is it the old problem with the back?'

'Aye. He says he can hardly get outa bed in the mornin', niver mind bend over the rings. An' now he says he hasn't the strength in his arm for settin' them either.'

When Thomas left them and walked on, turning down the lane to his own forge, they'd continued down the steep hill from the church and up the equally steep slope leading them past Alex's cart manufactory itself. All was silent, the grass already grown high between the waiting carts and the wheels that would now never be fitted.

As they walked on, John talked about the part of Alex's work he knew best, for he'd fitted new metal rims to the wooden wheels of the carts on the estate often enough, fixed others that had sheared or worn thin. A difficult task because the metal hoops must first be heated in a circular fire built on a stone ring, then the wheel dropped in and the hoop shrunk on to it.

'Sure the first time Thomas set me to do one didn't I set the wheel on fire because I got the rim too hot,' he said, shaking his head. 'An' the next time I couldn't get the rim on, because I was being so cautious with the fire the rim was so cool it hadn't expanded at all.'

'Thomas?' she said, puzzled. 'Did you once work for Thomas then? You never told me that.'

'I served my time with Thomas,' he replied, laughing at her amazement.

'But what about your father? I thought you said he was a blacksmith.'

'Aye, he were. But he didn't hold with father teachin' son. He said yer far better to go to a stranger. An' he knew Thomas was a good man. Sure the Scotts has been blacksmiths as long as anyone can remember.'

Rose laughed aloud.

'And we've been married six years and I never knew you were apprenticed to Thomas. What other secrets have you been keeping from me?'

He laughed and swore he had a dozen, and then began to tell her stories about the people who lived in the farms they passed as the lane rose again among the little rounded hills.

'Did I ever tell you about the children who lived down Bloody Lane?'

She smiled and shook her head.

'There was a new master at the school an' he was very strong on bad language. One mornin' he was filling in some form for the School Governors or suchlike and he asked this wee child where he lived. "Down Bloody Lane", says the child, and promptly gets caned. 'Of course, there are four brothers and sisters live in the same place,' he said grinning as he turned to look down at her. 'So three more of them get caned as well. Well, finally, we get to the eldest one and he's been figuring out what to do so that he won't get caned. "Where do you live?" says the Master. "In the lane the blood flowed down after the Battle of the Yellow Ford", says he, all pleased with himself. "And what date was that?" says the Master. "Don't know, sir." So he gets caned after all.'

'Our friend Thomas had business with Sir Capel the day,' John began, as they settled by the fire. 'An' he came down to see me afterwards.'

Rose was about to take up her needlework, but the tone of his voice stopped her. She sat quite still and waited for him to go on.

'He's asked me would I go into partnership with him, Rose. He says since Alex has been poorly there's so much extra work coming to him, he hasn't even enough room roun' the forge to line up the stuff while it's waiting. He's workin' all hours not to let people down that needs their machinery an' their carts but he says now he knows the manufactory is closed it can only get worse, he'll not be able to manage without help.'

'And what did you say to him?'

'I said I'd think it over an' let him know by the end of the week. I'd have to give Sir Capel a couple of weeks' notice, though by right it's only a week either way.'

'Would you want to leave Sir Capel then?'

'Ach, it's not Sir Capel, he's the best at all, it's the work. Sure, it's all the same. An' there's no company. To tell you the truth, Rose, I just want to be my own man. I'm tired of workin' for someone else.'

'Well, I can't fault you for that. Didn't I marry you for a change of boss?'

He looked at her blankly, saw she was teasing him, and relaxed with a smile.

'It would mean at times I'd be late home of an evenin' an' there'd be a lot more money than now, but sometimes in winter, or bad weather, I might be early home an' the money not so good,' he said, cautiously.

'Well, the money'll not worry us,' she said, reassuringly. 'If you get in my way I'll put you out in the wash house. Or maybe I'll teach you to sew wee dresses,' she said, laughing.

'I woulden be idle, Rose. There's plenty I could do round the house. We'd not be worse off, over all, but it'd be a change for you. What do you think?'

'If it's what you want, John, it's what we ought to do.'

Suddenly, she realised the room was lighter. She went to the window and saw the downpour had stopped. To the south, in the direction of Armagh, the sky was full of high piled castles of cloud, the first streaked patches of blue sky showing between them. Her spirits lifted and gave her the courage to go back to her memories of those cool, wet years.

She'd been anxious as she continued to read of the violence surrounding the actions of The League, but no harm had come to Sam, even though he'd worked long and hard in the countryside. And when he wasn't active in the field, behind closed doors he'd been helping Davitt to devise a Land Act that would secure ownership of the land for small tenants and give them security against eviction at last.

When Davitt persuaded Parnell to take up the land question, Sam's letters became ever more hopeful. He'd been right, too. If Parnell would only take up the cause of the tenant farmers, he'd said, then Protestants and Catholics would come to their support. And they had. In his last letter he said he was sure Lord Ashbourne's Purchase of Land Act would go through Parliament when it came up this coming August. Once it was active, the old, bitter question would be resolved, once and for all.

He was now working as a land surveyor, but he'd not abandoned the cause, as he made so clear in his letter.

She reached up to the mantelpiece and unfolded his most recent letter. She took it down from the mantelpiece and unfolded it.

*It can't ever have been right Rose, for 70% of Ireland to rest in the hands of 2000 landlords and for three million people to own no land at all. But Parnell has shown Gladstone what is needed. Provided the Land Act gives the land back into the proper hands, I, for one, am content. The British have done me no harm. Indeed, even Davitt says he has nothing against the ordinary working man in Britain. His only quarrel is with those who have exploited us and treated us unjustly. They deserve our condemnation.*

She shook her head. For him the issues had become simple. But when you thought about people individually, not as *landlords* or *tenants* or *working men*, it seemed to her very far from simple.

She put his letter back and reached for the one beside it, newly arrived from Lady Anne. Since her first years in Sligo, when her letters had been full of Race Meetings and Horse Shows, change had come about, as much of a surprise to Rose as Sam's involvement with Davitt and the Land League. Now they were full of stories of her efforts on behalf of the children on the estate.

Rose smiled as she saw the flowing hand on the envelope and felt the thickness of the folded sheets inside. Unfolding them once more, she thought of all the upsets she'd sat through in the schoolroom at Currane Lodge, whenever Miss Pringle had forced Lady Anne to put pen to paper.

*I thought once I'd got a schoolhouse and a teacher and books I would have the problem solved, but I hadn't. 'When the teacher showed me the rolls I could see that half the children came only one or two days a week. Not sickness, I'm happy to say, for Harrington has set up a dispensary now for each part of the estate, but what the cause of the absence was the teacher either couldn't or wouldn't tell me.*

*You know, Rose, how Harrington worries about me when I ride alone, since all this*

176

Land League business got started and I hate to upset him, but I decided if no one could tell me what was happening I'd just have to go and find out for myself. Oh, what a horrible shock I got. I went to the house of a sister of one of our grooms because I knew her name and that she had six children at school. Rose, when I got there this tiny child opened the door and there were all the other children, the youngest no older than your little Sam, sitting round the table at work.

The place was full of great paper parcels of linen, so there was hardly room to move and the mother and all the children were clipping and folding and drawing threads. When I asked why the children were not at school she said she had to have them to help her and that they'd be working all day and into the night because of the truck. I couldn't get her to explain what this truck was, but I asked our housekeeper and she says it's what they call the way the factory agent's work. They pay the women in goods from their own shops and if they're late with work they dock their pay so they can't buy as much food. That's why the children are kept off school.

What am I going to do, Rose? It's not as if Harrington hasn't reduced the rents, twice now, in fact, but even if they paid nothing in *rent I still don't think they'd have enough to feed themselves from these little bits of land, not with six or seven children.*

*I really don't know what Mr Davitt is going to do about women having too many children, but then you know I cannot forgive that man for calling Harrington a vampire and saying that he was an absentee landlord when he had his meeting at Ballysadare. He must expect us to be able to live in two places at once!*

She put the letter down and thought of the wild and intractable young woman she'd once known. That Lady Anne would ever find anything more important in her life than riding superbly she could not have imagined, yet she had. Firstly, she'd amazed herself by producing a son and a daughter whom she loved dearly, and then she'd surprised her entire family by encouraging her husband with his land improvement projects and his political activities. Lord Harrington was now a member of Parliament and a vigorous supporter of Parnell.

*Politics is so boring*

Rose could still see the girl of nineteen sitting at her dressing table complaining about the way Captain O'Shea always wanted to talk politics to

Lord Harrington. Now the same Lady Anne was eager to tell her of Gladstone's plans for Ireland and how Harrington was rallying support for Parnell amongst his friends in Sligo and Dublin. She was also able to tell her about her own meetings with Parnell and how she'd found out for herself the truth in the rumours about his relationship with Captain O'Shea's wife.

*Rose dear, Katherine O'Shea is really a very nice woman. I liked her when she came to Currane but was rather shy of her and especially of her fierce old Auntie Ben, but when I met her in London at Auntie Violet's she had one of her children with her. The image of Mr Parnell, exactly the same passionate eyes. Apart from his eyes, he is such a cold-looking man, and so quiet. He came every day while we were there. When he's with her in company, he doesn't say very much but he looks at her so tenderly anyone can see he loves her.*

*Poor man, she can't possibly get a divorce so that he can marry her, the priests would all go mad, but she doesn't seem to mind not being married to him. Horrible old Captain O'Shea hardly ever shows up, except when he wants something. Harrington says he's going to be the new candidate for Galway. Do you*

*remember, Rose, all those years ago you told*
*me that men's friendships are often based*
*on advantage? How right you were. I think*
*of you so often when I watch them talking.*
*I wish I had you here to ask you what you*
*think about so many things . . .*

'And I wish I had *you* here, just to have an old friend to talk to,' Rose said aloud.

As she folded the letter, a beam of sunlight struck the kitchen floor. The sun had come out at last. As she hastily returned the letter to its place on the mantelpiece and hurried to the window, she caught the sound of voices.

'I'll go and tell Ma ye'r comin'.'

'Don't run so hard, James, you'll fall.'

'No, I won't.'

She looked out. James was running full tilt towards the garden gate. A fair way behind, Hannah was walking sedately, yet with a certain briskness, young Sam firmly held by the hand.

Rose went and opened the door. She stood there, waiting till they came close enough to catch in her arms as the sun now poured down around them.

# CHAPTER TWELVE

A week later, the schoolhouse closed, the older children playing in the field behind the house, Rose heard the door of Sarah's room open quietly.

As she sat sewing by the open window, the small figure of her youngest child hurried across the floor towards her

'Ma, G'anny's making a funny noise.'

'I'll go in and see her,' said Rose quietly, a stab of anxiety passing through her. 'You can go out and play with the others now you've had your sleep,' she added, giving Sarah a quick hug.

Entering the room swiftly, she heard an irregular rasping noise. She'd never heard a death rattle, but it had been spoken of enough times these last ten years past for her to fear the worst.

'Sarah,' she said gently, taking her hand. 'Are you all right?'

There was no reply. For a moment, she thought the figure lying so still beneath the unruffled counterpane had left already. Then came another rasping breath. There was another long moment of silence, then the old woman turned her pale, worn face towards her.

'Right as rain,' she said weakly, her lips so dry the words were barely audible.

Rose took up a glass of water from the bedside table. Deciding she was too weak to raise she simply moistened her lips with drops of water on her finger.

Sarah smiled. Her eyes flicked open and she ran the tip of her tongue back and forth over her cracked lips.

'D'you know, Rose, Tom was here,' she said, more clearly. 'A few minutes ago, I saw him standing there by the door, as plain as I see you now. An' he's not one bit changed from the days we used to walk out over Moneypenny Hill and he picked wild strawberries and put them in my mouth.'

She closed her eyes again and Rose waited, not knowing whether to speak.

'Are you in any pain, Sarah?' she asked at last, when the heavy silence in the room grew too much for her.

'Pain?' Sarah repeated, a hint of puzzlement in her voice. 'No, I have neither pain nor ache. It's the best day I've had for months,' she said sleepily. 'I'll maybe get up after a bit and go and see the roses. Wee Sarah says they're all coming out together with the heat.'

She closed her eyes and drifted off to sleep. Rose

left her, but only long enough to send James to fetch his father from the forge.

An hour later they were both sitting with her when the tip of her nose began to go white. They stood up, still holding her hands, one on each side of the bed, and watched in silence as the rest of her face slowly took on the same ashen hue. A slight smile touched her lips. Her departure was so peaceful, it was some time before either of them took their eyes from her face, unsure whether she was still with them or not.

When finally they turned towards each other, Rose saw that tears were streaming down John's face and falling unheeded on his shirt, the large drops making clean marks in the fine dusting of grime from the forge. She came and put her arms round him and kissed his damp cheeks, comforting him as she would comfort a hurt child.

'What do we do now?' he asked, as he wiped his eyes on his sleeve and looked again at the peaceful figure on the bed.

'We'll bring the children in and tell them where Sarah's gone,' she said quietly, 'and then maybe you'd have a wash and go into Armagh to Loudan's. You could call in with Mary Wylie as you're passing and ask her would she come down to me. Go up to Thomas and tell him too. You might be lucky and get a lift into town. Loudan's will bring you back in their chaise.'

'What wou'd I do without you, Rose?' he said, shaking his head.

'And what would I do without you, John?' she said gently, as she wiped his tear-streaked face with her handkerchief.

As they went out together into the meadow where the children were playing in the sunshine, Rose suddenly saw herself as a child, sitting by a turf fire in Ardtur, the dust and smoke from falling cottages floating through the door, her father asking her mother what he was to do.

How strange it was that men, who seemed so strong, so able to go out into the world and achieve great things, sometimes so completely failed to see their way forward, turning to their women, as lost and vulnerable as a child. She recalled how often her mother had spoken of her own father in such terms, sitting by their tiny fire, in the room above the stables at Currane Lodge, a piece of needlework resting in her lap, her mind moving over precious things from long before.

'He was a good man, Rose,' she said softly, 'but there was little in his life to teach him about the important things,' she went on more forcefully. 'Living and dying, facing hardship and disappointment. That's what religion ought to do for us. Help us to live with the hurts of life. But that didn't seem important for your father's religion, it was so fixed on the life to come and being worthy of it. To tell the truth, mine wasn't much better. It was far more concerned with wrongdoing than with living well. But I had my grandmother to guide me. She was a wise old lady and she taught me that we all have courage if we can but find it and it's easiest to find if you have someone to love. Love is what releases courage, for men as much as women, but the difference between them is this, it's the women who see what has to be done. A man may have the courage of a lion, but if they have no loving woman to guide them, they can do nothing with it.'

Rose watched John as he picked up little Sarah in his arms and took Sam by the hand. She heard him say something about Granny as she bent down to Hannah and James.

'Granny has died and gone to heaven,' she said, as she slipped an arm round each of them. 'It's awfully sad for us, because we'll miss her so, but all her pains will have gone.'

'Will we bury her in the garden, Ma?'

'No, James, she wants to be beside Grandpa up in the churchyard.'

'And will they be together in heaven?' asked Hannah anxiously.

'Yes, I'm sure they will. Granny was looking forward to seeing Grandpa.'

'I know that. She told us all about heaven,' said Hannah firmly, as they went into the house. 'She said we weren't to be upset when she went, because she'd keep an eye on us from up there.'

Rose walked across the kitchen and into Sarah's room. John was standing by the bedside, little Sarah in his arms. She was pointing at the figure on the bed.

'G'anny said she'd be able to jump over a fence again when she went to heaven,' she said doubtfully.

'Aye, she will too,' John agreed. 'That old body of hers was wore out. She'll be given a new one. She'll not know herself.'

Rose looked from child to child, saw their eyes take in the unfamiliar stillness of a woman who had been animated even when she could barely move. Tanned by wind and sun, the face did not yet have the deathly look of chiselled marble. There were even slight signs of a smile, still resting on her lips. Rose caught John's eye.

'Say "Bye bye" to Granny for now. We'll bring her some flowers later. It's time you had your tea.'

Rose had visited enough bereaved neighbours to know exactly what was expected of her in the busy days that followed. They left her little time for grief or thought, as streams of visitors came to pay their respects to a figure who'd been as well-loved in the community as in her family.

The funeral was a large one, the church crowded, the forge silent, every blind and curtain in the cottages on Church Hill drawn as a mark of respect.

It was only as Rose and John walked away from the flower-covered grave that it occurred to her there was scarcely a house in the whole townland that hadn't a plant or two from Sarah's garden growing somewhere about the place.

A few days after the funeral, Rose set out for Armagh to do her weekly shopping and pay the rent. As she left the children with Mary Wylie, her closest neighbour, she felt a real sense of loss for the first time, the opening up of a space to be filled in her own life.

It was not Sarah's help with the children and her willingness to do any job she could manage that she was going to miss. It was her wisdom, for she was one of those people, like her mother, who had aged well, reflecting on all that had come her way, neither embittered by her losses nor overly impressed by her passing good fortune.

Sarah's wisdom wasn't all that obvious in what she said, rather it was in the steadiness and well-being which she spread around her. Even on her worst days, when the pain was bad, or she could hardly move with stiffness, she could find something to celebrate: a job well done, a plant coming into flower, a crack in the clouds, the warmth of the fire, or some wee remark of one of the children.

'Ah Rose, sure we all get depressed at times,' she

would say. 'It's just nature's way of reminding us we're tired or we're not thinking about things we should be thinking about.'

Rose could hear her voice and see the crinkle of laughter round her eyes as she went on.

'*Sins of omission and sins of commission,* the Prayer Book calls it. A very posh way of putting it, I'd say. I didn't understand what it meant for years. But then that's very elevated language for ordinary souls like you and me.'

'Sorry indeed to hear about your mother-in-law, Mrs Hamilton,' said the grocer, as she put her basket down on his counter.

'Thank you, Mr Frazer. It was very peaceful, but we miss her terribly.'

'Ach, 'tis hard. But worse to see an old one lingerin' in pain,' he said, tightening his lips, as he took his pencil from behind his ear and opened his order book.

Everywhere Rose went there were condolences. People spoke to her grief and then shared their own experience. She found it very comforting, though she was surprised they should talk about their own families so easily. It was only as she took out her rent book in Samuel Monroe's in Russell Street and waited for one of the clerks to come and take her money, that the reason dawned on her. After ten years here, they simply treated her as if she'd always been part of the community.

'Hallo, Peggy. I'm afraid I'm a day or two late,' said Rose, as she handed over the correct money.

'What does that matter? Sure we knew about old Mrs Hamilton. It's a hard time. We're all awful sorry up at home.'

Rose smiled and nodded, touched again by the real sympathy in the girl's voice.

'Your sister's been so kind to us. I don't know what I'd have done without her. Especially the way she helped with the children while we were getting ready for the funeral.'

'Mary loves children. The more the merrier, she says. Sure many a time you've helped her out when William was bad.'

Peggy wrote the amount carefully in the rent book, blotted it and handed it back to her. From a rack in front of her, she drew out a white envelope addressed to Mr John Hamilton.

'I don't know what that is, Rose,' she said, as she passed over the letter. 'I hope he's not putting up your rent. There's one or two landlords has raised them recently,' she added, a note of warning in her voice, as she dropped the shillings and pence into the appropriate slots in her cash box.

'I'll tell you next week, if I don't see you down at Mary's in the meantime,' said Rose, picking up letter and rent book and tucking them under the groceries in her basket for safety.

As well as the shopping to do, there were books to go back to the library. She also had to take Sarah's death certificate and her Friendly Society document to a solicitor to be witnessed before they could claim the money to pay the undertaker. In the meantime, she also needed to draw money from the bank, for John to pay the grave-digger and the verger and not keep them waiting till the policy money came through.

By the time she'd finished, walked back to Mary Wylie's, given the children their supper, prepared a meal for John coming in from work, read a story and put the little ones to bed, she was so tired she dropped gratefully into Sarah's old rocking chair and leant her head back against the padded cushion.

She was fast asleep when she heard John's footstep on the garden path.

'Hallo, love. Have you come home to your idle wife?' she asked, stretching and yawning hugely.

'Were ye havin' a bit of a rest?' he said, kissing her. 'An' why woulden you, an' you worked so hard this last week.'

'And so did you,' she said firmly. 'But there are no rocking chairs in the forge. Are you still as busy?'

'Aye, Thomas is still at it, but he made me come home. I worked on while he had his dinner at midday. Fair's fair, he said.'

'I hope you ate your piece.'

''Deed I did. I was ready for it,' he said, as she moved to the stove and took out their meal of bacon and cabbage.

'D'ye not want me to wash before I eat?' he asked, as she tipped potatoes from a saucepan into a dish.

'Just your hands,' she said easily. 'It's very late, you must be starving. You can wash properly before we go to bed.'

They ate in silence, hungry now the food was in front of them. Thoughtful too, as the weariness of the long day swept over them. They'd often sit silent over their meal on these long summer evenings, even before the last week had come to tax them both.

It was only when Rose put the tea caddy back on the mantelpiece after making a pot of tea that she saw the white envelope behind the clock.

'I nearly forgot. Peggy gave me this for you from Monroe's. She says she hopes it's not an increase in the rent.'

She saw the sudden look of apprehension on his face as he took it and began to feel anxious herself.

'If it's the rent, you're not to worry,' she said hastily, as she watched his eyes race back and forwards over the single, thick sheet. 'We can easily afford a few more shillings.'

John shook his head and looked at her blankly.

'Ah don't understand this at all,' he said flatly. 'There's some mistake. He says he wants to put us out next week.'

Rose read and reread the carefully written letter while John sat, his head in his hands, his tea untouched beside him. It didn't seem to her that there was any mistake. Rather, there had indeed been a mistake, but it had been made so many, many years ago, there was nothing to be done about it now.

'John dear, try to remember,' she began gently. 'Was there a new name put on the lease when your father died? You'd maybe have noticed because there's a penalty for putting on a new name and it would be a fair bit of money.'

'I woulden know, Rose,' he said, shaking his head sadly. 'I was working up in Doagh in the mill the time he died. I was only back for the funeral until I could find work here, so as to be company for m'mother. That was a couple o' months later. But she never mentioned anything about names. We just paid the rent regular week by week as we always did, though in those days there was a man came and collected it every Saturday mornin'.'

He looked at her, his eyes wide, the whites made whiter by contrast with his still unwashed face.

'Ye don't think there's anythin' in it, d'ye? It can't be right,' he said desperately.

But Rose could not reassure him. The letter was explicit. Sarah was the last of the three named lives. With her death the lease expired. They would have to consult a solicitor, certainly, but it looked to her as if the writer of the letter knew exactly what he was talking about. She very much feared they'd have to leave their home in a week's time and she had no idea where they could go.

# CHAPTER THIRTEEN

Early next morning, John wrote a note to Thomas, left it in the silent forge and walked in to Armagh. Dressed in his Sunday clothes, he arrived at Samuel Monroe's in Russell Street as the youngest clerk was polishing the brass plate on his door.

'Is he in?' asked John awkwardly.

'He is,' she replied, nodding towards a door at the end of the dark, narrow hall. 'Do you have an appointment?' she asked hurriedly, as John strode past.

John didn't turn back. He knocked on the door, went in the moment he heard an answering sound and drew the letter from his pocket.

'My wife brought this home to me yesterday, Mr Monroe. I'd like to know what you have to say about it.'

Monroe stood up, extended his hand, greeted John courteously and told him his fee for a consultation.

John simply nodded. Rose had warned him the

sum required would probably exceed his earnings in a good week. It would be a small price to pay if there was some way they could keep the home they loved.

Monroe peered at the letter, noticed that John was still standing, fidgeting anxiously, and bade him sit down.

'I'm afraid I'm not hopeful, Mr Hamilton,' he said, after a cursory reading of the single sheet. 'Naturally, I shall call up the relevant deed which will be in our files, but unless the lessor has made a serious mistake and the lease has indeed been modified as required, then he is quite at liberty to give you a week's notice,' he began, reaching for a bell on his desk.

He wrote something on a piece of paper and handed it to the clerk who had slipped quietly into the room.

'Right away, please,' he said crisply, as the young man glanced at what he had written.

'The point about these leases, Mr Hamilton, is that, by specifying three lives and allowing for a renewal fine on the decease of a named life they actually become leases in perpetuity,' he began. 'If they are maintained and the fine paid for the addition of a new life, that is,' he added, a hint of severity creeping into his voice. 'What the lessor is indicating in his letter is that the three lives named in your lease – your grandfather, your father and your mother, are all now deceased. Unless we find that some new name has been entered and the fine paid, then I fear nothing can be done, unless of course, we can assist you with the purchase of a new property,' he ended, with an encouraging smile.

The young man reappeared with the lease, handed it to Monroe, and withdrew, shaking the dust from his hands as he went. Monroe untied the bindings, opened the document and scanned it.

From where he sat, John could see that the document hadn't been opened for years. There was no sign of fresh ink anywhere on the faded parchment. He waited patiently, now he knew what was coming.

'A great pity, Mr Hamilton. A great pity,' he said, shaking his head. 'Do you remember when your grandfather died?'

'Aye, it's on his gravestone. 1845.'

'That might explain it,' said Monroe, nodding to himself. 'The omission, I mean. Your grandmother may have been unaware of the terms of the lease, but it is even more likely in that very bad year, she was unable to pay the renewal fine in order to have a new life inserted. It could, of course, have been done subsequently. But I fear it was not.'

Monroe turned the document round so that John could read for himself the neat copperplate writing, now faded from black to grey and the red seal that bonded together the two signatures on the document. The lease had been drawn up in 1785. Three generations of Hamiltons had lived for a hundred years in the same house. And now they were out on the street.

John stood up.

'We can, of course, advise you about compensation for improvements. I'm sure the property has benefited by your family's long residence,' Monroe began.

John registered what he went on to say about his fees for such a service, but he couldn't concentrate on the details.

'Do you know this man Ludlow?' he asked, abruptly.

'We do collect his rents. Yes.' replied Monroe, getting to his feet.

'Would he give us a while to find a place?'

'I'm afraid I don't think so. He's bought a fair amount of land round Annacramp and Ballybrannan and he's been looking for a house for his son for some time now. I'm afraid your misfortune has been to his advantage. He's not a man to be persuaded to kindliness.'

'An' what if we don't go?'

Monroe shook his head and looked severe.

'I'm afraid that would have very unpleasant consequences, Mr Hamilton. I would most strongly urge you not even to consider it as a course of action.'

John thrust his hand in his pocket and brought out the sovereign Rose had given him. He added a shilling to it and placed it on the desk, turned on his heel and strode out of the office, his head down, blinking his eyes blinking rapidly so that he could see where he was going. He walked the three miles home and strode into the kitchen before the sitting room clock struck ten.

'Rose, where are you?'

'I'm here, love. I'm here,' Rose said, as she ran into the kitchen, drying her arms. 'I was pounding clothes so I didn't hear you. I wasn't expecting you for a while yet.'

She took one look at his face and put her arms round him.

'When do we have to go?'

'Saturday. Four days time and the family here for a hundred years. Can ye credit it, Rose? That's the date on the lease. 1785. The year my grandfather was married. What are we going to do at all?' he asked, as he dropped down in an armchair by the fire and buried his head in his hands.

'We're going to have a cup of tea,' she said firmly. 'And you're going to eat a bit of bread and jam for you took no breakfast. Then we're going to take the children up to Mary so that I can go looking for somewhere for us while you're at work,' she went on. 'Now away and change your clothes while I get you a bite to eat. Your job is to tell everyone that comes to the forge that we've nowhere to go. Maybe someone will know of somewhere that's empty.'

For two days, Rose tramped the roads and lanes of Grange parish, from Ardrea to Drumcairn, from Cabragh to Lisdonwilly. She even went as far as Loughgall and enquired at the Post Office if they knew of anywhere available to rent. But within a three mile radius of Church Hill, the most she reckoned young Sam could walk to and from the schoolroom there was nothing to be had.

John had no better news. Everyone who came to the forge said the same thing. A lot of old houses had fallen beyond repair, and there were no new ones being built because so many young people were going to work in Belfast or into local mills with houses provided. Farm servants and labourers usually lived in the few farm cottages left between Grange and Armagh, and they were all occupied.

On Thursday evening John arrived home late, tired and utterly distraught.

'They can't just put us out, Rose. How can they do that to us with children?'

Rose smiled wryly.

'Of course they can, John. There's no use pretending they can't. They've been doing it for centuries. Don't tell me you want the police and the bailiffs here to frighten the children?

'No, of course I don't,' he said crossly.

'Now eat your meal before it gets cold. We'll think of something yet. We're not destitute and it's not winter,' she said soothingly.

'Aye, but we haven't even got friends with a good barn we could sleep in like your parents had. There's nothing for us but the hedgerows, like gypsies,' he said bitterly. 'Where will we put our furniture and all our good things? Your clothes and the children's toys?'

He bent his head and ate hungrily. She watched, distressed and anxious herself, not so much out of fear of what was to come, but at his bitterness. Suddenly, she saw herself, a little girl, leaning against her mother's knees by a turf fire in an old man's cottage.

As she began to eat her own meal, she tried to recall his name. She'd heard her mother speak of him so often. An old man. Blind from birth. Yes, that was it. Daniel. As the name came back to her, she remembered he'd told stories that night after they'd been evicted, the big room packed with people, the dark rafters with the crosses high above her head.

She looked up at the whitewashed boards of the low ceiling, above the table where she and John had eaten food together for ten years. She had always been so grateful to have food and clothes and to be able to pay the rent. It had never occurred to her that in this new, more comfortable world she would once again be evicted.

She remembered now Daniel's face and the way he greeted people he couldn't see. What she most needed to recall was not the stories Daniel himself had told, but the story he'd called upon her mother to tell. About her father and her uncle turning their backs on their homeland after being evicted and walking the length of Scotland. But there was more to the story than that. Something Hannah had said that was very important for her, here and now.

'Have ye written to yer mother yet,' John asked flatly, as he wiped his plate with a piece of bread.

As he spoke, her mother's words came back to her. Wise words about being bitter. She couldn't remember them exactly but she felt again the deep hush in the cottage as she spoke. She'd said it was all right to shed tears and be sorry. To seek comfort for what had hurt you. But bitterness, she said, was a destroying thing. You mustn't let bitterness get into you.

'No, John, I haven't. But I've been thinking what she'd say to us if she were here.'

She stood up and looked down at him.

'Would you go up and see that Sarah hasn't kicked all the covers off, while I make us a pot of tea. Then I'll tell you.'

She drew the kettle forward on the stove and went across the narrow hall. She'd changed nothing in the room since the old woman's death, a week earlier, except she'd refilled the vases with fresh flowers. She went to the sideboard, bent down and reached back behind the best china for a single cup and saucer that had sat there, safe and undisturbed since it arrived from Kerry. She blew a little wood dust from the cup.

This time, she heard her mother's words without any struggle of recollection.

*I want you to take that with you. And maybe sometimes if things go a bit hard with you, you'll sit down by yourself and drink from the cup, even if it were only spring water you had. My mother gave me that the night before my wedding and I did as she asked many a time when I was anxious or perplexed.*

Never before had she felt so alone. She wasn't by herself, true, but she'd seldom been so anxious and perplexed and here was her dear John, so full of anger and bitterness. She'd tried to comfort him, but he wouldn't be comforted. He had gone away into himself wrapping his misery around him. It frightened her, for the darkness of his mood and the bitterness of his outbursts seemed to take away her courage, her strength to keep up hope and act wisely for them.

She looked at the pretty cup and saucer in her hand and thought of the night before her wedding, when she and Hannah had sat by the fire in their room together knowing it might be years before they would meet again. She heard John's footsteps on the wooden stair, pushed the sideboard door shut and hurried back into the kitchen where the kettle was boiling furiously.

'Were they all asleep?' she asked as she poured John's tea into his favourite mug.

'Aye.'

She poured her own tea into the pretty china cup and sat sipping it slowly. The room was quiet, but for the tick of the clock and the faint murmuring of bees beyond the open window. A comfortable room, well-swept and always freshly whitewashed, the stone floor smooth with long wear, the embrasures of the windows full of geraniums, bright red in one, deep pink in the other.

As the silence deepened, she looked around, knowing that this was the last time she would sit in this room, the familiar objects in their proper places, the American clock on the wall, the brass candlesticks on the mantelpiece, one on each side, the two white dogs with black noses and the coronation tea caddy with a very young Queen Victoria. There were the curtains she and Sarah had made together, the saltbox in the alcove by the stove, the bookcase with the family bible and commentaries, and John's books about engines and machines. Under the window was an old metal box full of the wooden toys John had made for the children.

She remembered that last morning in the old home in Ardtur and how she'd watched her mother go round the room touching things, taking a last long look at the place where she had lived for half her life. Yet for all the pain of loss there was no sadness on her face.

Rose finished her small cup of tea and poured another. John's mug sat untouched as he stared into the fire. But still she did not speak. She was waiting. Hoping that something might come to her out of the silence and the depths of memory.

'John,' she said, breaking the silence at last, 'What's the worst thing that can happen to you?'

He looked at her in amazement.

'Need ye ask,' he said harshly.

'I remember you once saying you'd give your life for me and the children. Have you changed your mind?'

'What?'

She repeated what she'd said but he just shook his head, unable to make sense of what she was saying.

'John, would you not think it worse if we lost the children? Or maybe if I were to die and leave you to mind them?'

'Ach, Rose, what are ye saying?' he cried. 'Sure, it doesn't bear thinking about.'

'Would it be worse than losing stones and mortar?'

'But it's not stones and mortar, Rose, it's our home.'

Rose shook her head.

'John dear,' she said, her voice soft. 'I've been thinking of that morning all those years ago back in Donegal when we were put out. I tried to remember what my mother did while we were waiting for the men to get to us. And it's just come back to me.'

She paused and waited for him to lift his head and look at her.

'Aye,' he said flatly.

'Will you listen, John, if I tell you what she did?'

He nodded but said nothing, his head still drooped on his chest.

'She looked around her and gathered up her home into her head. I watched her do it, though I didn't understand then what she was doing. When we walked down the track with the cart and the cow and our few bits and pieces, this cup and grandfather's watch and the Gaelic Bible she gave to her friends in Ramelton, she had our home safe. She just needed somewhere to put it. Some bits of stones and mortar. Wherever we went, whether it was the barn in Donegal, or the servants quarters in Currane, she took out our home and brought it to life for us children, even after my father died.'

John looked up at her and said nothing.

'I'd rather live under a bush than lose you, John. Would you do the same for me?' she asked gently.

He dropped his head into his hands once more. She knew he was crying, but trying not to admit it.

'John, John, it's all right. If you'll just stop being angry and give me a hand, I can take our home in my head till we find a place to put it in.'

'Sure, I've let you down,' he sobbed, the tears running down between his fingers. 'I would have handed you the moon and stars if I could and now we're no better than beggars.'

She put her arms round him and let him cry, stroking his dark hair and rubbing the spot on his shoulder that always ached after a long day in the forge.

'Why don't we go up to bed now,' she said quietly, as the sobbing subsided. 'It's been a hard time and you've been late home, but maybe we'll gather up all the happiness we've had in that bed and take that with us as well.'

It was Rose who fell asleep after they'd made love, but as the moon rose and shone through the open window, she woke suddenly and discovered John wide awake beside her.

'Can you not sleep?'

'I was havin' a bit of a think,' he said, turning towards her and propping himself up on one elbow.

'What about?'

'There's somethin' I didn't tell you that I should have told you. An' I'm sorry for it.'

For one moment Rose's heart stood still. What more could happen in the space of one short week? And then she saw the softness in his eyes.

'When I told Thomas on Tuesday what had happened, he said if we were beat we could use the old house opposite the forge. It's been empty for years, but he says the roof is still holding, though it needs new thatch.'

'What old house, John? I've never seen one opposite the forge?' she said, propping herself up.

'Ach, it's kind of hidden from the road. There's a tree between it an' the lane and there's shrubs and weeds all growed up in front of it. Sure, I pass it every day when I go up the orchard for the spring water and I hardly notice it's there.'

'Why didn't you tell me, John?'

'Ach, I was ashamed. I went over to look at it and sure Mary Anne has her chickens in the wash house and the front windows have panes broken. I managed to open the front door and the cobwebs and dust would drown ye.'

'But it's dry?'

'Aye, bone dry an' no smell of damp. But there's no stove, only an old broken crane over the hearth. Aye, an' the ashes of a fire still there.'

'Would you know of a good blacksmith, John, that could make a new crane for us?'

'Two of them, not fifty yards away,' he said, smiling. 'Choose your man.'

'I chose my man ten years ago,' she said easily, her heart lifting when she saw him smile. 'I've not regretted it.'

'Even after what's happened?'

'Especially after what's happened.'

'An' you'll come an' look the place over in the mornin',' he asked, stroking her hair.

'Yes, I think I could manage that. What time would suit you?'

# CHAPTER FOURTEEN

The dew was still heavy on the tangled grass as Rose followed in John's footsteps to the door of the old house next morning. The brambles had sprung back already on the rough path he had beaten a few days earlier. They tore at her skirt as she waited anxiously for him to open the door.

It wasn't locked, but there was a dense mass of weeds growing against it and half covering the broad stone door step.

'There,' he said, stepping aside and letting her go ahead of him into the empty room. 'Can we do anythin' with it at all, d'ye think?' he asked anxiously.

'Yes,' she said promptly, even before she had run her eye right round the main room, for the air was sweet, a fresh current moving across the room from a broken window at the front to one at the back. The place was cool, silent, and very dirty. Tattered rags of curtains still hung at the windows and a scatter of sticks on the hearth told her birds had been nesting in the wide chimney. A few runners of ivy had penetrated the window frame of the back window and run diagonally up the walls, their leaves pale from lack of sunlight.

The whole empty space was filled with a strange greenish light. Nettles, tall plants of angelica and shrubby bushes of elderberry had sprung up all around, so completely masking the small windows at the back only a little light filtered through to make dappled patterns on the stone floor.

'I'll see if I can let a bit more light in.'

John strode across to the back door and pulled it open. Sunlight spilt across the floor and picked out his damp footprints in the dust. From somewhere nearby, they heard a lark sing. He turned to look at her, a half smile on his face as she stood watching him.

'Have you been in the other room?' she asked, smiling herself as she saw him cock his ear to the cascade of notes falling into the silence of the abandoned kitchen.

He came back to her side, prised away a bit of board wedged into place in front of the broken panes and leant it against the wall.

'No, I hadn't the heart,' he said, as another patch of sunlight fell on the dusty floor.

'Come on then, we'll go in together,' she said, moving towards a small, brown painted door to the right of the huge fireplace. It had a handsome brass knob, much in need of polishing. Pinned to the lintel with a horseshoe nail, a woven rush cross, faded to the colour of straw, reminded her of making crosses with Aunt Mary, long ago in Ardtur, to celebrate St Bridget's Eve and the coming of spring. She pushed open the door and went through, her boots echoing loudly on bare wooden boards.

'You can just see the forge,' she said, peering through the one corner of the front window that wasn't covered up by the ivy.

They huddled together as they peeped through. Almost opposite was the high pitched gable and the well-used path which ran from the forge to Robinson's farm and on, up the shady lane skirting the orchard until it emerged onto Church Hill.

They inspected the wooden partitions that divided the space into three parts. Two small rooms about seven feet square with a tiny window at the back of each had been separated off, leaving about fourteen feet by nine for the main room.

'It's bigger than I thought,' said John cautiously.

'We could maybe put Sarah's good sideboard in the bedroom,' Rose said thoughtfully. 'And the floors are stone and wood,' she added. 'We had earth floors at Ardtur.'

They heard the scrape of boots on the doorstep and turned to see Thomas stooping under the low lintel of the bedroom.

'Well, what d'ye think? Could ye make do for

a bit?' he asked, straightened up and looking from one to another.

'Ach, Thomas, you were right,' said John, smiling wryly. 'I should have told Rose on Tuesday. I wasn't thinkin' straight at all. Many a man would be grateful to have as good a roof over his head.'

'Sure there's no harm done,' said Thomas reassuringly. 'It's not what you've been used to at all, Rose, but it's better than nothing.'

'Far better indeed, Thomas,' she replied. 'I was reared in a house like this one, but it had earth floors. I wasn't expecting anything better.'

'Were you not now?' Thomas asked, his eyes bright. 'Sure I thought yer man here had stole you from some big house,' he said teasingly.

John grinned and looked sheepish.

'Ah told Thomas on Tuesday I couldn't ask ye to live in a place like this, even if it were all fixed up an' decent lookin'.

'Never mind,' she said, taking his arm. 'But we have a bit of a job in front of us to make it fit to sleep in tomorrow night. We'll have to contact the landlord first and get his permission. Who *is* the landlord, Thomas? Is it you?' she asked, turning to the older man.

He threw back his head and laughed.

'Ach no. I'm just a tenant like yourselves,' he said, 'though there's been Scotts here for a brave while. But I'd say you'd have no difficulty. The landlord is

Sir Capel, same as meself. He's not a hard man to deal with, as you well know. Ye may away over an' see him right away, John. He'll maybe give ye a bit of help to get fixed up. An' ye'll want to agree the rent an' get some agreement drawn up.'

He shook his head. 'After what's happened to the pair o' you, I'd better go in to Monroe's m'self and see what m'own lease says. Ye wouldn't find a house with a forge so handy,' he said, shaking his head ruefully. 'Away on now, John, an' see Sir Capel.'

'I hope he's not gone to Dublin.'

'Well, he was here a few days ago when Sammy came to get the black stallion shod,' he said quickly. 'Sure he won't let anybody but John shoe him,' he added turning to Rose. 'Did he iver tell ye that?'

'I think there's a fair amount he doesn't tell me, Thomas,' she said, laughing gently, 'but I'll be able to keep a better eye on him now.'

'I can't go off an' leave ye like this, Thomas,' John said, as they all stepped out into the sunshine. 'What about our work? Sure we're up to our eyes.'

'Aye, we are,' he agreed. 'A couple of hours will be neither here nor there in a hundred years,' he went on cheerfully. 'I'll light the fire to show we're still in business an' then I'll get my great new scythe and cut in as far as the windows to give Rose daylight. Ah see ye brought yer broom an' yer buckets with ye.'

'We did indeed, and a piece for my lunch,' she

213

replied. 'I think I'm going to need it, don't you?'

'Aye, ye've yer work cut out for ye,' he said, as he turned on his heel with an awkward laugh and headed for the forge. 'I'll be back over when I've the fire lit.'

'That's one good friend we have,' she said, as she saw him stoop under the doorway of the forge and disappear into the darkness.

'Aye, and Mary Wylie another,' John added, thinking of the children. He hesitated, then came and put his arm round her and kissed her. 'I'm sorry, Rose for the heartache I've caused ye. But I'll make it up ye. I'll be back as soon as I can.'

The day grew hotter as the sun rose higher in a cloudless sky. Rose worked methodically, pulling down cobwebs, sweeping the two small bedrooms out into the larger one, rubbing the unbroken windowpanes with a piece of torn curtain to remove the layers of grime. By the time she started sweeping the main room, Thomas had cleared the rampant growth from around all the windows and the smell of cut grass flowed through the open doors. It helped to offset the choking dust from the floors, but after a couple of hours, she was not only tired, but gasping with thirst, her bottle of cold tea long gone.

The well was in the big orchard behind Thomas's house, but she wasn't sure where. As it served the needs of the forge and of Thomas's wife and three children, she reckoned there'd be a well-worn path visible once she crossed the piece of common that ran between the two houses.

The heat struck her bare arms as she stepped out of the cool interior of the cottage. She stood by the back door, drawing in deep breaths of the clean air. It was full of the heavy scent of elderflower. Everywhere she looked, plants grew and flowered. There were creamy heads of meadowsweet and the bright spikes of purple loosestrife in the damp bottom of the hedgerow. Tall, branching stems of buttercup and pink flowering willow herb stood in drifts, towering over the shorter grass with its clusters of daisies and clover. Here and there, where the grass grew a little longer, were the delicate spikes of Irish orchid, one of her favourite flowers, some pink and speckled, some varying in colour from pink to mauve and lavender.

She smiled to herself. Once, long ago, when Miss Pringle threatened to stop Lady Anne riding if she didn't produce at least an attempt at watercolour by the next day, she'd gone out and sketched and painted them for herself. She'd been amazed at how much you saw in a flower when you really looked at it and even more amazed she'd turned out something that pleased Miss Pringle enough to keep Lady Anne out of one more piece of trouble.

From where she rested, propped against the windowsill by the back door, she could see there'd once been a sizeable garden behind the house. An overgrown stone wall on two sides and a hedgerow on the other enclosed a space humped and hollowed with the regular lines of spade rigs. In one corner, there were some fruit bushes almost completely overwhelmed by convolvulus, large white trumpets shimmering in the bright light.

She stood up, stretched her aching back and tramped around cautiously, the ground so uneven it would have been easy to twist an ankle. She smiled in delight when she found an old briar rose had grown outwards over the low wall into a small triangle of land with two or three old apple trees. Untended for years, it formed a dense thicket covered with a mass of tiny pink blooms. From the scuffles her movement had set off, the sudden vigorous shaking of sprays of bloom, it had to be home to a couple of bird's nests at least, if not something larger.

Completing her circuit of the old garden, she squeezed through a gap in the hedge where a single rotting post might once have supported a garden gate and stepped down onto the broad, grassy cart track that led to three small fields with no direct access from the main road.

'I'll just have a quick look at what's down the common,' she said to herself, when a glance towards Thomas's house failed to reveal the path to the well.

The soft, rich grass brushed the hem of her heavy, working skirt as she turned down the cart track, the grass soft on her now bare feet.

'Oh, how lovely,' she gasped, as she came out of the shadow of the trees overspreading the common and saw all three fields were in flax. Waving gently in the light breeze, the blue flowers swayed like an inland sea, ripples of wind flowing across the rich crop like eddies on a lake.

Suddenly, Currane lake came to mind and the darker blue waters of Ballinskelligs Bay. For one painful moment, she was overcome with such a longing to be there again, to stand on her hillside once more, with a view south to Eagle Mountain or west to the Atlantic. Then, quite suddenly, a lark rose into the still air, above her head, his song indifferent to the hum of insects in the hedgerow behind her and the muted ring of hammer on anvil as Thomas worked on through the heat of the day.

She brought herself back firmly to the present. Blessings she'd had, and despite all the heartache of the last week, blessings she still had. It was up to her what she made of them.

Refreshed by her walk and the cool shade of the orchard where she drank from the well and filled up her bottle, she took up her broom and pulled open the door of the small outbuilding placed at right angles to the back of the house. To her surprise, the floor had been brushed, but it looked as if it had been done rather hastily. The corners of the stone-floored wash house were still full of feathers and dried chicken droppings. The small window was tightly shut and the smell was horrible.

'Oh dear,' Rose said aloud, as the sharp stench enveloped her.

Intensified by the heat of the day, it made her eyes water. She struggled with the window but couldn't shift it. Then she realised a nail sticking out of the window frame had actually been driven right through it to prevent the window being opened. She sighed and thought she'd go and borrow a claw hammer from Thomas. Lever it out and let the air in. But she decided against it. Thomas was such a kind man he'd almost certainly put aside his work and come and do it for her and he'd had enough interruptions for one day.

She went outside, took a few breaths of fresh air, then started to pull down cobwebs and feathers as quickly as she could. She brushed out the corners one by one and carried the sweepings to the far end of the garden.

'Rose, where are you?'

Delighted to hear John's voice, she wiped her damp face on her apron and hurried back into the house. He turned towards her, the beam on his face telling her all she needed to know. Beside him stood a little gnome of a man almost half his own height.

'Rose, this is Sammy Hutchinson from Ballynick. He's come to fix the windows for us.'

'Pleased to meet you, Sammy, I've heard about

you many a time,' she said, as Sammy pulled off his cap and offered her a wizened brown hand.

'Nothing bad I hope,' he said, eyeing her sideways.

'Nothing but compliments,' she replied, laughing. 'But I've a poor welcome for you,' she went on apologetically. 'I can't even offer you a cup of tea and you've come all the way from Sir Capel's.'

'Ach, never worry yerself, Missus dear, ye've had enough to worry about, the pair of you, losing the old lady and then bein' given notice. All in the one week forby,' he said, shaking his had slowly. 'Sir Capel was not well pleased when he heard what had happened to ye's,' he went on, as he dropped his tool bag beside the nearest window and eyed up the broken panes and rotting frame. 'There's a few of these boyos around has made money one way an' other. Now they're buying land and puttin' people out. It's a bad thing losin' good people out of the place. That's what Sir Capel says, an' I agree with him. Sure, emigration has been the detriment an' destruction of this island. An' it'll start up again as bad as iver if young folk can't get work and homes.'

With a fierce nod towards them, he turned to the window and started scraping away the remains of dried and broken putty.

'How're ye gettin' on, Rose?' John said quietly as he cast his eyes round the clean, empty room, now filled with sunlight.

'Not bad. The wash house could do with a wash itself,' she said, waving a hand towards the open door. She led the way out to the back, glad to have an excuse to speak to him on his own. 'How did it go, John?'

'The best at all. Half the rent Thomas pays for his dwelling house an' he'll put in proper new windows an' renew the thatch before the winter, unless we can find somewhere better,' he said, as he stepped into the wash house.

'Rose, dear, the smell here's awful. Why didn't ye leave it for me?'

'I left you a nail in the window,' she said laughing, as he stepped quickly out again. 'If you could shift that, the draught would get the smell out.'

'Aye, it would. But ye shouldn't have cleaned it yourself wi' that smell. I'd have done it,' he said.

She smiled at him.

'I know you would, but you mustn't take any more time from the forge. Thomas cut all the nettles and weeds for us and he hasn't taken a break all day.'

'Did Mary-Anne not bring him a bite to the forge?'

'Not that I saw,' she said.

It suddenly struck her that she'd seen no sign of her neighbour in the course of the long morning, either going up the orchard for water or passing across the front of the house on her way to the privy.

'An' did she not come over an' say a word to you?'

'No, she didn't,' she replied matter-of-factly. 'Did you think she would?' she went on when she saw the puzzled look on his face.

'Well, it woulda been neighbourly,' he said quickly. 'Am sure Mary Wylie or Hannah Running woud've come to see ye, aye an' given ye a hand,' he said sharply, 'had ye been movin' in next door to them.'

'Maybe she wants to let us get settled. And I'm not exactly dressed for receiving visitors, am I?' she said laughing, as she did up a button on her blouse, below which she wore neither chemise nor stays. 'Now away an' get that hammer. I don't think I can face washing the place out till there's some fresh air in there to breathe.'

# CHAPTER FIFTEEN

'Did ye try the raw onions, Rose?'

She picked up the kettle from the hearth and carried it to the table where the teapot sat waiting. For a moment, distracted by the pain in her back as she bent over, she couldn't think what Mary Wylie was talking about. Then she remembered the stench of the chickens left behind in the wash house.

'Well, I'm not sure it got rid of the smell,' she said, laughing, as she put the lid on the teapot and lowered the kettle back down to the hearth without stooping. 'But John's started to complain about the smell of onion, so there must be an improvement.'

'D' you want to put wee Edward down on the bed while you have your tea?' she asked, looking at the sleeping baby Mary had been feeding while they talked.

'Well, we can try,' she replied, with a sigh. 'But this one has all the others beat for guile. He cries his head off as if I were starvin' him, then when he gets a few mouthfuls he dozes off. Happy as Larry, he is, unless I try to put him down. Ma says I have him spoilt, but she's half deaf, she doesn't have to listen to the cries of him.'

Mary moved the child gently away from her breast and raised her eyes heavenward when he didn't wake. She tiptoed across the room and through the open bedroom door. The silence continued. Mary shut the door quietly behind her and waved her hands in the air, fingers firmly crossed.

'Must have been the open fire made him sleepy. He wouldn't do that at home,' she said, shaking her head, as she settled herself comfortably back again in Sarah's rocking chair and did up the buttons on her blouse.

'Do you miss your stove?' she asked, as Rose passed her over a cup of tea.

'Yes, I do,' she confessed. 'But it'll be better when I have a new crane. It's the bending over all the time that gets me. Still, I was amazed how cooking on the fire comes back to you, if once you've ever lived with it.'

'Ach sure yer tired out, Rose. I'm not surprised yer back's botherin' ye. I don't know how the pair of you's managed at all. When did ye do the whitewash?' she asked, casting her eye round the freshly coated walls on which Rose had already hung some favourite pictures and the bunches of flowers she always dried for the winter.

Rose laughed.

'Don't tell anyone. We didn't go to church on Sunday. John says *the better the day the better the deed*, but I've heard our neighbour is very strict about Sunday, so we kept the doors closed and crept around very quietly. But we needn't have bothered. It seems she goes off to her old home in Battlehill to the church there, so she was away the whole day.'

Mary nodded her head and drank her tea gratefully, rocking herself gently in the comfortable old chair.

'She hasn't called yet?'

Rose shook her head and pursed her lips.

'Maybe that's for the best.' There was a significant pause before Mary added, quietly. 'She's got a bit of a reputation, you know.'

'Well, are you going to tell me like a friend, or do I have to find out for myself?'

'Ach, I wouldn't want to put you off. She might be all right if you take the right way of her. But she's very strong in her opinions.'

'And what are her opinions?'

Mary looked uncomfortable, her large blue eyes flickering round the hearth as if she were counting the pots and kettles gathered under the projecting canopy of the chimney.

'Well, she's a Methodist for a start,' she began awkwardly, 'Not that I've anythin' against Methodists, but she's awful strict. An' the family is all great loyalists. I've heard that her grandfather was a great friend of Dan Winter. There was Catholics killed back that time an' no one ever taken for it. The Courtneys of Battlehill was in the thick of it, so I've heard,' she said uneasily, 'but I've no head for history. I may not have the right way of it, for I think it's all far better forgotten. But Mary-Anne forgets nothin' and forgives nothin', so I hear.'

Rose listened carefully. The one thing you could be sure of, Mary Wylie would never say a bad thing of anyone if she could find a good thing to say instead. She was so good-natured indeed, she often wondered how she'd managed to get this far in life without being exploited.

'Tell me, Mary, how did our friend Thomas ever take up with a woman like that?'

'Ach, ye may well ask,' said Mary with a sigh. 'Ma says he was took in. Mary was gettin' on, she was thirty three an' her younger sisters all married. Robert was three years younger an' kinda shy. His own mother had just died an' he'd no sisters, none that lived, that is. When they met up she's as nice as pie. Sure it's an old story, Rose. Ye've heard it afore.'

She nodded.

'Did they have to get married?'

'Aye. It were a July weddin' as the sayin' is. An wee Annie was born the night o' the big snow in January '76.'

'What do you mean "a July wedding" Mary?'

'D'ye not know that one? Maybe that's an

225

Armagh one. No one marries in July unless they have to. It's bad luck,' she said. It had a name in Irish, my grandfather always used. But I never got my tongue round it. She made a try at the unfamiliar sound. I *think* it means bad luck,' she said tentatively.

Rose smiled to herself. It was seldom these days she heard a word of Irish, or had any cause to speak it herself, except for the cobbler in Armagh, an old man from the south of the county. The very sound of it still touched her and brought to mind the cries of children playing, the songs sung by their fireside, the stories she had heard. She recalled the last of the stories, the one old Daniel McGee had told. Her last story and his too, for he'd died in Letterkenny Workhouse a week after he was evicted.

'Yes,' she said, thoughtfully, 'it is unlucky. What you said means hungry month. July was hungry, because it was the month between the potato crops. The old ones were gone and the new ones too small to dig. Not a good time for a wedding.'

'Speaking of weddings, Rose,' said Mary suddenly. 'Is it not very quiet out the back?'

Both women stood up, went to the window and looked out. Half an hour ago, they'd watched Hannah, as chief bridesmaid, adorning the bride, Mary's eldest girl, Jane, in an piece of lace curtain. Little Sarah was making bouquets of pink roses for the bride and bridesmaids and James was being turned into a minister by Mary's boys with the help of an old black skirt of Rose's.

'No sign of them,' said Rose. 'Maybe the bride and groom are emigrating and they've gone on the convoy.'

'Should we away and look for them?' Mary asked anxiously, as she opened the back door and glanced around the empty garden.

'I don't think so,' she replied easily. 'Mine know they can only go as far as the top of the orchard unless they tell me who they're going to play with on Church Hill. Hannah's very reliable. She'd not go beyond the orchard without coming to ask. I'm sure your ones wouldn't go off and leave them. We'll give them a while and see if they come back to the garden. If they don't appear in ten minutes or so, we'll go then.'

'It'd be a pity to wake wee Edward,' confessed Mary, as she settled herself again. 'It's not that often he sleeps for me when I want him to.'

'Which reminds me,' said Rose, getting up again. 'I have a present for that young gentleman.'

She opened the doors on the new dresser, bought with the money from the furniture they'd had to sell. She took out a cardboard box and laid it across Mary's knee.

'A small thank you for all you've done to help us,' she said smiling. 'It might come in handy in a month or two.'

Mary looked startled, stared at the box as if it

might tell her what was inside. Rose had to smile. The box said *Ladies wool stockings – Large*. Cautiously, she opened it and gasped.

'Oh Rose, you can't give me this. It's so lovely. I've never seen anything half as nice, even in the shops I never go into.'

To her amazement, Mary burst into tears.

'Oh there, my dear, what's wrong?' she asked, crossing the hearth and putting her arm round her.

'Nothing's wrong,' she said, scrubbing furiously at her eyes with a corner of her apron. 'All that work, Rose, all those lovely wee flowers, an' lace and ribbon. An' you did it for my wee Edward. Sure he'll be like a wee Prince when he's christened. Nobody else ever gives me things like you do,' she said abruptly. 'Good old Mary'll do it. That's what they say. And sometimes not even a thank you . . . an' you go and make this for me . . .'

'Now come on, Mary, don't cry,' said Rose, kissing her cheek, 'or I'll be afraid to make you a blouse for yourself . . .'

Rose broke off. There was someone knocking at the front door. A loud and peremptory knock at that. Puzzled, Rose looked at Mary and glanced through the window to see who the caller might be. But there was no one visible, neither pedlar, nor gypsy, fish man or bread man. She opened the door.

A sour-faced woman in dark clothes stood on the step, her greying hair scraped back in a tight knot, her bosom high with strong stays and indignation.

'Missus Hamilton, I'll have you know that the path down the side of my house is not for the use of you and your collection of children. It's bad enough you using it to go to our well for water, which in charity we can hardly deny you when you have none of your own, but to let these children use it to make a playground out of the orchard is beyond all bearing. You will chastise them and see it does not happen again.'

So saying, she turned on her heel and strode off, her high buttoned boots crushing the weeds in her path. Rose watched, in amazement, until she disappeared under the trellis of roses which arched over her front door.

'Well,' she said, as she shut the door behind her, 'you said she had strong opinions.'

Poor Mary's face was a picture of anxious distress.

'Oh Rose dear, what *are* you going to do?'

Rose took a deep breath and realised she was shaking from the sheer effort of self-control. She smiled ruefully.

'I don't know, Mary, but I can tell you what I'm not going to do and that's "chastise" the children. "Chastise", Mary? Is that a good Christian way to deal with children?'

'That would be Mary-Anne's way. Her children have the fear of God beaten into them. Even wee Robert and him not breeched yet.'

'I've not seen one of her children since we moved last Saturday, and today's Thursday. Does she keep them indoors and it the holidays?'

'As far as I know, she does. The eldest girl, Annie, does all the housework. So I hear. Young Thomas lives with her mother over at Battlehill in the holidays to do her work for her, and Robert is only allowed out into that wee bit of grass behind the forge. She used to put him there in a horse collar when he was a baby so she could get her work done.'

'A horse collar?' said Rose, completely amazed.

'Aye. It's not such a bad idea, it keeps them safe for a wee while if ye're busy,' Mary explained. 'My own Ma used one with the boys, but wee Robert was in it all day unless it was pourin' with rain. One of the servin' girls at Robinson's used to stop and talk to him when she was sent over with the milk, but Mary-Anne put a stop to that,' said Mary sadly.

She hesitated, not sure whether she should say more.

'Ye see, Bridget was from away an' she spoke mostly Irish. That makes Mary-Anne mad. She hates the Irish.'

'But sure she's Irish herself,' protested Rose. 'Aren't we all Irish in Ireland?'

'Most of us are, I'm sure, but not Mary-Anne. She's one for not wantin' Ulster to have anythin' to do with the rest of Ireland. Don't for any sakes mention Parnell or Gladstone in front of her. Traitors the pair of them.'

'I don't think I'm likely to mention *anything* in front of her,' she replied, shaking her head. 'If today's anything to go by, she's a woman best avoided, but it's going to be difficult if we've trouble over the well.'

'Pay no attention to that. It's not her well. Sure it's on the Robinson's land for a start. Anyway, it's not a well, it's a spring. Someone has just hollowed it out a bit to make a pool of water for the buckets to go in. Ye can't own a spring, can ye?'

Rose was about to say she thought the same woman would lay claim to anything, when she caught a movement by the back door. One by one the children straggled into the kitchen looking downcast and miserable. James came last, still in his parson's robes. He was carrying little Sarah, who was crying.

She held out her arms for the child. She looked pale. Her small body was hot and damp as she buried her face in her shoulder, wound her arms round her neck and cried even harder.

'What's wrong at all?' asked Mary, looking from one silent child to another. 'Jacob, tell me what's happened.'

'We were taking Jane and Sam to the station. An' I was the engine driver. An' we saw this wee child sitting by itself on the grass playing with bits of wood. An' it comes over to us. "Can I play with you?" it says. An' I says, "What's yer name?" An it says "Robert Scott." So I says, "You can be the guard. Ye have to wave a flag and shout *Are ye right?*" So we took the train up to the top of the orchard an' roun' the far side an' when we get back doun again t' the back o' the house, there's this woman standin' there.'

'She smacked wee Robert an' he cried,' said Hannah, her own eyes brimming with tears, her arm round young Sam who was clinging to her.

'An' she said we weren't to come into the orchard down her path,' said Jane, her eyes large, her face solemn.

Mary stood up and held out her arms. Jane and William leant against her generous figure while Jacob, her eldest boy, a few months older than James, stood biting his lip and trying not to cry.

'Maybe I should take the children home now, Rose,' said Mary awkwardly, as she felt Jane and William cling to her and saw the look on Jacob's face.

Sarah had fallen asleep in Rose's arms, her skin still prickling with heat. She looked round the bedraggled company and shook her head.

'No, Mary, you can't do that. I promised these children fresh soda bread with butter and a little bit of golden syrup for their tea. How about that?' she asked, looking from one to another.

There were some rapid nods and a few weak smiles, a response better than she'd hoped. She made the best of it.

'James and Sam, have you shown Jacob and William the engine your Da made for you? she asked, nodding at the wooden box under the window. 'Hannah, could you slip into the bedroom very, very quietly, and bring me Sarah's blanket and a pillow. We'll put her on the settle for a wee sleep. Maybe Jane dear, you'd go out to the wash house and bring in the biggest bowl and the baking board for me.'

Rose and Mary exchanged glances as the children promptly moved around and did as they were asked, but it was not until they were all sitting round the table, fingers sticky with syrup dripping from the warm soda bread that the dark pall of Mary Anne's wrath finally began to disperse.


'What's she thinkin' about at all?' asked John, as they sat by the embers of the fire late that evening. 'Sure that's no way to treat childer, even if they have done wrong. An' I can see no wrong in it. Can you?'

Rose sighed.

'Well, I suppose if she told wee Robert not to move from where she could see him, then he was in the wrong,' she said, trying to be reasonable. 'But imagine keeping a child from playing with others,' she burst out, her anger getting the better of her.

John shook his head sadly.

'Sometimes Thomas bees very quiet. Ye'd not get a word outa him the day long. I think maybe now I see the way of it, if that's what he has to put up with at home.'

They sat in silence, the room growing darker as the long summer's evening turned towards dusk, the only sound the tick of the clock on the wall and the creak of the elderly armchair he'd been meaning to strengthen for weeks.

'What are we going to do about the water?' Rose asked quietly. 'Can she really put them out of the orchard?' she went on, her mind moving from one anxiety to another. 'The garden at the back is not that big and we'll be wanting to plant it anyway. Then they'll have nowhere to play but the bit of common.'

John twisted awkwardly in his seat and was about to reply when a sudden high-pitched cry startled them both.

'That's Sarah,' said Rose, already halfway across the room.

'What's wrong with her, Rose?' he asked, his face contorted with anxiety as she reappeared moments later, the distraught, screaming child in her arms.

'She's soaked in sweat, John. She's wet through,' she said, as she cradled the child and tried to comfort her. 'Go over to Robinson's and ask old Mrs Robinson if she could she come to me. Tell her it's fever of some kind, but I don't know what.'

* * *

By the time John was back, a small bottle in his hand, Sarah had exhausted herself and lay silent.

'She's comin,' but she's slow on her bad leg. She said give her a teaspoon of this an' wet a sheet in cold water,' he said, putting the small bottle down beside her and bringing her a spoon from the dresser. 'Where would I get a sheet?'

'There's one in the top drawer of Sarah's sideboard, right hand side, but there's only half a bucket of water left in the wash house.'

'Never worry, I'll get ye more. It's not dark yet,' he said, as he hurried into the bedroom.

Rose heard him speak to Hannah, telling her to go back to sleep, reassuring her that Sarah would be better soon. She looked down at the child in her arms. As pale as a ghost now the redness had left her face, her dark curls plastered damply to her small head, her tiny body no weight at all as she cradled her in her arms.

'Good man,' she said, as John brought her the sheet pushed into the half bucket of water. A step at the door told them old Mrs Robinson had managed it.

'Ach, dear, dear,' she said sympathetically, as she limped across the floor and looked down at the sick child. 'Did ye give her the feverfew?'

'Yes, we did.'

'Will I away into Armagh for the doctor?' said John, looking from one woman to the other.

Rose said nothing, she just watched Sophie Robinson, a woman well known for her skill with cures, as she took Sarah's limp hands in hers and concentrated open-mouthed on the erratic breathing.

'Sit yer ground man dear, or go to your bed,' she said briskly. 'The doctor might do her some good tomorrow, but she's got to get through the night. She might and she might not. We can only do our best,' she said matter-of-factly.

Rose glanced at John, saw the look of utter despair on his face and thought for a moment he was going to cry out. But he gathered himself.

'Have we any more buckets? I'll away to the well in case ye need more water.'

'There's one in the wash house that's not scoured, but you can fill it with a clean jug,' said Rose, as steadily as she could manage. 'Wait a minute and you can have this one as well,' she said, as she peeled off Sarah's sodden nightdress. Sophie Robinson squeezed out the sheet and wrapped it round the inert and naked child.

It was Sophie who insisted John go to bed and gather his strength for when it was needed. As it was, he only took his boots off, ready at any moment to walk into Armagh for the doctor. The two women took it in turns to hold the child, rearranging the damp sheet when the fierce heat of her body dried it in patches. Sarah herself lay still, barely stirring as they wrapped and unwrapped her. At moments, she opened her eyes, looked as if she might cry out and then lapsed back into stillness.

'What's wrong with her, Sophie?' Rose whispered, plucking up her courage at last, as the first hint of light showed itself beyond the curtains which had never even been drawn the previous evening.

'God knows, Rose, but I don't. I've seen it before, though, many a time. All I can tell you is it can go either ways. Another hour or two an' I'd say ye stan' a chance. All ye can do is keep yer heart up. Maybe you'd make us a mouthful of tea.'

Rose did her best to collect herself, but she knew she was moving round the room as if she were in a dream, seldom taking her eyes from the pale, sweating face that Sophie wiped gently with a damp handkerchief. It seemed to take so long to stir the fire, to get the kettle to boil. She had to make a huge effort just to remember she needed cups and sugar and the tea caddy from the dresser, milk from the far side of the wash house where the north facing wall was always cold.

'Would you eat a bite of soda bread, Sophie?'

'I would indeed, thank you. I get far hungrier when I sit up in the night than I ever do by day. Isn't that a strange thing?' she said cheerfully.

Rose nodded and wondered to herself how she could be standing here buttering bread and smiling and nodding at a neighbour when her little child, her littlest love, was so very bad she might die.

'I'll take her while you have a bite,' she said, as she arranged Sophie's bread on a plate and poured her tea.

'I'm so grateful to you for coming to me,' she went on, as she settled herself, the small body cradled in her arms, the damp warmth of the sheet penetrating her blouse.

'Sure that's what neighbours are for. Aren't we put here on earth to help one another?' she said vigorously, as she munched her way through the well-buttered soda bread.

Rose looked at her, an old woman, older than her own mother, and wondered if it was loss of some kind that had made Mary-Anne Scott so bitter and hard.

*'Take comfort for your grief and your distress but never let yourself be bitter. It is bitterness that destroys life.'*

Rose closed her eyes, feeling the prick of tears she couldn't prevent, as her mother's words came back once more in her hour of need.

'Dear Lord,' she prayed silently, 'give me back this child and I'll try all my life never to be bitter. And I'll try to forgive those that are.'

'That was great, Rose. It would put heart in ye,' said Sophie, rising from the table. 'Now come and drink a cup of tea at least. I'll have the wee one again.'

Rose drank the tea Sophie poured for her, surprised at how good it tasted and how thirsty she was. Fingers of light were now slanting across the stone floor as the sun rose through the lowest branches of the big pear tree beyond the forge.

'What time does John start his work?' Sophie asked suddenly.

'Eight o'clock in summer,' Rose replied, puzzled, but not anxious, for the tone of the question was steady and without alarm.

'We'll let him sleep till six, then he can go into town and leave a note for the doctor to call on his rounds. Have ye a clean nightdress and a wee blanket handy?'

'They're in the bedroom.'

'An' what time is it? Ah can't see that clock of yours now we've put the lamp out.'

'It's half five.'

'Near enough. Just slip in an' get it,' she said briskly. 'If ye wake him, it's no matter now.'

Cautiously, Rose slipped into the bedroom and took out a child's nightdress from the left hand drawer of Sarah's sideboard and a blanket from the cupboard underneath. John never stirred. Lying diagonally on the bed, face in the pillow, his stockinged feet pointing out over the edge, he'd fallen asleep where he'd thrown himself down.

Rose went back into the kitchen and found Sophie unwrapping the sheet and wiping the remaining dampness from the small body. As she watched, she saw Sarah shiver and put her thumb in her mouth.

'Put her wee nightdress on now and wrap her up well while I make up your fire,' said Sophie, laying the naked child on Rose's knee. 'Another hour an' ye might see a wee hint of colour in her face. But she may sleep the day out.'

Rose wrapped her in the blanket and sat rocking her by the fire as the old woman got to her feet.

'She's a pretty one. Aye and a fighter too,' she said, grinning as she looked down at the sleeping child. 'I'll come over around tea time an' see how you both are. Of the two of you, I'd say you were the paler,' she added, laughing and nodding to Rose, as she took up her stick and opened the door.

Sunlight poured around her as she raised a hand in farewell and hobbled across the broken, weedy ground to the path by the forge that would take her back to the farm and to her bed.

# CHAPTER SIXTEEN

Rose drew back a few threads of hair from the pleat she always wore when going out. Standing in front of the mirror on the bedroom wall above Sarah's sideboard, she thought of the pretty dressing table with the comfortable padded stool she'd found waiting for her when she arrived at the house in Annacramp. Laid out with crocheted mats, a posy of flowers and a cut glass perfume bottle, she'd been amazed and delighted by such unexpected luxury.

'Never mind, Rose, there are more important things, as you well know,' she said to herself, as she smoothed out her skirt and adjusted the collar of her blouse, one ear tuned to the monologue going on close by in the tiny bedroom where Hannah and Sarah slept.

'Now then, Ganny, you must tidy your hair like Ma, 'cos we're going visiting.'

Rose smiled. She still couldn't say 'Granny,' with an 'r' though Hannah and her brothers kept coaxing her. Hardly a common name for a rag doll either, but it was Sarah's own choice. She'd named it the day Grandma Sarah had given it to her, just a few weeks before she died and had never thought of changing it. Its dress made from one of Sarah's own old dresses, its apron cut from an apron little Sarah knew well; long, grey woollen hair neatly plaited as hers had been, there was much of Granny about Sarah's large, comforting companion.

'We're going to see Ganny Sophie and the kittens. You like the kittens, don't you?'

Rose sat down wearily on the edge of the bed, her back already aching with the effort of dressing and doing her hair in the small space between the head of the bed and the sideboard. She took her purse from the top drawer and counted out shillings from a worn leather pouch.

Little Sarah's voice carried on, just as if she were talking to her grandmother still. Rose smiled, grateful for the innocence that could replace the beloved old lady with the rag doll she had spent her last weeks making.

'Not so easy, Sarah dear, if you're grown up,' she whispered to herself. 'Not easy at all if we'd lost you the night Granny Sophie came.'

The memory of that longest of nights flowed back to her once more, as it had a hundred times during the weeks of the summer. When she changed the sheets on the children's bed, or found the best bucket half full of water, or encountered Sophie on her visits to

Robinsons, all the anxiety of that night would return, her stomach tighten and her mouth go dry. The best she ever managed was to recall as vividly as possible the comfort and hope of the day that followed.

Sarah had slept right through it, rousing briefly only when the doctor came and examined her.

'I can't tell you what it was, Mrs Hamilton,' he said sadly, as they stepped back into the kitchen, 'but this much comfort I can offer you. Children who survive such an event and have no recurrence often have long and healthy lives.'

To her surprise, Doctor Lindsey had accepted her offer of tea. After he'd washed his hands, he pulled his chair up to the hearth and settled himself comfortably. It was true he'd known John's family for a long time, treated her after both miscarriages and been a regular visitor to Sarah, but in ten years she'd never known him sit down as if he had time to spend.

'You're looking very tired, Mrs Hamilton. You've had more to cope with than your anxiety over the child,' he said matter-of-factly.

Rose admitted as much as she moved to and fro between dresser, table and hearth.

'You've a good man out there, working for you,' he said, nodding in the direction of the forge, where both anvils were going strongly, 'but he's a soft man, one not used to hardship or disappointment. How did he take the little one's illness?'

'He was totally distraught.'

'That doesn't surprise me,' he said, shaking his head, as he took a cup of tea from her hand. 'His father was the same. A lovely man, full of kindness and care. He and Sarah were as happy a couple as ever I've known, but without Sarah he'd have been lost. It can be hard on a woman to have that extra care, Mrs Hamilton. You must look to your own health and keep your strength up.' He paused deliberately. 'Your good neighbour Sophie Robinson might advise you better than I about women's matters,' he said, looking at her sharply to see if she caught his meaning.

When she nodded and smiled, he looked around the fresh, sun filled kitchen, his eye lingering on the red geraniums in the windows, the carefully arranged dishes and plates on the dresser, the bright fire and well swept hearth.

'I knew this house before the Colvins emigrated,' he said thoughtfully. 'It wasn't in great shape then. You've done well in such a short time.'

'We were in dire straits,' she admitted, 'but once I knew this place wasn't damp, I thought I could make something of it until we can find somewhere better.'

He nodded.

'Well, you might be fortunate there. I'm not well informed these days. I think nevertheless, I would not recommend it unless another move were very favourable to the whole family.'

Rose was surprised by the strength of his tone. Even more by the sheer relief she felt at his words. So much had happened, she realised how desperately she needed a quiet time. Even finding a house as nice as the one they'd left would make a demand she wasn't entirely sure she wanted to meet.

'It is possible,' he began slowly, 'only my own theory, of course, drawn indeed from observation, but certainly not supported by experimental knowledge – it is possible little Sarah may have come in contact with tuberculosis, either someone with the disease, or someone who carries it. And goodness knows it's common enough these days,' he said, shaking his head sadly.

He paused, as if he were passing through his mind some of those cases which had been part of his observation.

'If she has,' he continued steadily, 'this very alarming episode may have been her bodies reaction to the infection. That she *has* reacted so violently may protect her indefinitely from the disease, but it will also have cost. I advise you to take great care of her over the next few months. Don't mollycoddle her. She should be out and about and play with other children quite normally, but do watch carefully for signs of fatigue. That is the chief danger. If she is at all tired, she must rest. And you must see that she eats well. Does she like milk?'

'No, I'm afraid she doesn't,' said Rose uneasily.

'Neither she nor Hannah will drink it, though both the boys drink their share and more, any time I have it to spare. I didn't think it right to force her,' she went on. 'She's not an awkward child.'

'Quite right. Quite right,' he said, nodding vigorously. 'Children often know what's best for them, so long as we don't confuse them. But it's a pity about the milk. If she doesn't like cow's milk, you might just try goat's. But you're right not to force her. Do you ever give her oranges?' he asked cautiously.

'At Christmas,' she said honestly.

'If you can manage it, a couple every week for the next six weeks. And I'll make you up a bottle that will encourage her to eat more. She's very light for her age, but then, I expect her mother was too,' he said, grinning unexpectedly.

Rose laughed heartily.

'When I first met John, he used to pick me up and set me down like a parcel. It put me at a great disadvantage when we had words.'

Doctor Lindsay laughed and stood up.

'I could sit long enough by this welcoming hearth of yours, but there's work to be done. I'll call again and see the wee one when I bring the mare to be shod, so there'll be no charge for *that* visit,' he said firmly, as he pocketed the half crown she'd left ready on the kitchen table.

'Good day, now, and take care of yourself as

well. What would they all do without you?' he said, nodding once again, as he made for the forge where he'd tethered his horse in the shoeing shop.

With Sarah and her beloved Ganny safely delivered to Sophie at the farm, Rose strode out gratefully. The fresh autumn morning, the tracery of spiders' webs beaded with dew, the hedgerows bright with berries, lifted her spirits, bringing her an ease and a freedom she hadn't felt for weeks.

The last time she'd been in Armagh was the fateful day when she'd taken delivery of the white envelope at Monroe's. Two months ago now. With the children at home and so much to do to make the house workable, she'd had to rely on John's visits to Armagh for necessities. He'd pay the rent and buy oranges for Sarah when he had to go to Turner's for hardware for the forge. Sometimes, he had time to collect tea and sugar for her as well, but more often with the forge so busy she'd had to use what the baker's cart provided. It gave her much less choice and was considerably more expensive.

She'd missed her visits to town sadly. Missed the weekly books from the library, the changing fashions in the windows of the best shops, the familiar faces in the grocers and drapers shops, but most of all she'd missed wearing clothes other than her working skirt and her oldest blouse. She felt as if she'd not stopped dusting and brushing, scrubbing and sweeping, weeding and digging, since the day John pushed open the door into the abandoned house. For the first time in her life, her hands were so rough and dry they caught threads in her stockings when she put them on.

She'd had nothing to read but the newspapers, full of news that brought no comfort to anyone. No time to sew except for the usual collection of rips and tears, the backsides of James and Sam's trousers after they'd been climbing or the knees of John's when he'd been kneeling down to rim cartwheels on the stone circle.

Her only joy was clearing out the roots of the weeds around the front of the house and making two small flowerbeds under the windows. There, where she could keep a watchful eye on them while they were small, she planted out the first cuttings that had rooted from those she'd made from Sarah's garden.

In the dusk of that last, long summer evening at Annacramp, weary from the effort of the day and clumsy with tiredness, she'd worked methodically along both borders and used every small flowerpot and empty tin can she could lay hands on. Determined not to abandon the most precious of Sarah's plants when she ran out of containers, she'd cut much larger pieces from the most flourishing plants and put them in water in an old bucket with no handle, hoping she could take the cuttings later.

They'd had to wait till after the doctor's visit, but they'd taken no harm from the delay. The small fragments of Sarah's sweet-smelling herbs and shrubs had put out vigorous roots in an old wooden box she'd found in the wash house and filled with soil from the overgrown garden. Although she knew many of the cuttings she'd made would take years to mature, she'd been delighted she would be able to recreate the best of the Annacramp garden.

As she walked up Railway Street and made her way through the noise and bustle of the Shambles, she blessed Sophie once again for being so willing to have Sarah.

'Sure I miss having a child about the place,' she'd said, smiling down at her. 'All my grandsons are big lumps and the granddaughters are walking out or newly married, so it'll be a day or two before there are any wee Robinsons. At least, we may hope so,' she added wryly. 'Let me keep the wee one when you go into Armagh or down to see Mary Wylie,' she'd added sharply. 'Every woman needs to get away outa the house once in a while and have a quiet word with a friend.'

'Good morning, Mrs Hamilton, it's good to see you again. You've not been in for a while. What can I do for you today?'

Rose smiled and returned the greeting, exchanged news with the pleasant young man who always served her in the drapers, then gave her attention to choosing material and trims for the baby's dresses she made for a local outfitter. It would be good to have time to do fine work again. Indeed, it was very necessary she should make time. The expense of the move had absorbed all the extra money which came from the long hours worked at the forge in summer, money she always saved for the lean weeks of winter. She was already concerned she had so little to fall back on. The new rent might be less than the rent for the house at Annacramp, but they'd had to sell their cow and the chickens, because there was nowhere to put them. Instead of egg money coming in, there was now egg money going out to the farm each week. They had no milk or butter of their own, no potatoes or vegetables either, until next year's crop.

'Rose McGinley, well, well, this is fortunate indeed. Just the person I need.'

Still absorbed in her own thoughts while waiting for her purchases to be parcelled up, she turned towards the speaker, startled out of her reverie by a familiar voice she couldn't immediately place.

'Lady Ishbel,' she said, dropping a neat curtsy out of long habit.

'Indeed. A short ten years since we shared a carriage to Dublin with your good man trying to look like a groom rather than a bridegroom,' she said cheerfully, laughing a little at her own joke. 'Now, I need your help. My cousin asked me to match these threads for her and my eyes aren't up to it. They all look the same to me. I gave up embroidery years ago. Haven't the patience, never mind the eyes.'

Rose smiled to herself. Forthrightness was certainly one of Lady Ishbel's characteristics. It didn't always go down well, even with people of her own class, but she'd always preferred it to the sweetness with which some ladies behaved towards servants in public and the indifference and bad temper, they showed them when there was no one around to see how they behaved.

Lady Ishbel's cousin had been rather meagre in providing samples of the embroidery silks she needed. More than once she'd to go to the door of the shop to decide between two very similar shades. Meantime, Lady Ishbel stalked up and down between the counters, throwing out questions about velvet and patterns. By the time Rose had finished most of the staff of the shop were engaged in seeing to her requirements.

'Most obliged, my dear. You always were good with a needle and had an eye for dress. Just like your mother. Is she well?'

'Yes, thank you,' replied Rose, beaming. 'How kind of you to ask. She still hopes to visit us one day, but we've been unfortunate so far with children's illness. And it *is* such a long way.'

'Further than I can face these days. Never did

like bouncing along over bad roads. They get worse, or my bones get worse,' she said abruptly, as they made their way out into English Street. 'Bad news about Harrington, isn't it?'

Rose felt the blood drain from her face.

'Haven't you heard?' Lady Ishbel asked, catching sight of her expression. 'Lady Anne writes to you, doesn't she?'

'Yes, she does, but I haven't had a letter for several weeks.'

'Damned Land Leaguers took a shot at him while he was out on the estate. Missed him, thank God, but his horse threw him and he's broken a leg. Could be worse. The tenants are withholding rents and he's having to borrow from the bank to pay his people. Your friend is in a bad way I hear, trying to keep things going with no money to do it with.'

Lady Ishbel waved her umbrella at her carriage parked in the open space in front of the Post Office.

'Must be going. Supposed to be in Richhill for lunch with the Richardsons. Can I drop you anywhere further up the town?'

'No, thank you very much. I'm on my way to Russell Street to pay the rent.'

'Hah,' she said. 'How old-fashioned of you. I suppose if the Land Leaguers don't hound us out, Sir Capel will be ostracised by the Orangemen because he won't join their cause. Good day to you.'

Without a backward glance, she stepped up into

her carriage, said a sharp word to the groom and settled herself for the drive to Richhill Castle.

'Poor Lady Anne,' Rose said aloud. 'And she's worked so hard. They both have. It's not fair, it's just not fair,' she added to herself.

She had to wipe tears from her eyes before she tucked her parcel of fabric firmly under her arm and marched past her favourite dress shop without even noticing the elegant gown displayed in the window.


'Hallo, Rose, how are ye?' Peggy Wylie asked.

She came from behind her desk to take the rent money, her usual smile replaced by a look of real concern.

'Amn't I the sorry one to hear the bad news I gave you the last time you were in. How are you managing at all?'

Rose smiled and made an effort to respond to Peggy's kind enquiries. Although she knew her only slightly, it was clear she was just as soft-hearted and good-natured as her sister Mary. She did her best to reassure her about the house and told her it was nice to be so near to John while he was working.

'An' what about wee Sarah? That was an awful fright you had. Mary told me all about it.'

'She's fine. I look at her sometimes and think I imagined it all, she looks so well,' Rose replied honestly, 'though we have to be careful with her still, Dr Lindsay says.'

'Isn't that just the way,' Peggy replied, smiling at last, 'sure one never knows the day with wee ones, what they pick up. D'ye remember how bad William was with his chest when he first went to school and now there's no stoppin' him?'

Rose laughed. If there was a way of doing something which would cause damage to the object or William himself then William would find it.

'Another week or two, Rose, and you won't see me here,' said Peggy, dropping her voice and looking over her shoulder to see who might be still in the outer office.

'Won't I? Have you got a new job then?'

'Well, in a manner of speakin',' she replied, smiling shyly. 'I'm getting married the beginnin' of October.'

For the first time since she'd come into the office, she saw the light return to Peggy's lovely brown eyes. The effect was amazing. Her unexceptional features were transformed, just like Lady Anne, when Lord Harrington first appeared at Currane Lodge.

'Oh Peggy, what splendid news. Do I know the lucky man?' she said warmly, delighted to have such good news to take home to John.

'No, he's a big secret,' she said, laughing. 'I met him in Belfast when I went for my holiday to my uncle and aunt on the Donegall Road. He's a Catholic, so we decided we'd be married in Belfast in the registry office to save any fuss, but Mary an'

Billy are comin' down for the day. She'll maybe be askin' you to keep the we'ans,' she added wryly.

'Well, I'm always happy to have them, but I'll be even happier that day. Will you live in Belfast?'

'Looks like it. Kevin works in the shipyards. He's a boilermaker, so there's no work for him here, more's the pity. But the pay's good. He says we can come up on the train on Sundays for the day whenever I want. So I'll not miss the country too much.'

As she came out into Russell Street, she knew she still had no heart for window-gazing, for all her pleasure in Peggy's new-found happiness. Lady Ishbel news had cast such a dark shadow over the day, it was all she could do to keep her mind on the things she still had to do. She felt so downcast she almost decided to leave the library, but then she remembered there was a book John particularly wanted.

'Oh how fortunate,' she said, as she carried her books to the desk. 'I've been wanting to read Mrs Gaskell's last novel, but it's always out.'

'Very popular, Mrs Hamilton. We could do with extra copies. And this is for your husband?'

'Yes, I hope it's not as heavy as it looks.'

She slipped the volume of *Wives and Daughters* into her shopping basket, then rearranged her parcels to accommodate *Portable Engines and their Applications*.

'Can you manage? Or shall I hold it for you till next week?'

'No, I'll manage. My husband has so missed his reading over the summer. It's been a busy time.'

She was sure it was worth the effort of carrying it home for the book would give John such pleasure, but it made her return journey far from pleasant, with the weight of her shopping. To her own surprise she had to sit down and rest several times on the way. She had to admit she was tired, but what wearied her the more was the constant echo of Lady Ishbel's words. *Bad news about Harrington, isn't it?* By the time she reached home she felt completely exhausted.

'Shoo, shoo,' she cried, as she came up to her own front door.

She set down her basket, dropped her parcels on a grassy hillock, waved her arms furiously and chased the fat hens who'd been scratching in her newly-made flower beds, back towards the common. They raced off, flapping their wings and protesting, leaving behind a mess of scattered earth and the exposed fragments of her precious cuttings.

Tears streamed down her face and splashed onto the light fabric of her blouse as she closed the front door behind her and stood in the empty room, the fire smouldered on the hearth, the windows closed to keep out the smell of retting fibre from the nearby flax hole, the clock ticking its way to the point where the children would arrive home from school, hungry and full of their own concerns.

'Rose, stop it. Stop it. You can't cry over your wee cuttings when Harrington might have been killed. Stop it.'

There was a sudden rap on the door. She wiped her eyes on her sleeve. She no longer had to wonder who it was. She took a deep breath and opened it.

'Missus Hamilton, I'll thank you not to chase *my* hens. After the fright you gave them, it's enough to put them off laying. See that it doesn't happen again.'

Mary-Anne Scott turned on her heel in her usual manner after delivering one of her familiar reprimands. But this time was once too often. Rose was quick enough to stop her.

'Missus Scott, I'll stop chasing your hens when you ensure that they do not trespass on what small piece of land you can't actually lay claim to, nor cause damage to our property.'

'Property? What property?' she retorted, following Rose's pointing finger. 'A few weeds. You call that "property"?'

'A collection of cuttings from my mother-in-law's garden. Of great value to my husband and myself. Keep your hens in *the Robinson's* orchard or on *everyone's* common, but keep them out of *our* garden,' she said, her voice thick with emotion, as she closed the door firmly in her face.

\* \* \*

Standing in her own kitchen, staring at an apron and a towel, hung on separate hooks on the back of the door she had just closed so firmly, she felt a sudden aching sense of loss. It was quite different from the feelings she'd had in the last month or two, whenever she'd remembered a particularly happy thing about the old house, or how much easier it was to manage with more space. This was a more personal loss, something she couldn't explain.

For the first time since she'd left Kerry, she felt she no longer had a whole, bright new world beyond her door. It was not just a matter of having a garden where she could work with pleasure, a field for the cow and the chickens, a place where the children could play freely. Weary from her long walk, her face still damp with tears of utter distress and frustration, she sat down at the kitchen table to try and compose herself.

She sat staring at the new dresser, her eyes moving round the plates and cups, the striped mugs, the collection of teapots and jugs, the photograph of their wedding Mr Blennerhassett had sent and Sarah insisted on framing, the small souvenirs that had been precious to her, the small jars and vases she herself had collected to put her flowers in.

As she had promised to do the night before they left Annacramp, she'd gathered up their home and tried to recreate it in this very different house. She thought she had succeeded. Everyone who visited said how well the place looked, especially Mary Wylie. She'd been amazed at its transformation, the first time she came, the day Mary-Anne had been so angry with the children for speaking to little Robert and using the path down the side of her house to go into the orchard.

She sighed. You could make a home, but you couldn't keep the door shut. You couldn't protect the children from the threat of Mary-Anne's outbursts or the unease that spread out from her hostility, the feeling that so often hung over them like the smell from the flax hole when it was in use. She knew that every move they made, every coming or going of friends, or children, was observed. Whether she was sweeping the front of her own house for the second time in the day, feeding her hens, or cleaning her windows, she knew that Mary-Anne was always on the look out for something to complain about.

She'd forbidden her own children to speak to their new neighbours and hers had guessed as much. Then one day, James had come home in distress and confirmed it. High up in one of the trees behind the forge, he'd overheard her scolding little Robert and repeated every word.

'You just play there behind the forge where I can see you through the window, an' don't you dare go near yer wuman from Kerry an' her childer. You just keep to yer own ground. Have nothing to do with that wuman whatever.'

'Yer wuman from Kerry,' Rose repeated to herself, trying to mimic the harsh timbre of Mary-Anne's voice. 'What *does* she mean?'

Yes, there was dislike, hatred even, but she could think of no reason why her being from the other end of Ireland could have any meaning. But it *did* have meaning for Mary-Anne. Whatever that meaning was, she knew it was beyond any power she herself might have to make it any different.

She stood up, propped open the door, and fetched a bowl of water from the wash house. When the children came home from school, they found her down on her knees at the front of the house rescuing the small fragments that had survived the vigorous scratchings of Mary-Anne's hens.

'Ach dear, that's bad news indeed for poor Lady Anne. What'll she do, d'ye think?' John said, as he took his mug of tea from her hand, late that same evening. 'I mind ye once said to me that big people has to mind their money just as much as we do, though one wouldn't think it. How'll she manage, if there's no money comin' in and him not able to change his line of work?'

'I really don't know,' replied Rose, smoothing the work on her knee and rethreading her needle. 'He'll have some money from property in England, but that won't go far with nineteen house servants, never mind outside staff. And he has to travel to and from London and keep a coach. All big expenses. I don't know what the Land League is thinking off and him so strong a supporter of Parnell.'

John drank his tea and looked down into the glowing embers in the hearth. She waited, wondered if he'd ask whether Sam could tell them more, or even help. But what he said next put all thought of Lady Anne's troubles quite out of mind.

'I made a start on yer new crane today. There was a piece of metal just the right length. It was Thomas pointed it out and reminded me,' he said warmly. 'Not that I'd forgotten, but you know how busy it's been. I didn't feel I could start when we have so much waiting. He paused and looked across at her. 'Maybe I'll get it finished sooner than I'd thought.'

There was something about his whole manner that alarmed her. As if he were slowly acknowledging some anxiety, but could not bring himself to speak of it openly.

'And why might that be, John?' she asked, looking him straight in the face.

'We had visitors at the forge today,' he began, reluctantly.

'Yes.'

'A cousin of Mary-Anne's from Battlehill and a big farmer from over Cabragh way.'

He shook his head as if he couldn't go on, then it all came out in a rush.

'They wanted Thomas and me to join the lodge

and start drillin' with them. They say there's bound to be trouble over the Home Rule Bill an' we hafta be ready.'

Rose dropped her sewing on her knee.

'And what did you say?'

'Ach sure we both tried to say we'd think about it an' put them off that way, but they weren't takin' that for an answer. So when it came to the heels of the hunt, we had to say 'No'. That was not our way. Thomas is no more a man than I am for that sort of thing. That's why he niver joined the lodge in the first place.'

'An' how did they take that?' she asked, knowing he wouldn't volunteer the information.

'Not well. They argued and persuaded for a bit an' whin they seen there was no shiftin' us, they made to go. Then they came back to say it was a pity a good forge should go down the hill for want of business, but wasn't there as good ones in Ballyleny and Drumsill.'

'So you think they'll take work away,' she said steadily.

'I know they will,' he replied flatly. 'Yer man from Cabragh is a regular, four horses and the machines to go with them, forby a pony and trap. But it's not just that, it's what he'll put about the place and take after him. It's not good, Rose,' he said, shaking his head sadly. 'I don't know why all this bad luck has come upon us. I don't know at all.'

# CHAPTER SEVENTEEN

In Salter's Grange the winter of 1885 was damp and dreary, but there was little cold and almost no frost right up to Christmas. The falls of snow in January melted quickly as the weather turned wild and stormy. By the end of the month the mild dampness that had characterised the late autumn had returned. Then, suddenly and silently, on the very last night of March, to the enormous delight of the children, snow fell again. Waking to sunshine and blue skies, they could hardly wait to get outside.

Rose laughed as she watched them set off for school, Hannah absorbed in making footprints wherever she found pieces of undisturbed snow, James and Sam gathering it up in handfuls, circling around, watching for the best moment to pelt each other.

As she set about her morning tasks, Rose gave thanks for the quiet, uneventful months that had passed. Today was the first of April. Whatever hard weather early spring might bring, nevertheless it *was* spring.

'Winter is over and all's well,' she said aloud as she made up the fire, and began her preparations for baking a cake of wheaten bread and some soda farls. 'At least it's well for us,' she added, more soberly.

In the world beyond Salter's Grange all was far from well. The newspapers were full of turbulence and unrest they'd hoped the new Land Act would have put an end to, but it hadn't. Throughout Ulster, the situation was getting worse, if anything, as rumours about a Home Rule Bill were confirmed. There had been incidents and outrages, protest meetings, demonstrations and counter demonstrations. Happily, none of these events had touched them directly, but the uncertainties of the times were an ever present threat.

They'd come through the winter months without hurt. There'd been no unexpected expenses when least money was coming in. There'd been no illness in the family beyond the normal winter coughs and colds. However wearying life when dim, misty days darkened to night so early in the afternoon and mornings were bleak and cold, they'd suffered no real hardship.

She had no quarrel with the day's routine, for many small pleasures could be set against it. Except for little Sarah, all of the children were now reading and writing for themselves and even Sarah could manage her ABC and her numbers, though still too young for school. She spent much of her day 'reading' to Ganny, from whatever book she took from the shelf and when her brothers and sister arrived from school she'd insist they read to her.

Hannah loved reading aloud and was always willing, but James, who preferred railway engines to fairy stories, and even Sam, who was still on the first reading book, would take their turn. There was something about Sarah's directness and quiet determination that intrigued Rose. But what she particularly enjoyed was Sarah's sudden sharp delight in what she heard or saw. The laughter her pleasure provoked was a constant delight to her.

She fetched her baking board from the wash house, shivering as she came back into the warm kitchen. The board was so cold it felt as if it was damp. She set it a little way back from the hearth to get the chill off and picked up her sewing while she waited.

She'd had to work hard at it over the last five months, more than doubling her best efforts of previous winters, for the lean winter weeks at the forge were leaner than usual. John had been right. Some of their best customers had left them, taking their work to Drumsill or Ballyleny. Either meant a few extra miles, but that was nothing to men who'd made up their minds John and Thomas did not deserve their business, because they were not 'loyal.'

For such a mild man, Thomas's determination not to be intimidated by their threats had surprised them. He'd let it be known he had neither Protestant nor Catholic neighbours, simply neighbours. So far, there'd been no further visits from the Orangemen, but the drilling continued and they knew some of their neighbours had joined the ranks. It was not said openly in the forge, but it was well known many younger men allowed themselves to be roped in more to avoid bad feeling in their homes than from any commitment to the cause.

Rose finished her seam, put the sewing back in its clean cloth and took up her baking board.

'That's better,' she said, touching its surface, before she sprinkled it with flour.

Having been prepared for difficult times, things had turned out much better than she'd expected. Her very hard work of the summer months had made the house workable. Whitewashed for the third time, the wash house had finally lost its smell. John had made a deep shelf all the way round its walls and a wooden plinth, so that the sack of flour wouldn't take up dampness from the earth floor. She could now keep both milk and butter against the north facing wall, cool even in summer, and there was space underneath for the water pails, the sack of potatoes, the crock of oats. She'd made a rag rug to spare the cold feet of the children when they washed themselves in the space nearest to the back door.

The handsome new crane with its chain and

hooks, installed before Christmas and much admired by all who visited, meant she no longer had to bend over the fire to cook on the hearth itself. The backache that had plagued her during the summer disappeared completely and some of the anxiety as to what would happen if she were ever to fall ill went with it.

As the morning passed and she alternated sewing with making the bread and tending it, she glanced through the window and saw the snow was melting. From the high pitched roof of the forge, small avalanches slithered down and fell wetly among the long bars of iron that leant against its low walls.

John and Thomas had made her life easier as well. Whenever either of them went into town to buy supplies for the forge, they offered to pay the rent. As her own grocer had begun a new weekly delivery round, she had only to go to Armagh when she needed to buy fabric or change the library books. It was a relief to know that she didn't have to tramp wet or icy roads simply to fetch her groceries.

To her great surprise, she'd found she had a little more time for herself, even with all the extra hours she needed for her sewing, Some of it she spent reading to Sarah, but Sarah was often happy to play by herself. That was when she settled herself at the kitchen table and wrote letters to her mother, or Lady Anne, or Sam. For the first time too, she wrote to her sister Mary in Donegal, and brothers Michael in Scotland and Patrick in Nova Scotia.

Neither Mary nor her brothers had ever been correspondents, though they did write an occasional letter to their mother. They left it to Hannah to pass on their news to Rose, rather than write to her themselves. Now in these winter months, she was surprised and grateful to have letters in reply to hers. She enjoyed writing and found a strange comfort in setting down on paper all that had happened in the preceding months.

Her sister Mary had never left Donegal. After her father's death, she'd gone into service with the Stewarts of Ards, married a shopkeeper in Creeslough and had seven children, the eldest boy and girl now working in the shop themselves, thus giving their father more time to see to the out workers who supplied his drapery business. Mary's letters were mostly about her children, but in each of them she'd referred to their life together in Ardtur.

*Do you ever remember Owen Friel?* she'd written in one of them.

*He carried you home on his back one day just before we were put out. Maybe you were too young to remember.*

Rose remembered Owen perfectly well. He'd carried her when she could walk no further and he'd never told anyone where he'd found her or that she'd set off by herself to go up the mountain and look at the castle their landlord was supposed to be building.

*Well, it seems that he and Danny Lawn were part of a group that raided a prison somewhere in Canada. It seems that comrades of theirs had been imprisoned wrongly and there was no other way to save them. It was Owen made the plan to get them out, but something went wrong after they'd freed them and Danny got caught.*

Rose suddenly saw herself back in the schoolhouse trembling at the harsh sound of the Master's voice. She could never forget Danny Lawn, after all he'd suffered at the hands of the Master.

*Rose dear, they hung him. Poor Danny never had any wit. I cried when I heard it, though I'd never heard news of him since we left Ardtur. Could you ever have imagined such a fate for the poor boy when we saw him carrying creels of turf home from the bog?*

*I saw Owen Friel's sister in Letterkenny last month and she says he got away to California, but she's not had word of him for over a year. Maybe he got caught too after all.*

Her older brother Michael had no children, but he and his wife had three nephews living with them since the death of his wife's sister. Their small farm on the Galloway coast was enough to keep them fed and clothed, but Michael was looking forward to the eldest boy being apprenticed to a boat builder near Port William.

*It's always good to have some money coming in that doesn't depend on the weather and the price of cattle,* he'd said, in a letter that gave her an unexpectedly sharp picture of his family and the rich hilly landscape that backed the sweeping curves and sandy beaches of the Solway coast.

Rose gathered her thoughts, swung the crane away from the fire and held her hand an inch or two above the griddle. It was hot, but not too hot. She sprinkled it sparingly with flour, took the circle of wheaten bread from the baking board, lowered it gently on to the dark surface of the griddle, marked it into four sections with a sharp knife and swung it back over the fire. Dusting the flour from her hands, she took up her sewing again till the wheaten cooked and the griddle had reheated for the soda.

Her eldest brother, Patrick, three years older than herself, really surprised her by telling her he often made the bread for the family when he was at home. He'd married a girl whose family, the Rosses, had emigrated from Skye to Nova Scotia with the Earl of Selkirk in 1801. He had nine children, five boys and four girls. They farmed a portion of land that had come down to his wife from the original division made after their ship arrived. Most of the time, it was his wife and family who ran the farm while Patrick travelled back and forth, earning a very good living as a trader, just as his uncle had done before him.

'Kerry, Dublin, Donegal, Salter's Grange, Galloway and Nova Scotia,' she said to herself, as she drew the threads to shire the front of the small dress. She thought of the children who had once recited '*Ulster, Munster, Leinster, Connaught,*' in the brand new school house so close to Ardtur, scattered now far beyond the four provinces of Ireland, and of Danny Lawn, who couldn't recite the counties of Ulster, buried in some unmarked grave outside a prison compound for his part in an attempted murder.

The wheaten had risen nicely, opening along the cuts she'd made. She took a clean cloth and transferred it to cool on a harning stand John's father had made for Sarah sometime after the bent candlestick. She swept the griddle with a goose's wing, dusted it with fresh flour and set the soda farls to bake. She wiped her fingers on her apron and took up her sewing again.

The best news of the whole winter had come from Lady Anne just before Christmas. Initially, she'd had a very difficult time. She'd sold most of the jewellery she'd inherited from her grandmother to keep the estate going, then visited the members of the Ladies Land League who were active in the area. She wasn't sure she'd had much effect on them, but shortly afterwards rents were paid once more, though somewhat reduced. A month later, she'd written to say that Harrington had made a complete recovery, was able to ride again, and although he knew exactly who was responsible for his near miss, he'd decided not to proceed against them.

Rose smiled to herself. Lady Anne's next letter had so delighted her she almost knew it by heart.

*Rose dear,*

*After all Harrington's anxiety about my safety, I found myself worrying about him every time he rode out on the estate, so I invited the commander of our local militia and some of his officers to dinner and asked their advice about learning to shoot. They were really quite helpful, once they realised I was perfectly serious, so I sent to Dublin for a pair of pistols and practised with a rifle until they arrived.*

*I knew the most difficult thing would be to get Harrington's horse accustomed to the noise of gunshots after the fright the poor beast had, so I took the grooms into my secret and got them to fire off a few rounds every now and again when the horses were being groomed.*

*So, now I ride out with Harrington and am quite prepared to retaliate if he's shot at. Commander Pakenham says I'm rather a good shot, though I need more practice firing on horseback.*

*The strangest thing, Rose, if I'm to believe what Cook tells me, is that the two men we suspect of firing at Harrington, I'm sure rightly, have left for America. Cook says there's a rumour in the county that I'm so angry I've vowed to kill them both!*

She and John had read the letter over and over, Rose beaming with delight at the thought of Lady Anne setting up her targets and practising with her new pistols.

'Aye, she'd not let her man down, the same one. No wonder the pair of ye got on so well in the end.'

'I wonder, John,' she said, as she put Lady Anne's letter in the window, 'if Sam *was* able to do anything. He did say he'd try.'

The day after she'd bumped into Lady Ishbel and heard the news from Sligo, she'd sat down and written to Sam.

*What on earth do the Land League mean by attacking someone who has so completely supported their cause, lowered his rents, provided dispensaries and schools? How can they expect to keep the support of moderate people if they do things like this?*

*Can you really support them if they use such violence? I've read about other outrages, but the newspapers thrive on such events and I couldn't judge how much they had been exaggerated. But this is different. I know what happened and it's a mercy Harrington wasn't killed.*

*How can you reconcile this, Sam, with all you've said about being satisfied provided the Land Purchase Act went through? It has, and as I read, many are buying their land. Why then this victimisation when there is a process in place to achieve all the Land League's stated objectives?*

She'd read her letter through when she'd finished and decided she was being a bit hard on Sam, but she didn't change a word of it. He'd always been honest with her and she knew he'd always acted for the best, but deciding what the best was, was another matter. Sometimes she just didn't know what to think herself. However important it was to have general principles, there must always be exceptions, surely. You couldn't label people 'bad' because they were Protestant landlords, or 'good' because they were poor Catholics. It was never as easy as that.

Sam had written by return. He'd explained the way the League was organised, decisions were made locally. Someone in Sligo would have listed Harrington as a big landowner. Possibly as an absentee if he didn't know about the split nature of his estates. Harrington might even have been listed by someone who had a grudge against him.

*The problem, Rose dear, as I have found to my cost, is that in every organisation there are many interest groups. The Land League is no exception. There are people of high principle who are concerned, as I hope I shall always be, to right a social wrong, but there are others who see the organisation as an opportunity for their own advancement, in terms of financial gain or political power.*

*The genius of Parnell is that he is able to keep together all kinds of groups and factions, some of them extreme, without allowing himself to be identified with any one of them individually. He is himself totally committed to constitutional means, but some of the groups on which he depends for his support are not. You could say that the price of their support is his turning a blind eye to their methods. It is the oldest dilemma in the book. Can you tolerate doing something you*

*would not wish to do if you think it will lead
to a greater well-being for the majority of
people?*

Rose always passed her letters to John. Those
from Hannah and Lady Anne, he could sit back
and enjoy, but he'd take up a letter from Sam with
every sign of trepidation and read it with fierce
concentration. When he'd finished, he'd shuffle the
pages, and ask a question, not quite unrelated to
what he'd just read.

More than once, Rose had questioned him
closely. Did he think Sam was right? What did he
think the Orangemen would do if a Home Rule Bill
was passed? But John would shake his head and
refuse to engage with it.

'Some things I can grasp just fine. I see what's
fair and what's not fair. But the more ye go inta
things the more difficult it is. I wish I could live in
a world with no politics, an' no religion. No people
taking sides, arguin' and fightin' about the rights
and wrongs of things. Sure what's the point? Why
spoil the time we have when we're on this earth so
short a while?'

Rose had every sympathy with his agitation and
distress but she wasn't sure it made sense to try and
shut the door on what was happening when it was
so near at hand. Like Mary-Anne Scott, sooner or
later the threat out there in the world would come

knocking and you had to be ready to cope with whatever it threw at you.

By noon, the thaw had advanced so far that only where the forge itself and the pear tree on the path to Thomas's house cast a deep enough shadow were small patches of snow able to survive, lying like flour spilt from a sack. From the mended thatch of their own cottage, a row of drips splashed down on the layer of gravel John had laid in a shallow trench across the front of the house the previous autumn. The whitewashed walls gleamed wetly in the bright light.

She stood at the open door, took a deep breath of the mild air and peered down into her flowerbeds, now carefully enclosed by fine netting wire to protect them from the depredations of Mary-Anne's hens.

'My goodness, I wasn't expecting you so soon,' she said aloud, as she recognised vigorous grey-green shoots of aquilegia pushing upwards out of the dark earth and unfurling their first new leaves. 'Mary-Anne didn't get you after all,' she added in a whisper, with a cautious look towards the closed door of her neighbour's house.

The house always looked so dead, even when the smoke of a new fire rose each morning. Mary-Anne often kept her door shut, even in good weather, and she wondered what she did all day, apart from read her Bible and the sermons that the Methodists circulated.

She blinked up at the sun, grateful to feel its warmth on her face. In a moment, she would step back into the kitchen to put the kettle down for making tea and butter bread for John who'd be over soon for a quick bite. But not just for a few more minutes. She smiled to herself. Mary-Anne hadn't yet accused her of being idle, standing at her front door looking round her as if she had no work to do, but that might well come.

Nothing would surprise her, after the criticisms of the last months. Allowing her children to sit in the seats of the reaping machines awaiting repair, or to cluster round the stone circle when a turf fire burnt all the way round an iron rim before it was shrunk onto a wheel. Her children shouldn't be allowed to play outside on Sundays and certainly not to laugh. Nor should she let them talk to the two serving girls from Robinson's, who took it in turns to deliver the milk each day.

Sometimes she would actually respond to her hostile comments, even though she knew well enough neither quick retort or logical argument would have the slightest effect. More often, she would merely smile, hear her out and quietly shut the door. She never ceased to be surprised, however, at Mary-Anne's cunning. She always timed her visits when both hammers were going at full tilt so Thomas remained ignorant of her sorties, for she and John had long since agreed he was not to be told.

'Sure the poor man has enough to put up with,' he said, when she told him of the latest visitation. 'Can ye imagine getting' inta bed with yer wuman,' he went on, as they got into bed themselves, and he put out his arm to hold her close. 'Ah can't understan' meself how they come to have three childer.'

She smiled to herself. John's way of coping with Mary-Anne was to make fun of her behind closed doors, but they both knew Mary-Anne was no joke. Often enough she caught sight of Annie, the eldest girl, carrying out the slop bucket to empty in the privy. A poor, sad looking child with drooping shoulders, tall for her eleven years, but with no spring in her step.

The worst tirade in the winter months had followed a visit from Bridget, who had brought their weekly butter over one pleasant morning after the churning. Bridget and her sister Maggie came from a part of Donegal unknown to her, an Irish-speaking area around Dunlewy. Neither girl had much English and were delighted when they discovered Rose had Irish. Whenever they came over they would question her about words new to them.

'What is dishabels, Rose?' Missus said to Old Missus Robinson that she was 'caught in her dishabels'. We didn't like to ask.

'Dishabels' is old clothes, Bridget. What you wear to do the dirty jobs in the morning, before you dress yourself properly for the day,' she explained in Irish.

They'd stood laughing and talking by the door for five minutes or so, but hardly was Bridget out of sight before Mary-Anne was knocking fiercely at the open door, though Rose was plain to be seen inside.

'Mrs Hamilton, I'll thank you not to stand out in the street talking in a foreign language,' she began as she raised her head at the intrusion. 'It's bad enough that our neighbours employ these chits of girls that can't even speak the Queen's English without you encouraging them,' she went on, as Rose crossed to the door. 'I think you ought to be ashamed of yourself, talking the language of servants, now you've come up a bit in the world. I won't have my children hearing it,' she said, with her usual tone of complete finality, as she turned on her heel and stalked off.

She'd been tempted to curse her roundly in Irish as she departed, but she'd restrained herself for the hammers had stopped momentarily and Thomas had stepped out to fetch another bar of iron. She'd slipped back into the house before he caught her eye and taken out her frustration by pounding the sheets.

The last thin icing of melting snow slid down the roof of the forge and landed squarely in front of the open door just where the regular passage of feet had made a shallow depression in front of the threshold. On wet days, John and Thomas had to sweep it dry with a stiff broom, but today the drying wind had mopped up the moisture from each succeeding fall. Even as she watched, the tangled tufts of grass between bits of machinery straightened up as they shed their moisture. A few days of this and the trees might begin to leaf. Then she could really believe spring had come.

Just as she was about to go back indoors, she saw a carrier's cart come up the slope of the hill from the direction of Armagh. To her surprise, the heavy vehicle drew to a halt somewhere beyond the end of the lane. She looked down towards the road, but the cart had stopped out of sight, hidden behind the great ivy covered elm that stood a little way beyond their own gable. She turned away, but the voices she heard drew her back to the door.

She stood listening unashamedly as the conversation floated up to her, borne on the still air. Two men were speaking Irish with a familiar ring that took her straight back to the stable yard at Currane Lodge. The older, rougher voice, perhaps one of the carters that delivered for Turners or Hillocks of Armagh, was bidding good day and good luck to a younger voice who responded warmly, thanking him for the lift and for his conversation.

Moments later, the young man himself appeared outside the forge, his back to her, as he looked through the door into the dark. The shoulders were broader, the red hair less unruly, but there could be no doubt about it. It was Sam. The hammers fell silent and her young brother, now a grown man, stood talking to John and Thomas.

Every part of her wanted to run across and throw her arms round him, but she was so surprised to see him she just leant against the doorpost and stood staring at him.

He turned away, caught sight of her at once and came striding across.

'Rose, Rose, it's wonderful to see you.'

He held her so tightly and kissed her cheeks so gently that she knew something was wrong.

'What is it, Sam, what is it?' she said, as he released her. 'Are you in any kind of trouble? Tell me. Tell me quickly.'

'I'm fine, Rose,' he said, shaking his head sadly. 'It's Ma.'

'Is she ill?' she asked, a terrible feeling of dread passing over her.

'She died last week, Rose. I hadn't the heart to write you a letter, so I came as soon as I could.'

# CHAPTER EIGHTEEN

Sam's story was quickly told. The previous Friday, Hannah had been on her way downstairs to the servants' hall for the evening meal when she'd fallen. Not a bad fall, Cook had explained to Sam, for she was only a few steps from the bottom of the staircase when it happened, but there was just enough noise to bring Mr Smithers hurrying from his room. She was unconscious when they picked her up and at first everyone thought she'd hit her head. When the doctor arrived and found her still unconscious an hour later, however, he'd said 'No'. The fall itself had caused no great injury. He was more concerned as to what had caused the fall.

Hannah had been put to bed in her own small room and throughout the night her friends took it in turns to sit with her. She never became conscious again, but died peacefully just before six in the morning.

Rose listened dry-eyed. She could see so vividly the narrow wooden staircase, the dim corridor leading to the servants' hall, but she couldn't yet grasp what had happened. She'd tramped up and down those stairs thousands of times herself and her mother many thousands of times more. She knew them so well, she'd never have tripped and fallen.

'How did you find out, Sam?' she asked, agitatedly, springing up from the chair by the kitchen table she'd dropped down into only minutes earlier.

She walked unsteadily across the room and sat close to him on the settle.

'Sir Capel sent me a telegram in Dublin and I got the train down first thing on Saturday,' he said, taking her hand. 'The service was in the parish church where you and she used to go with the family. Every single person went from Currane Lodge. The church was so full they had to stand at the back.'

She saw the building again, so vividly, with its box pews, high pulpit and single stained glass window, a memorial to some previous Molyneux. For all of the years Hannah had been at Currane, she'd worshipped there and she'd gone with her every week. They'd sat side-by-side in their Sunday best clothes, their boots well polished, their stiff black skirts equally well-brushed, their best blouses starched and ironed. They'd sat with the family in the big pew below the pulpit, the only servants that weren't Catholic, apart from Mr Smithers, who insisted he wasn't anything and Sam, who had announced at fourteen he was an agnostic.

So often still on a Sunday morning, she'd thought of her mother as she and John walked up the lane to their much larger church, built by another Molyneux, a man, like his relative in Kerry, who'd also provided a chapel for his Catholic tenants. When she thought of her mother on a Sunday now, she'd have to think of the churchyard, not the church.

'So you're on speaking terms again with Sir Capel,' she said suddenly.

'Yes. He shook my hand when I arrived and asked me to forget the hard things he'd said when I joined the League. I dined with the family after the funeral and we drank port in his library. He said he still wished I'd come back to the estate. Even Lily was being nice to me,' he added, with a wry smile.

'Was she indeed, Sam?'

'Yes,' he said, stroking her hand. 'Do you remember me breaking my heart over her ten or eleven years ago?'

'Eleven now,' she nodded. 'And Ma was never able to come. I haven't seen her since my wedding day,' she went on, her thoughts following their own logic. 'We made so many plans, but either I wasn't well enough to travel or one of the children fell ill.'

'But you wrote, Rose, and she knew everything about your life. Whenever I had letters from her or got down to see her, she was always full of what you were doing and how the children were. You were never out of her mind.'

'And she was never out of mine. Time and again I imagined myself talking to her . . .'

She broke off as John's tall figure stooped under the lintel and came across to where they sat. She got up and put her arms round him.

'Did Sam tell you?'

'No, but I guessed. Is it yer Ma?' he said gently.

'Aye. Sam'll tell you while I make us tea. It's a poor welcome, Sam, and you on the road since goodness knows when,' she said, picking up the wheaten bread from the stand and carrying it to the table.

'It's only bread and jam, I'm afraid, but I've a bit of bacon and cabbage for tonight,' she added, apologetically, as she put the lid on the teapot and they drew over to the table.

'The bread smells great, Rose,' Sam responded, as she cut thick slices of fresh wheaten and pushed the dish of butter in his direction. 'Ma always said there was no bread as good as bread cooked over a hearth.'

'She's a great han' at the bakin', Sam,' said John, spreading his piece with damson jam. 'She's great han's altogether,' he added quietly. 'Just like her Ma.'

Whether it was the softness of John's tone, or the words themselves, or merely the passage of time since Sam had brought his news, but she felt tears spring to her eyes. She tried to blink them away, but they wouldn't stop. As they dropped like rain on her clean apron, she felt a pain rise in her throat. She put her head in her hands and cried as if her heart would break.

The tears brought some relief. Although she still couldn't eat, she was grateful for the tea John poured her. When she was steadier, he gathered up little Sarah, who'd fallen asleep over her reading on their bed, and told her he'd take her over to Sophie and go on back to work. He'd tell Thomas the sad news himself.

What no one knew was that Mary-Anne had returned from Armagh just as the carter dropped Sam at the end of the lane. She'd slowed her step, seen and heard all that had passed, then waited her moment to pass the forge when no one would see her.

Through the long afternoon, she seldom left her window.

'What time do the children get back at?' Sam asked, as he watched her clear away the remains of their meal. 'I'm looking forward to meeting my nephews and nieces.'

'Shortly after half three. Sometimes I can't believe how fast James and Sam get here. Hannah takes a bit longer.'

'I'd have liked to bring them presents, but I just hadn't time,' he said apologetically.

'But you've brought yourself. They'll be very excited about that. They're not used to presents. They never expect them, even at Christmas.'

'Are times hard for you, Rose?'

'No,' she said slowly, 'not compared to some. We've enough to eat and the children have shoes for Sunday. We've a little money in the bank from Sarah's burial fund, but I've not been able to add anything to it since she died. The forge isn't doing quite as well as it should.'

'I wondered about that,' he said sharply, casting his eyes round the room for the first time since he arrived. 'Rose, we've not much time. I have to catch the last train to Dublin from Portadown at seven this evening, so I'll have to be in Armagh for six,' he said hurriedly, looking at his fob watch. 'There are things I need to know from you and other news I want to give you. You can tell me what the Orangemen are up to and I'll tell you what I can't put in my letters. It's hard on you with the shock of Ma's death upon you, but she wouldn't be well pleased with me if I didn't think to our future.'

They sat side by side on the settle, the glow of turf at their feet, the light haze of smoke winding its way straight up into the broad canopy and on into the blue sky that arced above the low chimney. They spoke quickly and urgently about Sam's immediate concerns, about Parnell's plan to persuade Gladstone to bring in a Home Rule Bill in the summer, about the failure of the Land League to hold the support of the Protestant farmers in Ulster, who'd backed them in the early eighties and about the sectarianism growing again in Ulster after a period of calm and relative prosperity.

'*Are* they really drilling, Rose?'

'Oh yes. And it's not just lodge members. They're trying to draft in all Protestants.'

Sam shook his head.

'We've tried to tell him, but there are times Parnell simply doesn't listen. He still goes around saying it would only take a thousand RIC men to deal with the Orangemen if they give trouble, but if they do hold out against Home Rule it leaves three quarters of Ireland still a part of an empire instead of being its own country. That can't be fair, can it?'

'No, it can't, Sam, I grant you, but do you really think life can be? Is there any way of creating a world in which one group doesn't exploit others? Where no one imagines they're superior because of birth or wealth, or what they think, or even how they worship?'

'Yes, but then one has to ask, "*Is it worth trying*?"'

She studied her brother's face closely. Apart from her parents, Sam was the first person she had ever loved. The creamy skin and the light freckles had changed little with the passage of time. At twenty-seven, his bright eyes and open look still made him seem younger than his years. Suddenly and unexpectedly, she thought of the child she'd held in her arms, in a turf cart, sheltered from the sleet by her mother's shawl the day they were evicted and had to face the bitter chill of that April day. Twenty-five years ago, this very month.

'Sometimes I think I don't understand anything, Sam,' she began slowly. 'I read the papers and talk to John and borrow books from the library. The more I read, the less I'm sure of anything,' she said sadly. 'Maybe it's because I'm a woman, but what matters to me is living and loving and hoping for better times for the children. It's a weakness I'm sure. I can bear things for myself, but I cannot bear to think of those I love being ill, or hungry, or made homeless.'

'That's why I fight, Rose. I can't bear it either. I have to fight against greed and exploitation, though you're right, it's not as simple as I thought it was. I'm in two minds about the way things are going, but I have to give it one more try. I've been commissioned to go to America in September for the League to take letters to our supporters there and to raise money. I'll be gone for two months. Things may be clearer by the end of the year for both of us,' he said, dropping his voice, as a shadow fell across the floor.

'Hullo. You're Uncle Sam, aren't you?'

'I am indeed, young man. How did you know?'

said Sam, smiling as he stood up and offered his hand to his eldest nephew.

'I've seen your photograph in the book Mr Blennerhasset sent of Ma and Da's wedding. You were the best man. I didn't know you had red hair same as mine.'

'I told you he had, James,' Rose protested.

'Yes, you did, but I'd forgot,' said James cheerfully, as he shook hands with the only one of his uncles he'd ever met.

While James went to fetch Sarah from the Robinsons, Sam and Hannah settled down to question their new-found uncle about Dublin. Hannah wanted to know where he lived, what it was like and whether he was allowed to have a kitten. How wide was the river in Dublin? How long had it taken him to get to Armagh? Sam's questions were even more specific. He wanted to know what engine had pulled the train. Did it have a name? If he didn't know, then did he remember its number?

When Uncle Sam admitted he didn't know where to look for either, young Sam, not yet seven, surprised even his mother by telling him where he could find them next time he came to see them.

'James and I are both hoping to be engine drivers when we grow up,' he informed his uncle solemnly, as Rose began preparations for a very early meal.

With such a very short time before Sam had to

go, she decided not to tell the children about their Granny Hannah's death there and then. She thought she'd say he was going to America in September and had come to tell them, but in the end she offered no explanation for his sudden appearance. Happily, the children were so totally absorbed by the excitement of having a real live uncle over for supper, they required none.

When Sam rose to go and said his goodbyes to the children, the thought of saying her own goodbye, so suddenly, almost overwhelmed her. How could she let him go with so much unsaid?

'James and Hannah,' she said quickly, as inspiration came to her. 'I want to walk to the station with Uncle Sam. Will you look after Sarah for me? I'll only be about an hour and Da's in the forge if you need him. All right?'

They assured her they'd be fine. Hannah fetched her shawl from the bedroom, while James took down one of Sarah's story books. Sam picked up the bag he'd put down on the settle and extracted a heavy, awkwardly-shaped parcel of things he'd brought from Kerry and left it where he'd been sitting.

'They're grandchildren, Rose. All different and all lovely. They'd tempt a man to find a wife,' he said cheerfully, as they strode down the lane after they'd looked in at the forge and spoken a few words to Thomas and John.

'You know, Sam, it's the first time my children have seen anyone from my family. Isn't it sad the way we're scattered to the four winds. And John's side's no better now we've lost his mother.'

'He has brothers, doesn't he?'

'Yes, two of them. But they never write. When Sarah died, John wrote to the last address he had for them, but there's been no reply. Ma always said there are some who go away and try to pretend the past never happened.'

'You can't do that, Rose, can you? Your past shapes you whether you like it or not. And if it's given you a bad hand you'll not improve it much unless you know you have it.'

'We didn't do so bad, did we?' she said, taking his arm.

Sam kissed her cheek.

'No, we didn't. We might be dead and gone, perished in Derryveagh, or in Letterkenny workhouse, or buried at sea from the *Abysinnia*. But we're not. We're walking into Armagh on a lovely April evening, full of your good dinner. Ma would be pleased to see the pair of us.'

Rose nodded, afraid the tears might catch her again just when she had no wish to be sad. In the small piece of time they now had left to them before they reached the station, she wanted them to be happy.

'Rose, there's something I must ask you. I'm sure I ought to know, but I don't. When I was sitting in the church last week, I suddenly thought. 'Why Kerry?' I know what happened when Adair put us out and the Rosses in Ramelton gave us their barn and fed us. But how did we come to Kerry, Ma and you and me?'

Rose laughed again, amused at the thought of the years that lay between herself and this lively young man.

'Well, you were only a baby when it happened,' she began. 'After the news came about Da, the Rosses heard through their church that the Stewarts needed a housemaid. So it made sense for Mary to apply. *In own handwriting*, as all the advertisements say,' she continued with a smile. 'So she was called to interview. But Ma wasn't sure whether she'd be happy or not living-in. So she went with her. She told Mary that if they offered her the job she was to say that her mother wished to speak to the housekeeper before she could say yes.'

'That sounds like Ma.'

'Well, Mary was offered the job and Ma is called to the housekeeper's room where she proceeds to ask *her* questions about the situation. By the time she'd finished, the housekeeper has a few questions of her own. When she hears mother came from Ardtur and is now widowed, she asks if she'd like her to find a situation for her as well. So mother says "yes" and Mary Laverty, I think that was her name, sets about finding her a position.'

'And she found one in Kerry?'

'There was a Lady something visiting the Stewarts who knew another Lady something who was a cousin of Lady Caroline. And Lady Caroline needed an assistant housekeeper who could sew. That's how we ended up in Kerry.'

'*Ah, God be with you Kerry, Where in childhood I was merry,*' he sang cheerfully, as they passed the gates of the Richardson estate and came within sight of the spinning mill at Drumcairn.

'There hasn't been any trouble at Currane Lodge, has there? Not like poor Lady Anne in Sligo,' she said, her thoughts moving back to the peaceful times that now seemed so far away.

'No, no trouble at all. Don't forget they still have Old Thomas and my friend Tom.'

'How do you mean?'

'Well, those two were both founder members of the League in that area. They'd make sure the Molyneux were never on anybody's list. While Sir Capel lives, there'll not be trouble at Currane, but his successor might be a different matter.'

'And does he keep well?'

'Fairly well. Cook says he has gout and gets pains in the chest if he rides out about the estate.'

Rose sighed. Ma had gone and with her the link to the family they'd known so well. When Sir Capel died, the family itself would have to go. He had no heir and Sam, whom he'd cared for and educated, with the thought he might adopted him or marry him to one of his daughters, had abandoned him for the sake of a cause. Poor man.

They reached the level crossing and Rose waved to the signal man. They'd been exchanging greetings for years now, though only once had they met face to face.

'How does wee Sam know so much about engines?'

'That's his father fault,' said Rose grinning. 'John loves anything that moves by itself. I'm becoming an expert myself on pistons and steam pressure. Sometimes on a Sunday afternoon he takes them in to the station to see what might be there, waiting to go out, or being turned round. My friend, Mary Wylie, has an uncle who works in the engine shed so they sometimes get climbing up into the cab. There's no stopping them talking when they come home,' she said, beaming as they walked through the station gates.

'I'll see if I can find a book or two for them, now I know what they're keen on. What'll I send Hannah and Sarah?'

'Oh Sam, don't trouble. It's cost you dear to come up today and I doubt if you're very well paid.'

'Too true, Rose. And only proper. But I've no wife, or child, so I can spare a bit. There'll be a parcel for them in a week or two,' he said warmly, as he took out a tiny square of cardboard and the ticket collector waved them both on to the platform.

'And speaking of a parcel, Rose. What I left you is some of Ma's stuff. There wasn't much. I gave her clothes to Cook. I hope that was right, for they were good friends. But there was a blouse she was making and I knew by the size it must be for you and some nice pieces of material. And buttons. Thread, too. So I parcelled it up for you in case it would be useful. There was a good shawl and I sent that to Mary. Did I do right?'

'You've done wonderfully, Sam. I'm so very glad to have seen you, even if it was bad news that brought you. I hope we'll meet again soon,' she said, as a distant whistle told her the train was approaching. She looked down the platform and watched the gates of the level crossing swing out and clack into place.

'I've been over there on the road so often when the gates have closed in front of me, but I've never stood here looking out at them before.'

'Maybe, if things go well with us, we could make use of the trains. Sometimes there's cheap day returns. They're half the price. That's why I couldn't stay the night. But maybe next time.'

The train was approaching. She could see it coming under the bridge on the other side of the Loughgall Road. Now it was on the level crossing. Smoke and clouds of steam swirled around them as the brakes squealed and carriage doors flew open as it came to a halt beside them. There were no more hours, or minutes, only seconds.

Sam put his arms round her, kissed her cheeks and hugged her.

'Take care, Rose. Take care. Write very soon,' he said, and was gone.

Even before he'd thrown his empty bag up in the rack, the train had creaked, moved silently for a few seconds, then pulled forward more quickly, gathering speed as the huge clock above the platform jerked from six o'clock to one minute past. A further cloud of smoke and steam enveloped her. By the time it cleared, the guard's van was already growing small in the distance and Sam was looking out at the countryside through which they'd walked together only half an hour previously.

Rose slept badly that night, her dreams haunted by questions she couldn't answer and people who turned out to be not the people she thought they were. She saw herself climbing a mountain with a bleeding foot and woke up trying to remember the name of the boy who'd carried her part of the way back home. She felt clumsy and confused and had to take a headache powder when the children went off to school.

She sat down with her sewing as soon as she'd cleared away the remains of breakfast and washed up the porridge bowls. Even the sound of little

Sarah's voice reading to Ganny seemed to make her head ache. It had been an effort to get the children off to school without snapping at them, but she had a strict rule that she never took out her temper on them when she herself felt bad.

The head had begun to ease when she heard a slight scuffling sound and looked up sharply. An awkward-looking youth stood on the threshold, gathering himself to knock the open door. He dropped his hand, then mumbled indistinctly as she put her sewing down and came over to him.

'Thomas sez t' tell ye, the pair of them is gone over t' Robinson's,' he began, jerking his shoulder in the direction of the farm. 'The big cart is stuck in the sheugh and the wheels is jammed. He said t' tell ye if anyone comes wi' a horse, they'll be a while. They're beyond in the back lane if they're wantin'.'

She nodded encouragingly as the lad turned away and strode off past the empty forge towards the Robinson's. She went and drank a cup of water from the pail in the wash house and sat down again to her sewing. She'd hardly put her needle back in the seam when a shadow fell across the floor and she looked up to see Mary-Anne standing at the door, her knuckles poised for her familiar tattoo on the door.

She got to her feet quickly enough to prevent further action and stood waiting for what was to come. To her surprise Mary-Anne's tone was more reasonable than usual.

'Missus Hamilton, I understood that when you were put out of your last house you came here as a temporary measure until you found something suited to you. I'd like to know when you intend moving on for I see no signs of it at the moment.'

The cheek of the woman. Somehow she found her apparent reasonableness far more insulting than her habitual rudeness.

'No, indeed you don't, Missus Scott. We're quite well settled thank you,' she said coolly. 'Sir Capel has been most kind in mending our roof and replacing the windows. We have no intention of moving.'

'So yer not moving, aren't you?' Mary-Anne spat out. 'Well, we'll see about that,' she went on, putting her hands on her hips. 'I let my husband talk me in to havin' you and your family here against my better judgement,' she went on furiously. 'An' I've put up with it nine months now, using our water and making free of our land an' showing no respect for the property. It's one thing havin' a man workin' at the forge who's foolish enough not to support his own people, but it's another matter having you and your family, forby your followers from Kerry, comin' to spy out the land, I suppose, for the other side,' she said, pouring out the words with such venom she had to pause for breath.

'I take it you are referring to my brother who came yesterday,' said Rose, in an icy tone.

'A right red-headed Fenian whoever he was,

standin' at the end of the lane sayin' his piece to yer man from Blundell's Grange, gettin' his information, or passin' it on, no doubt. What good woud he be up to an' not willin' or able to speak the Queen's English?'

The pain in her head vibrated like the sound of a heavy hammer in the forge and she felt a tightness in her chest as if her heart were going to burst. How dare she? How dare this woman speak of Sam like this? How dare she treat her as some lower form of life, to be tolerated for a time and then moved on as no doubt she moved on tinkers or gypsies?

'Missus Scott, first I'm going to tell you why my brother Sam has red hair, and then I'm going to tell you what I'm going to do unless you go away and leave me and my children in peace.'

She spoke so softly, she realised Mary-Anne was having to pay close attention in order to hear her, but she couldn't have spoken louder if she'd wanted to. Her chest was so tight with anger and tension she had barely breath enough to get the words out.

'My brother Sam has red hair, as has my son James, because their grandfather had red hair. He was a Scot, a Covenanter, as bitter and as hard as you are, a real, good Christian, reading his Bible and cursing those who weren't like he was. And do you know what happened him? Well, I'll tell you. He died, like everybody dies. And you'll die to. And just like him, there'll be no one to mourn you, not even your own children.'

'I beg your pardon, Missus Hamilton . . .' said Mary-Anne, her face flushing a hectic crimson.

'I haven't finished,' snapped Rose, sharply. 'If you don't leave us alone, I shall tell Thomas exactly what you've been doing. I'll tell the Robinsons you've tried to deny us spring water from *their* orchard and I'll ask Sir Capel to give us a plan of this property with your boundaries marked on,' she went on, taking a quick, gasping breath. 'We pay our rent, we are good tenants and he is happy for us to be here. We owe *you* thanks for nothing, not even the practice of the Second Commandment. Now go away and don't come back,' she ended, raising her voice for the first time, as she closed the door firmly in Mary-Anne's startled face.

She closed her eyes and leant against the door, shaking with the effort of control she'd made and wondering whether she should put in place the wooden bar they seldom bothered to use except on very windy nights.

'Not nice lady,' said Sarah, her eyes round, her arm firmly enclosing Ganny. 'Don't like her, Ma,' she went on, her voice wavering.

Rose gathered the little girl in her arms and walked her up and down dropping little pecking kisses on her cheeks till the child responded with a big hug that almost throttled her.

'She's gone now, Sarah. We'll forget all about her. Would you like a wee, tiny drop of Ma's tea with sugar in it if I make some?'

'Yes, please,' she said excitedly. 'And Ganny too. She always liked her cup of tea.'

'You read her a little story while I go and fill the kettle.'

Rose just managed it to the wash house before she burst into tears. She wept, leaning against the cold north wall so that little Sarah wouldn't hear her. She wept tears of fury that life should be made so much harder than it need be by the nursed resentment of a bitter woman. She wept tears of sorrow that the one person who would understand about the loss of her mother, dear Sarah, was herself gone before. And she wept tears of anxiety, the nameless fears of the night returning in the broad light of day, growing into a sense of menace that the future was about to ask of her a strength she would not be able to find.

# CHAPTER NINETEEN

The early spring was particularly lovely in that spring of 1886. After Sam's visit and the news of her mother's death, Rose moved through her daily routine with only half her mind on what she was doing, her head full of strange random thoughts and memories. She paused often to take in the loveliness of the day, only to find herself sitting or standing, minutes later, lost in her own thoughts.

When she went up the orchard for water she would pause by the well, make sure there was no sign of Mary-Anne, and sit down on the mossy slope nearby, careful not to crush any of the newly opened wood anemones that flourished in the dappled shade. Despite the sunlight pouring down upon her through the budded apple trees, she felt all her pleasure in the day drain away. Try as she might, she seemed powerless to prevent a painful restlessness welling up and obliterating the joy such moments of ease so often gave her. It happened so often, she began to think, joy and ease were features of the past.

Sitting by the well one morning towards the end of April, she closed her eyes in the sun's warmth and saw herself walking out into the garden at Annacramp to see what had bloomed with the morning sun or pick flowers for their table. Often, she would carry one of the children in her arms, repeating for them the names of Sarah's plants.

'No, that's not the way, Rose,' she whispered to herself, alarmed at the wave of longing that swept over her.

She followed the flight of a huge bumble bee moving across the long, rich grass in front of her, its hum the only sound in the stillness. But the image of the garden at Annacramp wouldn't leave her.

'You can't go back. It's not good for you to think so,' she went on berating herself. You can't go back, you can't.'

Even as she spoke, she knew she wasn't longing for the past, nor wishing herself back where once she had been so happy. She was looking for something that had gone from her life.

'Sarah and Ma?' she said tentatively.

It was one thing to miss Sarah, who'd been so much part of her daily life for ten years, sharing her joys and sorrows, helping her and appreciating her, another to feel such loss for her mother so far away in Kerry. Dear as she was, how could her going call up so bitter an ache of loneliness, when she had a husband and children living she loved so dearly.

But perhaps it was not her mother in herself, rather it was all she stood for. She and Sarah were both rich in experience. Though Sarah appeared to have had the easier life, she'd always shared the lives of those around her, grieved for their losses, supported them in their anxieties and what she'd experienced, she'd pondered deeply in her quiet hours, just as her mother had done.

'*How do you know so much, Rose?*'

She smiled to herself. So long ago now, the moment when Lady Anne reached out to a shy, awkward man who could only talk about horses.

It was so obvious really, once you thought about it. Her mother was her first teacher and Sarah had followed after. With them, she'd not learnt French, or English, or geography, but how to live. How to understand people. And now, for the first time in her life she was on her own. She would have to use all they had taught her to go on teaching herself.

She stood up and filled her buckets from the clear water. John had made a marker that showed the fluctuations of the water level. It seldom varied. Even in the driest weather, the shallow pool restored itself almost immediately. Mary-Anne's fears for her water supply were unfounded. But then, as Hannah would have said, 'It's not about the water, it's about meanness of spirit.'

She followed the new path they'd tramped along the side of the orchard and through the gap in the hedge she and John had enlarged one summer evening, after one of Mary-Anne's early visits. It was just wide enough for her to pass through sideways with the buckets. Once through, she had only to cross the common and push open the unlatched new gate into her own back garden.

'Out of sight, out of mind,' John had said, as they worked out what to do to keep out of Mary-Anne's way. But keeping out of Mary-Anne's sight had not avoided her displeasure. A mild word that, she thought, as the gate clicked shut behind her.

'It's hatred, Rose. That's what it is. And hatred's hard to bear,' she said to herself, as she put down the buckets in the wash house and went back into the kitchen.

She crossed immediately to the open door and looked out. Sarah was sitting exactly where she'd left her in her own wooden chair, on a small grassy mound overlooking the stone circle where the cart wheels were rimmed. She was totally absorbed in what her father and Uncle Thomas were doing.

She laughed. The other children would be sorry they'd missed it, seeing a wheel rimmed was one of the things they most enjoyed and Sarah was sure to talk about it all afternoon. She was just going to turn away and pick up her sewing when she saw Thomas pause and greet someone, a woman, certainly, for he'd touched his cap. A moment later, Rose gave a little cry of delight. It was Mary Wylie.

'Mary, how lovely to see you. Will you have a cup of tea.'

'No, Rose dear, I can't stop. Ma's got wee Edward an' he's teethin' an' I have to go inta Armagh. I only called for a minute or two. Couldn't bear to go past an' not get a look at ye. How are ye?' she said, with a sharp look at her, as she dropped down on the settle.

'Not bad,' said Rose honestly, touched by the real concern in the simple question.

'Has she been back?'

Rose shook her head and Mary pursed her lips.

'I've trouble forgivin' that woman anythin',' she said, shaking her head slowly, 'but comin' at ye when she knew ye'd just lost yer mother . . . I can't believe the badness of it. She *must* have known. Thomas would have told her. She knew he came to see you, an' she'd never have let him near ye if it weren't a bereavement. I think that woman's jealousy forby everythin' else.'

'Jealous?'

'Ach aye, there's some people made that way. They always see others with somethin' they think they should have. You wouldn't understan' for it's not in your nature.'

'Isn't it?'

'No. I've never known ye grudge anyone their good fortune. Sure, look at Lady Anne. Do you ever grudge her the money, or the big house, or

308

the dresses, an' you just as clever as she was, an' probably better lookin'?'

To Rose's amazement she found herself blushing. Lady Anne was no great beauty, but she'd never given it a thought.

'Well no, but the poor girl has her own troubles,' she said quickly. 'She was in a bad way over her husband. He might have been killed, Mary.'

'There ye are. That's what I mean. You only think of the person themselves. But the likes of Mary-Anne looks at you an' thinks about *herself*. An' then she thinks of what *she* wants an' whether or not ye're any use to her. Maybe she'll leave ye in peace now you've spoke up. I don't know how you stuck it so long. Are ye sure yer not lettin' her get in on ye?'

'I couldn't swear to it, Mary, but I'm trying. I'm not in best form, I know, but I don't think it's Mary-Anne. I still keep going for the notepaper to write to Ma, but I suppose that's not surprising.'

'No, not a bit. An' ye were close to her for so long. It's not as if there were half a dozen young ones roun' her. There was only you an' wee Sam.'

'Which reminds me, Mary. I've something to show you and a wee present for you. D'you remember Sam brought me some stuff of Ma's? I hadn't even looked at it when you came up to see me. And I forgot all about it when I came down to you. Hold on a minute,' she said, hurrying into the bedroom.

She returned a few moments later with a half finished blouse in one hand and a length of fabric in the other.

'Look,' she said, holding out the blouse, a fine, dark plum-coloured silk which shimmered in the light. 'She was making it for me when she died,' she said, sadly. 'Sam knew it was for me by the size, but what he didn't notice was this. Look, Mary.'

'Ach, a lovely wee brooch,' she said, unpinning it from the hem of the garment and turning it over in her large, red hands.

'It belonged to my great-grandmother,' explained Rose, 'but my mother never wore it. The day we were put out at Ardtur, she gave it to me to wear under my shift, in case any of Adair's men might see it and steal it. I haven't laid eyes on it since.'

'It has the date on the back. Did ye know that?' said Mary, peering at the tarnished metal. 'J. M. it says, 1745. That's a queer while ago,' she added, her eyes bright. 'There's maybe a story there, did we but know it.'

'Yes, I'm sure there is indeed,' said Rose, as she looked for herself. 'J. M. is probably James Mackay. Or maybe it's Jane Mackay . . .'

'Rose dear, I must go, much as I'd like to stay. But I must tell you what I came for. I have good news. Peggy and Kevin was up on Sunday on the train, looking powerful well. Peggy has one on the

310

way. July or thereabouts, she says. And Kevin is as pleased as Punch, as the sayin' is.'

'Oh, that's lovely, Mary. Isn't it great to have good news. I'll start a wee dress for her one of these days,' she said firmly. as she picked up the length of material she'd set down beside them. 'And this is for you,' she said, handing it over. 'I'm afraid you'll have to make it up yourself, I'm doing so much for Leeman's, these days, but the minute I saw it I thought of you. Blue's your colour.'

'Rose, you can't give me this,' said Mary, startled, as she stared at the folded length of blue fabric.

'I just have.' Rose laughed and gave her friend a little kiss. 'I've not got much to give away these days, but that had your name on it from the minute I opened Sam's parcel. I'm just sorry I can't make it up for you.'

She walked to the door with her and stood watching as she set off down the lane with a cheery wave to Sarah and a word to Thomas and John.

'Give thanks, Rose,' she said to herself, as she stepped back into her kitchen and picked up her sewing. 'You may have lost your wise women, but at least you've a kind friend who's no fool. Mary's not great at thinking things out, but she'll never let you down.'

The apple blossom that May was lovelier than anything she had ever seen before. Even the three very elderly trees just beyond their garden wall were laden with blossom. For a week or more, their delicate perfume blended with the perfume from the orchard and flowed through the open doors and windows of the house. The insects were busy, the bees drunk with nectar. Though the night skies were clear, there was no frost. As the days passed and there was still no wind, the blossom fell like snow in summer. Minute green fruit appeared in great quantity promising a rich harvest.

But the spring weeks that brought more work to the forge and the first signs of growth in their newly cultivated garden, also brought growth of a different kind. As the days lengthened and the news that the Home Rule Bill was to come before parliament, senior men from the lodge made a further visit to the forge. The drilling now was out in the open.

Thomas thought the outdoor drilling might only be because of the good weather, but John was less sure. His guess was that there were now too many to accommodate in the small Orange Hall in the middle of Robinson's bog. From what the lodge men had said, he felt there was a growing confidence that no one would lift a finger to stop them, were they now to parade openly in the streets of the city.

Sometimes on fine evenings when the children were in bed, Rose and John would sit on the bench under the young pear tree at the gable wall of the shoeing shed. From there they could hear any sound from the children's rooms while still enjoying the fading light and the antics of Robinson's calves in the small field in front of them.

There was seldom any movement on the road beyond this late in the evening, except maybe an empty cart coming back from market, or a neighbour leading home a new cow, pulling awkwardly at its temporary rope halter. But more than once as the evenings lengthened towards midsummer, the sound of tramping feet reached them. They moved out of sight into the shoeing shed until the marching column passed.

'What do you think will happen, John? Will it go through, do you think?'

He shook his head sadly and studied the toe caps of his working boots.

'There'll be trouble over it. That's the only thing that I'm sure of. Whether it were to go through or not, there's been so much bad feeling stirred up it'll come out some way or 'nother. Ye've only to read the reports in the paper. It's all very well saying it's just talk, but people talk themselves into badness. An' it's been goin' on for months now.'

'Sam says there'll be trouble in Belfast either way. But what about here, John?'

'Ye can't tell. One o' the men came to us las' week I've knowed since we were at school together. A right kind of a man, ye'd think, if ye met him in the ordinary way, the sort who'd always help a neighbour out. But he was talking big, about what they was goin' to do. You'd think he'd taken on the whole of Italy, he was that hot about the Pope. 'An sure wasn't his gran'mother a Catholic from over Moy way. She used to visit m' mother an' swop wee plants wi' her.'

He paused and watched the swooping flight of the swallows over the field of calves.

'They were a lot harder to talk to than the las' time,' he said awkwardly.

'Did you not tell me the half of it, John?'

He laughed wryly and looked sheepish.

'Well you'd better tell me the whole of it now,' she said, with a lightness she certainly didn't feel.

'I thought maybe it was a threat with nothing to it, and maybe so it will be, but your man from Cabragh said there was people had approached him about buying the cart manufactory and gettin' it goin' again. That was meant as one in the eye for us for "*not bein' loyal*" as they call it. I don't know who owns that land, for Alex was just a tenant, but if it's only money that's needed then yer man has it, or could raise it if he wanted to. An' ye know what that wou'd mean.'

'I do, love,' she said steadily. 'I know perfectly well what that would mean. But we'll not worry till we have to. We'll meet it should it come.'

A few days later a groom from Sir Capel's estate came to the forge and told them the old man was failing. The doctor had been sent for. By the end of the same week, they were getting out their Sunday clothes to go and pay their respects as he was laid to rest in the family vault, a few yards from the Scott grave and a short walk from the Hamilton one.

Rose was overcome with anxiety lest they'd be turned out again and this time they really did have nowhere to go. For days she told herself not to be so silly. Was it likely that Sir Capel's successor would want their poor cottage for a relative? Would he want to get rid of the Scotts and the Hamiltons to make more room for sheep, like Adair of Glenveagh? She tried to laugh at herself, but all to no avail. She shared her fears with John, who did his best to comfort her, but the sense of menace would not leave her. Only when a greater storm broke did she realise it was coming from somewhere quite different.

Riots started in Belfast even before the Home Rule Bill came before Parliament. According to Kevin Donaghy, Mary's new brother-in-law, the whole outbreak had begun with jeers and taunting in the shipyards. A Catholic had said something to a Protestant during their lunch break about the days of the Ascendancy being over.

The story got around and was added to in the telling. Kevin said he'd heard later that the Catholic was supposed to have said that a Protestant wouldn't be able to earn so much as a loaf of bread when

Dublin was in charge. The following day, a gang of Protestants attacked the Catholic workman and his friends in the dinner hour, beating them up and chasing them for their lives. Some tried to escape by jumping into the docks. The first death was a lad who couldn't swim and was drowned.

But that was only the beginning. Day after day, there was news of more riots and more deaths. Even when the Home Rule Bill was defeated, it did nothing to cool tempers. Protestants lit celebratory bonfires and Catholics set their chimneys on fire as a protest. Smoke hung like a pall over the city as pent up energy erupted into a violence that grew by what it fed on.

Rose almost came to dread John's coming home. There was little that happened in Belfast during the night that didn't reach the forge by late morning. What was in the morning papers, or reached Armagh with the railway workers would come by way of the carters and the postmen. The latest news always reached the forge by the end of the working day. And the news was always bad. John was weighed down by it in the telling as much as she was in the hearing.

Nor was it an easy time for the forge. It had always been a meeting place and a clearing house for the news of the locality, but the old easy feeling had gone. No longer did people talk about the weather, the state of the crops, the health or otherwise of their neighbours. Now it was only the latest riot and which side had done what.

Both John and Thomas knew that men of the lodge were coming to the forge to hear what was being said, so they said as little as possible themselves. But it put a strain on their relationship with each other and with their neighbours.

But worse was to come. One August morning Mary Wylie appeared tear-stained and distraught.

'Rose dear, I'm on my way to Belfast,' she gasped, out of breath on a morning already hot and windless. 'I can only stop a minit. I can hardly bear to tell you what's happened.'

'Mary dear, sit down. Let me get you a glass of spring water. Now, tell me. Please.'

'Last night,' she said, drinking gratefully in large gulps, 'there was trouble in the Donegall Road. Some Catholics went for an Orange Band that was leading a Sunday School excursion back home. Some wee lad got hit with a stone, and Kevin went out to help,' she went on, tears streaming down her face. 'Someone hit Kevin on the back of the head as he was bendin' over him. We don't know whether it was a Catholic or a Protestant,' she said, sobbing. 'It doesn't make any difference now. Kevin's dead, Rose, an' Peggy's wee baby due any time.'

# CHAPTER TWENTY

Though Rose dreaded the cold of winter and longed for the warmth of summer, the long, warm and very dry spells of that summer brought her little pleasure. It seemed as if the heat itself had encouraged the nightly rioting in Belfast. The tiny, overcrowded houses spilt their human contents into the streets to continue ongoing battles and keep up the avenging of insults the other side was supposed to have perpetrated with a succession of stonings, burnings and looting.

The riots went on through July and August, coming to an end finally after three days of heavy rain that flooded some of the poorest areas of the city and left crops damaged throughout the countryside. The newspapers put the official number of deaths at thirty, but the personal stories that reached Armagh to be passed on to the forge made it clear the actual number had to be much higher. In addition to the deaths, hundreds had been injured, many of them seriously.

'How is she, Mary? Is she going to stay in Belfast?' Rose asked, when one damp and misty September morning, her friend appeared at her door.

'No, she says she can't bear the sight o' the place, though the neighbours has been kind. Catholic and Protestant alike. She says the whole place is entirely different from when she an' Kevin were married and that not a year ago. It's the feel in the air she can't stand. An' forby, she's no money. The little bit they'd saved for things for the baby has gone in rent an' sure there's nothing comin' in. Peggy's not that strong yet to go out to work an' she's got no one to mind the wee boy.'

Rose sighed. Hardly a day passed when she hadn't thought of Peggy and wondered how she was coping with the shock of Kevin's death and the long hard labour which started the day he was buried. There were times when the enormity of Peggy's loss came close to overwhelming her. What would she do if she lost her own beloved John? Where would she go? How would she live without his love and comfort. It was not so much providing for the children, but coping with a life that would have lost all its meaning.

'So will she come home?' she said, pushing away her own sad thoughts.

'There's nothing for it,' said Mary matter-of-factly. 'Me Ma's not keen on having the child, she says she's too old to go through all that again. She does her bit comin' down to help me, but she doesn't want a baby in the house. Still, when it comes to it, I think she'd be glad to have Peggy back. Da's getting awful crotchety with the arthritis. Ma says he only opens his mouth to complain. Isn't old age awful, Rose. D'ye think we'll be like that if we live long enough?'

She had to laugh. It was the directness and lack of calculation about Mary she so loved. What she thought, she said. But what she may have lacked in tact, she more than made up for in kindness.

'I can't imagine being old, Mary,' she said honestly. 'Oh, I can imagine failing. Being a bit deaf or losing my sight. Not able to walk very much, like poor Sarah. I dread the thought of it, but I can't imagine not being the person I am now. Do you know what I mean?'

'Aye. I can't see you different, somehow. But there's many that are,' she said, a frown on her face. 'There's people I used to know when I was a girl. Some of these men marchin' around in hard hats. They were only a few years older than me. Sure, I made hay with some of them an' had a bit of fun behind the haystack,' she said, winking mischievously. 'What gets inta them d'ye think that they go so serious an' get so puffed up in themselves. Behavin' as if they knew it all an' most of them have no idea. They don't know the half of what goes on.'

Rose shook her head.

'I sometimes wonder if it's fear, Mary. Fear of

losing their farm, or their job, or of being ill, or getting old. So they build themselves up. Pretend nothing can touch them. Forever playing "I'm the King of the castle and no one can knock me down." And to prove it they have to find someone weaker to knock down, and so it goes on,' she ended abruptly, straightening herself up and pulling a sour face.

Mary laughed.

'Ye might be right, Rose. It wouldn't be the first time,' she said, grinning. 'But tell me this an' tell me no more, as the saying is,' she went on leaning forward and dropping her voice confidentially. 'Why is it only the men?'

'You're forgetting Mary-Anne,' said Rose, with a smile.

'An' isn't she better forgotten?' replied Mary, so promptly that Rose burst out laughing again.

'But why only the men?' Mary persisted.

Rose was silent a moment. Why indeed? She'd never thought of that, though it was true enough.

'Perhaps it's because men don't bear children,' she said seriously. 'Because we carry life, we're more concerned with the ordinary business of living. For us there'd always be something far more important than marching or rioting.'

'Aye, maybe ye have it there, Rose dear. Sure what attention wou'd ye pay to anythin' if ye'd a child sick?'

The two friends moved on then and talked of

other things. Mary confessed her anxiety about Jane, now eight years old and not as tall as her little brother William. She was never without a cold and now after the hot, dry summer she had a cough. In return, Rose confided that John was in very low spirits, because Thomas had grown so silent he could hardly get a word out of him.

They agreed as they parted that the doctor might well do something for Jane, but there was little anyone could do for Thomas with Mary-Anne around.

On a pleasant Monday afternoon in October, Rose was startled by what sounded like a cry from the direction of the forge. Immediately, she dropped her sewing and went to look out. As she reached the door, she saw a young horse burst out of the shoeing shed and race down the lane, his leading rein trailing on the ground, a young lad in hot pursuit.

'John,' she cried, as she flew across the space between the house and the forge, dodging round a parked cart and a hay float waiting for repair.

But the figure who lay just inside the shoeing shed was Thomas. His grime-streaked face was deathly white and dark bubbles of blood were pushing through a long gash on his forehead. As she knelt down beside him the hammering stopped next door.

'John, come here. Come here quickly,' she shouted.

'My God, Rose, what's happened?' he cried,

kicking aside a still glowing horse shoe and dropping to his knees beside the crumpled figure.'

'I don't know, but we've got to get him to the hospital,' she said as the blood began to stream down his face.

'Robinson's trap is our only hope,' she went on. 'Run and ask George will he take him. Then ask Sophie has she anything for bleeding,' she said, cradling Thomas's head in her lap.

Rose had never before seen a head injury and she was horrified by the blood now pouring down his face. If she didn't do something to stop it she knew he would bleed to death, where he lay, on the hard earth floor of the shoeing shed.

'Lord, tell me what to do,' she prayed, tears of anxiety and frustration welling up in her eyes.

'Stop it,' she said to herself fiercely, as a tear dripped down on Thomas's face, making a clean mark.

Before she actually thought about what she was doing, she'd felt around the wound for the pulsing vein that was pumping out his blood. She couldn't halt the flow, but she could reduce it. She kept her fingers pressed to the vein and used her other hand to wipe the blood and grime from his face with a loose corner of her apron.

He moaned, his eyes flickering and closing again as if the sunlight penetrating the outer area of the shed was too bright to bear. He tried to say something, but she could see his lips were too dry. She moistened the other corner of the apron with spittle and wiped them gently.

'Rose?'

'Yes, it's me Thomas. Don't move now, like a good man, till John comes back. I think we'll need a doctor to stitch you up,' she said softly.

'I think it was maybe a wasp stung the poor beast,' he said, with an effort. 'M' leg's broke. I heard it crack afore I fell,' he said, looking up at her with a wry look on his face. 'I've an awful pain in m'head.'

Rose laid her free hand across his forehead and listened for any sign of John's return. He'd been gone a few minutes only, but already it seemed like hours. Though the bleeding had slowed it still seemed such a lot as it trickled between her fingers and down her bare arm. It would take half an hour at least to get him into Armagh and up to the Infirmary. Would there be any blood left by then?

She heard a step behind her and tried to turn her head to see who it was, but she couldn't move her head without disturbing Thomas, who now lay still again, his eyes shut.

'Is he dead?'

The voice was familiar but for a moment she couldn't place it.

'No, but his leg's broken. John's gone for Robinson's trap.'

There was a rustle of skirt and a moment later, Peggy Donaghy was kneeling beside her, her once rounded face pale and drawn, her eyes lifeless, their sparkle gone.

'Can I do something to help, Rose?' she said coolly.

'Yes. Go over home and bring me a bowl of spring water, a cup and a clean cloth. There ought to be one in the wash house. See if wee Sarah's still asleep and tell her to stay where she is if she's awake.'

Peggy left without a word. The events of July, the blood spilt so liberally in the street where she'd started her married life with such hope and joy, Kevin lying as Thomas now lay, came into her mind so sharply.

'How is he, love?' John said breathlessly, as he dropped to his knees beside her. 'George is harnessing the mare. He'll come round by the lane and back up here. Maggie's away lookin' for blankets to put under him and Sophie sent you this,' he said quickly, handing her a soft pad of linen saturated in some sharp smelling liquid. 'She said to feel for the throb and press it, but not too hard and not all the time. Put this on the wound and hope it'll clot. Don't for any sakes wash it, she said.'

'I knew that much,' she said briskly, 'but I've sent for a bowl of water to make a cold compress. He said he had an awful head.'

'Did he speak t' ye?' he asked, his voice almost breaking with emotion.

'He did. He says his leg's broken. He thinks a wasp stung the horse.'

'Ach dear, dear. Such a wee thing to cause such grievance. That beast couldn't be a quieter animal if it tried.'

He got to his feet as the wheels of the trap sounded on the cobbled lane and Peggy appeared with water and a cloth.

Maggie Robinson had padded the floor of the trap with blankets for John had made it clear that it wouldn't be possible for Thomas to sit up.

'Will you go with him, Rose?'

'What about Mary-Anne?' she said, thinking of her for the first time.

'She's away out.'

'I'll go, surely,' she said, relief breaking over her.

'I'll stay till you come back, Rose, and see to the wee ones,' said Peggy, as she arranged herself on the floor of the trap and strong arms lifted Thomas gently back into her lap, his broken leg bound firmly against the good one with a piece of rope.

While the door of the trap was wedged open to accommodate Thomas's length, Peggy made a compress for his head and Rose put the cup of water inside the empty bowl and placed it beside her so she could moisten his lips as they went.

'Are ye right, Rose?' George asked, as she braced herself against the back of the driver's seat.

'Yes, I am. Take it easy on the lane till I get the knack of it,' she said, looking at John, trying to reassure him with a soft look. 'Peggy'll make you a cup of tea,' she added when she saw how white he'd gone. Peggy nodded calmly and Rose herself felt comforted.

She was cramped and uncomfortable, her back aching with the awkward angle she needed to sit at, so she could keep her fingers on both Sophie's pad and on the throbbing vein. She wondered how she would ever manage to keep going the whole way to Armagh when she was in such pain herself by the end of the lane.

She concentrated on Thomas, not sure whether to be pleased or anxious he was no longer conscious. She kept the pad damp on his forehead and his lips well moistened in the hope that the slight comfort might somehow touch him, but in truth, it was she herself who was comforted. As they neared the outskirts of Armagh and the hot sun was shut off by the cool shade of the chestnuts opposite the gates of Drumsollen, she suddenly remembered being just as painfully cramped in a strawlined cart, a red-headed baby in her arms, a bag of turf poking through her thin shift.

The baby had survived and so would Thomas. If

thoughts and prayers could keep him safe, then he'd not lack for them. She made the sign of the cross on his forehead and spoke to George.

'I think maybe we could risk going a wee bit faster.'

'Whatever you say Rose. Anything that'll help Thomas.'

A group of men were standing awkwardly outside the forge when George drove her back up the lane. John was the first to reach the trap, swinging her down in one easy movement, his eyes on her apron and hands, still covered in dried blood.

'Well,' he said, anxiously.

Rose looked at George, but George shook his head.

'Rose'll tell you,' he said, nodding to the onlookers. 'I didn't understan' the half of it.'

'They said the leg is broken cleanly and should heal well enough,' she began, looking at the sombre faces. 'The head wound is more serious, but they've got the bleeding stopped and put stitches in. They can't tell if there's a fracture to the skull. The doctor said that would show up in a day or two.' She paused and went on as steadily as she could. 'He said another half inch and Thomas would have lost his eye.'

There was a sharp intake of breath and relieved comments as the men looked gravely at each other. As they dispersed, they said they'd be back tomorrow for the latest news.

Left alone after George had turned the trap and set off down the lane, Rose leant against John, suddenly desperately weary.

'Come on over home,' he said encouragingly, as he slipped an arm round her. 'Peggy'll have ye a cup o' tea in no time. She's one great girl, that Peggy, after what she's been through, playing wi' wee Sarah an' gettin' Hannah to help her make the supper. She had them all peelin' or scrapin' or washin' stuff to have it ready for Ma comin' home.'

'Have you told Mary-Anne?'

'She's not there to tell. I went up when school was out an' wee Annie came to the door. She says she's at Battlehill at some class or other. She'll not be back till the night.'

'What did ye say to Annie?'

'I said nothin,' for the poor wee thing was half afeerd to open the door. She didn't ask.'

Peggy was pouring tea as they stepped into the kitchen.

'I heard the trap,' she said, 'or rather Sam did. So we made the tea,' she said cheerfully, her eyes meeting Rose's, full of the question she would not ask in front of the children.

'Poor Uncle Thomas's has had an accident and he's got a bad head,' Rose said, as four pairs of eyes met hers, 'but they'll make him better in hospital.

329

I've heard they give patients oranges every week. Wouldn't that be nice?'

She put out her hand for her tea and saw for the first time the blood that had trickled down her arms.

'I'll be back in a moment,' she said, as she made for the wash house. As she shut the door behind her, her hands began to shake uncontrollably as she'd known they would if she'd tried to take the cup of tea Peggy had held out to her.

'Come on, Rose,' she said to herself as she washed. 'If Peggy Donaghy can do what *she* did this afternoon, you can keep up a bit longer.'

John got up early next morning, put on his Sunday clothes, walked into Armagh, and was just about to knock at the entrance door of the hospital when it was opened by two night nurses coming of duty. They pointed him to the Matron's office. The news was encouraging, she said. Thomas was conscious but confused. He told her he'd had a headache after he fell, but his mother had come and kissed it better and he'd slept the best at all. She'd told him about the visiting hour that afternoon and wished him good morning.

By eight o'clock, he was back in the forge. Rose was sure she could hear the relief in the rhythm of hammer on anvil as he began the days work on his own, for the first time in years.

She spent most of it sewing, grateful to be sitting

down, for she felt so weary, her mind preoccupied with going through every minute detail of yesterday's calamity.

After she'd managed to drink her cup of tea, she and Peggy had taken a little walk down the common, both of them glad to leave the children to their books and be quiet together.

'Peggy, I've thought of you so often,' said Rose. 'Is there anything in the world I can do to help you?'

'Thinkin' about me *is* a help. If I didn't know there was a few people knowin' the hurt of it, I couldn't keep goin'. An' as for ministers and priests, they should be banned. Tellin' ye the man ye love is in a better place when all he ever wanted was to lie in my arms. That was his heaven, he said. And mine,' she added, tears tripping down her face unheeded.

They put their arms round each others waists like old friends, though they had only been friends at a distance until now.

'The only people who understan' are people like you and Mary that love their men. My mother's sorry enough for me, but she's forgotten what it was like to love my father. An' to tell you the truth, lookin' roun' me I don't see many that loves their husband more than they love themselves, though maybe I shouldn't say it.'

'Say what you feel, Peggy. That's what a friend is for.'

They turned back at the bottom of the common,

the air beginning to cool. Already dew was forming on the bright bunches of hawthorn berries and the fronds of golden bracken in the hedgerow.

'Promise me, you'll come up again soon, Peggy, and we can talk properly. You were wonderful today. You gave me such courage.'

'Me? Me give *you* courage? I thought it was the other way round.'

Rose shook her head and kissed Peggy on the cheek.

'I'll be thinking of you *and* Thomas tonight,' she said as they parted at the foot of the lane.

Now that he was in safe hands and there was little more that she could do practically, she found the evening the hardest part of the day.

Being on his own, John had to use all the hours there were and besides, this evening he had to wait for Mary-Anne to come home. She knew he dreaded telling her of Thomas's injury, but she had to leave that task to him.

'Well, have you seen her?' she asked, when he came in at last, threw his cap on the settle and dropped down beside her.

'Aye I saw her, an' short shrift she gave me,' he said, his face stiff with anger.

'What did she say, love?' she asked gently, putting a hand on his.

'I had to go up to the house, for she lit past the forge so fast I coulden catch her,' he explained. 'She said the Lord's will would be done an' as much as closed the door in my face.'

'And did you explain the blow to the head nearly killed him?' Rose went on, hardly able to grasp what John seemed to be saying.

'She diden give me half a chance. I said, "I'm afraid Missus Scott, Thomas has had a bit of an accident," thinking maybe she'd say "Come in, John and tell me what's happened," but no, not a word. I must have told her he was in the hospital, but all I mind now was her saying about the Lord's will being done. As if the Lord would strike down a good man like Thomas. Is it any kind of a religion at all that wuman has?'

'People believe what they want to believe, John dear. Now go an' have a wash while I heat up your dinner. Sure you must be starving and it nearly nine.'

The week passed and by the end of it there was no doubt at all about Thomas's well-being. When it became clear that Mary-Anne had no intention of going to see Thomas in hospital, they took it in turns to visit him on the few days visiting was allowed. His head was swathed in bandages and his leg in plaster, but he was already out of bed and walking on crutches. Rose sat with him in the glass veranda that looked out over the city and told him the news, and the names of all the people who'd been to the forge to ask after him.

'I don't think I've ever known Thomas talk so much,' she said that evening when John asked her how she'd got on. 'He's looking really well, if you can forget the bandages and so on. He says the food is great and the nurses are kind.'

'Well, he'd better enjoy it, he'll not get much kindness when he comes home,' said John sharply. 'She's been down to the forge each day to collect the takings, an' divil the enquiry about him. She must have some of her own people goin' to ask about him, but wouldn't ye think she could just ask if I've heard anything fresh from anyone whose been in town?'

By Friday, George Robinson brought back the good news that Thomas would be allowed home sometime the following week if he continued to mend as well as he was doing. John walked over to the house at once to tell Rose.

It was a pleasant autumn day and after she'd heard the good news, everything she did seemed to go well. Her spirits rose and she sang as she went about her work. Even the bread turned out nicer than usual. She hoped John might get in a little earlier than he'd been able to do all week, but she knew he was trying to keep up with the most urgent work, so that Thomas wouldn't be anxious about letting their neighbours down. But he was late and when he did step into the house and she greeted him with a smile, he hardly managed to return it.

'James and Hannah, time you were off to bed now,' she said easily.

They kissed their father and left him sitting dispiritedly on the settle.

'What on earth is wrong, love. It's not Thomas, is it?'

'No, Thomas is fine. It's that wuman, Rose. God forgive me the thoughts I have about her. She came down a while ago and gave me my pay,' he said, his face tight with anger.

'Did she say that?'

'No, she didn't have to. I don't mind the word, but the face said everything. She was treating me like you wouldn't even treat an apprentice.'

Rose saw him drop his head in his hands.

'Maybe I was wrong to leave Sir Capel, just because I wanted to be my own man. When it's brought us to this.'

'To what, John?'

By way of answer, he put his hand in his trouser pocket and pulled out some money.

'To that, Rose. For a week's hard work. Count it.'

But she didn't need to count it. One glance told her it was the amount she usually set aside for the milk, eggs and butter from the farm.

'Was it a bad week, John? Did no one pay for anything?

'No, there was money in every day. I didn't take

a note of it when she came askin', but there was a fair bit. People made sure they paid up, knowing Thomas was in hospital.'

'And did you ask her how it came to so little?' said Rose gently, not wishing to upset him more than she need.

'Aye, I did. She said there was bills to pay. That I needn't think the work was all profit.'

'And were there bills?'

'Surely, there's always bills, but Thomas spreads them out. She must have paid the whole lot at once. You'd a thought she'd know better,' he said bitterly.

'Oh yes, John, she knows better,' said Rose, nodding her head. 'She's done it deliberately. That woman would starve us out of here if she could. But we'll not let her. If we go, we'll go of our own free will. Now don't worry,' she said, squeezing his hand, 'I've a bit in the top drawer and Thomas will be home next week. He may not be working, but he'll not let her do that again.'

She took up the shillings, made a little pile of them and set them in the window ready to go to the farm in the morning.

'Next week, keep a wee note of what comes in. We'll not let her beat us, John, will we?'

# CHAPTER TWENTY-ONE

After the continuous bad news of the summer and the shock of Thomas's injury, his return from hospital was one of the happiest moments in a difficult year. Throughout the townland, Thomas's progress was a daily topic of conversation and many of his neighbours would tramp down to the forge simply to ask for news of his progress.

When Rose saw him go down to the forge on crutches on his first afternoon home, she slipped over to ask him how he was.

'Ach sure it's a good thing me curtin' days is over,' he said, 'I'd have to go about it at nights or I'd frighten the girls away.'

Sitting later with her sewing, she realised he'd actually laughed about the fierce looking scar that arced from his temple across his right eye. He'd been full of wry humour about his accident, and greeted the men who'd come to see him with far more warmth than usual. Yes, there was no doubt about it. He seemed a much happier man, despite his ordeal, quite changed from the Thomas whose growing silence and withdrawal had so dampened even John's habitual good spirits.

'Well, there ye are, love. That's a bit more like it,' he said, as he came through the door that evening and handed her a grubby envelope with his name written on it. 'He gave me that as soon as we were on our own.'

Rose was relieved and delighted as she tipped the battered note and the grubby coins on to the kitchen table. She'd be more than able to replace her tiny reserve in the top drawer, but she was puzzled nevertheless.

'Was this week a very good week, John?'

'No, not that I could see. Not much different to last week. But then, there'd have been no bills to pay. Or at least nothin' pressin'.'

Sitting by the fire late in the evening, enjoying the quiet hour after the children were asleep and the day's work done, he looked across at her and nodded.

'There *is* somethin' strange about the money this week, Rose,' he began, fidgeting with the books he'd been working with earlier in the evening. 'I don't know where the extra came from, but there's a kind of a smile Thomas has when he's pleased, an' it was there when he gave it to me. I asked him how it came to be so much an' he really didn't answer me. He just smiled to himself.'

'To tell you the truth, Rose, I think he had it out

with Mary-Anne for what she did last week,' he continued after only a slight hesitation. 'I saw her comin' back home early this evening and she gave me a good day like she hasn't done in years.'

'Maybe he asked her what she thought wou'd become of her if he'd died and her with three we'eans,' he suggested, with a grim shake of his head. 'There'd be no help from Battlehill for all her runnin' to these classes of hers, for there's no love lost between her and her mother, so I heer tell.'

'Maybe that's what's wrong with her, John,' she suggested. 'If her mother was hard on her, maybe she knows no other way to behave.'

'Aye, they say "like mother, like daughter", an' I suppose there's somethin' in it, but surely a grown woman of her years shoulda learnt to think a bit for herself as to how she treats others.'

'Well, maybe and maybe not. Remember the men who came after you and Thomas to join the lodge. They were in their fifties and still hadn't much time for anyone who wouldn't see things their way.'

'You're right there, Rose,' he said sadly. 'An' I don't think we've seen the back of them. Our wee ones are lucky to have you to teach them what's right an' wrong. But even you can't do it all for them. They'll have to make up their own minds as they get older. Ah hope to Heaven they don't end up like some o' the ones we've had talkin' at us and arguein' the bit.'

She finished her seam, concealed the end of the thread and clipped off the remainder neatly with tiny scissors.

'They're getting older every day,' she said, laughing across at him. 'This time next year, if we're spared, James'll be ten and wee Sarah'll be at school.'

She wrapped up her work in its cloth and fetched a candle from the dresser. John waited till she'd lit it and then put out the lamp.

'Long days for you, love, till Thomas is mended,' she said, as she led the way to the bedroom door.

But the days weren't as long as Rose had expected. Even before Thomas was fully recovered and able to start work, the seasonal dip in work began. And it was worse than usual. Agricultural prices were down, said the Robinsons, and many small farmers were in difficulties once more. With many references to past years, the newspapers began to report the return of evictions and the violence they led to, though there were few from their own part of the country.

In the months before Christmas, farmers delayed the maintenance work usually done after harvest, bent teeth on the reapers, missing points on the harrows, worn winding gear on the hay floats. Horses were put out to grass for the winter to avoid the expense of shoeing. To make matters worse, work that did come in was often not paid for when it was collected. To press old customers in difficulties was not something Thomas or John would have thought right, but the bills for iron, horseshoe nails, and coal, came in regardless.

But that was not the worst of it. After Christmas, the weather turned cold. There were high winds and snow and the water froze in the pails in the wash house. Three times in as many months, Rose went to the bank and drew enough money for a fresh load of turf from Annaghmore. Each time she hoped the cartload would see them through to the warmer weather, but it didn't. There was still snow on the ground in early April and only a few pounds of Sarah's little legacy left.

Sadness and loss had punctuated the winter months. Maggie Robinson had found old Sophie dead in bed one bleak, cold morning. The adults of the community had celebrated a long life and an easy going, but little Sarah had wept day after day, old enough now to feel her loss as she'd not felt it when her beloved Granny Sarah had died.

Hard as Rose found it to comfort Sarah's loss, she found it almost impossible to sustain her poor friend, Mary, as she nursed little Jane. When Dr Lindsay had shaken his head sadly and spoken the dreaded word, 'tuberculosis', Mary was devastated. The ordeal that followed, as Jane faded before her eyes, left Mary failing herself in both body and spirit.

The little girl's death brought on anew all Rose's anxieties about her own children. Every time one of them caught a cold or started coughing, she felt panic stricken, as if she could not bear one more blow.

Day after day, she'd do her best to raise her spirits. She told herself there was little use spending good money to keep up a bright fire, if there was no warmth and welcome to go with it. But little came to help her. Everyday tasks seemed harder when the cold bit to the bone, the snow lay piled deep in the orchard and you had to take a hatchet to break the ice on the well before you could fill a bucket of water. Mary was so locked in grief over Jane that Peggy had to look after her children as well as her own baby, just when she felt strong enough to look for work. The roads were so treacherous, visits to Armagh were rare, even changing the library books became infrequent. Necessity drove her to do more and more sewing and turned it from a pleasure into a wearying chore.

Spring came, late and cold, the trees still not in leaf at the beginning of May. For the first time since she'd had a garden to tend, some of her precious plants failed to appear despite the layers of straw she'd put down to protect them. Work in the forge picked up only slowly, hard frost and then heavy rain making it impossible to begin work on the land.

When Rose looked out through the open door

on the first damp, but mild morning in the middle of May and saw the postman heading toward her, her heart leapt at the thought of news. Even letters had been rare over the long winter. Her sister Mary had been ill for weeks, her brothers silent. Lady Anne was unusually silent, though there'd been a handsome monogrammed card at Christmas with a hasty message of love and remembrances to all the family. Sam had returned to America on League business for a second time.

'Here you are, Missus Hamilton. Someone has news for you,' said the postman cheerfully, as he handed her a fat letter.

Rose beamed at him. She could not possibly mistake the great sweeping curls. The postmark was Dublin, but the hand was Lady Anne's.

*My dearest Rose*, she read, as she settled herself by the window.

> *You are the loveliest friend I could possibly have for you write me such long and interesting letters when I really don't deserve them. I so love hearing from you and I write you wonderful letters in my head, but I've been such a poor correspondent these last months. I am determined that this morning I shall make amends for my neglect, which was in deed and not thought.*
>
> *Harrington has gone to London again,*

my little boy is away at school, and Charlotte is with her governess. So I have told everyone that I am definitely not at home. Except to you, dear Rose.

I am so sorry that the winter has been such a gloomy time for you. Poor Mary. I worry just as you do whenever Charlotte or Alexander get a cough. There is just so little one can do if it's consumption. The school master tells me that in the Ballysadare school they expect to lose as many as twenty children each year with it. And it's not as if the illness were due to lack of food or poor conditions. Auntie Violet's sister-in-law, the Duchess of Langley, lost her eldest son last year. He was seventeen and such a beautiful looking young man.

I wish I had some happy news for you, but apart from Harrington and I being well, most of what I have to tell you makes me very sad, though I don't quite know why it should. Perhaps you will understand, you always did understand things about me better than I ever did.

My mother died last October, only a few months after yours. She'd been an invalid for so long it was hardly a surprise, yet it seemed to upset my father terribly. He said he couldn't bear the place without her, so

*although we tried to encourage him to wait
till the spring, he decided to hand it over to
the cousin who is to inherit it when he dies.
As you see from this address, he has moved
to our Dublin house where he is close to
libraries and the Royal Dublin Society, which
has always been his major interest.*

*Lily and I have supervised the move. We
had no idea he had so many books! She is
going to live with him. She's twenty-seven
now and still not married. She says she never
meets any young men in Kerry, but perhaps
she's said no to all the eligible ones left. At
any rate, she thinks Dublin may suit her
better.*

*It seems that cousin Oliver has no wish
to live at Currane Lodge. At the moment it
is shut up and he is planning to let it, but all
our dear people are gone, except Mr Smithers
and Cook who've come to Dublin with us.
Old Tom the coachman had retired and had
a cottage on the estate. We don't know what
will happen to the retired staff.*

She dropped the letter with a little cry.

'Oh no, not Currane too . . . and poor Thomas . . .'

She saw herself standing in the tiny sitting-room
she'd shared with her mother in the rooms opposite
the new stable block. Empty rooms now. Dust and

sunlight in their small room, dust and sunlight in the great rooms where glass chandeliers hung above fine furniture and family portraits.

Try as she might, she couldn't prevent tears welling up as she thought of all the people who would now have to find new work and a new home. She imagined the house shuttered over as it sometimes was when the family were in Dublin, the carriage yard empty, the stables silent. The clock stopped.

Gone. All gone. That world which had seemed so stable, so fixed.

*I can't understand, Rose dear, why I am so upset at Oliver not wanting to live there. Not that we would have visited. I doubt if he has the slightest wish to know us. And I wasn't all that happy for much of my time there, as you very well know. But I cried when we left and all the house staff came to wave us goodbye before they cleared up the mess of packing and left themselves.*

The letter continued, but she had no heart for any more of it, just at that moment. Lady Anne had tried to cheer herself by telling Rose the good news from the Sligo estate, the results of her own hard work with the school and Harrington's efforts to improve farming practice, but she hardly registered it. In the quiet hours before the children came home from school, all she could think of was Currane, as it had been all through her growing years, and as it was now, empty and desolate, but for the floating memories of days that would never come again.

'Are ye very tired this evenin?' John asked, as Hannah and James closed the bedroom door quietly behind them.

'No, no I'm not tired,' she said quickly.

She went on with her sewing, then sighed suddenly and put it down.

'No, not tired.' She stood up and fetched Lady Anne's letter from the windowsill. 'I've had news today that's made me so sad. Will you read it yourself, or will I tell you?'

'Ye'd better tell me. She has so many curlicues on the words that I lose the thread o' what she's sayin' by the time I've puzzled out what the words are.'

She laughed, grateful to feel a spark of pleasure return.

'Lady Caroline died in the autumn and Sir Capel's signed over Currane to the cousin, but the cousin doesn't want to live there,' she began. 'The place is empty, boarded up since before Christmas. He's hoping to let it.'

'Is that the English cousin? Hertfordshire or thereabouts?'

'Yes, I suppose it is. How did you know?'

'Old Thomas. I learnt a lot from the man, sittin' waitin' for my lady love to come from her work,' he said, smiling slyly at her.

'I seem to remember you did a great job putting the world to rights that summer,' she retorted. 'Young Tom was as deep into the Land League as our Sam and no doubt a few of those visiting grooms carried it back to their own places.'

'Who knows what was started there, Rose. But you and I had some grand evenin's, along by the lake, diden we?'

'We did,' she said softly, wondering if he could understand what the loss of so well-loved a place really meant to her.

'I still don't know how ye ever give up that place for the likes of me. I've never seen the equal of it, all that water and sky, an' the evenin's that warm ye'd never think of a jacket. I know we niver did hear the nightingale, though Sir Capel swore there was one, but sure there were all the wee water fowl and the swans. D'ye mind tellin' me when I asked ye that ye went up that bit of mountain to hear the lark sing.'

She smiled weakly and nodded, her mind so full she could find no words to speak of her loss, even to John. In a handful of golden days, she and Lady Anne had each found the love of their life. Perhaps that's what made the news so poignant. The sharpest memories you have are when you meet that person, but those memories dim with the passage of the years. You treasure a piece of a dress, a faded photograph, a handful of dusty pressed flowers to convince you it really did happen as you remember it. We all lose the time when we first loved. But we don't always lose the place.

Even if all her plans to return to Currane Lodge had come to nothing in the end, knowing its life went on, just as she had left it, was a solace and a hope. A hope that one day, she would stand again by the water's edge or climb her favourite hillside. Now that hope was gone, extinguished for ever. Currane Lodge had become a big, empty house in a far country, its vibrant life dispersed for ever and with it some of the most precious of her memories.

'I wonder what'll happen to the retired staff that live on the estate,' said John slowly. 'They'd no pensions, but they had their house and their turf and Sir Capel saw they never went short. D'ye think yer man'll do the same.'

She shook her head sadly.

'They're not *his* people. They're just people in houses he may want for other purposes. He owes them nothing.'

'Like ourselves the other year at Annacramp?'

'Just like ourselves indeed, love.'

They fell silent as the long, dim evening finally faded to dusk.

'Will I light the lamp, or have ye done enough?'

he asked quietly, his tone shot through with a sadness she knew he didn't know was there.

'Yes, light it for me. I want to see you properly,' she said firmly.

'An' what d'ye see, Rose dear?'

'I see there's something you're not telling me,' she began. 'I've told you my sadness, now you can tell me yours.'

He sighed and dropped his head in his hands. It was always a bad sign. She waited.

'Yer man from Cabragh has bought the cart manufactory like he said he woud,' he began. 'He's a man and his son comin' to start it up at the beginnin' of June,' he went on, his voice as colourless as the darkening evening sky.

# CHAPTER TWENTY-TWO

Throughout the month of June the cart manufactory took from them the business of Lodge members just as John and Thomas had expected. Some of them still came to have their horses shod, but the stone circle for rimming the wheels remained cold. Amongst the men who used to sit so comfortably on the bench inside the door, exchanging the news, there was a wholly new sense of unease and constraint.

The weekly income dropped predictably and they reckoned it would drop further as soon as the manufactory was able to offer machine and tool repairs along with its work on carts and traps. At its best, the summer income would be little more than half what it had been when the two men started out together, some five years earlier.

During slack times in the previous years, Thomas and John had tried various ideas for keeping up their winter takings. They'd approached Turners and Hillocks, with the possibility of making implements for them. They were listened to most courteously, but it was made clear the price either firm could afford to offer for handmade tools would barely cover the costs of making them. They'd be in direct competition with machine made tools, they said, and machine made tools were cheaper and did the job just as well.

At the end of June, the decisive moment came. The partnership between Thomas Scott and John Hamilton was ended, as it had begun, in friendship and mutual respect. Their good neighbours found it hard to tell which of the men was more distressed, Thomas by the prospect of having to go on alone, or John, who now faced the daunting prospect of finding work elsewhere.

For Rose, the first week of July took on a nightmare quality. Each evening the Lambeg drums thundered out on the warm air, an unhappy reminder of the previous year's bitter agitation. The vigour of Lodge members drumming so late into the night, underlined the hurt done to both men, the veiled threats now become a reality.

They lay awake, talking in whispers, light still in the sky as the longest evenings of the year began to shorten imperceptibly. She knew John dreaded the morning. She could guess only too well how he would feel walking past the forge, greeting Thomas as he went. Harder still to bear was what she knew he must feel walking into Armagh, a man looking for work.

He'd been so happy at the forge. Despite the periods of Thomas's depression and withdrawal, and the troubles that had finally driven him out, he'd always been at ease there. He admitted he'd sometimes found the work repetitive but it had never troubled him. Only a month ago, he'd talked openly about it.

'Ach sure when I'm making the fortieth horseshoe, I'm thinkin' about what I read in the books ye bring me. That's how I manage it. Figurin' things out, an' imaginin' things. Wonderin' how long it'll be before we have horseless carriages and ploughing machines. Aye, an' maybe flyin' machines,' he added with a smile.

'Do you really think there'll ever be flying machines, or are you just teasing me?' she'd asked.

'No, I'm perfectly serious,' he said promptly. 'I'm sure James and Sam will live to see road vehicles, even if I don't. Think of it this way, Rose,' he said, looking at her so directly she was almost startled by the brightness of his blue eyes. 'It was 1825 when George Stephenson created Locomotion No. 1. An' it was 1851 when the railway got to Armagh. Now its 1887 and there's railways all over Ireland, with bigger engines and better power weight ratios. They've come on so fast ye could hardly believe it.'

Then he'd laughed unexpectedly.

'Sure my father told me that some people thought that the railways would bring on the end of the world. They said the birds would die with the smoke and the cows lose their milk with fright. But sure nothing happened at all and now anybody can travel anywhere, if they've the price of a ticket, that is.'

'Now there was a time, Rose, when people like Stephenson were experimentin',' he went on, warming to his story. 'Ye see, ye hear nothin' about all that until there's somethin' to try out. But the work's goin' on all the time. Some day we might look back and think "Sure had we but known it, So and So was inventing the steam plough or the steam thresher or the flying machine an' now they're as common as the train."'

Although her main worry was the loss of the job and what they'd do for money if John couldn't find work quickly, she couldn't help being sad at the two men being separated just now, when they'd been getting on famously since Thomas recovered from his accident. There'd always been good fellowship between them, but it had become something deeper and created a light-heartedness which brought pleasure to even the hardest days. Tending her plants in the front flowerbeds, she'd hear them laugh. Now, poor Thomas had lost his friend and colleague through no fault of his own, just as he'd freed himself from the burden he'd long carried.

In the event, she need not have worried, for John found a job immediately. She couldn't quite believe it when he arrived home at midday on the Tuesday of his first week of looking for work.

'Well,' she said, as he came in and sat down at the table, a look of relief on his face.

'Well, we'll not starve yet a while,' he said soberly.

'You've got something already?'

'Yes, second place I tried,' he replied, nodding. 'Drumcairn Mill. Maintenance and repairs. Eight in the mornin' till seven at night. A week's annual holiday for the Twelfth. Good money and steady each week. Unless the demand for cotton drops or the management go bust, that is. Not very likely at the moment from what I heard. Every spindle going and a full order book.'

'But what'll *you* be doin' John?

'Oh, mendin' boilers. Fixin' the looms. Makin' new parts, I expect, when they're past fixin'. There's a big workshop out at the back with anvils and suchlike. An' they've a stable o' horses for the drays that do the deliveries to the weavers. They'll need to be shod. An' the drays kep' runnin' forby.'

'So you won't be indoors all the time?'

'I woulden think so.'

'An' when do you start?'

'The morra,' he said promptly. 'That's the whole point ye see. They've a man off sick and they're desperate. They diden even ask me if I knew one end of a loom from another, though I did tell'em I'd worked in Doagh fifteen years ago.'

'Oh John, are you sure you're doing the right

355

thing?' Rose asked, suddenly full of an unease she couldn't explain.

'Sure it's a job, love. Haven't we got to earn our keep?'

She had to admit that having a known amount of money coming in each week would be a great relief. She hadn't really realised what a burden she'd found it trying to guess how much she needed to save in the summer months to get them through the winter and last winter she hadn't managed it. Even with Hannah helping her with the seams and hems of the babies' dresses and Sam and James fetching the water and doing the dishes to give her more time, it had still been a struggle to turn out enough to keep food on the table and fire on the hearth.

By Christmas, she'd even regretted renewing her subscription to the library. When it became due in October, things hadn't looked too bad, but two months later the five shillings yearly subscription seemed like an extravagance she should not have allowed.

'Well, it'll be different this year,' she promised herself, as she got ready to go into Armagh on a pleasant October morning, leaving the house tidy and empty behind her.

She still hadn't got used to Sarah going to school, but Sarah behaved as if she'd never done anything else. She loved school and was already showing signs of being able to read far more quickly than any of the other children. With no reading book of her own, she couldn't wait to try out her day's work on Sam's as soon as she got home.

'Pity there are no children's books,' she thought, smiling a little at the idea of asking for fairy stories or animal tales at The Armagh Natural History and Philosophical Society, the actual name of the library. 'When they're a little older, I'll can pay the extra two and sixpence and let them come with me. We could all read the magazines in the reading room together and go and look at the cases of birds eggs and the samples of rock when we got tired of sitting down.'

She wondered if she might try some volumes of poetry for Hannah, but the books John enjoyed puzzling over still seemed a bit difficult for James and most certainly were for Sam.

As she walked into Armagh, a train passed just where the line ran close to the road. As the train whistled and let off steam she looked up and saw a red-headed child wave its hand from a carriage window. She waved back, smiling, as the carriages rolled on, towards the complex of sidings and engine sheds at Armagh Station.

She tried to remember what ambitions her brother Sam had admitted to when he was as young as his two nephews. Going fishing with Old Tom seemed more to his taste than trains, but then he'd never seen a train. No, what Sam really loved was books. He'd had the run of Sir Capel's library from the day the old man caught him sitting on the bottom step of a ladder, so engrossed he hadn't even noticed him coming into the room.

Dear Sam. In a few weeks he'd be with them again and this time, he'd be able to stay two nights, for he had a whole week in Belfast. The thought of his coming filled her with excitement and anticipation. He'd have so much to tell about his four crossings of the Atlantic, his visits to New York and Boston and the small towns of up country Pennsylvania. His letters had been brief for him, but she knew there was much he preferred not to put down on paper lest it fall into the wrong hands.

She laughed at herself. 'You're as bad as the children,' she said aloud.

In his brief visit last year, Uncle Sam had made such an impression on them, they were talking excitedly already about all they were going to ask him. He'd kept his word and a few weeks after his visit, a large parcel arrived for them. There were books on railways for James and Sam, ribbons and a little brooch for Hannah, and for Sarah, a frame with brightly coloured beads to help her with learning to count.

She walked on, enjoying the morning, till she came to Mill Row. She remembered the very first time she'd gone into town. She'd waved to some children playing in the dust and they'd stared at her unblinkingly. Though the doors of the tiny houses stood open, there was no one about. As she passed the mill itself, she heard the roar and clatter of the looms in the great four-storey building and thought what John had once told her about it.

'Drumcairn and Gillis,' he'd said. 'Gillis was where the brothers worked till they got the money for America. Powerful noisy things looms, ye'll hear them as ye go past on yer way inta town. The spinnin's not so bad for noise, but the pouce fillin' the air is worse than the roar of the looms, I'd be thinkin'. The brothers used to say the forge was dirty work, but sure that sort of dirt you can wash off.'

As she looked up at the rows of windows she wondered just where he was and what exactly he'd be doing. And whether, once again, he'd told her the half of it.


From the moment Sam arrived on Saturday afternoon to the time he left for the six o'clock train to Portadown on Sunday it seemed he'd always one more good story to tell. The children were insatiable. What was it like on a ship? Where did he sleep? Was it stormy? Was he frightened? Did he see any whales?

Rose laughed as she moved back and forth preparing a tasty stew for the evening meal. She'd always been proud of her brother. As a little boy she'd helped him with his lessons and been pleased when he'd turned out to be so able. Now she was just as delighted with Sam, the model uncle, impressed by his willingness to answer honestly whatever they asked, and equally ready to ask his own questions in return.

Not surprisingly, he found it easier to talk to the boys. She listened as he described the new railroads stretching right across America and the differences between the modest engines they'd seen in the maintenance sheds in Armagh and the very much larger ones that steamed across the continent. As she listened, it surprised her to discover just how much James and Sam knew already. She'd seen John, sitting at the table explaining things to them, making sketches for them at the back of the notebook where he made his own notes, but she'd hadn't appreciated what a good teacher he must be.

What touched her particularly was the way Sam talked to Hannah and Sarah, making sure they had as much of his time and attention as the boys. He'd remembered what they'd said to him on his last visit and he did his best to find out what interested them now.

'Now then, bedtime for all of you,' she said firmly, as Sarah leant against Hannah with her eyes closed and James and Sam fell silent at last. 'Uncle Sam will be here in the morning, if you haven't worn him out completely.'

She lit the candle while they all went out to the privy and gave it to Hannah when they came back, one by one, shivering from the chill of the dark starry night.

'I'll come in five minutes to tuck you in,' she said, as she swung out the crane and hung the kettle on its chain over the glowing fire.

'Not a sound out of them,' said Sam a little later, as he took his cup of tea from her hand.

'Are ye surprised, Sam?' said John laughing. 'Sure, they've never stopped since ye arrived. I hope ye didn't think ye were comin' to get a rest from the big city.'

'No, I didn't,' he said, honestly. 'I came to tell you all the things I didn't feel I could put in a letter. The good and the bad.'

Rose saw a shadow pass over his face as he said 'the bad' and was immediately anxious. So often these days, even now life was so much easier than a year ago, she still found herself worrying over trifles, imagining misfortunes that might yet befall them.

'America is extraordinary,' he began. 'It's the best and the worst, full of opportunity, yet riddled with poverty and disease. You always hear about the good things when people write home, and I think I understand why they do it, but I've seen things in New York that upset me far more than when I was helping poor souls evicted from their cabins.'

They sat silent, surprised at the whole change in Sam's tone and watched as he collected himself.

'I joined the Land League to help people who

361

had little to eat and no land of their own and no one to speak up for them. Yet those people, poor as they were, had fresh air and neighbours in the same boat. The same people now, in New York, live in one room in a tenement, bound to long hours of hard labour which they were never used to, just to pay the rent. They earn so little, once the rent is paid, they can't afford to buy the food they need.'

He paused and sighed, his face grown lined and grim.

'The death rate from consumption is higher among Irish immigrants than among any other group, even those living in the same filthy tenements, a family to a room.'

'An' they're no better off, after all their hardship?' asked John, his eyes wide, his brow furrowed with concentration.

'Not one bit better, and more likely to die in a year or two, hungry and homesick, than they might have been where they were,' he said sadly.

'So you don't recommend America, Sam?' said John quietly, shuffling his boots on the edge of the hearth.

'Oh I do, yes, I do,' he said nodding vigorously. 'But that's the contradiction of it. Go up country, away from the cities, into the Alleghenies or deeper into Pennsylvania, and you're in a different world. Great country, rivers and woods, small settlements, good land for cultivation and grants still available.

It's a paradise compared to the city, sheer heaven for any poor people who can get that far. Plenty of work on the land, or in the settlements, a good climate and rich crops. But that's not where you'll find many Irish. Most of them arrive with nothing, and end up with nothing. More's the pity,' he said, picking up his teacup and drinking thirstily.

They sat silent, each of them absorbed in their own thoughts. It was Rose who spoke first.

'As always, Sam, it's those who need help the most that get the least.'

'Aye, and it's the ones in most need that are most tempted by the advertising. You've only to read what the shipping offices put in their windows or in the newspapers. Three meals a day. Sounds wonderful if you're only used to one. But it's a different story when they're onboard. I had men tell me about the rotten meat they threw overboard, the weevils that fell out of the biscuits when you broke them. Half-starved people went on starving at sea. Some of them died as soon as they arrived. And that's still been going on through the 70s and 80s. Even the poorest of the poor can be exploited by men who have ships to fill,' he said bitterly.

She looked at her brother closely. She read his distress and his need to share it, but she couldn't understand why he was now painting such a dark picture, when he'd shown such enthusiasm when talking to the children.

'I'm going back myself in the springtime to Pennsylvania,' he said slowly, naming a small town, with such a strange name that Rose didn't quite catch it. 'I met a girl when I stayed there, both times I went.' He paused and looked sheepish. 'There's a job waiting for me. Her father's a government surveyor and they're crying out for trained men. As soon as I arrive, we're going to be married.'

He stopped abruptly and looked from one to the other, almost as if he expected them to protest. When there was only a gentle nodding of heads, he went on.

'To tell you the truth, I feel guilty,' he said unhappily. 'Guilty for leaving the movement. Guilty for going away when there's work to be done here. I was passionate about the Land League, you know that Rose, don't you? But I've seen all sorts of corruption set in. People join up now for what they can get for themselves. And I don't think Home Rule will solve anything even were it to come. There are too many people who are too selfish, too greedy, too full of their own way of thinking . . .'

He broke off, overcome with emotion. John looked across at Rose, not knowing what to do. She dropped her eyes, which told him to stay where he was, though she knew he was acutely uncomfortable. Expressing his own feelings was hard enough for him, but sharing someone else's he found almost impossible.

'Sam, there's no point feeling guilty,' Rose began. 'What good is that going to do anyone? If you go and make a successful life out there, that could put you in a position to do more than you ever imagined for those in need. You've tried so hard, I know you have. But sometimes the way we choose first isn't really the right way for us. Had you thought of that?'

'No, I hadn't. I'd always imagined that if you looked at the facts and you didn't think what you saw was fair, you ought to try to change them. That's just simple logic.'

'Yes, I agree. But sometimes logic doesn't work for individuals. You must hold to the good that you did,' she said, looking at him directly. 'There are many people have cause to be grateful for what Davitt achieved and you must take credit for your part in that. But maybe now you're called on to tread a different path.'

'It may be so,' he said quietly, with a long look at both of them. 'But I can't stop feeling somehow I'm abandoning my fellow men. Running away to make myself comfortable.'

'Yer not doing that at all, man dear,' said John abruptly. 'Sure you're an educated man and who knows what's in ye yet. Sure ye might be inventin' some great idea. Ach, I'm not thinkin' of steam ships and flyin' machines an' suchlike, that we were talkin' about earlier. I'm thinkin' of the likes of Tom Paine and Keir Hardie that have tried to make life better for ordinary workin' people. Sure who knows where ye'll go inside yer head when yer not so close to the problem?'

'John's right, Sam. Sometimes one has to get away from a problem to see it more clearly. You might manage far more for Ireland in America than you ever could in Dublin.'

'I think that hope might reconcile me a bit. I'll sleep on it and tell you tomorrow,' he said, standing up. 'I hate to admit it, but suddenly I'm so tired I could sleep on a wooden shelf,' he added, yawning hugely.

'Well, I'm glad to say we can offer you a little better than that,' she said, as John went into the bedroom and returned with a borrowed mattress and she reached for a bundle of blankets she'd thrown over the arm of the settle to air in the heat of the fire.


'I'll only be an hour, John. Is that all right,' Rose said, as Sam put on his coat and closed up his bag.

'As long as you like, love. But are you sure you don't mind comin' back in the dark?'

'Not a bit. I know the road like the back of my hand, as the saying is. Anyway the moon's nearly full. It'll be well up by the time Sam's on the train.'

The goodbyes were said. Sam kissed Sarah and Hannah, who had gone very quiet, then shook hands with the boys in a very grown-up way. He hugged John and said nothing at all.

'Good luck, Sam,' John said, as he left them at the end of the lane, having lit their way through the scattered debris in front of the forge.

The night was still, the sky pierced with myriads of stars. Their breath rose on the cold air.

'A bit different from last time,' he said, falling into step beside her in the middle of the deserted road.

'Very different, indeed, Sam,' she said, remembering the pleasant summer evening when they'd last walked to the six o'clock train.

'Do you remember Ma ever saying to you that we like to think change comes gradually, building up quietly to the point where we recognise that something is different. But it's not like that at all. Sometimes life can change in a moment,' she said, as they strode out.

'Yes, she did say that to me. But I didn't grasp it at the time. It's true, nevertheless. It happened to me one night in a club in Dublin when I first heard Davitt speak. Then it happened again at a barn dance in Pennsylvania. I'd only gone because it would have seemed rude not to when I'd had such generous hospitality.'

'And you met Eva?'

'Yes,' he said, laughing. 'How did you guess?'

'Well, it wasn't very hard. Something had to have happened very quickly to have you going back to get married. It wasn't much different with me and John.'

'He's a good man, Rose. I think I understand him better now than I did a year ago. Maybe I've changed.'

'I think you have. But then, I think he has too. A lot has happened.'

They walked on steadily, their journey punctuated with the tiny lights from the few cottages on their way. They talked of Sam's wife to be, American born, from a family of Bavarian immigrants, most of whom still spoke only German. And they talked about the long future, hoping they would meet again. They promised each other they'd take up their old way of writing now there'd be nothing of which they might not speak freely.

'Do you think John is happy in the new job, Rose?' Sam asked as they passed Drumcairn, the solid black mass of the mill outlined against the starry sky.

'I'm not sure, Sam. I'm biding my time. Even if he's happy enough, I'm not sure I am. It could just be that in the end, we'll follow where someone we trust has led. You'd give us advice, wouldn't you?'

'Rose dear, I'd give a lot more than advice if I thought I could have my big sister on the same continent. You'd only have to say the word.'

# CHAPTER TWENTY-THREE

Four months later, on a mild April morning, Rose beamed at the postman as he handed over an envelope covered with brightly coloured stamps. She took it indoors and sat down at the kitchen table. It was all she could do to stop herself ripping open Sam's first letter from America, but she knew the boys would want to save the stamps. By the time she'd extracted the closely written sheets, she was so excited and agitated it was all she could do to hold the paper steady enough to read.

> *My dearest Rose,*
>
> *I am writing this on board ship, but the captain says we will arrive at midday tomorrow. By the time you receive it, I shall be in Pennsylvania with Eva and her family. I can hardly believe it has all happened so quickly. The Atlantic crossing will have taken only eight days, though this ship, the Germanic, has previously done it in seven*

*and a half. You may tell John from me Ulstermen build great ships and Harland and Wolff have every right to the fame they've won.*

*I have thought of you so often on the crossing and I wonder if you and John will follow me. If you do, I must insist you come by steamship. Yes, it is more expensive, but I am convinced that the shorter journey will be better for all of you. My first crossing was under sail and it was often rough, people were sick and the children frightened. Even with similar heavy seas, the effect is much diminished on a steamship.*

*As I am travelling on my own, I have the cheapest possible ticket. I will not pretend it is very comfortable. Once again, I feel you should think about second class. It may seem a great extravagance, but I'm convinced it would be money well spent, a little rest and pleasure for both you and John and an experience to be remembered for the children.*

*I wish I could say that I would help with the expense, but starting out as I am myself, I just don't know what the immediate future will bring. Eva has saved up a little money for us, but as you know my work with the League was poorly paid, which means that*

*I have no resources of my own to add to it. What I do hope is that, by then, we would have a home, however modest, where you would be welcome for as long as you need to find your own place.*

*I have asked Eva's father about the prospects of work for John and he says that skilled craftsmen of any kind are in such demand that he would have a choice of jobs and in most cases will also be entitled to a grant of land.*

Rose put the letter down and stared out of the window.

'A grant of land,' she said aloud, as she focused on the path from the forge to Thomas's house.

The tall pear tree almost opposite was already showing grey points as the buds grew thicker in the mild air. The year was moving upwards, the confinement of winter's dark and cold would soon be ended. She longed for the warmth and light of summer days when she could sit outside with her sewing, when the washing dried in a long morning and going to the well was a pleasure.

'A grant of land,' she repeated.

She smiled to herself. Yes, the phrase had something quite magical about it. A promise of openness, of space and light.

She drew back sharply from the window as she

caught a glimpse of movement under the archway of Thomas's house. A moment later, her Bible under her arm, Mary-Anne tramped down the path, looking neither to the right or to the left. Nor did she pause a moment at the forge to say a word to Thomas.

Rose sighed. Perhaps she should be grateful that Mary-Anne had never again knocked on her door, since the morning after Sam brought the news of their mother's death. But then again, she'd never spoken when they'd met in the lane or on the shortcut over to Robinson's, choosing to lead her life behind closed doors. Nor was there any obvious softening of her resentment towards herself and her family. For all she knew, she was still referred to as 'yer wuman from Kerry.'

When she was sure Mary-Anne was on her way, Rose moved back into the sunlight and read the rest of Sam's letter. He wrote of the preparations being made for their wedding. In a small township like Eva's, the real importance of a wedding was the opportunity for a huge celebration. Eva had warned him a special beer was always brewed and he'd be expected to prove his manhood, not by abducting the bride, but by lowering a very large tankard all at one go.

Rose laughed and let her thoughts move into this new world of Sam's. A kinder climate, he said. Though there was often more snow in winter, the cold that came with it was not so hard to bear. Often there was sunshine and there was less of the damp, misty weather she found so depressing.

Sometimes she wondered if it was the lack of space in their home and in their immediate surrounding that weighed down her spirits so. Other times, she felt it had to be the pervasive presence of Mary-Anne, her closed door, closed face and lack of joy.

Suddenly and quite unexpectedly, she found herself walking round Sarah's garden in Annacramp. A great longing overwhelmed her. She could see so vividly the tall stems of delphinium, their heavy blooms carefully supported with sticks hidden in their foliage, the prolific foxgloves which never needed planting, only thinning out. She saw the bright flame of geraniums in window boxes, their descendants in her own windows, tended and slipped each year, so that Sarah's garden would never totally disappear.

After their move, she'd scolded herself whenever she'd caught herself longing to return to the old house, but now she let her mind move as it would. She thought of the field behind, the cow they'd bought when James was on the way, the chickens who'd earned her egg money. For all her years there, she'd been so happy.

And now? Could she say she was unhappy? Or was she just older and wiser? Yes, she was that, but sadder also. Sarah once said the longer you lived the more there was of sadness and loss. You couldn't avoid it, so you had to find what there was to set against it.

She and John had had their hard times, indeed they had, but there'd never been any hurt between them. She'd never regretted marrying him, or leaving behind her known world. The children were good children, even when they were cross, or upset. They'd never been hard to love, or hard to please. When she'd been in poor spirits herself, it was the stories they brought from school, the games they invented, the questions they asked, that brought her to herself again, ready to find some little treat, some small pleasure to share with them.

What would it be like for the children if they left all that was known and secure and set out on such an adventure? What would they gain in a new place, among such different people, to balance the loss?

She sat for a long time, letting the thoughts move back and forward, as if she sensed it was important to have a very clear picture of what was at stake. Only when the fire needed making up did she move for there'd be no bread if she didn't. Even so, only a fraction of her mind was given to the familiar task.

A little later, the bread hardening on its stand,

her hands washed and well dried, ready to take up her sewing, she paused again, picked up the newspaper from the window sill and looked at the long list of advertisements for sailings to America. There were plenty to chose from and many from Belfast, both sail and steam. She went back to her sewing, her mind occupied with figures and calculations. All the while she sat, she could hear Sam's words, 'A grant of land,' echoing in her mind. She really hadn't the slightest idea why the phrase should have lodged there, teasing continually on the edge of consciousness, but sooner or later its meaning would emerge. As Sarah used to say: 'If you wait long enough, time solves most of your puzzles.'

Rose didn't have to wait long. A couple of weeks later the April weather turned bitterly cold right at the end of the month. There was no snow but heavy frost made the ground hard as stone and the road into Armagh icy and treacherous.

'Mind yerself, won't you,' she said to John, as she gave him his piece.

'Don't worry love, the boots has a good grip,' he said kissing her as she walked to the door with him, the children still asleep at this early hour.

John didn't fall on the road, but three nights later, arriving home later than usual, he almost fell into the kitchen when he opened the door. His face was ashen as he began to shake. A few minutes later he was violently sick.

'James, help me get Da to the fire,' she said, putting an arm round him and trying to steady him the short distance across to the settle.

'Was it raining out there?' she asked startled, for his clothes were wet through, the sodden fabric icy to the touch.

'What?' he said, screwing up his face.

She repeated the question, but he still didn't hear her.

'No, it's not raining Ma,' Hannah said sharply, her eyes grown round with shock. 'It hasn't rained all day.'

John was sick again and upset at the mess he made. A few minutes later, he began to waver back and forth on the settle, his face taking on a greenish hue. It was only the quick action of Rose and both boys that stopped him falling heavily when he passed out.

'James, go and see if Thomas is still working,' she said quickly. 'If he's not, you may go to the house. If it's Mrs Scott, say you've a message for Thomas. Ask him would he come over.'

Rose and Hannah prised off the sodden jacket and found his shirt was just as saturated.

'Get me a towel, love,' she said to Hannah, who had put her warm hands on her father's icy chest. 'Sam, put more turf on the fire, please. Small pieces at a time to keep it hot. Sarah, sit well back in case the sparks fly. Don't worry now,' she added, seeing Sarah's eyes large and bright, firmly fixed on John's crumpled figure. 'Da'll be better soon.'

'Ach, dear a dear, what's happened at all,' said Thomas, crossing the room in a couple of strides and dropping down on his knees beside her.

'Could we get him to bed, Thomas. His clothes are soaked through and he's been very sick.'

Thomas felt John's head, which burnt with fever, while his naked chest remained icy cold, despite the warm fire so close to where he lay.

'Come on now, man, up ye come,' said Thomas, his arm firmly round John's waist.

To Rose's surprise and amazement, he lifted John to his feet and held him there till John opened his eyes and looked at him bemused.

'Come on till yer bed, man. Ye've wrought too hard,' he said reassuringly, as he half marched, half carried him across the floor, Hannah darting in front of them to open the bedroom door.

They stripped off his clothes and got him into bed, rubbing him vigorously with dry towels, then wrapping him in the blankets Hannah and Sarah had warmed in front of the fire.

'Do you think I should send for the Doctor, Thomas? Would he come out at this hour?'

'He might. It's not that late. I'll see if George has the mare in the stable. If he hasn't, I'd be as quick walkin' into town as fetchin' her up from the meadow and harnessin' her. Do yer best to get him warmed up in the body. I'll be back as soon as I can.'

Thomas was as good as his word. He arrived back in less than an hour, but the Doctor couldn't come. He was out with a woman in labour and daren't leave her until the situation was resolved one way or another. He'd be sure to come first thing in the morning.

Rose would never forget that night. Like the night when she and Sophie had sat up with Sarah, she didn't know whether or not she was going to lose the love of her life. Thomas tried to reassure her, but John was so sick he couldn't even keep water in his stomach. His head was wet with perspiration, but his body remained chill for all their efforts to warm him.

'I wish I had a few good bricks I could heat in the fire,' said Thomas, as they wrapped him again in warm blankets. 'Have ye anythin' like old stone bottles or maybe a flower pot?'

'Yes, I think I have. They're only small though.'

'No matter. They're better than nothin."

She took a candle to the wash house and poked around at the back door, found the flowerpots and two old ginger beer bottles. They were clean for she'd used them for bunches of flowers, but the pots were still full of soil. Hurriedly, she scraped them out with a knife and rubbed at them with a wet cloth, feeling the weight of every passing minute, so anxious was she to get back to John, lying inert as if he would never move again. At last they were clean and she ran back into the house.

'Great girl. You sit here now and we'll see what we can do,' he said, as he took them from her and went out into the kitchen.

He came back after a very short time, towels wrapped round the bottles he'd heated with boiling water and the pots he'd cooked up in the fire. They kept replacing them with fresh ones, until finally John's body lost it's deadly chill. Only then did Thomas speak of going.

'Get in beside him, Rose. Sure wouldn't that bring any man back from the dead,' he said, gently as they went to the door and she tried to find words to thank him. 'I'll be over in the mornin' as soon as I see your smoke.'


The Doctor arrived shortly after Thomas's visit. He looked older and more tired than when she'd last seen him, but he'd lost nothing of his sharpness nor his kindliness.

'Not often I see you, Mrs Hamilton,' he said cheerfully. 'I congratulate you on your healthy children. It's years since I was last here. Now what's this about your good man?' he added kindly.

John had woken at the sound of voices, but made

no move. His ghastly pallor had been replaced by a slightly yellow look. When the doctor asked him to sit up, to sound out his chest, he had to let Rose help him.

'How long have you been in the mill now, John?' Doctor Lindsay asked casually.

John looked quickly at Rose, who repeated the question.

'About nine months,' he replied, very weakly.

'And when did you move to the spinning rooms?'

John screwed up his face, opened his mouth slightly and waited. Doctor Lindsay repeated the question.

'I'm not in the spinnin' rooms, not usually that is,' John began. 'I'm mostly in the workshop. But there was new looms went in this week. The heat in them rooms is desperate,' he said, shaking his head.

'And the noise, John?'

John nodded.

'And the heat, and the smell and the spray of water to keep the fibre moist,' the doctor added, deliberately raising his voice.

John nodded and looked slightly sheepish.

'Well, I'm glad to say there's nothing wrong with your lungs. I can't tell about your hearing, but it doesn't usually deteriorate this quickly. It's probably a result of the last week and will improve with rest,' he said thoughtfully.

'But you've had a warning,' he said, looking

severe. 'Never, never again, if you want to live, come out of those rooms with your clothes wet and walk home in the cold night air. I've know men do that, catch pneumonia and be gone in three days,' he said matter-of-factly. 'Fortunately, you're made of tougher stuff and you're not half-starved. But be warned. Keep dry clothes at your work and get into the fresh air at the meal breaks. Stay in bed today, stay in the house tomorrow, and don't go back to the mill till you have your full strength. A week if you can afford it. If you're not on your feet in three days send for me again,' he said, putting his stethoscope back in his bag and snapping it shut.

Rose shut the bedroom door behind them. As he washed his hands in the water she'd left ready at the kitchen table, she offered him a cup of tea.

'Sadly, I must say no. I remember the last one I had here, by your bright fire. How is the little one. Sarah, was it?'

'It was indeed. My goodness, what a memory,' she said, beaming at him.

'I try, but old age plays havoc with it. Especially after a short night,' he said, as he picked up the clean towel and dried his hands vigorously.

'It was a woman in labour. My neighbour, Thomas, told me,' she said, tentatively.

He nodded briefly and Rose didn't ask the question shaping in her mind, for his face told her quite clearly the woman had not survived.

'Your good man should feel better quite soon. Plenty of spring water and food when he wants it, but not until he asks. It's a pity about the partnership with Thomas,' he said sadly. 'I heard what happened to them. It sometimes makes me despair that men can behave in such a way, making enemies to fight when there's enemies in plenty round every corner. But illness and poverty are not as exciting as waving banners and playing soldiers,' he added bitterly.

He picked up his half crown from the table and put it in his pocket.

'I hear you're a loss yourself to the healing profession. It doesn't surprise me.'

'What do you mean?' she asked, totally surprised by his remark.

'The Matron of the Infirmary's an old friend of mine. She was rather impressed by the way you coped with Thomas's injury. She thinks he's lucky to have survived.'

'Thanks goodness he did. He saved me last night. I was wild with worry.'

''Tis a weakness of women, I fear. Yet it usually comes from love, so I tend to forgive it. Even when it causes me a mite of trouble,' he added with a dry smile.

He opened the door and the bitter cold air touched her face.

'You did right to call me, but you've no cause

for worry today,' he said, reassuringly. 'You must think ahead, however. The spinning rooms can cost a man dear.'

John's recovery was much as Dr Lindsay had expected. At Rose's insistence, he took a week at home, despite the fact that he felt perfectly well after three or four days.

She found it strange to have him all to herself in the morning hours. Once he was on his feet again, he wouldn't sit idle, but helped with her work and fetched water from the well. After a day or two, the weather changed again. Suddenly, it was warm enough to sit on the wall of the back garden where he'd set a broad plank in cement to make a seat for them beyond the shadow of the house.

Sitting there one afternoon, she decided the time had come to share what she'd been thinking about, ever since he'd come home and collapsed on her.

'Ye've it all worked out in yer head, haven't you?' he said, looking at her in amazement, when she'd finished.

'Yes,' she agreed, laughing. 'I have to admit it. I've been thinking about it ever since Sam's visit. I even made some calculations a month or so ago. But it was the day you slept the clock round it really came to me. I know you were glad to get the job, John, and I know we can be careful, like Doctor Lindsay advised us, but I don't want you going on at the mill, year after year. I think we'll have to find some other way of earning our living that's better for you, and better for all of us.'

They sat in the sun, the insects now busy with the flowers that had bloomed in the sudden warmth.

'So when would you see us goin'?'

'It'll take a year at least to save up enough for the fares, more if we have a bad winter like the one before last,' she said easily. 'And maybe five to six months for rail fares and something to keep us going while you see what's best for you.'

'An' woud ye think the childer could face it?'

'They're growing up fast, John. Even Sarah is no baby. I'm sure they'd be sad to leave wee friends and the place they know. But then, so will we. It can't ever be an easy decision, but I think we should consider it as a real possibility.'

'Rose dear, there's no considerin' to be done. You've always shown me the way when I couldn't see any way meself, like when we were put out at Annacramp. Tell me what ye want an' I'll do what I can to help.'

'What I most want, John, is for you to stay well,' she said, touching his cheek. 'You gave me an awful fright.'

'Sure I think I frightened m'self, Rose. I've niver been as sick as that in me life. When Thomas lifted me up off the floor, I couldn't have got up if ye'd paid me.'

They sat silent for a little.

'Will we tell the children d'ye think?' John asked tentatively.

'No, love,' she said, shaking her head. 'We'll not tell *anyone*. We've a fair way to go. We don't know what lies ahead of us that might hold us back. We'll wait till we're ready to buy the tickets.'

'It'll be a wee secret, Rose,' he said grinning. 'Sure we've not had many of those, have we?' he laughed. 'An' then again, sure if it didn't come off, we'd be none the worse, for nobody knowed in the first place.'

# CHAPTER TWENTY-FOUR

A year later, on Easter Monday, Rose and John took the four children up to Todd's field, a steeply sloping meadow where generations of children had trundled their Easter eggs. It was a wild, blowy April day, full of great towering white clouds, but there was no cold in the breeze that caught Rose's skirts and threw Hannah's long dark hair across her eyes.

'What's the prize, Ma?' said James, as she opened her bag and handed them each a hard-boiled egg.

'It's a surprise,' she said, laughing.

'They're yellow, Ma. How did you do that?' asked Sarah, as she examined her egg carefully, her brow furrowed in concentration.

'James and Sam collected whin blossom for me over in Robinson's bog,' Rose began, 'where the rocks break through at the far end. They got a few scratches between them,' she said laughing again and turning to the boys as they eyed the slope. 'It takes a lot of blossom to fill a can.'

'And then you boiled it up?'

'That's right,' said John, looking down at her. 'Same as last year, but they were brown then.'

'That was tea leaves,' she said firmly.

All around them children were rolling their eggs down the steep slope, the air full of cries of triumph or despair.

'Now remember,' said John, 'not too hard. And don't throw. Only whole eggs win prizes.' he said, settling himself on the grass beside Rose.

'Best of three, Da,' said Sam.

'Best of three, it is then,' he agreed, taking four small pieces of stick from his pockets. 'Whose doing marker?'

'I am,' said Hannah, 'Sam did it last year and James the year before.'

'Right then, off you go.'

They sat for a while, watching the four children organise themselves and pick a spot where their eggs wouldn't collide with anyone else's as they rolled down the slope. James gave the signal and all four children launched their eggs downhill, running after them and encouraging them as they slowed down.

'James has got tall, hasn't he?' said John, as they watched him come back up the slope.

'And he looks more like you every day,' she replied, as she saw him stoop to pick up a small child who'd fallen over.

'Who's Sarah like?' he asked suddenly, as he watched her retrieve her unbroken egg from a clump of grass.

'Like herself, I think,' she replied. 'She's nearly as tall as Hannah and she's only six in June. She's already passed Sam at school, in reading anyway.'

There was a whoop of glee from the slope as Sam's egg far outstripped anyone else's on the second throw. Hannah looked crossly at her own egg and went and changed Sam's marker.

'They seem so happy here, Rose. Are we right, d'you think, to take them away?'

'If I were sure they'd go on being happy, I might say no. But it's not just for the children that we're going. You've had a good year, I know, and not been ill again, but we can't depend on that. And there's your hearing to think of as well. Sometimes by Saturday you can't hear me properly if you've had a lot of work indoors.'

'Aye, you're right. There's times I coulden stick it at all if I thought there was no end to it,' he admitted, turning his head away to look out over the green countryside in the direction of Cannon Hill, where the obelisk was just visible in the clear light.

'How are we doin' with the money?'

'Better than I expected. I planned to save so much a week, all being well. Then I deducted a bit for emergencies, but we haven't had any, thank God. We've the full passage money and a bit more.

The summer should give us all I'd allowed for.'

'So, we'd be lookin' at September?'

'All being well, yes.'

A huge cheer went up from the slope below. Sarah had outstripped them all on the third roll. Hannah had her turn and fell short in a clump of grass, the boys did their best, but Sam's egg hit a stone, and James's just failed to match Sarah's carefully planned effort on the smoothest piece of slope she could find.

Rose and John clapped hard and as the children raced back up the slope towards them. Rose brought out the buttered scones and the bag of sweets she'd brought for a prize.

'Eggs first,' she said, as she held out a paper bag for the discarded yellow shells. 'Here you are, Sarah. Well done,' she said, giving her a kiss and handing her the bag of sweets.

Sarah beamed with delight, opened the bag and peered inside.

'You first, Ma. Then Da,' she said, as she held out the bag towards them.

'That was a great day, Rose. I wish we had more like it,' John said wistfully, as they sat by the fire in the quiet hour they so enjoyed before they themselves went to their early bed.

'I was thinking we might take them to the seaside in June,' she said quietly.

'And how would we do that?' he asked.

'I hear the Methodists are planning an excursion to Warrenpoint. The children were told about it in school. Everyone's welcome, though I think the Methodist children go free. They say it'll be a shilling each, but we've done so well, we could manage it. The biggest expense would be your losing a day's pay, but I'd love us to go. Sure, when did you and I last see the sea?'

'A brave while ago, now Rose.'

'Maybe if we're planning to cross the ocean, it would be a good thing to take them to the sea,' he said thoughtfully. 'Though Warrepoint's hardly the Atlantic,' he went on. 'It's better than nothin'. I'll certainly ask for the day off. Is the date settled yet?'

'Yes, it is. Twelfth of June,' she said with a little smile.

'Ach is it? Your birthday and Sarah's,' he said, delighted. 'Sure, wouldn't it be worth a week or two's savings for such a big day. That's settled then. I'll put in a word with the foreman tomorrow.'

Two weeks before the 'big day', as all the family came to call it, she bought the tickets from the young Methodist Sunday School teacher in her drapers in English Street. An old friend, she'd been buying her fabric and trimmings from him since he'd begun to serve his time.

'Good news, Mrs Hamilton,' he said, as he took

the small rectangles of cardboard from a box under the counter. 'They've dropped the price to tenpence and children are going for half. A few more pennies for ice-cream and rock,' he added, as he counted out the tickets.

'That *is* good news,' she said warmly. 'I really had to think twice about it. Six shillings *is* a lot of money.'

'You're right there,' he agreed. 'I think many people felt the same. It's been non-stop since the price came down. This is my third box of tickets and I'll have to ask my superintendent for more. They're nearly gone. Let's hope we get a lovely day, there's been a right few wet ones recently.'

The tickets were viewed excitedly when she got home. Sarah insisted in reading every word of print aloud, wanting to know what *Non-transferable* meant and why it said *Available only on day of issue*. Hannah asked if there was going to be a band. She'd heard the Methodists had engaged The Royal Irish Fusiliers to walk them to the station. James and Sam asked if they could go and see the engine before they left.

She did her best to answer their questions, make appropriate promises, and keep their excitement within bounds. She was anxious lest they be sadly disappointed, but it was she herself who had the biggest disappointment before the day came.

'No go, I'm afeerd, Rose,' said John, the previous

Friday evening, as he handed her the envelope with his wages. 'Yer man was sorry himself, said his own wee ones was goin' with his missus, but there's two new looms goin' in that day, so I have to be there,' he said sadly. 'Now don't worry about the new looms,' he went on quickly, when he saw the look on her face. 'Two looms is only a few hours work, an' sure it's summer. I'll not take any harm, I promise you. But I'm sorry I can't come. Can ye get a refund for the ticket and have a few more ice-creams?' he suggested, trying to put a good face on it.

Rose hid her own disappointment. She wasn't going to spoil the biggest outing the children had ever had. She entered into all their plans, discussed what they would take in their bag of food, whether they would have to wear their shoes or not and how early they'd have to get up to be in good time for the ten o'clock departure.

In the event, all the children were awake before she and John had stirred at half past six and they were all ready to leave by eight o'clock.

'Go and say hello to Thomas,' she said, wanting a few minutes by herself to collect her thoughts.

She stood in the middle of the kitchen, trying to think what she might have forgotten. The tickets were safe in her purse with some money. Hannah and Sam had already taken charge of the two bags of food.

'Of course,' she said, bending down to the fire and beginning to rake the hot embers to the centre. 'Not a good idea to come home to no fire when we're all tired and wanting a cup of tea,' she said to herself, as she covered the hot embers and made sure they were thoroughly damped down.

She got up, brushed the fine flecks of dust from her best skirt and went and looked at herself in the bedroom mirror.

'Happy birthday, Rose,' she said, as she tidied away a few stray threads of hair and adjusted the stand up collar of her blouse.

She touched the little brooch her mother had pinned inside the blouse she was making for her when she died. A simple brooch. More of a pin really. A thin bar of gold supporting a single red stone. It looked so pretty against the white of her finest cambric blouse.

'Thirty-six, today, and no grey hairs yet,' she said aloud, laughing at herself as she put her comb in her bag, checked that she had handkerchief as well as purse and went to collect the children from the forge.

Although it was not yet nine o'clock, the station was full of people. Traps and carts were arriving every few minutes and dropping families and little groups of friends. There was a long queue at the ticket office. Some people must have decided at the last minute when they saw how glorious the day was going to be.

Rose had never seen so many people she knew all in one place, not even at church.

'Ma, when's the band coming?' asked Sarah.

'Can we go up and see the engine first?' James countered.

She looked at the station clock and reckoned that the Methodists would hardly leave their hall in Abbey Street before nine-thirty for the walk to the station.

'Yes, we'll go and see the engine now. Then we'll come back here for the band. All right?'

To her surprise, a long row of carriages was already standing at the platform and she had to give up their tickets to get through the barrier. But the collector promised they could have them back again if they wanted to see the band.

'Isn't it a long train,' said Sarah, eyeing the carriages, some of which were already occupied. 'It wouldn't go without us, would it?' she added anxiously, as they walked along the platform.

'Can't go anywhere without steam, Sarah,' James said, reassuringly as they came level with the engine.

Sitting in the dazzling sunshine beyond the shelter of the roof that arced over the platform, the engine gleamed in the sun. Rose looked from James to Sam, anticipating the pleasure John had so often told her about after one of their visits to the engine sheds on his Saturday half day.

To her surprise, they said nothing and stood watching the driver and the fireman who were talking together, it being far too soon to raise steam.

'It's a very handsome engine isn't it?' she asked, as the boys bent down to study the wheels.

'Yes,' said James, thoughtfully, 'but it's not very big.'

'Maybe they're goin' to bank it,' suggested Sam.

'What's that mean?' said Sarah sharply.

'They put another engine at the other end to push it up the hills,' explained James. 'You often see two engines with goods trains.'

'But there aren't any hills on a railway line, are there Ma?' said Hannah.

Rose hadn't thought about that one. She looked at James.

'Are there hills?' she asked.

'Yes, but they don't look like hills,' he replied steadily. 'They're called gradients. The Warrenpoint line has some steep ones, much steeper than on the line we see going to Portadown and Belfast.'

'Can we go back to hear the band now, Ma?' Hannah asked, as she saw Sam take out his notebook and write down the number of the engine.

Just at that moment, the driver caught sight of them. He leant down from his cab and smiled at the little group inspecting his engine.

'Good mornin' ma'm. Lovely day for your excursion,' he said amiably.

'Yes, indeed,' Rose replied. 'My boys are admiring your engine.'

'Aye, a great wee engine. Have ye got her number, lads?'

'Yes, thank you.'

When they said their goodbyes, she was grateful to walk back under the shade of the platform roof. She was beginning to feel very hot indeed standing in the sun, the light reflecting back from the engine and the acres of railway lines that crossed and recrossed outside the station.

The platform had filled up and they had some difficulty passing through a crowd of dignitaries milling around outside the only first class carriage on the train. From some distance away, they could hear the sound of the band.

'Ma, the train's near full. If we don't get in, we'll not get seats,' said James, surveying the carriages as they passed.

'There's Aunty Mary,' cried Sarah, waving her hand at a familiar figure four or five carriages away. Mary turned as she lifted young William up into a carriage and beckoned to them to join her.

'There's space here, Ma,' said James firmly. 'I think we should take it in case there's no more room down there.'

One glance at the crowded platform and the banging doors of carriages told her he was probably right.

'Up you go, then,' she said, 'We'll stay and listen to the band this evening when we come back. I just don't know where all the people have come from.'

The carriage was still cool and she breathed a sigh of relief as she sat down and settled Sarah beside her. There was one window seat left and it was agreed Sam and James could take it in turns to look out until they left the station, then Sarah and Hannah could take turns as they went through new countryside.

'A lovely day, isn't it,' said a gentleman sitting opposite, with his wife and three little girls.

Rose smiled, wondered if he might be a Methodist superintendent. She exchanged a few remarks with his wife, a pleasant woman whom she suspected was feeling the effects of firm corsetry, her dress very fashionable, but rather too heavy for comfort as the day was turning out.

The other occupants of the carriage were two young girls who whispered together and looked as if they might be in service and two young men, very well spruced up, but too shy and awkward even to exchange pleasantries.

Rose was pleased with Sam and James. They reported on everything they saw, but they did it quietly and without undue excitement. The only time they both pushed their heads together out of the carriage door, tramping on the feet of one of the young men as they did so, was when Mary Wylie's young brother, now a station porter, came past locking the doors.

'What are ye doin' that for?' asked James.

'To keep ye from fallin' out.'

'No need, Davey,' said Rose sharply, 'I'll see they don't fall out.'

'Right ye be,' he said agreeably, as he moved on.

'Are ye comin' with us?' asked James, leaning out as he locked the adjoining carriage.

'No, I'm on the next train. Passenger. The 10.35 to Newry,' he said as he passed on.

'We'll be going in a minute now,' said Sam, taking his turn at the window, 'the Guard has just blown his whistle. I can see him waving his flag.'

Seconds later, there was a minute movement in the carriage, followed by a distinct lurch, a long whistle and a passing cloud of steam and smoke.

'We're away,' said Sam, his face wreathed in smiles.

'Yes,' said Rose, sitting back, glad they were underway at last, after all the waiting and the delays.

They rolled out of the station between high banks, the sides of the cutting steep and smooth, the light glinting in long, undisturbed grass with nodding heads. Briar bushes grew in tangles, pink with opening buds. Hannah changed seats with Sam and looked up at the blue sky high above them, surprised and delighted when the cutting became an embankment, and her view was now over meadows and hayfields.

'My turn now,' said Sarah.

Smiling agreeably, the woman beside Rose said what good children they were and how well they shared the window seat.

'Susie, you change with Helen, then Mary can have a turn,' she said to her own children, while her husband smiled benevolently and consulted his fob watch.

'Fifteen minutes late,' he said. 'Good thing we're not going to work, we'd be in trouble,' he added, looking at the four young people.

One of the girls managed a smile.

'You'd have a stoppage for that, sir, where I work,' said the older of the two young men.

'We're slowing down,' said the gentleman. 'I hope we haven't got a cow on the line.'

James thrust his head through the window.

'My turn,' said Sam, urgently a few moments later.

At the moment he spoke, the train stopped.

'I think they'll have to bank her, she can't get up the slope,' said James, turning to Rose.

'So we'll have to wait for another engine to come and give us a push?' asked Hannah.

'They'll not make it otherwise,' he replied, soberly.

While the train was moving there had been a

comfortably breeze through both open windows. Now the air was still and getting hotter every moment. The amiable lady was perspiring visibly and Sarah was beginning to get cross as the sun beat down on the thin roof of the carriage.

'James, see what's happening,' said Rose, who was beginning to feel uncomfortable herself.

'They're going to divide the train,' said James, suddenly. 'They've uncoupled the first five coaches to take them up the gradient first. Then they'll come back for us.'

'Let me look,' said Sam, urgently. 'Let me look.'

James gave way reluctantly under Rose's glance.

'A man's put stones under the wheels of this carriage,' said Sam, abruptly. 'The other man says he's mad to take the vacuum off. What's that mean?'

By way of answer, James stuck his head out of the window again. As he did so, the carriage received a bang loud enough to startle everyone. It began to move imperceptibly backwards. He spun round, his face taut with urgency.

'Ma, the stones have crumbled, we've got to jump out?'

'Why James?' Rose asked, alarmed by the tone of his voice.

'There's no brakes on us now the vacuum's off, and the 10.35 is coming up behind us. We'll run straight back into her.'

Rose stood up immediately.

'Open the door James and jump out. I'll drop Sarah down next,' she said without any hesitation.

The movement in the carriage was very small. The young girls looked at her in surprise as she lowered Sarah into James's waiting arms.

'You next, Sam, and catch Hannah.'

Rose was about to jump down after her when she realised no one else in the carriage had moved.

'Please, *please*, follow me immediately,' she said, looking at the gentleman and then at the young people. 'Something dreadful is going to happen, I can't start to explain, but I know James is right,' she said as the carriage wavered more significantly. 'I must go to my children,' she said, with a final backwards glance.

She paused at the door to get her balance and jumped down, almost falling forward, but managing to steady herself. She ran back the dozen or so yards to where the children were standing waiting, Sarah with tears running down her face.

'I'm all right, Sarah, but I've got to go and see Auntie Mary. James, take them well off the line, out of the sun. Wait for me.'

She picked up her skirts and ran as hard as she could to catch up with the runaway carriages, trying to work out how far away Mary's had been. She was gasping for breath as the coaches picked up speed and she tripped several times on the rough stone as she tried to navigate the narrow space between the rails and the edge of the embankment.

Heads were now poking out of windows, arms trying to open locked doors. The carriages were gaining speed, minute by minute, running quickly down the gradient that had defeated the engine on the way up.

'Mary, Mary, she called, as she drew level with a coach that might be the one. A man was struggling with the door. Mary's face appeared beside him at the window white with fear.

'It's locked, Rose. It's locked,' she shouted, shaking her head in despair.

'Try the other side,' she yelled. 'Jump out, Mary,' she cried, with one last effort to keep pace with the carriage. 'For God's sake, jump.'

She straightened up, a violent stitch in her side, as the last carriage of the divided train rattled past at speed. She took a deep breath, crossed the line and looked down the embankment, hoping against hope to see a figure, standing, sitting or even lying on the grass. But there was no one there.

The screams of the trapped people sounded in her ears. And then a yet more ominous sound, the long, long whistle of the oncoming passenger train. She covered her face with her hands, sobbing and waited for what had to come. The smash of metal on wood, the cries of people whose bodies would shatter like the wood of the carriages.

The pain in her chest was so bad she couldn't breathe. She tried to move and couldn't. Finally, she let herself slump to the ground and buried her face in the warm grass. She gasped, panting madly, found she could breath again. Then she staggered to her feet, shaking violently and crossed the railway line.

'The children are waiting, Rose,' she said aloud. 'Don't look back. Just don't look back.'

# CHAPTER TWENTY-FIVE

The children were sitting under a hawthorn hedge at the bottom of the embankment. James had his arm round Sarah who was still crying. Hannah was making a daisy chain. Sam was watching out for her and waved the moment he saw her come over its edge. As she began the steep descent, she saw Hannah offer the daisy chain to Sarah, but Sarah shook her head and went on crying.

'There's Ma, now. I told you she wouldn't be long,' said James, as she came up to them, immediately dropping to her knees and putting her arms round Sarah, who wrapped her arms round her neck and wept even more loudly. Above her dark curls, she ran her eyes over the other children.

'Did you find her, Ma?' asked James.

'Yes, I did,' she said calmly.

James dropped his eyes and asked no further question.

'Are all the people killed now?' Sarah burst out, lifting her tear-stained face from her shoulder.

'A lot of people will be hurt, Sarah. Some will be killed. But we don't know yet how many.'

She looked closely at Sam and Hannah. She'd seen already that James was very steady. At twelve, he was grown up for his age and she knew he'd worked out exactly what was going to happen when the passenger train ploughed into the runaway carriages. Sam was unusually silent, his face pale, his dark hair catching the sunlight. Hannah stood looking at her, the daisy chain was crumpled in her hand, her eyes dry, but unnaturally large, without their usual sparkle.

'What we must do, Sarah, is go home. And on the way, we must go and tell Da we're all right. He'll be so worried about us. It's a long way, across to our own road, so you'll have to be a very brave girl.'

'Can we not go and help?' said James roughly, nodding his head in the direction of the runaway carriages.

'Yes, you and I could,' she said, looking him straight in the eye. 'But I don't think we should.'

She saw his lips tighten as he grasped her meaning.

'What's the best way to get to Killuney, James?'

'Over the fields, you mean?'

She nodded. They would have to cross the embankment. The wreckage might well be visible and even worse, they might still hear the cries of the injured, but it would have to be faced.

'Go ahead, James, see can you spy out the best way across the fields towards the bridge. If we can reach it, it's an easy walk up the lane over Drummond and down on to our own road.'

'You mean the lane that comes down by the wee chapel beyond the mill?'

'That's right, we've walked it the odd Sunday, but we've never gone as far as the bridge.'

'I'll go with James, Ma,' said Sam suddenly. 'I always see the wet bits long before he does.'

'Don't get too far ahead,' she warned, as she wiped Sarah's eyes and stood up. 'Can you manage that bag, Sam, or will I carry it?'

'I can manage.'

'What about you, Hannah?'

'I'm all right,' she said, straightening up.

The tramp across damp meadows was slow and wearying, especially when they had to find gaps in the hedgerows large enough for them to climb through. Sarah had never been a good walker, she tired quickly and, although she didn't ask to be carried, Rose knew she was soon exhausted. They had to stop more than once to let her rest.

Although the distance to the bridge was not more than two miles, to avoid a full view of the disaster area, James's chosen route took them nearly an hour. With wide, boggy patches to thread their way through between the sloping fields, their progress at times was painfully slow. The final steep pull up to the lane running over Drummond Hill in the full glare of the hot sun left Rose breathless and nearly as exhausted as Sarah and Hannah.

But she didn't stop, urging them to press on, for even at this distance she could hear sounds that filled her with dread. As the lane sloped downwards under the shade of trees and became the familiar place of Sunday walks, she began to feel her courage return. Once they were back on the Loughgall Road, it was less than two miles home and there were shady places where they could stop and rest. She might even make them eat a bite from the picnic Hannah and Sam still carried.

As they neared the foot of the lane, they stopped to rest once more and she called James to her.

'It's not far now to the mill, James. Go and ask for the foreman. Tell him what's happened,' she said, speaking very quietly. 'Say you'd like to speak to your father to tell him we're safe. You'll probably catch up with us long before we're home. I'll have to carry Sarah soon.'

'Right, Ma. I'll not be long.'

She watched him run down the lane and disappear round the corner of the small chapel that marked the end of the Asylum grounds. Once he was out of sight, she moved them on, Sarah hanging on her hand, Hannah silent with fatigue. Only Sam plodded forward steadily just a few yards ahead of them. His role as scout was over, but he always took the lead when James wasn't with them.

They were resting again under the trees near the gates of Drumsollen when he caught them up.

'Did you see Da?' she asked, before he had caught his breath.

He shook his head.

'Da's gone to Killuney, him an' three men with tools and the big dray. They sent down from the station for transport an' the foreman asked for four volunteers. The looms was in, so he was free to go. He's away half an hour ago.'

'So he doesn't know we're safe,' she said, her heart sinking at the thought of what lay before him.

'I'll carry Sarah for a bit,' he said, looking her full in the face.

'Just for a bit, James,' she said, trying to keep the distress out of her voice. 'We can stop at the pump for a drink of water.'

In all the hundreds of times she had walked from the gates of Drumsollen to the pump opposite the old limestone quarry, a distance little more than half a mile, it had never seemed so long. Just putting one foot in front of another required all her thought and effort. She tried to focus on the gush of water that would quench their thirst and cool their hands and faces.

She was annoyed with herself for having brought nothing to drink, but they'd planned to buy lemonade when they got to Warrenpoint. Bottles were heavy and difficult to carry and always leaked, no matter how hard you tried to cork them up.

Suddenly she thought of the trainload of passengers they'd left behind. So many in such need and no water. No shelter from the hot sun.

She stopped herself, knowing if she let herself think, she'd not get the children home.

James was so vigorous with the pump he splashed them all, but no one laughed. They all drank deep, hands held out to cool in the very cold water. Rose wiped Sarah's face with her handkerchief where she was already reddened by the sun. They would have to walk under the hedgerow for what shelter they could get on the last open stretch to their own lane.

They were just about to set off when they heard a vehicle approach from the direction of home. They stayed where they were in the shade to see who it might be.

'It's George Robinson with Thomas and two of the boys. I think it's young George and Sammy,' said Sam, stepping out into the road to wave at them.

The trap was coming at speed, but it slowed down as soon as it saw them and came slowly to rest beside them. Thomas leapt down and put his arms out, trying to embrace them all.

'Thank God, Rose. Thank God yer safe. Are ye hurted at all?'

Totally overcome by the tears streaming down

Thomas's face, she could only shake her head.

'How did ye hear?'

'They sent for help to Castledillon, an' one of the grooms rode over to me in case they needed tools. He's away up to the cart manufactory. They've asked for vehicles fit to bring people to the hospital. Can ye's make it home, d'ye think?' he asked, eyeing them doubtfully.

She nodded vigorously.

'You go on, Thomas, we can manage. John's away with the dray from the mill. Tell him we're safe. Please tell him if you possibly can,' she said, quickly, afraid her tears would let her down.

'I'll tell him all right,' he said, as he sprang up into the cart again.

As he sat down beside George and his sons, she saw that the two young men, broad shouldered and newly married, were looking as pale and vulnerable as her own Sam.

She managed to wave to them, as George shook the reins, but she could think of no words to wish them well on the journey they had in front of them.

'I'll take her now,' she said, sometime later, as they came up the hill and caught sight of the forge, a thin trickle of smoke still rising in a leisurely way up into a perfect blue sky.

As she took Sarah from his arms she could see that even James was now exhausted. She led her little party up the lane, picking her way between a hay float and the reaping machine on which Thomas had been working when the call came.

She waited for Sam to open the door and they went in to the empty kitchen. It was warm and stuffy.

'Prop open the back door, Sam, will you,' she said, as she put Sarah down and opened the front windows as far as they would go.

'We'll have our lunch now,' she said firmly. 'Would anyone like a cup of tea with some sugar in it?' she asked quietly.

All she got was nods as she bent to stir up the fire and put the kettle on its chain. She glanced at the clock on the dresser. It said ten to twelve. Not yet noon and already it felt like the longest day in her whole life.

As soon as they'd eaten, she put Sarah to bed. To her surprise, Hannah went too, without being asked, and she was followed shortly afterwards by Sam and James. She sat herself down in Granny Sarah's rocking chair and stared at the table, where the scattered remains of their picnic still waited to be cleared up. It was only when the creak of the bedroom door startled her that she realised she'd been asleep.

'Can I bring you a glass of the spring?' said James, as he crossed the floor in his bare feet. 'I'm so thirsty.'

'Yes, please,' she said, yawning and stretching,

her mind still caught in a pleasant dream.

Before James put the glass in her hand, the pleasure had evaporated and enormity of what had happened flowed in upon her like a dark cloud. With it came the knowledge of what she had to do.

'James, I'll have to go down to Wylie's. Can you look after the girls? Sarah might sleep till I get back. I'll not be long.'

She'd have liked to change her clothes but she was afraid of waking Sarah, so she set out for Annacramp still dressed in her Sunday best, though her well-polished boots were now streaked with dried mud and the hem of her skirt stained with grass.

What could she say? To Peggy, of all people, who had lost so much. Could she have done more? Could she have gone back and searched for Mary and the children leaving hers in the care of James? Could he have got them home by himself? Or would Sarah have screamed uncontrollably, once she was not there to reassure her?

Rose argued the case back and forth as she tramped the familiar road, empty and quiet in the early afternoon. Could she have helped? Comforted a distraught child, a dying mother?

'*Don't look back, Rose. Don't look back.*'

The words had come to her as she stood on the embankment, the carriages running away from her. They echoed in her mind from long ago. She could hear the voice, kind, but firm. She knew she'd done as she'd been told, but where the voice came from or when it had spoken would not come back to her.

She turned into the yard of Wylie's farm and made for the dwelling house that sat back behind the stable and byres. The back door stood open as it always did. She was about to knock when she heard a movement, a slight rustle of a skirt. Peggy Wylie stood in front of her, her face red and swollen with crying, her arms outstretched.

'Rose, Rose,' she cried, tears pouring down unheeded. 'I thought I'd lost everyone now, but you're still alive. Are the children all right?'

They wept in each other arms, tears of sorrow, tears of relief inextricably mixed.

'How did you know what had happened, Peggy?' Rose said at last, as they grew steadier.

'Sam Loney at Richhill station heard from the guard on the 11.15 down train from Armagh,' she began, doing her best to not to cry. 'He said a man had just run back down the other line and asked John Foster to telegraph for help to all the railway stations. Then Sam came over for Billy and they're away to help with two of the Gibsons. What happened Rose? Whatever happened?'

Rose told her all she knew, though nothing to raise her hopes about Mary or the others. She was in one of the carriages nearest to the guard's van at the back of the train, she said. The doors were locked and the runaway coaches were gaining speed all the time.

'Poor, poor Billy,' Peggy said, 'He's such a good sort, but he hasn't much go about him. Sure, look at the way he went to bits when wee Jane died. What'll he do if he loses her? An' the wee ones too? Ach, Rose, I don't understand about God at all. First Kevin and now this. How can He let such things happen?'

Rose shook her head.

'My mother used to say that God wasn't for doing things for you, He was for helping you bear what comes. I didn't understand her then and I'm not sure I understand yet,' she said sadly. 'I prayed for a miracle on that embankment but the Lord certainly didn't put out his hand and stop those carriages.'

They were silent for a long moment, then she roused herself.

'Peggy, I'd like to stay with you, but I've left Sarah asleep and James can't manage her if she starts to cry again. She feels things more than's good for her, that child.'

'Thank God you're all safe. I'll have news by tonight. Davey'll be back from work around seven and he'll know, one way or the other. He was on duty at the station all day.'

She said her goodbye. She simply hadn't the courage to tell Peggy that Davey's duty had been changed, that it was Davey who had been sent to lock the carriages and Davey who was to follow on the passenger train behind.

By the time she arrived back home, Hannah was peeling potatoes and James and Sam had gone to fetch more water. Careful not to wake Sarah, they'd cleared the table, washed the cups and left the room straight. Though the hours passed slowly, no one had the heart to say a word.

At five, Rose woke Sarah and gave the children their meal. She sent James over to Robinson's to see if they'd heard any news. They hadn't, so she read them a story. Then another. And another.

Shortly before eight o'clock, there was the sound of wheels on the road. Before she'd even spoken, James was out the door and into the lane.

'It's Da and Thomas,' he called back. 'The Robinson's have dropped them on the road. They'll be up in a minute.'

'Good boy. Stay here, I'll be back in a few minutes.'

Rose ran down to the foot of the lane and stood watching the two men walk slowly up the hill, while the trap made its way up into the farmyard.

John put his arm round her, but said nothing, his face a mask of exhaustion, pale under a layer of dirt and grime. Thomas looked down at the road and then up at the sky. Both men's trousers and forearms were streaked with blood.

'What about Mary Wylie?'

They shook their heads.

'And Jacob and William and Ned?'

'Jacob and William were with their mother. Wee Ned's all right. She threw him out into a bush,' said John, his voice so tired it seemed an effort for him to speak the words.

'And Davey?'

'He was there helpin' us, poor lad.'

They walked up the lane together and paused outside the forge.

Thomas looked in through the door at the silent anvil and the cold ash of the fire.

'I took tools in case there was people trapped in wreckage,' he said in a level tone, 'but sure I didn't need them. Those poor people might as well have been sitting in match boxes for all the difference it made. I've never seen the like of it,' he said, his voice failing him.

Pressing his lips together, as if to choke a cry, he raised a hand in salute, turned his back on them, tramped up the path, pushed open the closed door of his house and disappeared inside.

'Come and have your supper, John,' she said quietly, as she took his arm. 'You may not feel like it, but we must keep our strength up. We've an awful lot to give thanks for.'

The children waited silently while he went out to the washhouse with a kettle of hot water and the clean shirt Rose fetched from the bedroom. They let him begin his supper, but when he began to ask his own questions, they could restrain themselves no longer and poured out their story just as they had experienced it. The boys told him about the size of the engine, the dividing of the train and the stones that gave way. Hannah described the long walk home, the boggy bits where she and Sarah had almost got stuck and said how glad Thomas had been to see them at the pump.

'Are all the people killed now, Da?' said Sarah, repeating the question she had asked at intervals all through the day.

'Some were killed, Sarah, but most are all right,' he said reassuringly.

'Could we have been killed, Da?' she went on, fixing him with a piercing gaze from her dark eyes.

'No,' he said, slowly. 'Not with your Ma to look after you and your brothers to be so sensible. If you'd stayed in the train now, you might have got hurt.'

'But we didn't. We jumped out. And James caught me,' she said, her eyes lighting up unexpectedly, as she came and climbed up onto his knee and threw her arms round him.

He held her until she released her limpet grip. Then he kissed her and looked wearily at Rose, who picked her up and took her off to bed.

'You'd have been proud of them, John,' she said,

when an hour later the other children had followed her.

She told him the parts of the story the children had left out or could only guess at, then rose to make them a pot of tea. It was when she came back to the table with the teapot, she saw how pale he'd gone.

She came and put an arm round him, felt his shoulders tight as a board. He was holding himself rigid.

'John dear, you haven't told me the half of it.'

A bleak smile flickered for a moment as he nodded his head.

'I daren't, Rose. It's not fit for you to hear,' he said wearily. 'An' I might disgrace m'self.'

'Sure Thomas disgraced himself this morning when he saw us by the pump,' she said quickly. 'What's the shame in that, John? Isn't there a river of tears flowing tonight in houses all around us? Some that we know of and some that we don't. Why should we spare ours?'

She poured the tea into two mugs, so that she could sit beside him on the settle and hold his free hand.

'Come on, love. Tell me from the beginning.'

To her surprise, he set off quite steadily. Told her how he'd just finished work on the second loom when the foreman came up looking for him, the message from the station in his hand. They'd hurried down and out to the cart sheds without a word, each knowing the other's wife and children were on the train. John harnessed the horses with another man, some of the spinners brought cans of water and bales of the clean, spoilt cloth they used for wrapping full spindles. They had to go the long way through the town, for the dray was too wide for the lane over Drummond.

'By the time we got there, they'd started to lay the bodies out under the hedges. Most of the dead was lying down at the bottom of the embankment, so we left the dray with the youngest man an' went down there. I saw Captain Prescott from The Mall giving brandy to a man. I went over to ask him could I help an' I heard the man say, "It's no use, Captain." An' he died. So we carried him up an' put him under the hedge. I'm sure we carried a dozen, men and women, an' I managed rightly. I kept tellin' m'self you'd a' been away up at the front, for the boys wou'd want to be near the engine. That's what kept me going. An' then Prescott saw this young lad. "Give me a hand with this one," says he to me. An' I put my hands under his shoulders an' Prescott took his feet, an' the head came off in my hands and the feet came off in Prescott's. So we put him under the hedge in three pieces.'

He put down his mug and dropped his head in his hands. She thought he was crying, but he wasn't. He was just rubbing the skin of his face, for it was stiff with exhaustion. In a moment, he went on.

'Yer man Prescott offered me a mouthful of brandy, but I said no. I wasn't used to it, it might make my head light. So he told me to go and get a drink of water, or milk, and come back to him. An' I did that. I climbed back up the embankment an' I met Thomas an' he told me he'd seen ye. An' after that I was fit for anythin',' he said, his voice taking on an unexpected note of strength.

'And did you and Thomas stay together?'

'Not to begin with. I thought I ought to go back to Prescott, for I'd been helpin' him. So I went back down. An' when I come to him, he was talking to two wee childer. They were sitting on the grass making daisy chains as if there were nothing amiss. "Were you on the train?" says he to them. "Yes," says one of the wee girls, a wee fair-haired child no older than our Sarah. "An' so was she," she says, pointing to another wee girl, her sister by the look of it, just lying there dead with not a mark on her an a wee smile on her face.'

'Were there many children killed?' Rose asked, amazed at how cool they both were managing to be.

'Not that many that I saw, but there was nurses from the hospital lookin' for them. Women threw childer out of the windows when they found the doors was locked. Like Mary did. Sure they found wee Ned crying in the middle of a briar bush because he couldn't get out.'

They sat silent, Rose wondering if she had the

courage to ask about Mary, but he read her thoughts.

'Prescott went to see what the arrangements were for taking the bodies to Armagh, so I went and found Thomas and the Robinsons. They were moving axles to get at the ones underneath. Though they were all dead,' he said, matter-of-factly. 'It was Thomas who found Mary. He was standin' up on the embankment an' he sees somethin'. He diden say a word to me, just went down and turned over this woman who'd been thrown out, down the embankment. He said he knew it was her before he turned her over because he'd seen her passin' on their way to the station and she had on a blue blouse. An' when he looked up at us, we went down to him an' carried her over to the hedge. She wasn't marked at all. Thomas said he thought her neck was broke. He said he minded waving to her as he came out of the forge to start in on the reaper.'

'And the boys, Jacob and William?'

John shook his head and pressed his lips together.

'There was an army doctor there,' he said, slowly. 'The Barracks sent down their ambulance corps forby military, an' I heard him say to Prestcott he'd seldom seen such carnage, even on a battlefield.'

Rose knew the blue blouse only too well, made from the length of material Sam had brought from Kerry after her mother died. It was Mary's colour, perfect with the lovely blue eyes so ready to glint with humour, or with mischief. It was the thought of Mary's eyes, wide with surprise and delight, the morning she'd given her that piece of cloth that finally breached all her defences.

She wept, as if she'd never have enough tears for all the pain and loss of the day. John put his arms round her and comforted her, his own tears falling unregarded in the mass of her soft, dark hair.

'How many were there, laid out like you said?'

He shook his head.

'We made two journeys to the Tontine rooms with ten each time. And I saw the Army wagons follow us on the way to the market house. Thomas said he and the Robinsons had seen the first carts leave for Armagh Station. It won't be less than sixty and there's hundreds injured.'

They sat silent. She wondered if she'd seen all that John had seen whether she would be able to grasp any better the sheer magnitude of what had happened, for the scale of it seemed outside her imagining.

'I'll tell you a funny thing, Rose,' he began.

She stared at him, the idea of anything even remotely amusing coming out of the day quite unthinkable.

'D'ye mind yer man from Cabragh, that did me out of my job?'

She nodded silently.

'He was there with the father and son that has his

cart manufactory. I heard him askin' the Reverend Jackson Smyth if there was a priest about the place, for he thought his neighbour wasn't goin' to live an' he wanted to get him the Last Rites.'

'And was there a priest?

'Yes,' he said, nodding. 'Smyth pointed him out and yer man away and got him. Him that was so hot on Rome. Ach, sure maybe somethin' good might come of it, Rose, but it's not for us to see. We may just do our best an' try to help our friends. An' give thanks we were all spared.'

# CHAPTER TWENTY-SIX

Rain came in the night. Waking from a restless sleep, Rose heard it drumming on the windows. Next morning when she knelt to stir the fire, the room was as dim as many a winter's morn. The downpour eased as John left for work at the usual time and stopped altogether just before the children left for school. She looked out on the sodden garden and the deep puddle at the entrance to the forge. The heavy grey cloud hung overhead like a pall which the days news would do nothing to lift.

The children arrived back half an hour later. There was no school. The master had lost his sister-in-law with her two children and a little niece who'd come to stay especially for the excursion. His young assistant had been at the schoolroom to send the children home. She told them one of their classmates, little Edith Kane from Ballybrannan had lost an arm and was very poorly. They were to be sure to remember her in their prayers.

Rose listened with a sinking heart, knowing that

it would be days before the bad news could come to an end. Between the newspapers and the forge, there'd be no avoiding every scrap of information that each new day would bring.

She set about her immediate task of occupying the children so she'd be free to go down to Wylie's to see Billy and Peggy and offer to look after little Ned and Peggy's baby while they made arrangements for the funeral.

'Sam and I could go and give a hand at Robinson's,' said James helpfully.

'What would you do?' she replied doubtfully.

'There's always work,' James assured her. 'They might be eyeing potatoes for the next plantin', or cleanin' out the byre or the stables. They do that on bad days,' he explained.

She agreed gratefully, knowing that Hannah and Sarah would be quite happy to stay indoors and read. It was always the boys who got restless on wet days when there was no school.

She had just finished baking the day's bread and was tidying herself for going down to Annacramp, when John himself arrived back home. So few spinners had reported for work, the mill had been forced to close and would not re-open until all the funerals were over. The morning newspaper put the death toll at sixty-seven, but the number of seriously injured was high. The hospital was full, it said, and some badly injured people were being cared for at home. One Armagh doctor had 102 of his patients on the injured list. But what was emerging was that people had not only come from a radius of three or four miles around the city, but also from much further afield, as far away as Moy and Caledon and Clones.

'When ye get as far as the mill, ye can hear the bells o' the cathedral tolling. It's a powerful mournful sound,' John told her. 'An' I diden see a face since I left home that would know the remembrance of a smile.'

'Will you come with me to Annacramp?' she asked.

For a moment, he said nothing and looked out across at the forge, as if he'd just come over to speak to her and needed to get back to the job right away.

'I will if ye ask me,' he said honestly.

'I won't ask you, John,' she said shaking her head. 'There's little enough I can do for Billy and Peggy. I doubt if your going would help all that much and I know it would be hard on you. There's maybe things I'll have to ask you to do later on.'

He nodded, his relief obvious.

'I can get in the water and dig the spuds for the dinner,' he said quickly. 'Is there anything else I can do? I thought I might give Thomas a bit of a hand. It's too wet for the garden.'

She nodded, touched by his willingness to help and his inability to face the grief he would meet at

Annacramp. Like the boys, he needed to occupy himself.

'That's a good idea. Thomas'll not have had much comfort last night. I'd be glad to see you out there with him,' she said quietly. 'Sarah's got her book and Hannah's going to do some of my sewing for me,' she said, dropping her voice even lower and nodding across to the settle where the two girls were already absorbed. 'If I'm not back by twelve, make them a piece, but I should be and I may have Ned and the baby with me.'

'Whatever ye think best, love. I'll do what I can.'

He sat down abruptly in a chair at the kitchen table as if the effort of talk had exhausted him. She came and touched his cheek.

'It'll pass, love. However long it takes, it'll pass.'

'Aye, your mother used to say that, diden she?' he said looking up at her. 'Whenever things was bad?'

'She did. And strange enough your mother use to say it too, though in a different way. 'All things pass, Rose, both pleasant and unpleasant. Those were her words.'

'D'ye know, I think I mind that from those old copy books we had at school. Maybe that's where they both got it from,' he said, looking pleased with himself.

She saw the hint of a smile touch his lips and was grateful. Maybe it was harder for men. They couldn't face the grief of others and they didn't know what to do with their own.

'Did ye tell Lady Anne ye were goin' on the excursion?' he said unexpectedly.

'What made you think of that?' she asked, startled.

'Ach, mentioning yer mother I somehow thought of her. Did ye tell her?'

'Yes, I'm sure I did. It's a while since I wrote, but I'm sure I did.'

'She'll be desperate upset if she reads about what happened in the newspaper.'

'I never thought of that. D'you think it would be in the Dublin papers?'

'Och yes, and the English ones too. Sure all the newspaper offices has the telegraph.'

'I could write her a note,' she said distractedly, already wondering about her sister in Donegal and her brother in Scotland.

'I think you should, love. Write it when you come back and I'll go into the Post Office in Armagh. She'll have it in the mornin'.'


Rose's visit to Annacramp was not as hard as she'd expected. The farm house was full and little Ned had half a dozen women and girls fussing over him. Billy had gone up to the churchyard to show the gravediggers where the unmarked family grave was to be opened. Peggy was dry-eyed and steady.

'I knew yesterday that Mary was gone,' she said quietly, when they walked out into the damp lane behind the house to have a moment alone together. 'You were very honest, Rose, an' I'm grateful. If I hadn't known to expect the worst, I couldn't have coped as well when Billy came back.'

She turned to face her.

'He and the Gibson's had just found one of the Gibson girls when Thomas came up to him. He said last night he thought Thomas was going to collapse, he was that distraught, when he had to tell him he'd found Mary. That was before one of the nurses found wee Ned.'

'Was he really in a briar bush?'

'He was. Right in the middle. And not a scratch on his face, though his arms and legs are covered,' she said, shaking her head. 'He's not four yet, Rose, do you think he'll remember?'

'He might remember indeed, but if he has all the comfort he's having now, it may take away the hurt,' she said, thinking of Sarah and the length of her memory. 'But it's harder to do that for Billy,' she said, looking at her friend with concern.

'He surprised me last night, Rose. I thought he would be absolutely helpless, if he lost Mary, but when he came back with wee Ned and told me about her and the boys, he said "We're both in the same boat now, Peggy. We'll have to do what we can for these two wee'uns, Kevin's son and Mary's son."

Oh, he cried. Sure we both did. We cried till our eyes were sore, but then he said to me. "Go to your bed, Peggy. We'll need our strength for the morra." An' he's away up to the churchyard, quite composed. Three o'clock tomorrow, Rose.'

She nodded, not trusting herself to say the simple words that she and John would be there. Billy might be acting bravely for his part, but she was not sure how she herself would feel seeing the one large and two small coffins going into a wide grave and one of them her dearest friend.

'Is Davey all right?' she asked suddenly, as she remembered his face at the carriage window when he came past locking the doors.

'Yes, thank God. He was in the Guard's van of the 10.35, but the driver managed to get the train stopped. Oh, it didn't prevent the accident, but there were sixteen people stepped out safely and they were the first to help. Davey says there were a couple of very fashionable ladies with big hats and feathers in one of the coaches. They just took off their finery and left it in a pile and went up the track to help. There was a doctor and a minister too, he says. He came down this mornin' before he went to work. He's very bright, full of talk,' she said, shaking her head dubiously. 'But he's not injured in any physical way.'

'Did he tell you he was the one locked the doors?' Rose asked quietly.

'No, he never mentioned that. Was *all* the doors locked?'

'Most of them,' she said, nodding.

'We heard last night the Constabulary had arrested the men from the G. N. R, the driver and the supervisor and two others. They wouldn't come after Davey, would they?' she asked, suddenly alarmed.

Rose shook her head firmly.

'No, Peggy. Davey was only acting on orders. It wasn't his fault. But it may suddenly come to him that it was. That's why I'm telling you.'

'Thank you, Rose. You've been such a good friend to me,' she said, tears springing to her eyes. 'An' I used to think it was just because I was Mary's sister.'

'Not a bit of it, Peggy. Not a bit of it,' she said, slipping her arm round her waist as they turned back to the house, gathering themselves for whatever awaited them.


'Sit down an' rest yerself,' said John, as he followed her back into the house. 'You're lookin' desperit pale. Sit there and Hannah an' me'll make us a bite,' he said, putting the kettle down.

Hannah wrapped up her sewing and began fetching cups and plates from the dresser.

'Is Ned all right?' Sarah asked sharply.

'Yes, he's fine, Sarah. He's got some scratches.'

431

'Why did Auntie Mary throw him into a bush?'

'Because she couldn't jump out like we did. Their doors were locked.'

'Why were they locked?'

'In case children might fall out?'

'Did Auntie Mary know they were going to crash?'

'Yes, she did.'

'Why didn't she throw Jacob and William out as well?

'They were too big to throw through the window?'

'Why . . .'

'Sarah, your Ma is tired out. That's enough of questions,' said John firmly, as he cut slices of wheaten bread and put them on a plate. 'Now come to the table and have some bread and jam. Will I butter it for you?'

'I can butter my own bread,' she said abruptly.

'Thank you,' prompted Rose automatically.

The 'thank you' was dutifull but sulky.

'I think maybe we'll all have a little rest after our lunch,' she added, looking from Hannah to Sarah.

'I don't need a rest,' said Sarah, crossly.

'But I do, Sarah. I'd like you both to keep me company.'


To her surprise she fell asleep as soon as she lay down on the bed, though she'd only intended a pretence until Sarah was asleep. It was always a bad sign when she kept asking questions and was irritable. She was still over-tired after yesterday's walk, never mind all that she'd seen and heard. Unlike Hannah who was happy to sit and sew and became totally absorbed in what she was doing, Sarah's active mind never seemed to stop. She was always telling stories, asking questions, thinking things out and puzzling her head to make sense of whatever came within her experience.

Rose slipped quietly off the bed. She was fast asleep, clutching Ganny, Hannah asleep beside her. She moved quietly out into the kitchen. John had cleared up the remains of their meal. Everything was tidy, except for a small scatter of crumbs on the floor. She wondered why it was that men never seemed to notice such things.

She went to the window and saw that it had been raining again. The hollow at the door of the forge, swept dry when she came back from Annacramp, had a small, new puddle. John and Thomas were bending over a reaper, testing the raising and lowering mechanism. Suddenly lonely, she walked out to speak to them.

'Ach Rose, how are ye?' said Thomas kindly. 'I hear you were down at Annacramp. I must go down m'self the night,' he said, looking no easier at the prospect than John looked earlier in the day.

She told him what she could to reassure him and

was pleased when she saw relief dawn as she quoted Billy's words to Peggy.

'Sure maybe the pair o' them'll make a family of it in time,' he said thoughtfully. 'I've seen it afore. Sure haven't they both been hurt an' will understan' one another.'

She nodded, surprised that Thomas had spoken with such insight, though the same thought had come to her when she walked with Peggy in the lane.

'Well, what news this morning?' she said, looking from one to another. 'I didn't ask John in front of the girls,' she said, glancing up at Thomas, who was leaning against the seat of the reaper.

'All bad, so far,' said Thomas. 'Five more has died overnight. An' there's two wee lassies among the dead you'll know. Minnie and Elizabeth Rountree. They'll be burying them tomorrow as well. An' wee Mina Reilly. Do you know her? Works in the stationers in Scotch Street.'

'Yes, I buy writing paper there,' she replied, nodding sadly. 'Minnie and Elizabeth are apprentices at the dressmakers in Thomas Street. I used to meet them walking home if I went in on their half day. We always talked fashion and dresses though we all had to make our own,' she said shaking her head.

They stood silent for a moment, John crouched down, plucking a stray piece of grass from between the teeth of the newly reset reaper, Thomas staring at the lever mechanism. A soft footstep behind them made them all turn round sharply. George Robinson, in large Wellington boots came striding towards them, carrying a crowbar. He tipped his cap to Rose and nodded to both men.

'Jimmy forgot this one this mornin' when he brought the rest back, Thomas,' he said, leaning the heavy bar against the reaper. D'ye's know John Hughes?' he went on without a pause.

'Aye, of course we do. Sure he delivers for Turners. Don't tell me he was on the train?' said Thomas, looking at George in disbelief.

'No, he woren't. He said he was far too old for such capers, but he let the three children go with some neighbour, for half the street was goin'. When he heard the news, he away out with the cart to look for them an' give a hand. It seems he took one look at the train and the carriages an' dropped down dead. An' the worst of it is the three childer were away up at the front beyond where they divid the train an' they were all safe and sound.'

'That's another one,' said John sadly. 'That's seventy-three now.'

'Yer none the worse, Rose?' George asked, awkwardly, looking down at her. 'What about the wee ones?'

'I'm all right thank you, George. And the children are as right as any of us are. I'm a bit concerned about Sarah, but sure she's alive and not hurt. I hope the boys aren't in your way?' she said apologetically.

'Not a bit, not a bit. They're always ready to tackle things. T' tell you the truth they're company for my boys, for they're all through themselves, them an' their wives. Sure they're like childer themselves today they're that upset. Maggie said to tell you the boys are welcome any day till the school starts, she's glad of them for a bit of distraction. She says she can't face any of the funerals, so she'll be at home, if you want to send the wee girls over to her when you go.'

Rose smiled her thanks, touched by the sudden thoughtfulness of a woman not normally very aware of the concerns of others.

'I'm very grateful, George. We must go to the Wylies and the Rountrees and . . .'

'Rose, have ye forgot that letter ye were to write?' John said quietly.

Rose gasped and put a hand to her mouth.

'I keep forgetting things,' she said.

'Sure we're all distracted,' said Thomas, 'but if ye want to catch the post, John wou'd need to be on his way soon.'

Hastily, she sat down at the table and wrote three short notes, to Lady Anne, her sister Mary and her brother in Scotland. It still seemed so strange they might have heard of what had happened already and them so far away, but she knew John was right. The world had changed since the coming of the telegraph, and even the post from America now only took eight or nine days.

'I'm sorry to give you the walk, love,' she said as she handed him the envelopes.

'Ach it's no bother. I'm better kept busy. Is there anything ye need from town?'

'No, we're all right for groceries, I went in on Tuesday, so I could buy a few wee treats for Wednesday,' she said wryly.

'I'll not be long. I'll maybe get the evenin' paper,' he said casually as he looked up at the threatening sky and put the letters under his jacket.

John was soaked when he got back a couple of hours later. He had an ashen look about him as he opened the door that brought the old anxiety leaping into Rose's chest.

'The rain caught me just past the pump,' he said, peeling off his saturated jacket. 'I coud a' stood in, but I knew it was near supper time. An' a wanted to get home,' he said, his voice strong, his liveliness somewhat forced.

She relaxed as she saw him dry his hair on the towel Hannah brought him.

'Wou'd I need to change the trousers?' he said, tentatively. 'There's no cold in that rain, but it was right heavy.'

Rose nodded, relieved that he sounded so much better than he looked. She saw him slip the folded newspaper from under his jacket into the embrasure of the window as he passed into the bedroom. She went on peeling potatoes and watched him as he came back into the kitchen, sat down by the fire and asked the girls did they have a good sleep.

'I had a dream,' said Sarah, whose dreams were famous for their complexity and the zest with which she told them.

John just nodded. She wasn't surprised that he didn't encourage her to tell her dream just at the moment.

'What about you, Hannah?'

'I've nearly finished my first whole dress,' she said, her face beaming. 'Ma's says I can cut out the next one by myself,' she went on proudly.

'Ach that's great, just great,' he said with as much enthusiasm as he could manage.

He was about to say more when the door opened and the boys arrived, gasping for breath, each holding a potato sack over their heads.

'Did you get caught too?' he asked, as Rose inspected them.

'No,' said James. 'We were waitin' for it to stop, but it showed no signs of it, so George got us the sacks. We knew it was near teatime,' he said, 'and Ma'd be lookin' for us.'

'I was indeed,' she said. 'Did you have a busy day?'

'Aye. Young George was mendin' a harness

an' we helped him,' said Sam, enthusiastically. 'An' he explained the way it all worked. An' then we explained to him about engines and vacuum brakes. He'd no idea there was only one brake at the front and one on the guard's van an' that once the vacuum was broke, there was only the guard's brake left.'

Rose cast a quick glance at Sarah, saw she was listening and looked across at John.

'What kinda harness does George use?' he asked, picking up her hint. 'There's a new lighter harness these days a lot of farmers have. Some say it's not so good. What does young George think?'

Rose put the potatoes to boil, began chopping vegetables and wondered how she could manage to get through the remaining hours of this endless day. Despite her rest, she felt exhausted, every task a huge effort, even peeling potatoes. It felt as if she were cutting out a new pattern for the first time.

After the meal, John read the children the story in the weekly magazine and she was able to look discreetly at the paper he'd brought. There were long lists of the dead but fortunately there were no new names since the morning. What was strange, however, was that the list was much shorter than the numbers everyone in Armagh knew about. But what did upset her was the way the paper indicated that many of the seriously injured were unlikely to live. As if the poor relatives haven't enough heartache without the newspapers adding to it, she thought as she turned the pages quietly.

Some eye-witness observers were saying there'd been twelve hundred or more on the train and that the engine was a poor choice, even for the nine hundred that had been expected. It also seemed there were numbers of people travelling illegally, eight soldiers and two civilians in the front brake van and fifteen people in the luggage compartment and rear guard's van.

There was also speculation as to what would happen to the officials who had been arrested by the constabulary the previous afternoon, growing concern the hospital wasn't big enough to cope with even the seriously injured and a report that a party of Red Cross nurses had arrived from Dublin to assist Dr Palmer and his staff.

There were also enormous lists of family notices for funerals on Friday and Saturday.

Rose refolded the paper carefully. It made very unhappy reading, but it brought no new shocks. That was about as much good news as they could hope for till the next week had passed.

Rose sent the boys to bed as early as she could, expecting that she and John would not be far behind. They sat gazing into the fire, the quiet and the warmth a comfort on the bleak, grey evening.

'Have you looked at the paper?' she said as she

got up and made them their usual late cup of tea.

'Aye, I had a look in Armagh. I stood in out of the rain in McCann's doorway,' he said, a catch in his voice that made her turn quickly, the tea caddy in her hand.

'Ye wouden know Armagh, Rose,' he said cautiously. 'Ivery house has the blinds drawn. Ivery shop is shut with a notice on the door as to who they've lost. Sure, I saw three coffins comin' down Banbrook Hill while I was standin' at McCann's and the whole street out behind them walkin' up to the new cathedral. An' at the same time one comin' along Railway Street headin' for St Marks. Sure, it woud a broke yer heart to see it.'

'John, I'm sorry,' she said sadly. 'The letters could have waited. I shouldn't have let you go into town.'

'Ach, no. It wasn't the letters. To tell you the truth, I wanted to go up to the hospital and ask for news.'

'Did you, love?' she asked quietly, wondering what it was he hadn't told her.

'Aye. That wee lassie, Elizabeth Kane. Sure she's as like our Sarah as if they were sisters. The wee dark, bright eyes of her,' he said, looking into the fire. 'I was at school with her father an' we were great pals at one time. I hadn't seen him for months. But I saw him yesterday. An' I couden get him out o' me mind, standin' there with a nurse that was binding up the shoulder where her wee arm shoulda been.'

'And did you get any news?'

'Aye. She's no worse. There's still hope,' he said quickly. 'It was one of those Red Cross nurses I spoke to,' he explained. 'They take it in turns to come and talk to the people waiting outside. There's a whole crowd of them for they've no room to let them in, there's that many. And she said she'd tell us a wee story to give us heart,' he said, with a flicker of a smile on his face.

'She says they have a wee child that's doing well, but they were concerned it had something wrong with its hand. It was all screwed up,' he said, tightening his own hand into a fist. 'They tried and tried to get her to open her hand, but finally she tells one of them she has three pennies in her hand. "It's for excursion," says she, 'an' I mustn't let it go.' And the wee thing had them held in her hand since yesterday mornin.' But the nurse says she'll be all right, thank God,' he said, wiping the tears from his eyes.

She gave him his tea and they sat together on the settle drinking it.

'I think today has been worse for me than yesterday,' she said honestly, 'but you've had two bad days. And it'll not get better for a while.'

'No, it won't, but we're maybe through the worst,' he said, taking her free hand. 'We'll maybe have to remember the copy book.'

'What copy book?' she asked, completely baffled.

'The one our mother's used to quote, about time passing. I'm that tired, I can't mind it now.'

'All things pass, both pleasant and unpleasant,' she said, her voice thin with exhaustion.

'Aye, that's it. All things pass,' he said. 'Even this,' he added, putting down his empty mug and drawing her to her feet. 'Come on now, you should be in your bed,' he said gently, his arm close round her, as if he were coaxing a weary child.

# CHAPTER TWENTY-SEVEN

The days did pass, more quickly indeed than Rose and John had expected. It was true they left behind them images that would never be forgotten, but these too they shared, walking home in the rain from the funerals on Friday at Grange Church, on Saturday at St Marks, where thirty-seven graves stood open at the beginning of the day and thirty-seven mounds of rain-soaked flowers marked its close.

Through the drifts of grey rain, the first small pieces of good news glinted like longed for sunshine. No more seriously injured people died. Little Elizabeth Kane made progress. A fund had been set up to help the victims and Queen Victoria herself had sent fifty pounds.

The sun at last broke through on Sunday afternoon and on Monday morning the day was already fine and warm when John set off for work. When the children had gone too and Rose went into the garden to pin up the clothes, she found the pink rose that sprawled over the wall covered in a mass of bloom.

She sat down beside it, touching the close-petalled blossoms and listening to the birds, still active at this early hour. All around her, the luxuriant growth of summer was pushing leaves and flowers up into the sunlight, so warm on her shoulders, she felt her tight muscles relax and some sense of well-being return.

For the first time since she jumped from the moving carriages, she was alone, free from the need to think of others. She felt as if she'd been tramping for days through a long, grey tunnel, washed by rain and tears and had emerged at last into the light and life-giving warmth of the sun.

'You're alive, Rose, you're alive,' she whispered to herself, though there was no one to overhear. 'Your children have been spared.' She thought of John striding off to work, knowing he left behind him a family safe and whole, unbroken by the tragedy, unlike so many men setting out this morning to the work that must go on, however heavy their hearts might be.

She watched the washing swaying in the slight breeze that had sprung up, the sheets from the girls' bed flapping and billowing, white against the blue sky like the sails of a brave vessel heading out to sea.

'America,' she said, as if testing the word, a word she'd all but forgotten in the pain and distress of the last days. 'America?' she repeated, wondering if their plans would be changed by what had happened. After all, why not. The world had changed in an instant for hundreds of other people. Though she'd escaped unscathed she knew she'd certainly not escaped untouched.

No, nothing would ever be the same again. And yet . . . She looked around the familiar garden, as if seeking an answer to an unasked question. The potato plants were just beginning to flower, the breeze gently fluttering the leaves of the old damson tree that overhung the common. Wherever she looked she could see only the continuity of life, and feel only the comfort of things that didn't change.

She went on sitting, treasuring the quiet, reluctant to break the spell that the warmth and loveliness of the morning had cast round her like a comforting arm around her shoulders. Perhaps what she most craved after the long days of heartbreak was the solace and security of known, continuing things.

She smiled as she heard Thomas's hammer in the forge. When he fixed machinery there were long periods of silence while he measured and cut. Then, his hammer rang yet more vigorously, as if to make up for his silence, the long, slow notes interspersed with the rhythmic tap dance on the anvil.

She listened to the familiar sound, thoughts moving in her mind that still would not form into words. Not until she stepped back into the kitchen, took up the routine of the day and fetched her baking board from the wash house, did she realise that she felt that life had begun again. She paused for a moment and sent up a silent prayer of thanksgiving that it had, then set about baking the bread with a cheerfulness she thought she'd never know again.

On Tuesday, Thomas had to go into Armagh to order iron and supplies for the forge. As soon as he got back he came over to bring her the morning newspaper.

'You could hardly believe it was the same place, Rose. The shops are open and the market was held as usual,' he began, leaning against the doorpost, to indicate his visit would have to be short. 'Sure there was plenty of talk of how many was hurted and who was still away from their work, but it was amazin'. It wouda put heart in ye,' he said, smiling unexpectedly.

'It said over four hundred injured in last night's paper, Thomas. They'd an awful job counting those who just went home. Did you see that?' she said, picking up the evening paper John had brought.

'No, I must a missed it,' he said wrinkling his brow. 'George Robinson brought me the paper, but it was that late by the time I got to read it I was maybe asleep,' he said laughing wryly. 'Are ye goin' inta town yerself, Rose?'

'Yes. I need groceries. I thought I'd go tomorrow.'

'You'll see it well improved. It's hard to believe what a week can bring, I've niver known one like it. But you'll not be set back if ye go the morra,' he said, as he strode back across to the forge, took his jacket off and put his leather apron back on.

Thomas was quite right. Although there was only one topic of conversation in all the shops, still the whole place felt different. People were anxious to pass on what encouraging news there was to be found. The story of the little girl with the three pennies had been passed around the whole town. By the time she left hospital, well wishers had added a good deal more than three pennies to her store.

Rose did her shopping, looked in the dress shops, changed their library books and bought the local weekly paper. She knew it would have little new to add to all the columns of newsprint they'd read in the last week, but she'd discovered John's way of coping with the disaster was to read every word he could lay hands on, as if the more detail he absorbed, the easier it was to bear the facts. Whether it was the progress of the Board of Trade enquiry, or the experiments done with similar engines to see what might be learnt from the results, or the condition of the seriously injured people still in hospital, John skipped none of it. As each day passed he became steadier.

'You were right, Thomas,' she said, coming up the lane, and dropping down on the low bank by the shoeing shed. 'Everybody is trying to move on, I think.'

He lowered the horse's hoof he'd been examining

and leant against the animal's rump, stroking its back with one hand.

'Aye. I thought ye might say that. A queer a difference, isn't there?' he said nodding.

She took out the newspaper and handed it to him.

'Have a look when you go up for your tea,' she said getting to her feet again. 'John said he'd be a bit later this evening.'

'You've a letter, Rose,' he called after her. 'I told the postman to leave it on the table for you.'

'Thanks, Thomas, thanks.'

She opened the door, pushed the door stone into place with her toe and caught up the letter.

'London,' she said, taken aback, as she recognised Lady Anne's handwriting. 'But I thought she was in Ballysadare,' she cried, as she tore open the envelope.

*My dearest Rose*, she read, as she subsided into the nearest chair.

*A million blessings upon you for writing. I got your letter this morning, after the most awful, endless days I have ever spent. We had just arrived in London, unexpectedly, as I shall explain, when we heard of the disaster in Armagh. The London Illustrated News had a most gruelling report and I was frantic with anxiety.*

*Poor Harrington didn't know what to do with me I was so distraught, so he went and telegraphed the Lord Lieutenant to ask who was in charge of the rescue operations. He got passed on from one official to another and finally was advised to telegraph the constabulary in Armagh.*

*They did reply quite quickly. He was told that a Mrs Hamilton had thrown her children out of a window, but had survived herself and was not badly injured. I could just imagine you doing that, Rose, and I was beginning to try to collect myself when we heard that it couldn't be you because this Mrs Hamilton was the wife of a Royal Irish Constabulary officer.*

*Oh, the relief when your letter appeared today, forwarded from Sligo. I could not contain myself. The servants think I have gone quite mad, because I couldn't stop crying and saying how happy I was.*

Rose put down the letter, because she couldn't see to read any more, her own tears tripping down her face and dripping unregarded on her second best blouse.

'Oh, you dear girl,' she said aloud. 'You are so incapable of pretending. And you care about us so much.'

She wiped her eyes and pushed aside a piece of blank paper that had fallen out of the envelope.

*I have been so full of joy and relief that if Harrington didn't need me here, I'm convinced I'd take the first train to Liverpool or whatever is the port for Belfast and come straight to Armagh and see you. But I can't, so I want you to do something to help me.*

*I have never dared send you a gift of money before because I knew you would be so fierce with me, even when you were so poor and I was so concerned about you. But now, after all I have been through, you cannot possibly deny me anything. I want you to spoil yourself and your dear John and the little ones. New dresses for yourself and the girls, of course, and whatever might please the boys, though I expect if my son is anything to judge by it will not be clothes.*

*And then I want you to go and get a family photograph taken. I have nothing to comfort me here, but the ones I begged from Mr Blennerhassett, fourteen years ago. Please, Rose, don't say no to me, I simply cannot bear it.*

*Harrington has just inherited a vast estate in Gloucestershire from some cousin he hardly knew and will have to decide what to do about it. That's why I came with him unexpectedly. I saw Katherine O'Shea the day after I arrived at Auntie Violet's and I'm afraid I cried all over her when someone told us the news from Armagh. She remembered you and spoke of 'your lovely Ulster blacksmith.' I shall be writing to her today as soon as I finish this to tell her my good news.*

*Please write soon my dearest Rose and tell me that you are recovering from all the unhappiness you must have suffered. I think of you so often and am determined we shall meet before very long. Harrington sends his good wishes with mine. He has said little, but I have never known him so devoted to the telegraph office.*

*Your loving friend,*
*Anne*

Rose stared at the pages, read them again, and picked up the blank piece of paper she'd pushed aside, turned it over and found it wasn't blank. It was a cheque drawn on Coutts. She looked at the figure three times before she worked out that it was twice the amount John had earned since he started work in the mill almost a year ago.

She put her head down on the table and wept.

The remaining two weeks of June were marked by fine weather and the hectic activity generated by the hay harvest when each hour without rain is precious. The boys spent every possible moment at Robinson's. When school closed on the last day of the month, George asked them to help through the summer holidays, if that was all right with Ma and Da.

The boys were so pleased with themselves and the small weekly sum he'd offered them, Rose wouldn't have had the heart to refuse them. Besides, the money apart, she agreed with John that it was a very good idea.

'Sure it's all experience for them, Rose. By the end of it, they'll know more about farm work and more about themselves forby,' he said, one fine evening when they sat beneath the gable of the forge looking down at the empty road and the cut stubble of Robinson's fields beyond.

'I mind I worked at Lydney's in Annacramp before I left school an' sure it made up my mind,' he said wryly. 'I couldn't wait to get back to school at the end of August before there was any more diggin' and plantin'.'

'You never told me that,' she said, surprised. 'I thought you liked working in the garden.'

'Ach yes, a bit of a garden. It's one thing plantin' a few rows of potatoes, or beans, or cabbage, it's another thing altogether if ye've a whole field t' plant.'

It was the way he said it which made her laugh. He turned to look at her.

'I haven't heard ye laugh like that for a long time,' he said happily. 'I think it must be that wee fortune you've come into,' he added, his tone light and teasing.

'It's not mine, John, it's ours.'

'Well, that's good news,' he said firmly. 'At least you're not going to upset the poor girl by refusing it.'

'Did you think I would?'

'Well, I had m'dou'ts, as they say. But there's no doubt at all the same Lady Anne has you well figured out,' he went on. 'She knew the poorer you were, the less chance she'd have you'd take anythin'. You're very proud, Rose,' he said, not looking in the least displeased.

'Is that a bad thing, then?'

'Aye, it can be, when there's those that want to show how much they appreciate you. Like she does. Sure, if it weren't for you she'd never have known how to go about a man like Harrington, he was that shy. He'd never have plucked up his courage even to speak t'her, if she hadn't helped him out.'

She beamed and laughed.

'What's so funny?' he asked.

'I remembered one night I was getting her dressed and she suddenly said, "He's very shy", and I nearly put my foot in it. I thought she was still talking about his horse.'

John grinned and stretched out his legs more comfortably.

'We've had no drummin' this evenin'. Had ye noticed?'

'Yes, I had. This time last year, they were at it every night. And drilling as well. Maybe what's happened will change things,' she said thoughtfully. 'D'you think it might?'

'Maybe, for a wee while. Certainly there'll be no bother this year. But then, there's no talk of another Home Rule Bill. That'll be the test of it, if we're here to see it?'

'What do you mean, John, "if we're here to see it"?'

'Well, we might be in America. I suppose we'd have enough now, even when you do all Lady Anne asked ye to do, new clothes and the photograph and suchlike.'

'Yes, we'd have more than enough,' she said nodding. 'If we bought our tickets in the morning, we'd still have enough to see us through the first six months or so. We'd be really well off compared to most emigrants.'

'An' ye still have a mind to go?'

She paused for a long moment, looking away into the distance.

'I'm not sure, John, not as sure as I was before our 'big day', she said uneasily, at last. 'I don't know why what happened should make any difference. Especially as we lost one of our best friends. I suppose that should make it easier to go, shouldn't it?'

'Ach things often goes by opposites. But sure, we've time enough to think about it before the winter.'

'Yes, we have,' she agreed. Though the evening was warm and still, the thought of winter and the overheated spinning rooms made her shiver. 'We'll have to think before the end of the school holidays,' she said carefully. 'We don't want the children to miss out on too many weeks schooling.'

'No, yer right there, I hadn't thought o' that,' he admitted. 'Though with all yer readin' and helpin' them, I'm sure they're well ahead o' other students.'

'Not just me, John Hamilton,' she said, poking him in the ribs. 'Who is it has us all up to date on fan belts and pistons and drive shafts?'

He smiled sheepishly.

'Sure you carry me home the books all the way from Armagh,' he said, a note of protest in his voice. 'I want t' see ye get yer value for your five shillin's a year.'

As she climbed the steps of the library on The Mall, a week later, Rose smiled as she recalled John's words. The only thing stopping her from paying her half crown for family membership was the thought that they might be half a world away by the end of September.

'Good day, Mrs Hamilton. Is there anything special I can find for you today?'

She thanked the young man who was always so

helpful with his detailed knowledge of the entire stock of the library, and handed him a piece of paper on which John had noted two books he'd seen mentioned in the bibliography of the last one he'd read.

'Ah, yes,' he beamed. 'We possess both, Mrs Hamilton, but one of them is on loan. The other I shall fetch for you while you choose your own reading.'

He turned away, greeted a gentleman who was just leaving, and climbed his ladder to the higher shelves.

Rose walked up and down the rows of books. She'd read almost all their volumes of the history and exploration of America, as well as their smaller collection of fiction. She was still standing gazing at the spines of the volumes of autobiography, her head turned sideways, when young Mr Reid came up to her.

'Mrs Hamilton, if I might ask a rather personal question,' he said uneasily. 'Do you have four children?'

'Yes, I do,' she replied, looking at him in amazement.

'And would I be right in thinking the boys are James and Sam, the girls are Hannah and Sarah?'

'Yes, you are quite right,' she nodded, wondering what to make of the look of mixed unease and satisfaction on his face. 'Have you taken up crystal gazing for a hobby, Mr Reid?' she asked, laughing merrily.

'Not at all, Mrs Hamilton,' he said, beaming himself. 'A gentleman whom I know well asked me to find out for him. Mr Sinton is waiting in my small office,' he went on, lowering his voice and using a tone which implied she must have heard of him. 'He would be most grateful if you would go and have a word with him.'

'Mr Sinton?'

By way of answer, Mr Reid listed a number of draper's shops in the town, including the one she'd been using for years and the one where she studied the most up to date and the most expensive fashion whenever she came into town.

Overcome with curiosity, she made no further protest, but allowed herself to be escorted to a tiny overcrowded room where a familiar figure stood waiting.

'My dear Mrs Hamilton, I have found you at last,' he said, bowing courteously and placing a chair for her so that she could sit down in the rather confined space. 'James Sinton, in your debt and at your service,' he went on, holding out his hand and shaking hers firmly.

Mr Reid scuttled away, closing the door behind him, leaving Rose face to face with the benevolent-looking gentleman she'd last seen across the width of a carriage on the ill-fated Methodist excursion.

'My wife and I have been searching for you for some weeks now,' he said beaming at her, as he seated himself opposite her. 'Clearly you do not live in the city itself?'

'No, we live about two miles away, at Salter's Grange on the Loughgall Road. I only come in once a week to shop and change our books,' she said easily.

'What a happy chance that I should have glimpsed you as you walked past. I use the reading room a great deal, but seldom in the afternoons. It is indeed an answer to our prayers,' he said smiling broadly.

Rose really could not imagine how she could be the answer to anyone's prayers, but his delight was so obvious that she merely smiled and waited for him to go on.

'Mrs Hamilton, I will come straight to the point. It is because of you that I am sitting in this chair, that my wife is at present visiting some of the injured, and that my three small daughters are alive and well. It is my dearest wish, and that of my wife, that we can find some means of acknowledging our great debt to you.'

Rose was totally taken aback. For a moment, she couldn't even think what he might possibly be referring to.

'My dear Mrs Hamilton,' he said very quietly. 'It was you who prevented the young railway man from locking our carriage. It was your son who alerted us so promptly to our danger, and you who underlined the fact when we were slow to respond. Even a few more minutes and there would have been a risk of injury, but we were all out before the carriages gathered significant speed.'

Rose gasped and shook her head.

'But I only . . .'

'Saved our lives,' he prompted.

'If there is any question of that being the case, I think my sons must take the credit,' she said, somewhat flustered.

'Certainly much credit is due to those young gentlemen,' he said agreeably, 'but may I say that, had you not shown such confidence in your son's judgement, we would all be in a much less happy state than we are today. You do realise, don't you, that even in the adjoining carriage, as far from the impact as it was possible to be, there were fatalities, both adults and children.'

Rose shook her head. 'I didn't know that. I thought they were all from the first three coaches.'

'No, there was not a single coach without a death or serious injury. The coach in which we were travelling was derailed. You did not know that either, I suspect.'

'No, I didn't,' she said, suddenly made anxious and uneasy as images crowded back to her mind from those last minutes in which she'd got the children out.

'Please, don't distress yourself,' he said, his pleasant face, suddenly grim. 'I would not for the world remind you of that day but to make my point, in the hope that you will do me the great kindness of accepting some gift or benefit for you and your family.'

She dropped her eyes, distressed and confused. If she had indeed done something to help his family, it would be ungraceful to reject his offer. She thought of Lady Anne's letter. 'You would be so fierce with me.' She couldn't be fierce with this good-natured man. But what was she to say?

'I have to confess that life has been very kind to me,' he said, grasping something of her difficulty. 'I have enough for all my needs and to spare. If without giving any offence I might suggest some assistance with the further education of your family, I could go back to my wife and know that she would be delighted and share my joy,' he said, watching her face carefully.

'What a kind offer,' she said, suddenly seeing the way out of her dilemma. 'We should indeed be happy to give our children every opportunity, but it is likely that we shall shortly be emigrating. Were we not, I should accept most gratefully for my children.'

She saw his face fall and was almost sorry she had not asked for some token, some books for James and Sam, paint boxes and paper for the girls, the gifts she'd already decided on out of Lady Anne's generosity.

'That is very sad, indeed,' he said, looking truly downcast. 'For such a talented family to leave us. If it is not too great an intrusion, may I ask why you are going?'

She sighed and decided she had to tell him the truth. In the short time of their conversation, she'd confirmed her first opinion of him, made during the delays and discomforts that had preceded that shortest of rail journeys. He was a thoroughly likeable man. Despite his manners, his elegant clothes and his affluence, he was as open and honest in his manner as John or Thomas.

She explained about the ending of the partnership between the two men, about the job at the mill and her anxieties about John's health. Mr Sinton listened with fierce concentration.

'If your husband were to have his own forge, do you think he could be persuaded to stay?'

'I think any metal-working employment, outside a mill, would probably solve the problem,' she said, answering him as honestly as she could. 'Though I think part of the attraction of America is the possibility of working with machines. My husband is fascinated by engines of all kinds. He's even convinced we'll soon have horseless carriages,' she said easily, glad to see that his look of sadness had quite disappeared.

'Was it your husband, Mrs Hamilton, who taught the boys about vacuum braking?'

'Oh yes,' she laughed, pleased by the smile on his face. 'And power weight ratios and drive belts and pistons and steam compression. He's read almost everything here in the library on moving vehicles. I can't say I understand it all, but I've carried all the volumes home,' she said laughing.

'Mrs Hamilton, you have made me the happiest of all men,' he said, unexpectedly. 'My brother is a linen manufacturer and a very wealthy man, with a great passion for machines. For some months now, he's been searching for either an engineer that can work metal, or a blacksmith that understands engines, to help him on his current project,' he explained, a broad grin on his face. 'Could I persuade you to tell your husband that I think I have the solution to your problem and mine?'

# CHAPTER TWENTY-EIGHT

James Sinton would be as good as his word, Rose was sure, but even she was amazed at the vigour with which he forwarded the task he'd set himself. Nothing was too much trouble for him. Difficulties he resolved with the greatest of ease. Although he was never hasty or overbearing, he pursued his objectives with a devotion that seemed totally out of character for such an apparently placid and equable man.

'Sure that's why he is where he is today, Rose,' said John laughing as they set out for an evening walk, leaving James in charge of his brother and sisters and Thomas still working at the forge.

'Ye don't come to own half a dozen shops an' run them successfully if you haven't got somethin' up top. I know he says he reads a lot, an' looks as if he were a gentleman of leisure, but when it comes to the bit, it's he makes the big decisions about them shops, mark my words. An' that's what counts.'

'Yes, I think you're right,' she said. 'But you like him, don't you?' She went on, as they turned out of the lane and down the deserted road.

'He's a lovely man and she's nice too,' he said warmly. 'Nothing fancy about her, except the dress. An' sure I expect she feels she has to dress up an' him in the business,' he added sympathetically.

Rose laughed, remembering the short time she'd spent alone with Mary Sinton when the whole family had gone to tea the previous Sunday, so that James could meet John and the children "Could renew their acquaintance", as he so tactfully put it.

'My dear Mrs Hamilton,' she'd said, almost as soon as they'd arrived, 'I hope you will call me Mary, and I may call you by your first name. We've talked of you and the children so much since that dreadful day I feel we have known each other a long time already.'

'But, of course. My name is Rose,' she replied warmly.

'Oh, how lovely. My dearest sister was called Rose, a pretty, lively child. We lost her when she was not quite eleven, just the age of your dear Hannah,' she said sadly. 'I hope our little girls will make friends.'

The children had indeed got on very well together. While the adults talked, they clustered round a table in the window of the tall, Georgian house overlooking The Mall and enjoyed the board games James Sinton had laid out for them.

'How do you feel about tomorrow?' Rose asked, as they turned up Church Hill and she realised she'd been silent, lost in her own thoughts.

'Well, it can do no harm,' he said easily. 'There's no doubt if the brother's anythin' like James an' he thinks I can give him a han,' it woud be great. Woud ye mind movin' Banbridge way?'

She laughed and took his arm.

'John dear, if I was prepared to go to America for the sake of your health and the future of our children, I'll hardly blink at fourteen or fifteen miles into the next county, will I?' she said, shaking her head and making a face at him.

'Aye, well. I suppose it's manners to ask,' he said, grinning himself.

They walked up the hill and paused outside the church yard.

'Not tonight, John,' she said gently. 'We'll come up again, whatever way it goes.'

So they walked on, down the hill, past the old oak that had been there in 1598, so everyone said, when the Battle of the Yellow Ford was fought over the fields and lanes between it and the river. The cart manufactory lay on their right, the windows of the workshop facing on to the road. They were still at work, father and son. John waved and gave them good evening as they strolled past.

'Maybe we'll not walk this hill again, Rose.'

'Maybe not, indeed,' she said, her mind moving from past to future. 'What time is James collecting you?'

'Eight o'clock.'

'Wasn't it lucky that this was your week's holiday?'

'Aye, I was just thinkin' that. It's as if everythin' was just fallin' inta place.'

When Drumcairn mill reopened after the annual holiday a week later, John gave his notice. One look at Henry Sinton's workshop was enough for him. He could hardly wait to examine the models that stood half-built on the benches. While Sinton talked enthusiastically to him, moving from one idea to the next, his brother followed silently behind, a discreet smile on his face, knowing that he had indeed contrived a situation of benefit to everyone.

When John returned late that evening, he was so excited that their evening tea was long gone before Rose could bring herself to put forward the question which had been in her mind since he'd arrived home, a broad grin telling her the result before he'd said a word.

'Where would we live, John? Did anyone mention that?'

He put his hand to his head and laughed.

'Ach yes, I clean forgot. There's a farm empty not

half a mile away. James says that if you like the place, he would make it over to you, freehold. It would be yours to do what you like with, his gift to you.'

'And did you see the place, John?' she asked.

'Yes, yes, I did,' he said, nodding vigorously. 'But mind you, so much has happened since, I can't be entirely sure how many rooms there are. I know there's a parlour, for it reminded me of Annacramp. An' there's a kitchen with a stove and a kind of a dairy place off it with a Belfast sink an' runnin' water,' he went on matter-of-factly. 'I loss count of the bedrooms, though some of them's wee an' I near hit my head wi' some o' the doorways. But I do mind I could see the mountains from the front one,' he said firmly. 'I couldn't have told you what direction we were for it's all hills, far bigger hills than these wee ones roun' here. But I looked out to see the garden an' there was the mountains o' Mourne, plain as plain, ye coud a put out yer han' an' touched them,' he said, his face beaming with pleasure.

'Did you say a garden, John?'

'Yes, I thought that'd please you. Ach, it's a bit neglected, an' I think there's plants has died wi' that dry spell in June, but sure you'll have it your way in no time. The flowers is at the front, an' there's fruit bushes an' an orchard at the back. James says there's a small parcel of land forby, but only about ten acres. It was gettin' late so we didn't walk it.'

Rose shook her head in disbelief.

'I hope I don't wake up in the morning and find I'm dreaming all this.'

John laughed.

'You're more likely to wake up an' find James on your doorstep with some paper to sign,' he said, yawning hugely, as he bent to unlace his boots.


His last week at the mill and the one that followed were busy ones for Rose. She wanted to keep her promise to Lady Anne and send photographs before they moved. There were clothes to buy and letters to write.

She spent a long afternoon with Peggy and left heartened by what she saw of the growing understanding between her and Billy.

'I don't love Billy, Rose, not like I loved Kevin, but I'm fond of him. Maybe in a year or two we might marry. I've no heart for any other man after Kevin and I know he'll always love Mary, but we've been through so much together I know we'd always be good to each other. An' sure that's half livin' to have someone cares for you. You know that.'

'I do, Peggy. If I had to choose between this lovely new place and having John, I wouldn't have a moment's hesitation.'

'Sure, I know that, but I'm delighted about the new job. You deserve your good fortune, the pair of you. You'll write to me sometimes, won't you?'

'Of course I will, Peggy. I won't have to work as

hard at the sewing. I'll have more time to myself, unless I decide to have a cow again and a few chickens,' she said, laughing.

For Rose, the only real sadness in leaving the house opposite the forge was the loss of Thomas. He'd always been a kindly presence, even in the days before his accident when she daren't go over to speak to him for fear of Mary-Anne's fury. Since then, he'd been much more forthcoming, often walking down to see them of an evening. In the days following the disaster, he'd been a regular caller, he'd gone with them to all the funerals, brought newspapers and news. Their friendship had strengthened just as they were about to part.

'Ach now Rose, don't take it amiss. Sure I'm that delighted for you both. An' isn't it a great start for the childer to have yer man Sinton concerned about their education. James'll go far, an' sure all of them's bright. Isn't it the best thing ever happen'd ye's.'

He'd looked at her downcast face as he sat by the gable with them one thundery July evening

'Sure wouldn't it be worse if ye's were goin' to America or Australia?' he said cheerfully. 'Our paths may cross again,' he added thoughtfully. 'Sure ye may yet come to see me in one of these horseless carriages John keeps on talkin' about. An' ye'll maybe write me a line or two, Rose. I'm a bad han' with a pen, but I'll write back to ye.'

\* \* \*

The photograph was prepared for and duly taken in Loudan's of English Street. Rose wore the first shop-bought dress she'd ever owned. According to John, she looked like a Queen. But Sarah protested. The Queen was fat and looked cross, but Ma looked lovely.

To Rose's surprise the boys were perfectly amenable to the photographer's arrangements and Hannah did as she was asked. It was Sarah who sat with furrowed brow, staring crossly at the lens and the antics of the young man under his velvet cloth.

Nothing would induce her to soften her gaze, until the young man had the brilliant idea of letting her look through the lens for herself. Having viewed her family critically, she rejoined them in a more agreeable mood and the resulting picture was pronounced a success, not only by the photographer, but later by Lady Anne herself.

The days sped by with a rapidity that left Rose feeling breathless and convinced there was something she'd forgotten. As she packed small items in newspaper and fitted them into the cardboard boxes James Sinton had retrieved for her from one of his shops, she tried to gather up her thoughts.

There was no doubt, she'd been right, a year or more ago when she'd said they should keep their plan to go to America a secret. Sam would have been so disappointed if he'd known how close they'd come to buying their tickets, but now he'd be able to enjoy their good news unclouded by regret. Soon to become a father himself, he was happier than he'd ever been, free for the moment of the old driving need to help others.

She worked slowly and carefully, aware that every object going into this particular box was precious. Some souvenirs of Sarah, including the picture of Niagara Falls sent by her sister and Grandpa's leaning candle-stick, as the children called it. The old brown handbag in which she still kept the rent book and some paper money. The cup and saucer from Galloway her mother had carried away from Ardtur and given to her the night before she'd left Currane Lodge to begin her married life.

She'd never actually been reduced to drinking spring water from it, but it had come very close. There'd been weeks when they couldn't afford tea or sugar, time enough, but she'd been so busy sewing she hadn't even had time to stop and drink. Besides, she hadn't been perplexed then, for she'd known exactly what she had to do to keep them going.

Now, it seemed those old anxious worries would be no more. There'd be others, of course, you couldn't have life without them, but something unbelievably good had indeed come out of the most heartbreaking experience of their lives.

A sudden movement caught her eye. Mary-Anne strode down the path on her way to Battlehill, her

Bible under her arm, looking neither to right nor left.

'Ye'll not shed many tears for yer neighbour Mary-Anne, I'm thinkin', said John, as he'd watched her take cuttings from the flourishing bushes by the front door.

'No, indeed I won't. My tears will be for Thomas. I hope you won't be jealous.'

'No, sure I know yer fond of him,' he said easily. 'an' he of you. Why wouldn't he be, an' you gave him heart to stan' up to her.'

'I wish it were different, John. He's a good man and deserves better. An' those wee ones have no life.'

'Yer right about that. But sure, there's always puzzles we'll never solve. It'll fall to others to see the why of it.'

Rose wondered if she could ever see the 'why' of Mary-Anne. What possible good did a woman like Mary-Anne do in this world, so bound up in her religion she'd not a moment to offer a word of kindness to the bereaved, or a helping hand to any of the families with injured to care for. Maybe she was a reminder. If you'd known a Mary-Anne and seen the hurt in the eyes of her children and the loneliness in the eyes of her man, it made you so determined to do better yourself.

As she closed the box and tied it firmly round with string she decided that would have to do for an answer, for she could think of nothing better.

*  *  *

Before July was properly over, the day of the move had come. The draymen arrived at noon from Sinton's of Banbridge, ate a bite with them and loaded up their furniture and all their possessions, carrying it down the lane piece by piece, because the dray was too wide to back up.

Rose was grateful Thomas had gone into town, their goodbyes already said outside the forge, where so much news, had been shared, good and bad.

The place was empty now, well-swept, with only the ash from the cooling fire to sweep up and throw on the garden. The children were sitting under the gable of the forge watching for the chaise, ready with picnic baskets and Ganny to climb aboard and wait while the last few jobs were done.

'Well, is that it?' asked John gently, coming back into the kitchen and seeing her standing there looking at the hearth.

'Yes, that's it. All clean and tidy for whoever might come. If they come,' she said without moving.

He waited, watching her. She smiled suddenly.

'I wish I could take the crane you made for me. I do love it dearly,' she said easily.

'Ach, sure they're almost a thing of the past,' he said. 'Maybe someone will come and put it in a museum. Sure you'll have a stove and gaslight forby. Yer man has his own gas plant an' has it laid on to the farm.'

'You didn't tell me that.'

474

'Sure I forgot,' he said, sheepishly.

She laughed happily as she turned towards him.

'Do you know, John, I've been wondering. Do you think when we meet the neighbours in our new place, anyone will call me "the woman from Kerry."'

'Not at all, Rose,' he said, grinning, as he pulled the door closed behind them. 'Sure you're that grand now with your new dress, nobody would ever know.'

# ACKNOWLEDGEMENTS

My own great-grandmother came from Kerry. I must thank her for inspiring this tale.

Without the help of my friends in Armagh I could not have recreated the world in which she lived. Once again, I thank Armagh Ancestry, the Irish Studies Centre, the Robinson Library and Armagh Books, who took such trouble to find me material I never knew existed.

But my greatest debt this time is to my husband, Peter, a historian, who not only helped me thread my way through the many accounts of the period 1861 to 1889, but kept me company on windy mountainsides and in damp churchyards.

My mistakes are my own and I hope will not detract from a story I have long wanted to tell.

NEXT IN THE SERIES

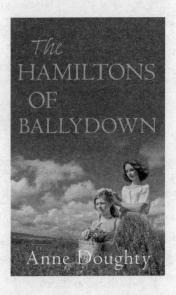

At the close of the nineteenth century the Hamilton family is enjoying new-found security and modest prosperity. John is a respected employee at the local mill and Rose's four children are growing into young men and women of whom she can feel justly proud. When John and his employer, Hugh Sinton, come against difficulty at the mill – challenged by the demands of keeping machinery and processes up to date, John feels responsible for the large workforce. At the same time, Rose, back at home, is concerned with the difficult choices her children are forced to make.

To discover more great books and to
place an order visit our website at
www.allisonandbusby.com

Don't forget to sign up to our free newsletter at
www.allisonandbusby.com/newsletter
for latest releases, events and exclusive offers

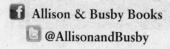

 Allison & Busby Books
 @AllisonandBusby

You can also call us on
020 7580 1080
for orders, queries
and reading recommendations